6/30/16

Enjoy!

F/BAN

$15.00

#3

This Signed Edition of

☑ **W9-AZM-929**

SAFE AT LAST

by
MAYA BANKS

Has Been Specially Bound by the Publisher

Love

Maya

Banks

xoxo

SAFE AT LAST

BY MAYA BANKS

Slow Burn Series

KEEP ME SAFE
IN HIS KEEPING
SAFE AT LAST

Surrender Trilogy

LETTING GO
GIVING IN
TAKING IT ALL

Breathless Trilogy

RUSH
FEVER
BURN

The KGI series

THE DARKEST HOUR
NO PLACE TO RUN
HIDDEN AWAY
WHISPERS IN THE DARK
ECHOES AT DAWN
SOFTLY AT SUNRISE
SHADES OF GRAY
FORGED IN STEELE
AFTER THE STORM
WHEN THE DAY BREAKS

SAFE AT LAST

A Slow Burn Novel

MAYA BANKS

AVON

An Imprint of HarperCollinsPublishers

SAFE AT LAST. Copyright © 2015 by Maya Banks. All rights reserved. Printed in the United States of America. No part of this book may be used or reproduced in any manner whatsoever without written permission except in the case of brief quotations embodied in critical articles and reviews. For information address HarperCollins Publishers, 195 Broadway, New York, NY 10007.

HarperCollins books may be purchased for educational, business, or sales promotional use. For information please e-mail the Special Markets Department at SPsales@harpercollins.com.

FIRST EDITION

Library of Congress Cataloging-in-Publication Data has been applied for.

ISBN 978-0-06-231250-1

15 16 17 18 19   DIX/RRD   10 9 8 7 6 5 4 3 2 1

SAFE AT LAST

ZACK Covington simmered with impatience as he waited for the go signal from his team leader. He didn't know exactly what was going on in the basement of the McMansion—not unlike the house he'd once dreamed of building for the girl he'd planned to spend forever with—but he knew it wasn't good. Sometimes bad lurked in seemingly benign locations. People existed in denial that it could happen in their little corner of the world. How very wrong they were.

It was a lesson he'd learned the hard way. Coming from a small town nestled against the shores of Kentucky Lake, he'd thought—just as most of its citizens had thought—that they were impervious to bad. And Zack? He was more confident about that than most, because his father was the chief of police, and he'd grown up knowing his father's job was to ensure the safety of the town, regardless of size.

But he'd damn sure failed when it came to Gracie. Everyone had failed her and Zack had led the pack. His father's refusal to use county resources on someone who didn't belong anyway had caused a rift between Zack and his father that to this day hadn't been mended.

It never would be.

Zack sighed as he contemplated the stately homes, the expensive cars, the swimming pools behind high privacy fences, the immaculately landscaped yards. The white-collar families who resided in the gated community that boasted top-notch security would be horrified to know that evil lurked in their midst. The irony of it all was that the affluent neighborhood had recently been voted the safest and most desirable community in the greater Houston area. Hell, it had scored in the top five in the entire state of Texas and in the top twenty for the whole country. So yeah, these people were utterly convinced that they were safe.

But he knew better. Inside was a child. Just a baby. Well, not so much a baby, since she was only two years younger than his Gracie. Goddamn it. Not here. Not now. It was no time for the past to intrude. Besides, Gracie was hardly the beautiful, innocent sixteen-year-old girl he'd loved more than a decade ago. She'd be twenty-eight now.

If she was even alive.

And she wasn't "his" Gracie anymore. She wasn't his anything.

Maybe he hadn't been able to save Gracie. Maybe he'd failed her. But over his dead body would he fail this young girl whose dreams were as big as the sun. Not when the two most important people in her life—or at least the two who *should* have been the most important—had failed her in every possible way.

Alyssa Lofton had been a very promising ballerina at an

early age, a fact her mother had taken pride in when she'd participated in kindergarten recitals and received high praise and glowing accolades both locally and across the state. Later, when the demands of her training had encroached on her mother and father's social life, Alyssa had fallen far down the list of their priorities.

Until the father had received pointed threats, aimed at Alyssa.

The Loftons had five children, with Alyssa being the middle child, between two older brothers and two younger sisters. When Howard Lofton had called in Devereaux Security Services, it had disgusted Zack that the man seemed irritated not that his daughter was being threatened, but that *he* wasn't the subject of the threat. It was a blow to his ego that evidently he was not as important as his daughter.

A pompous, arrogant pig who had no business having children. His wife was no better. Zack could only dream of the life they had—a life he once thought he *would* have—with a houseful of children. Happy. And yet the couple was more concerned with their social standing than the care of their children.

They'd hired a nanny and it was the nanny who attended all sports events and dance recitals and provided the love and support the parents should have. And now she was dead, shot when trying to protect one of the younger Lofton children after masked men had burst into the auditorium where the dance recital was being held and cut the lights, causing instant chaos as gunfire erupted.

The father? Had dropped like a fucking coward, hiding behind his *wife*, while the nanny had saved his son. Zack would like to put a bullet right between the asshole's eyes for that alone.

Howard and Felicity Lofton hadn't even been there so they could see their daughter shine. They'd attended solely because the CEO of another oil company also had a daughter performing and Howard was in negotiations to merge the two companies because the competitor was looking to retire and Howard wanted to take over both companies and expand his "empire." Hell, he and his wife hadn't even sat with their children. They'd left the nanny to tend to the kids while they sat a row back talking business and their daughters performed.

The target had been Alyssa. And Alyssa had been Zack's responsibility. Hell, she was all of DSS's responsibility, but Zack had been the closest, and in the clusterfuck that had ensued, a hysterical woman had blocked his pathway to Alyssa, a mere foot away, getting shot in the process, and Alyssa had been abducted in a professionally executed hit.

This was no amateur operation, and Zack had to wonder why someone would go to such lengths to kidnap the child of a high-profile oil mogul when the man took absolutely no security precautions, and if any research on Howard Lofton had been done at all and ransom had been the aim, he would have been the obvious choice.

Lofton would give up a hell of a lot of money for his own life. But for his children? Even Zack knew the answer to that, and he'd only briefly made the man's acquaintance. He'd despised Lofton on sight because he grudgingly had to part with some of his precious money to protect his daughter for "appearance's sake." After all, it wouldn't do for it to get out that a father had ignored threats to his child, and above all else, Howard Lofton had an ego the size of the state he resided in.

When the silence through his earpiece continued—and he'd

already waited an interminable amount of time—Zack lost what was left of his patience. Fuck it. He was going in. The Loftons might not give two fucks about their daughter, but Zack did, and he wasn't about to sit on his hands when each passing second could mean the difference between life and death.

Stealthily, he crept toward the window of the guest room. DSS had pulled the floor plans of the housing developments—they were cookie-cutter houses, after all—and quietly inserted his knife around the edges and bottom of the window to loosen the panes. Only when he was able to slide the window upward did he whisper into the comm, "I'm in."

He ignored the curses of Dane, heard Eliza mutter an "about time," while Capshaw and Renfro said nothing at all.

Zack slid into the bedroom with ease and quickly drew his gun and attached silencer with one hand and reached for a flash-bang grenade with the other. He knew the layout by heart, having studied it until it was ingrained in his mind.

The house was eerily dark when he slipped from the bedroom, but in the distance, the sound of a television could be heard. His partners could cover the front. His aim was the lower level and he homed in on his target with absolute focus.

A shadow appeared in his periphery and he immediately flattened himself against the wall just as a man rounded the corner, heading directly toward Zack. A quick assessment told him this wasn't a resident of the house. He was dressed in fatigues and a black shirt, with a shoulder harness holding a pistol and several Kevlar knives secured to his waist. What the fuck did these jokers want with a fourteen-year-old girl? Were they running some sort of human trafficking ring? And if so, why the *one* girl? There had been more than two dozen girls between the ages of eight and eighteen at the recital. In the utter chaos that had ensued, they could have grabbed several others.

Zack yanked his gun up just as the other man spotted him and did the same. But Zack had the element of surprise and only the thud of a dead body falling broke the quiet.

"One down," Zack said quietly into the comm. "And these guys are trained. Watch your sixes."

"Goddamn it, Zack," Beau hissed. "Wait for backup."

"Alyssa may not have time for backup," Zack bit back, moving toward the stairway at the end of the hall.

He paused at the top and peered downward, his ears straining for any sound to indicate movement up the stairs. What he heard froze him to the core.

Soft weeping. The sound of pain and despair. And it broke his heart.

Resisting the urge to rush recklessly the rest of the way down the stairs, he forced himself to take it step by step, making sure he made no sound as he descended when his every instinct was to charge in and take out the fuckers who'd taken and *hurt* an innocent child.

He paused at the bottom because there was only a small area between the bottom of the stairwell and the wall. He would have to round the corner to enter the larger area of the room. Where Alyssa was being held. Where soft weeping could still be heard.

He couldn't lob the flash-bang grenade, because it would be devastating to Alyssa, and she could be executed in a split second once her kidnappers were aware they'd been found. As schooled as Zack believed them to be, they'd likely been exposed to them before—and trained to withstand the effects while adequately defending themselves. Or taking out the enemy.

Inhaling a quiet breath, he gripped his knife in his left hand and curled his fingers on his right hand around the stock of the pistol, just brushing the trigger. The sight that greeted him would live with him until his dying breath.

Alyssa, bloodied, bruised, pale with shock, eyes glazed with pain and the sheen of tears, was manacled to the brick chimney base. It was like something out of a medieval horror movie.

But worse was seeing *who* her tormentor was.

Zack didn't move. Didn't so much as breathe, praying that the girl holding a knife to Alyssa's neck wouldn't be alerted to his presence and slice through the delicate skin.

"Why are you doing this to me, Lana?" Alyssa whispered, choking on her tears as she stared dully at her tormentor. "I thought we were friends!"

"Because with you out of the picture, *I'll* be the best. Not *you*," the teenage girl hissed. "It's always been about you. I'm sick of hearing about how great Alyssa is. How talented. How you're destined for stardom. What does anyone say about me? Runner-up. To you. Always second place. Now *I'll* be the star and no one will even remember your name."

Jesus. Zack recognized the girl. She'd performed just before Alyssa, and obviously displayed talent, but from the moment Alyssa had taken the stage, it had been equally evident that Alyssa had clearly outshone the other girl.

The sheer hatred for Alyssa was obvious in her rival's voice. The malicious triumph in her voice sickened Zack. A thin rivulet of blood slipped down Alyssa's neck and she gave a small cry, more of distress and fear than of pain.

What was more horrifying was that there was no way this girl could have pulled off a plan so flawlessly. Nor would she have knowledge of such men capable of executing a professional hit. Which meant her parents not only knew what was happening in the basement of their home but had likely masterminded the entire event.

Zack had to act fast. He was very good at reading people and he didn't doubt for a second that the jealous teenage girl would kill Alyssa if he didn't step in now. In no way did he want to kill a teenage girl, just a child—but no, this was no child. She was a cold-blooded psychopath who thought nothing of removing someone she perceived as competition.

And then the decision was ripped from him when Alyssa glanced past her captor and betrayed his presence by widening her eyes in alarm. Thankfully, the girl lowered the knife and turned, perhaps thinking he was one of the men who'd abducted Alyssa. But when her gaze settled on him, she raised the hand holding the knife, her expression so vicious it gave him chills. Then she turned, clearly directing the knife toward Alyssa's chest.

It all happened in a split second, and yet it was as though everything were in slow motion.

Alyssa screamed, straining sideways to avoid the wicked edge of the knife. Zack fired, his aim precise, penetrating Lana's arm just above the wrist, causing the knife to drop. Lana's scream mimicked Alyssa's own and yet the obvious pain the bullet wound must have caused didn't deter her from her determined vendetta.

She lunged at Alyssa, scratching furiously at Alyssa's face while her other hand hung uselessly at her side.

Goddamn it!

Zack hurled himself forward, grabbing a fistful of the hell cat's hair, and yanked her back. In his ear, two voices were demanding a status report. He ignored both, more worried about defending Alyssa from further harm if someone not on his team came down the stairs.

"I'll kill you!" Lana screamed, turning her fury on Zack.

And just as suddenly, her anger turned to triumph as she turned a spiteful look in Alyssa's direction.

"You're too late anyway," she said smugly.

Zack didn't pause to consider what the crazy-ass girl meant. He shoved her down into a nearby chair and handcuffed her uninjured wrist to the arm. This time it was she who gave away the presence of another. Relief flared in her eyes and Zack immediately dropped and rolled toward Alyssa, placing his body between her and any possible threat.

His gun was up and he didn't hesitate when he saw a man who was similarly attired as the one Zack had already taken down on the upper level. He didn't have time to go for the kill shot but put a bullet in the assailant's upper leg. Judging by the blood pumping from the wound as the man went down, it was likely Zack had hit his femoral artery. If that was the case, the man was finished and would bleed out in a matter of seconds.

Still, not one to assume anything, he took aim and put a second bullet through the downed man's neck.

"Goddamn it, where the fuck is everyone?" Zack demanded, addressing his teammates for the first time. "Alyssa's in the basement and two of the kidnappers are dead. Anyone care to offer some backup here?"

"Well, if you'd been a little more patient, you'd have gotten your backup," Dane said dryly.

"If I'd waited any longer, Alyssa would be dead right now," Zack snapped.

"We've cleared the main level," Eliza broke in. "On our way now. And Zack, this is some fucked-up shit we're dealing with."

"You don't even know the half of it," Zack said grimly.

Satisfied that he'd encounter no further nasty surprises, Zack picked himself up and quickly freed Alyssa's wrists, using the key lying on a table just a few feet away. As soon as she was free, she threw her arms around him and sobbed into his neck. He closed his eyes, cupping the back of her head as he gently stroked her hair.

"It's all right now, sweetheart. You're safe now."

"No it's not," she said with gulping sobs. "It'll *never* be all right again."

She clung tightly to him, her grief causing a knot to form in Zack's throat. The world was filled with all kinds of sick, twisted fucks, but even this had the power to surprise him. That someone so young was so evil and . . . sick. He didn't have words.

"Can you get up or do you need me to carry you?" Zack said, using a soothing, calming voice. "How badly are you hurt?"

At his question, she completely fell apart, her cries so hopeless that it enraged him that such innocence had been destroyed. But even then, he wasn't prepared for her answer.

"She broke my *knees*," Alyssa sobbed. "She made it so I'll never dance again. Dancing was all I had and now it's *gone*. She was supposed to be my friend. We were going to room together, go to the same performing arts academy. Oh God. What if I never walk again?"

Zack went utterly still with shock. As gently as he could, considering he was shaking with rage, he pulled her away, just enough that he could evaluate her legs. He hadn't seen them before. He'd been too focused on Lana and the knife she'd held and the fear in Alyssa's eyes.

And what he saw horrified him.

The leotards she'd worn in her recital were torn and bloodied, impossibly stretched by massive swelling caused by trauma to the kneecaps. He'd never felt so sick in his life. Not since the day . . .

He shook his head, refusing to go back to that time in his life. There was a young girl who needed him right now. He was all that had stood between her and death. And to her, such a devastating injury was tantamount to death.

He very carefully slid one arm underneath her thighs, above the backs of her knees and below her behind, and secured his other arm around her upper body, hooking it underneath her armpit.

"This will hurt, honey, but I have to get you out of here and to a hospital where it's safe. Perhaps your injuries aren't as severe as you fear."

Devastation and doubt were clear in her tear-swollen eyes, but she clamped her lips shut and leaned into him, not uttering a single sound as he lifted her and carried her past Lana, who was still handcuffed to the chair.

"What about me?" Lana shrieked. "You *shot* me!"

Zack turned his cold gaze on her, ensuring Alyssa's head was tucked firmly beneath his chin, her face buried against his neck so she would no longer have to lay eyes on her torturer.

"Sue me," he growled.

TWO

ZACK shifted position on an uncomfortable stool in a bar better described as a dive, several blocks from his apartment. It was a place he used as an escape, because no one knew him here. Despite his regularity, he kept to himself, never talking to others and definitely not using it as a place to pick up women for one-night stands. It was simply a place to blow off steam after a particularly bad assignment or the times when his past came back to haunt him despite his best efforts to move beyond it.

In this case, it was a double whammy.

Because the job from hell—literally—had brought back painful memories that he'd been able to keep at bay for a period of time he was proud of. He'd even thought he was beyond the worst. Moving on. Finally letting go and accepting. Accepting that the life he'd planned—the life he'd dreamed of—was never going to be a reality, and that it was time to focus on a new dream. A new vision. Or sacrifice forever any semblance of happiness and a satisfying, fulfilling life.

Yeah, when put like that, it didn't take a rocket scientist to figure out he'd been a prisoner of things he had no control of, for far, far too long. It was time to get the fuck over it and pull his head out of his ass.

"Hey." A soft voice interrupted his litany of self-castigation.

He turned gratefully, relieved to have a reprieve from his current train of thought even if he preferred not to be disturbed when he was here, a place he could usually count on being left alone because everyone kept to themselves and minded their business.

He smiled when he saw Tonya, a nurse at the hospital where Alyssa had been taken earlier in the evening. She worked in the ER, which was how Zack, as well as other members of DSS, had become acquainted with her. It certainly wasn't an uncommon occurrence for DSS to be in and out of the ER on a regular basis, whether it was an injury to one of their team members or someone they brought in as the result of a job. Like Alyssa.

"Rough night, huh," Tonya said quietly, her gaze flitting over Zack's features as if his inner torment were a flashing neon sign.

Zack sighed and took another long swig of his beer, setting the now-empty bottle back on the bar and motioning to the bartender for another.

"Yeah. It sucked. You want a drink?"

Tonya slid onto the stool beside him, hauling her purse into her lap between the edge of the bar and her midsection. "I'll have what you're having."

Zack lifted his hand to gain the attention of the bartender and held up two fingers.

"The girl wasn't my patient, but the entire ER was talking about it," Tonya said, a grimace twisting her pretty features. "If you can't talk about it, fine, but is it true that her *friend* did that to her because Alyssa was the better dancer?"

Zack made an indistinct garbled choking sound. "Some friend, huh."

"Jesus. So it's true. What the fuck kind of maniac teenagers are parents raising these days?"

"I think the problem is they aren't being raised at all," Zack said in disgust. "Rather, the parents are being managed and manipulated by their spoiled brats who have gross senses of entitlement. Whatever happened to pouting or throwing tantrums over not getting their favorite toys, for fuck's sake? Apparently taking out a hit on your competition is the new norm."

Tonya snagged one of the beers the bartender set in front of them and then clinked her bottle against Zack's before taking a long swallow.

"Sure makes you think twice about procreating."

Zack nodded, even if a large family had been exactly what he'd always wanted. If things had gone as he'd planned ... He closed his eyes, but not before the unfinished mental statement drifted through his mind as a fully formed thought. If things had gone as planned, he would be retired from the pros and have his second, possibly even third child by now instead of taking a bad hit as a quarterback in his second year and opting not to go back.

"Hey, you okay?" Tonya asked.

He glanced her way to see concern in her eyes. He didn't attempt to lie, because she saw this kind of shit on a daily basis, and she wasn't any more immune to the effects than he was.

"Yeah. Just another bad day at the office."

She laughed and held her bottle to his again. "I'll drink to that. But then isn't every day a bad one when you have jobs like ours? Makes you wonder if we have rocks in our heads."

Zack knew why he hadn't gone back to the pros. Why he'd pursued a career in law enforcement. Some would say he was just following in his old man's footsteps, even if that was the very last thing he'd ever do. And he also knew why he'd ended up taking a job with DSS at an important crossroads in his life when he was being recruited by a government agency.

But he liked DSS and the people he worked with. And he liked the fact that certain gifts that most people viewed with skepticism or outright derision were not only accepted but witnessed through the extraordinary powers that both Caleb's and Beau's wives possessed.

Because Zack had firsthand experience with the extraordinary. Gracie had possessed one such gift. The ability to read minds. There was no explanation for it. It certainly wasn't genetic, because her parents were complete wastes of human DNA and yet somehow they'd managed to produce an extraordinary daughter, so divergent from her upbringing and surroundings that it was astonishing. It brought to mind the possibility of being switched at birth or that the entire scientific argument of nature versus nurture was a bunch of bullshit thought of by brilliant minds with nothing better to do than hypothesize about why people become the people they do.

Because Gracie defied both nature and nurture. If one looked at her gene pool, she was fucked and doomed to life as a complete loser. If one looked at the nurture aspect, she was equally fucked, because in no way had she been brought up in an environment conducive to forming a responsible, empathetic, intelligent and sweet individual. And yet Gracie was all of those things. Her reward? He had not a fucking clue, but his imagination had come up with all manner of gruesome possibilities over the years and every single one of them tortured him endlessly.

"Hey," Tonya said, once more diverting his thoughts from the blackness into which they'd descended.

And once more he glanced her way, meeting her sweet smile, warm, sparkling eyes and inviting features.

"Want to go blow off some steam together? Your place, my place. Doesn't really matter. And no, before you ask, I'm not proposing marriage and no, I'm not looking for a relationship. I'm happy with my life the way it is at present, but that doesn't mean I'm blind, nor would I turn down a night of mindless sex with a gorgeous hunk of alpha male."

Her question rattled him, even though he considered himself as steady as they come and a master at masking any sort of reaction he might be feeling. He stared blankly at her a moment, pondering why he was even hesitating.

Tonya was a beautiful, intelligent woman. More than that, she had a sense of humor, didn't have an ego and didn't take herself too seriously. And she was a good woman. A woman any man would be damn lucky to have, and not just on the temporary basis she was proposing.

So why the hell was he sitting here staring like he had no idea how to respond instead of already herding her toward the door?

What the hell was wrong with him?

Shame twisted in his gut, filled his chest until it was tight with it. She was offering what most guys would give their left nut for, but damn it, she deserved more than some mindless fuck from a guy not completely and utterly focused on her. And tonight he couldn't give her that kind of guarantee. He couldn't give her anything at all except an orgasm, and well, that was questionable too. Because neither of his "heads" were focused, and while he didn't need his dick to get a woman off and rock her world, he just wasn't feeling it tonight.

Tonya slid her hand down his arm and then wrapped her fingers around his wrist, squeezing gently, her smile never faltering.

"I don't have a fragile ego, Zack. The look on your face says it all, so stop beating yourself up trying to figure out what to say to break it to me gently that you aren't looking for a one-night stand. I get it, okay? Well, and if you ever want a rain check, it's not like I'll harbor a grudge over being rejected and punish you for eternity."

Zack slid his fingers up her jawline, his features intent and serious as he cupped her cheek.

"That right there is a prime example of why you deserve better than me, even for one night."

Her hand fluttered upward to lie across his before she gently pulled it away, squeezing his fingers when she returned his hand to the bar top.

"Whoever she was did a real number on you."

His eyes widened in surprise at her perceptiveness when it came to the fact that his reluctance involved a prior relationship, but he also recognized that the conclusions she'd drawn were wrong. But he didn't correct her.

"Shit happens to the best of us," she said ruefully. "What separates the weak from the strong is what they do with the shit once it falls."

Zack leaned forward, framing her face in his hands before kissing her forehead.

"Thank you. I needed to hear that tonight."

As he slid from the bar stool, she frowned. "You need a ride home? How much have you had to drink?"

He smiled at the chiding tone of her voice. Yes, she was beautiful, fun, smart and witty, but she felt more like a sister than a lover. Why couldn't he be attracted to her? Sexually. It sure as hell would uncomplicate a hell of a lot of things for him right now. But then none of his previous sexual encounters could hardly be considered a matter of attraction beyond simple lust and a brief moment of blowing off steam.

If he was attracted to Tonya, or rather felt more than the affection one felt toward a sibling or good friend, then it *would* mean a more serious relationship, because she deserved that. For that matter all the women he'd been with deserved better than he'd given them, but at least he hadn't lied or misled them in any manner and both parties had gone in knowing the score. He wasn't *that* much of a bastard.

But Tonya? Despite her spiel about not wanting marriage and commitment—and he believed her because she was inherently honest and refreshingly straightforward—she was the bring-home-to-meet-the-family type woman.

"I've had exactly one and one-fourth beers. I'm good. Want to test my blood alcohol?" he teased.

She rolled her eyes. "Okay. You get a pass. I just don't want you in my ER when I'm off duty. So be careful."

"I will. And Tonya, thanks. I mean that."

"Anything for a friend."

"I'm going to take off and get some rest. Been a shitty day.

Ready for it to be over and start over again tomorrow. And hope to hell it's not a repeat of today."

She saluted him with her beer bottle as he gave her another hug and then headed for the door.

The cooler air was welcome after the suffocating interior of the bar, and it also served as a wake-up call from the maudlin direction his thoughts had taken over the last hour.

He slid behind the wheel of his truck and paused before cranking the engine. He hadn't lied. Today had been epic on the shit scale. Rivaled by very few other events in his life. And maybe that's why it had hit him so hard.

Losing Gracie. Not knowing how or why. That was the most difficult thing to swallow. And he *still* hadn't gotten over it.

His old man had been furious with him because Zack had seriously considered not even entering the draft his senior year of college after a stellar four years as starting quarterback for the University of Tennessee. But his head and heart hadn't been in it. How could it be? If the one person he wanted most to share his dream with was gone—disappeared without a goddamn trace, leaving him to think the absolute worst—then what was the point?

His father had railed at him that he was throwing his life away over white trailer park trash who wasn't worth his time. He'd never liked Gracie. *Disliked* was too mild a term. He *despised* her. The one and only time he'd brought Gracie to his home to meet his father, the bastard had humiliated her by calling her white trash and making it all too evident that she had no place in Zack's life, his priorities and that she wasn't good enough and would never amount to anything.

He'd never taken her back there. And it had forever caused

a rift between him and his father. One that hadn't been repaired to this day.

After her disappearance, he'd gone to his father. Asked for his help. It was his father's goddamn job as chief of police to protect the citizens of his town. His father had laughed. The asshole had actually laughed and celebrated the fact that she was out of the picture. He hadn't lifted a goddamn finger to investigate her disappearance.

And then when Zack had hesitated to enter the draft because he feared above all else that she would return and he wouldn't be there, that it would appear he'd simply given up on her, abandoned her, his father had lost his shit.

Only his friends talking him down and assuring him that if Gracie did return they'd sit on her and let him know gave him the impetus to pursue his dream of playing in the pros, something he'd never imagined doing without Gracie at his side.

They were going to be married. Have a big family. He'd play in the pros ten years, bank enough money so his family would be financially secure and then retire so he could devote all his time to his wife and children.

The first two seasons, he'd led a previously struggling, bottom-rung team to the playoffs. He'd been heralded as saving the franchise and putting it back on the map. Making it relevant. And then a bad hit sustained while he was making the game-winning touchdown pass had resulted in a torn rotator cuff, which had taken him out of pro football after only two seasons.

It didn't signal the end of his career but he was at a crossroads. He had two options. Undergo extensive rehab in the off-season, work his ass off and come back. Or take the guaranteed signing money from his contract and simply walk away.

He'd chosen the latter.

He could have rehabbed. He could have gone back and likely played for many more years. But instead, he'd joined law enforcement, because Gracie was still uppermost in his mind, and he couldn't give up the idea that one day he'd find her. Or at least find out what happened to her.

His father was enraged. Apoplectic. Told him that if he'd had his goddamn head in the game in the first place, instead of being so hung up on worthless white trash, he'd have never taken that hit in the first place. And that he was ruining his entire future for a *woman*. His father was a misogynist pig who couldn't imagine sacrificing anything for a female. Especially a career that would make him millions.

As a child Zack resented his mother for bailing on him and his dad, but as he'd grown older, he understood. How could any woman live with a man like his father? His only source of blame or anger was that she'd left him with a man who was clearly a self-centered, egotistical asshole.

So he chose a career that gave him access—opportunities— and channels that enabled him to be more proactive in his search for Gracie. And after that last confrontation with his father, he had never gone back home. There was simply nothing for him there, and every time a body would be found, he'd die a thousand deaths wondering if it could be Gracie. It was simply too painful to go back to a place that was so integral, such an important part of his life, his past. Where he and Gracie met, fell in love and shared their hopes and dreams for the future.

He hadn't lost his virginity until he reached the pros because it never felt right in college, though there was certainly no lack of opportunities. And the memory of that night was still a source of humiliation for him because it had made him sick to his soul. So sick that he'd stumbled out of bed and went into the bathroom and heaved the contents of his stomach into the toilet. Because that part of him was supposed to be for Gracie. They'd waited. It had been important for him to wait until they married. With her being four years younger, he never wanted to feel as though he'd taken advantage of her in any way. He wanted their wedding night to be special. Hell, he couldn't even remember the name of the girl he'd lost his virginity to. What kind of ass did that make him?

Thank God she thought he'd just had too much to drink, since they'd met at a team party after a successful playoff win.

He pounded his hand against the steering wheel, anger rising, self-loathing overwhelming him. He'd dissed a perfectly good woman tonight because of his own personal hang-ups and his inability to move on and get the fuck over it.

Twelve years. Twelve goddamn years. Enough already!

This was bullshit.

Either Gracie was dead, or she'd simply chosen to disappear. Neither was a possibility he could do a damn thing about and it was time to stop existing like a fucking zombie and get on with his sorry-ass life.

This shit had to end right now. It *was* ending right now. Because he refused to spend another goddamn day thinking about what could have been when any sane person would have gotten it through their thick-ass head that what could have been wasn't ever going to happen and no amount of regret or wishing would make a damn bit of difference.

He cranked the engine and curled both hands tightly around the steering wheel, resolve surrounding him like a steel case.

Let go.

Move on.

Quit being such a miserable fuck.

Be happy.

And starting tomorrow, that's precisely what he was going to do. Tonight was about saying goodbye to old dreams and what would never be. Tomorrow?

It was going to be about embracing a future without all the fucking baggage he'd been carrying around for more than a decade.

THREE

ANNA-GRACE lifted her arms toward the wall, frowning in concentration as she tilted and turned the painting to allow the light to strike it just so.

"If only you'd ever look at me that way," a male teased.

Instantly losing the frown—and concentration—she turned, a ready smile on her lips as she registered Wade Sterling's presence.

"I had no idea you preferred women who scowled at you," she said lightly.

It was a familiar repartee, one that had taken considerable effort to establish between her and the wealthy, handsome gallery owner. Most, if not all women, would consider her a fool for not returning Wade's overtures, which had grown subtler, not bolder, with time.

He snorted. "You may scowl when the light is not quite right, but then, when it is, you gaze at your painting as one would a lover."

She hated the faint heat that stole over her cheeks. And the fact that she instantly averted her gaze, looking away, anywhere but at him. He was no threat to her. Logically, she knew that. But logic never won over fear because fear wasn't rational. It defied all the rules of logic.

He sighed but didn't comment on her rejection. But then he'd grown quite used to them in their acquaintance. At first they'd been purposeful and adamant. Even forceful. Over time, however, she'd tried to relax, to soften the often unconscious rejection, but it was simply too ingrained in her to halt them all together. And her regret grew with each one rendered, unintentional or not.

"Here, let me," he said, seemingly unruffled by the awkwardness of the moment.

He took the painting, affixed it to where she'd found the best lighting and then stood back, studying the effect.

"It's good," he said simply. "But you know that. You wouldn't agree to display it otherwise and neither would I, despite our friendship. This show is going to launch you, Anna-Grace. About the last piece . . ."

He purposely trailed off, looking inquisitively at her, and she fidgeted self-consciously under his scrutiny.

"It's done," she hedged.

Or at least it would be once she let it go. Figuratively speaking. Thank God, Wade understood it—and her. That the painting in question wasn't merely an object of commercial art meant to showcase her talent. For that matter, it wasn't even for sale. It was too deeply personal to ever part with, and was the method of communicating her vow to *herself*. Not to others. She'd questioned even showing it at all, what purpose it truly served. But, it was, in many ways, symbolic of . . .

Well, there were many words applicable to the painting and its symbolism. Moving on—she nearly laughed, though there was nothing remotely amusing about the situation. Moving on indicated getting past something ... difficult. The end of a relationship, perhaps. The death of a loved one. Personal recovery. Reaching a point where one decided to take a stand and refuse to allow oneself to dwell—and exist—solely in the past. Well, at least that last one was applicable to her situation.

For her, the title said it all.

Dreams Lost.

"Destroyed" was more apropos, but too dramatic for a painting that was almost whimsical when viewed through unknowing eyes. An image that would invoke nostalgia for the sheer innocence that seemingly radiated from the light and shadows captured on the canvas.

It had taken her many attempts before she'd settled on the look she wanted to achieve. And in fact, the title had been indicative, and settled upon, after her *first* rendition of the place that had played such an important role in her formative years.

It had been dark, haunting to look at. One couldn't help but feel sadness when viewing the barren landscape and the sense of loneliness that was prevalent in the painting. For that matter, she wouldn't have been able to look upon something that brought back such heartbreak and despair.

She readily admitted that it was the more accurate version, the one that most represented her pain and grief. It was just simply too personal to share with strangers, those who didn't—who couldn't—understand. How could they? But the original depiction represented the person she'd been for far too long now and it was time to portray herself differently to the world. Even if the world, for her, was still a narrow, shielded familiar path she never ventured from. No one else knew of her demons. She shared them with no one, and she preferred to keep it that way. Only in Wade had she confided, and it had taken a long, winding road to open up to even one person. She had no desire to broaden her circle of confidants.

And so, instead of simply portraying a gnarled, sprawling tree, weathered by time, its limbs thin at the ends as if no longer offering protection beneath its awning and an empty landscape with the lake beyond looking gray and stormy as though it were angered by the betrayal the title represented, she'd painted herself—alone—a survivor. Standing beyond the once-protective shelter of the limbs and intricate roots of the huge oak, only her back presented as she stared over the lake.

It was a sunny day, not even one wispy cloud to mar the canvas, and the blue of the water sparkled like tiny diamonds that had been scattered by a playful child. And the tree, while showing its age, looked more of a timeless guardian, spreading its arms outward, ever watchful and mindful of those in its protective embrace.

Escape. Freedom. Once it had been those very things to her. And now things had come full circle because the finished painting represented her freedom from her destructive past.

Now she only had to hang it. The final step in her metamorphosis from hopelessness and helplessness to strength and optimism.

"Have you changed your mind about displaying it?" Wade asked.

There was a note of hope in his voice, almost as if he knew that putting it out there was ... acknowledgment. Baring all the things she'd hidden for the last twelve years. And he was afraid she wasn't yet ready. He was worried she'd revert to the woman she'd been when they'd first met. God only knew why he'd persevered. Why he'd shaken off the countless aloof and cold rebuffs from her and dug persistently through the layers of numbness, fear and paralysis to the heart of her. Then settled for the only things she *could* give him. Friendship. And finally, inexplicably, her *trust*.

No, he didn't think she was ready at all.

He was wrong.

She *was* ready. It was something she should have done so much sooner. She'd spent so much time numb, refusing to allow herself to feel . . . anything. Because emptiness was preferable to the overwhelming pain and grief she'd long ago resigned herself to, as though she had no choice but to suffer such a barren existence.

No, she didn't feel desire for Wade. Not the kind of the lover he'd referenced. But she *did* need him. His friendship and unwavering support. She needed those things more than she was comfortable admitting, but she was also done lying to herself and living in constant denial that she was okay, that everything was fine, and she was all right. Normal.

Because she wasn't. And she'd likely never be. But she'd finally accepted that and opted to make the best of what she *did* have and stop dwelling on all she'd lost.

She looked at him again, this time not masking any of the vulnerability she knew he could read in her eyes. There was a time when she would have died rather than allow anyone to see her so weak and . . . fragile.

His face softened and his eyes warmed with the friendship

she'd come to define their relationship by. The very thing she needed most but had never embraced. Until now. And in the lines of his face, a face that could in fact be quite hard, unyielding and even dangerous, she saw *his* acceptance of the only thing she could ever offer him.

She knew he'd accepted it long ago, but perhaps had never truly *seen* until now. Or wanted to see. Because she feared his giving up and her losing the one steadfast thing she now had apart from her art.

Her shoulders sagged imperceptibly, and she realized she'd been holding her breath, harboring the fear she'd vowed to no longer live with, because she'd been afraid of his rejection and of being alone. Again. As she'd been for so very long.

He wrapped his arm around her shoulders, easing the painting down with his free hand until its edge rested gently against the wall. He gathered her close, offering her the warmth and strength of his hug, something she'd come to cherish rather than dread for the physical contact she'd always avoided at all cost.

"You're ready," he said, as if having read her thoughts and answering his own question in the process. "I'm proud of you, Anna-Grace."

"Don't you dare make me cry," she warned, already feeling the betraying sting of tears.

He gave her another affectionate squeeze and then relinquished his hold on her.

"So where do we place the guest of honor?" he asked, his gaze sweeping the gallery and the other paintings of hers that were artfully displayed to their full advantage. "I think center stage, don't you? This means something, Anna-Grace. *You* mean something. And it—like you—needs to be celebrated."

Okay, so he *was* going to make her cry. She wiped the corner of her eye with the back of her hand in disgust and glared accusingly at him. He merely smiled back, and she marveled at the feeling of closeness—a connection—to another person. So what if she wasn't ready for a romantic relationship? Maybe she never would be. A woman didn't need a man to be whole, and she was more than happy to prove it.

But a friend? Everyone needed a friend. And she realized, not for the first time, that part of the reason her grief, her piercing and gut-wrenching sense of betrayal over what Zack had done, was so sharp, unrelenting and ... life changing ... was that he hadn't just been the man she had loved, had adored beyond reason, had planned to spend the rest of her life with, and have his children. The man who had shared her hopes and dreams and every secret she'd never dared expose to another living person.

He'd been her best—and only—friend. The one she turned to for comfort. Love. Acceptance. The very best part of her very being, her heart, her soul. He'd been her confidant. The one person she trusted never to let her down, as so many had in her young life.

And yet those past betrayals paled in comparison to Zack's.

She shook her head, furious with herself for going back. Again. And she set her lips firmly, sending Wade a determined look he couldn't possibly misunderstand.

Zack had been her entire world, and he'd turned it completely upside down, discarding her like the trash she'd been called by the people of their town. By his own father, for that matter. How could she have thought he would be different from anyone else in a place where she simply didn't exist or matter?

But now her world was what *she* made it. And she had no liking for the world she'd previously lived in, one of her making. Only she could change it. Create it. Make it better—*perfect* even. And it was high time she got on with doing just that.

Impulsively, she slipped her fingers through Wade's and squeezed his hand, startling him. She could understand why. She never initiated any sort of intimacy, even in the capacity of friendship. She had a carefully constructed protective barrier that surrounded her and she allowed no one to breach it, nor did she ever venture beyond it out of self-preservation.

But as she'd already acknowledged, everyone needed a friend. And losing one friend didn't preclude the existence of another, as stupid as it was for the time it had taken her to have that particular epiphany.

Wade was safe. She was safe *with* him. And she wanted him to know she ... trusted ... him. She inhaled sharply at merely allowing the word *trust* to drift through her thoughts.

Because after Zack, and until Wade, she'd trusted no one. It was a lesson learned the hard way, and one that had been repeatedly taught, but it had taken the most devastating lesson of all to finally make her realize that giving her trust was akin to taking a knife and thrusting it through her own heart.

Her chin trembled slightly, but Wade, ever observant, saw it and reached his hand to cup her chin, holding it between his thumb and fingers.

"Don't ever think it, Anna-Grace," he said softly, reminding her once again that he wasn't harmless, despite her observations to the contrary.

He was a dangerous, tightly controlled man whose vision of the world differed from most others'. The artist in her saw in bright colors—colors that had been dimmed for a long time until finally she'd set them free. But Wade's world was steeped in gray and shadows. Much like the initial rendering of her *Dreams Lost* painting.

She shivered at the intensity in his gaze and swallowed nervously, because she wondered if she'd finally lost her mind. Befriending a man like him? Trusting him when she'd sworn never to trust anyone—*especially* a man—again? A man, who like her, seemed to have no friends, not to mention had the same trust issues she herself suffered. It could well be the second-biggest mistake of her life.

Or? Perhaps . . . just maybe . . . it was her first *smart* move in twelve years and in Wade she'd found not a lover, husband material or romantic interest, but a kindred spirit who was offering her what she needed the most.

Simple friendship and the opportunity to reimmerse herself in the real world, where trust and friendship weren't bad four-letter words and were a normal part of everyday life—for most people.

But she could change all that *now*. He was offering, unconditionally. All she had to do was what she'd *already* resolved to do. Accept. Make peace. Move on.

Let go.

Free herself from her self-imposed prison of isolation and loneliness, and embrace the future that awaited her with hope and optimism, two emotions she'd once taken for granted but which were now completely alien to her.

She was in control of her own destiny and she could make it damn well whatever she wanted it to be.

Hatred. Grief. Betrayal. Hurt. Despair. Sorrow. Regret?

Those things no longer had any place in her life and she re-fused to live her life that way a single moment longer.

This showing was her moment to shine. She was stepping into the sun after avoiding its rays and any semblance of warmth for the first time since she was but a young girl with all the en-thusiasm and naïveté that only belong to the innocent.

She was living her dream. *Finally*. And she was poised to share that dream—her talent—with others. People who might reject her. But she was no stranger to rejection, and having been through the worst, she could honestly say that nothing could ever hurt her more than she'd already been hurt.

The only direction for her to go was up. There was no other option when you've hit rock bottom. She knew it. Wade knew it. And God only knew why he stuck with her. Why he reevaluated his wants and needs once she'd made it clear that she wouldn't—couldn't—return his romantic interest. And why he then com-promised and accepted only what she *could* give him.

It was on the tip of her tongue to *ask* him why. But when she looked his way once more, he wore the same determined, pierc-ing gaze, one that had always made her uneasy, because she knew what it was like to have the gift of reading others' minds—their innermost thoughts. And Wade had an uncanny knack for al-ways knowing precisely what was going on in hers.

FOUR

ZACK pulled into the parking lot of an upscale art gallery on Westheimer Road, on the opposite side of the interstate from the Galleria, an area known for its chic boutiques that catered to the fashion-conscious and wealthier crowd, or at least those who wanted to maintain the façade of wealth.

He wasn't impressed with the outer trappings of wealth. He could be considered wealthy in his own right. He had a million. Ten of them to be exact, managed and invested by his financial advisor, Wes Coyle, who worked in the Woodlands, a suburb north of Houston that had quickly become a haven for the privileged.

With the guaranteed signing money from his contract when he'd been drafted in the first round of the pros, and then walking away after an injury in his second straight playoff year instead of getting rehab and continuing to quarterback, he'd been guaranteed financial security, even though he lived frugally, choosing to stash the money instead of running through it in just a few years.

His truck was used when he bought it a few years ago and he still drove it. He lived in a modest one-bedroom apartment and preferred jeans and T-shirts to designer clothing. The *GQ* look didn't suit him and he felt fraudulent even contemplating the lifestyle of someone considered wealthy.

So his money was secured, gaining interest in moderate-risk investments instead of sitting in a bank drawing a measly .01 percent interest rate, and he lived on the salary he drew from DSS. It was more than enough for his modest needs. It wasn't like he had anyone to share it with anyway. No one to lavish gifts and surprises on. A matter he intended to rectify soon.

After his come-to-Jesus meeting with himself two days earlier, he felt at peace for the first time in more years than he could count. He had a sense of purpose. Direction. One that didn't have a lost cause at the heart of it all.

Gracie was gone. Lost to him. She wasn't coming back. He'd never have his dream. So it was time to get the fuck over it and deal. Find a new dream and live it.

He wasn't surprised to see Dane already there, parked two vehicles away. Dane was punctual to a fault. Well, not even punctual. His idea of being on time was to show up well in advance of the appointed time. Zack was pretty much the same. He liked to size up the situation. Get the lay of the land and a feel for what they were signing on for. He suspected Dane's reasons were similar.

Dane got out of his SUV along with Isaac and Capshaw and started toward Zack just as Beau pulled in beside Zack. Eliza was with him and Zack turned to open the passenger door for her. She smiled and gave him a saucy thank-you as she slid out of the seat.

Eliza was an exceptionally beautiful woman. Not that she had the distinctive look of a woman that most men found stunning. Nor did she have the carefully cultivated look of a woman who went to great lengths to enhance her looks. Not that he had an issue with women who did. He was all for whatever made them happy and confident—he had a healthy respect for all women, in all their shapes, sizes and looks, natural or not. After all, it was what was beneath it all that mattered—at least to him.

Eliza just had a fresh, natural beauty that people responded to. She was absolutely genuine and she shot from the hip. No bullshit about her. But what capped it for Zack was the warmth in her eyes, how easy with a smile she was and the fact that she could kick ass with the best of them and was a crack tech wiz to boot. Even if Quinn, the youngest Devereaux brother, was in denial when he swore his computer skills were superior to hers. Zack's money was on Eliza in a tech war throw-down. She could probably hack into the CIA. Hell, for all he knew, she already had, because the woman did have an uncanny knack for producing information that raised eyebrows with her coworkers.

Her diminutive stature made her look harmless, but Zack had seen her in action too many times to ever make that error in judgment. He pitied the fool who underestimated her, because there was no doubt in Zack's mind she was capable of taking down a man twice her size and weight. Hard. And hand him his balls in the process.

Brent and Eric got out of the back just as Dane and the others caught up to them. Brent had come off injured reserve a few months earlier after being involved in a crash involving him, Beau and Ari, who was now Beau's wife. It amused Zack to see

Brent riding since he was usually the one driving. He was a former race car driver and was usually behind the wheel personally or professionally. Judging by the disgruntled look on his face, he wasn't happy about his backseat status.

"Shall we?" Dane asked dryly. "Or are we just going to congregate in the parking lot and sip champagne?"

The irony was that Zack could see Dane doing just that. He had that wealthy, cultivated look that fit well with the environment they were about to venture into. Dane wore khaki slacks, a polo shirt and expensive sunglasses. Zack wasn't entirely sure what Dane's story was. Zack hadn't worked long enough with the other man to draw an accurate picture of him, and Dane kept a tight lid on his personal life. Not that Zack faulted him for that. DSS did their jobs, didn't tend to be too up close and personal, though Beau was the closest thing Zack had to a friend outside their partnership. But at the end of the day, they all had each other's backs. No questions. And wasn't that the most important thing?

But the man had money and there was no way his job at DSS gave him the kind of wealth he obviously possessed. Even at double Zack's salary, as generous as it was, Dane's lifestyle, though quiet, exceeded what DSS paid him. And though Zack admitted to a passing curiosity about Dane's history, he didn't spend a lot of time dwelling on it, nor did he ever attempt to pry, because he sure as hell didn't want anyone prying into his personal life. He offered his coworkers the same respect he himself demanded.

"Nice chunk of real estate," Dane observed as they headed toward the glass double doors.

Isaac whistled in appreciation. "Too rich for my blood. Wonder what the hell an art gallery owner wants with us normal folks and why he's pulling out all the stops for security?"

Beau shrugged. "It's a job. Pays the same as any other. Gets the same treatment as any other."

No arguing that point.

JOIE DE VIVRE, the name of the gallery, was positioned over the door, not readily noticeable from the busy street or to people driving by. It was obvious to Zack that either the owner had shitty marketing or that the art in his galleries sold by word of mouth and he didn't *need* to have a flashy display to draw customers inside. He was betting on the latter.

As soon as they walked through the doors they were greeted by an impeccably dressed woman. Her heels tapped on the polished marble floors, several strands of her upswept hair bouncing against her neck as she smiled in greeting.

The gallery was noticeably empty of patrons and Zack hadn't seen a "closed" sign. The doors were open, but perhaps that was because DSS had an appointment and was expected. In fact, the gallery looked as though it was being prepared for the showing, presumably the reason for the request for security. Maybe a big-name artist was going to be exhibiting here. Zack was woefully out of touch with the art world. What little he knew had come from Gracie and listening to her dreams of one day becoming an accomplished artist.

Despite his resolve to put her and the past behind him, he couldn't help but think that this could be her. Living her dream. Happy. Painting. Him supporting her in her endeavors.

Damn it but he had to stop this shit. Move forward. The irony of taking a job providing security for an art exhibition mere days after his vow to put his past firmly behind him wasn't lost on him. Fate was a fickle bitch and right now she was having one fuck of a laugh at his expense. Or at the very least testing his commitment to the promise he'd made to himself.

After Beau introduced his group to the woman, her eyes lit up in recognition.

"Of course. Mr. Sterling told me you'd be arriving at noon. Unfortunately he's on the phone with an important client, so it will be just a few moments before he's free. Would you care for coffee? Wine?"

If she'd offered champagne, none of the DSS members would have been able to keep a straight face after Dane's sarcastic remark in the parking lot. Even so, Eliza smirked, but then she was the most irreverent of the bunch.

The employee's smile was natural, not practiced like a lot of salespeople's were. Her comportment was impeccable, and she fit into the image of an exclusive, high-end art gallery with her designer clothing, heels and makeup that made it appear as though she wore none. Her ears were adorned with simple diamond studs that might not appear expensive but were at least two carats apiece and undoubtedly cost a hefty chunk of change.

When no one took her up on her offer, she politely excused herself and said she'd notify Sterling that they had arrived. Then she briskly walked away, her heels once again tapping a sharp staccato on the Italian marble floor.

"Size her up enough?"

Beau's dry question shook Zack from his observations. The other DSS operatives liked to give him shit for having a keen eye for detail. He sat back and studied people, and let others do the talking. More often than not he found out far more by merely watching and listening than he would by simply talking to the person. When people thought no one was looking they tended to relax, to lower their guard, and in those moments they'd become careless or simply betray their character.

Zack could be depended on to recall the minutest details his coworkers often missed. Body language. Subtle nuances that gave people away. Fidgeting, nervousness. He didn't miss much.

In this case, though, Beau thought Zack was viewing her with male interest, not sizing her up in a businesslike fashion. But Beau was wrong. Not that the woman wasn't beautiful, but this was a job. Not a pickup bar.

Zack shrugged. "She's got money. Not sure how much a gig like this pays, but I'm betting she's got another source, whether it's a husband, boyfriend or money she made herself. Could be a bored heiress, but she seems quite intelligent. I'd bet my next paycheck her knowledge in this field is solid. I would also bet that she has an advanced degree."

Eliza quirked an eyebrow upward. "You got all this by looking at her for five seconds? I would hate to see how *I've* fared in your analyses, since we've spent a hell of a lot more than a few seconds together."

Zack grinned. "You're the shit and you know it. You don't need me to give you pretty compliments."

Eliza rolled her eyes. "Well, duh! I know I don't *need* them, but they are nice to hear from time to time. Women like compliments and I'm no exception. Hanging around all the testosterone at the office hasn't made me grow a penis and forget all about my girl parts."

Beau and Dane cracked up, their shoulders shaking. Zack shook his head ruefully. Yeah, he adored Eliza. She had a sharp wit and tongue to match. She was intelligent, compassionate, loyal and was damn good company when Zack's melancholy kicked in more than usual.

Though he'd never shared any of his past with Eliza, or with anyone else at DSS for that matter, he knew Eliza saw more than she let on. As a result, she gave him shit on a regular basis, prodding him and basically refusing to allow him to feel sorry for himself. She had an uncanny ability to peg his moods when they were at their worst, and as a result she never let him withdraw from the others when he would have otherwise retreated into isolation for days at a time. Hell, she even routinely showed up at his apartment to watch a football game with him. Or she'd make him buy her dinner, have a few beers and shoot the shit. It was Eliza's equivalent of an ass kicking with a side of get the fuck over it.

It occurred to him that maybe he *should* have confided in her. Her skills were impeccable and she could very well have been of help in his search for Gracie and his attempt to find out what happened to her. But he was beyond that now and he wouldn't indulge in regret for what he'd sworn he was putting behind him. Not to mention she'd have likely thought he'd lost his goddamn mind for hanging on to a ghost for twelve years.

Zack shoved his hands in his pockets and glanced around the gallery impatiently. He hated waiting, and even more, he hated that they'd been summoned here when clients usually came to them, not the other way around. Why it was important for the meet-and-greet to happen on the client's turf he wasn't sure, but he suspected it was a power play. A dick-sizing exercise so DSS would know how "important" this guy was—or thought he was.

Whatever. He didn't call the shots. Caleb and Beau did, though Caleb had pulled back considerably since marrying Ramie, and Beau and Quinn had taken more of a lead in the day-to-day running of DSS, even if it had been Caleb's brainchild.

DSS had been formed in the wake of the horrific abduction, torture and rape of Tori Devereaux, the baby sister and only sister of Caleb, Beau and Quinn. Caleb was determined that no one in his family ever be threatened again, and if they were able to help others in the process, even better. The company had suffered a few setbacks in its infancy. But it had only made Beau all the more determined to learn from those mistakes, hire better—the best money could buy—and expand. As a result, DSS was thriving, with more requests than they could logistically take on. They carefully vetted their prospective clients, particularly since some came under the guise of wanting access to Ramie and her extraordinary powers. And Caleb was insanely protective—and rightfully so—of his wife because the price she paid in using her powers was utterly terrifying.

A few moments later, a tall, well-dressed man walked from the back of the gallery, his stride confident and purposeful, his gaze direct and indecipherable. He wasn't at all what Zack would have expected, though he wasn't sure exactly what he had expected. Whatever it was, Wade Sterling didn't fit any preconceived notion Zack might have summoned.

He wore wealth while not appearing to wear it. There were no gaudy trappings or overdone dress. He wore expensive but simple slacks, and a silk button-up shirt. No tie. His watch was several G's but again didn't scream expensive. And the shoes likely cost one of Zack's entire paychecks.

But he had a hard look to him. Dangerous even. Again, not

the look of the stereotypical art gallery owner or at least Zack's idea of one. Something about him hit a nerve with Zack, who bristled, immediately on guard.

A quick glance at his teammates told him their reactions were mixed. Dane was unruffled and as unreadable as ever. No one ever really knew what he was thinking. Beau looked pensive while Isaac, Capshaw and Brent just studied the owner intently.

Eliza seemed to have a similar reaction as Zack's. In fact her eyes narrowed and her lips thinned, almost as if she was calling bullshit on the whole thing. But she was smart as a whip and he trusted her instincts. Her reaction validated his own.

Sterling's expression, neither a smile nor a frown, was as bland and unreadable as Dane's as he approached.

"I apologize for keeping you waiting," he said in a calm voice that despite his statement didn't reflect genuine apology. "I was unavoidably detained by an important business matter. I hope you weren't too inconvenienced and that Cheryl, my personal assistant, took good care of you."

Dane was the lead on assignments even though the Devereauxs were actually the owners and "in charge." Dane was the face of DSS. He handled the media and statements and headed the negotiations. Caleb and Beau both deferred to him as the front man. Everyone answered to Dane. Well, except Zack, who answered solely to Beau. It was an unspoken agreement that Dane seemed to take in stride.

So it was Dane who addressed Sterling.

He was also a get-to-the-point kind of guy and not keen on wasting time on bullshit and pleasantries, something Zack appreciated and also had in common with Dane.

"What can DSS do for you, Mr. Sterling? I understand you want a full security detail for an upcoming exhibit in a week's time. That doesn't give us much time to prepare so we need to know exactly what you expect from us and what our duties will be. You want the best and that's what you're going to get. But you can't expect the best if we don't have all information and any potential liabilities exposed and assessed."

Sterling sized up Dane quickly, fleeting respect flickering in his eyes. Zack suspected this man didn't offer his respect often, nor did Zack suspect he needed to. He was a man who commanded it.

"I imagine this will be a routine matter for a firm of your reputation," Sterling said, revealing that he'd at least done his homework. "No *expected* threats. I merely want a presence, a subtle presence, to ensure that all goes smoothly. This is an important event for this gallery and the artist. It will be a debut showing and I've put a lot of money into publicity and marketing. There will be much curiosity, as I've been very vague about the identity of the artist."

Eliza's eyebrow arched, but she remained silent, studying Sterling intently.

"I expect a certain dress code, which I assume won't be a problem," Sterling began.

Zack could almost hear the mental collective groans going up from everyone except Dane, who was no stranger to looking the part of a wealthy art patron.

Sterling had opened his mouth to continue when the sharp tap of heels alerted them to Cheryl's presence as she hurried up to them, carrying a large, unwrapped canvas, excitement clear on her face.

"I'm so sorry to interrupt, Mr. Sterling, but I knew you'd want to see this right away. The last piece was just couriered over. Shall I place it where we discussed?"

Everyone's gaze swept curiously to the source of her obvious enthusiasm.

When Zack looked, all the breath left his body, crushing his chest as his world tilted on its axis.

Voices sounded around him. Sterling was speaking with his assistant. But Zack was utterly numb. He stared at a scene so perfectly rendered, a scene that took him back to another time and place. A place he'd once shared with Gracie.

Exactly as it had existed when he and Gracie had spent so much time under the awning of those tree branches, nestled in the roots, Gracie wrapped securely in his arms, Zack a barrier between her and the rest of the world.

And the woman in the painting?

Even with her back turned, he'd know her anywhere.

This wasn't a current depiction of that spot. Too much time had elapsed for it to remain unchanged. The parts along the lake owned by a paper company had been sold off years ago, and now, where it had mostly been untouched forest, it would be developed, trees gone, the landscape irrevocably changed by housing subdivisions.

His vision blurred, eyes stung, and the two initials acting as the artist's signature wobbled into view. A simple *A.G.*

Anna-Grace. His Gracie. Dear God, she was alive?

But if she was alive. Well. Painting, even. Then why the hell had she disappeared and why had she never made an effort to contact him?

The painting meant something to the artist. It was evident in every brushstroke. Emotion jumped off the canvas and grabbed the person viewing it by the throat. He was besieged by nostalgia, knowledge of a time when everything was new, innocent, the world a vast opportunity in the making, life not to be survived but to be lived to the fullest, with every day savored.

But if he drew the conclusion that the painting—the place depicted—held value to the artist, then wouldn't it follow that *he* meant something to her? Because someone who cared about another person in that fashion didn't simply vanish, never to be heard from again, unless some great tragedy had occurred. And if he did in fact hold any memory or feeling to her, then why the fuck wouldn't she have made a minimal effort to alleviate the nightmares he'd been victim to for more than a decade?

Then his gaze fell on the title of the painting and his heart began to pound even harder.

Lost Dreams.

It was certainly a depiction of that. For *him*. But what would have caused *her* to give it such a title?

There was an inherent sadness to the drawing, as if the memory indeed was painful, a depiction of lost hope, and as the painting was titled, lost *dreams*.

Even the silhouette of the girl facing the lake seemed lonely and barren somehow.

Unwanted tears burned the edges of his eyes and he was besieged by a sense of sorrow. The painting didn't suggest that she had willingly parted ways with him and instead suggested regret . . . grief over the past.

"Zack?"

His name registered sharply and he shook himself to awareness to see the entire group staring at him, an array of expressions on their faces.

Sterling and his assistant stood to the side, also staring at Zack. Sterling wore a slight frown, his eyes intently studying Zack's reaction.

"What artist is the exhibit for?" Zack asked casually.

But there was no disguising the betraying tremor and hoarseness to his voice, despite his best effort to contain his reaction.

"The artist isn't what matters," Sterling said neutrally. "The security in no way involves the artist. It involves the art."

Eliza's head snapped up, her eyes flashing fire. "Wait a minute. You want to hire a security firm for the exhibit, but you don't give a fuck about the actual artist?"

Zack saw red, his thoughts so jumbled and chaotic he couldn't even give voice to the thousand what-the-fucks going through his mind.

"The artist prefers anonymity," Sterling said in a biting tone. "It's not even decided as to whether the artist will attend. The exhibit isn't about the artist, but rather the art."

Eliza snorted. "And this helps us do our job how?"

"Who is she?" Zack asked quietly.

Sterling immediately stiffened, his entire stance becoming both wary and menacing.

"I don't recall specifying the artist's gender."

At the same time Cheryl quickly turned the painting around, obscuring it from view with her body.

"The initials *A.G.* Do they stand for 'Anna-Grace'?" Zack asked hoarsely, no longer even attempting to disguise the demand in his voice.

"I specifically said the artist in question prefers anonymity," Sterling said, his jaw tight.

Frustration simmered in Zack. He was perilously close to losing his shit right here and now. And it was not going to be a pretty sight. For twelve fucking *years*—more than a third of his *life*—he'd worried and agonized over Gracie's fate and now this fuckhead was playing goddamn mind games when Zack was on the cusp of the impossible?

Oh *hell* no. That untouchable "I'm wealthy and powerful" act might work on others, but not on Zack. He worked for extremely wealthy but down-to-earth people. He himself was wealthy and he didn't act like an arrogant douche bag, smug and confident that his words and actions were law. Or above the law.

"Just answer the question," Zack said through a tightly clenched jaw. "The initials. *A.G.* Do they stand for 'Anna-Grace'?" His tone was frigid, suggesting without actually stating that he wouldn't ask again.

At that Sterling's expression became absolutely glacial. Frost formed in his gaze. His eyes hardened, his jaw ticking as he continued to size Zack up. For whatever reason, as soon as Zack had said her name, Sterling had gotten pissed, where before he'd just been a smug, arrogant asshole. Anger vibrated from him in waves. His eyes became shuttered, masking any hint or clue as to what he was thinking. Zack wanted to put his fist right through the bastard's jaw.

The sudden tension between the two men was palpable. Eliza threw Dane an uneasy glance and took another step closer to Zack's side, almost as if she knew the shit was about to hit the fan.

"We're done here," Sterling said in a rigid tone. "I no longer require your services. I'm more than happy to pay a consult fee if you leave your billing information with my assistant on your way out."

His response enraged Zack and Eliza quickly stepped between the two men, turning her back to Sterling and placing her hand on Zack's chest.

"Let's go, Zack," she said in a low voice. "This asshole's taken up enough of our time." She tossed a pissed-off look over her shoulder at Sterling and said in a tone as icy as his had been, "And you can bet you'll get that bill before we leave."

"Lizzie," Dane said, carefully enunciating each word so she got the message, "get the fuck away from him."

The threat in Dane's tone, and his body language, was clearly evident. Eliza turned but pulled Zack with her, trying to herd him toward the door.

"Eliza, *stop*," Zack said quietly, not wanting to vent his seething emotions on the other woman. But he planted his feet all the same, making it impossible for her to budge his much larger frame. "This is important. The most important thing in my goddamn *life*. I can't leave here. Not until I get the info I'm looking for. I'll kick the motherfucker's ass if it gets me the intel I want—that I *need*."

"Sir, should I call the police?" Cheryl inquired anxiously of Sterling.

Before Zack could follow up and make another demand, the glass entryway swung open and a woman hurried through, her gaze immediately focused on Sterling and his assistant.

As she took in the other DSS members, her face reddened

in embarrassment. Several things happened simultaneously. Wade rushed toward her and she hastily babbled an apology for interrupting.

Zack went completely still, not so much a single breath escaping his lungs as he drank in the sight before him. His throat closed in and he couldn't speak. Couldn't think. All he could do was stare.

"I'm so sorry, Wade," she said in a rush. "But I've changed my mind. I don't want to display the last painting. I just . . . can't."

The pain on her beautiful features was clearly evident. Her eyes were haunted by ghosts of the past. Ghosts that mirrored Zack's own. Because he was staring at one right this very moment.

He finally managed to rip himself from the stupor enveloping him and force the single, choked word from his mouth, his entire mind quaking with disbelief.

"Gracie?"

FIVE

GRACIE'S head snapped up, obviously seeing Zack for the first time after she'd burst through the doors in her haste to recant the agreement to hang the painting Cheryl was still clutching nervously.

Her gaze was horror-stricken and her face was deathly pale. Utter terror was reflected in her wide brown eyes.

She immediately started backstepping, turning as if to flee, and she would have if Sterling hadn't made a grab for her arm to prevent her from falling. As it was, she slipped from Sterling's grasp, sprawling onto her backside on the marble floor, and still, she pushed herself backward, her body language signaling horrific fear as she frantically tried to escape.

Zack stepped forward, unbelieving. God. This was his dream come to life and she was *running* from him? Looking at him like he was a goddamn monster? What the fuck was going on?

"Gracie," he said, his voice cracking with emotion. "My

God, Gracie, I thought you were dead! All these years. You can't imagine . . ."

He never got to finish his statement because her expression grew even more horror stricken—if such a thing were possible. Tears filled her eyes and devastation bathed her entire face. Gut-wrenching, terrible grief, betrayal and heartbreak. All the things he himself was feeling and had felt for more than a decade.

"You meant for them to *kill* me too?" she choked out, her words so garbled and panic-stricken that he nearly didn't comprehend them. But he heard every one and it only increased his bewilderment a hundred times more. *Kill her?* This was his dream turned worst nightmare of his entire life.

"What are you talking about?" he demanded. "Who are you talking about? *Who tried to kill you?*" Didn't she know that he'd take apart anyone who ever tried to harm her? That there was nothing he wouldn't do to protect her? Had she had no faith in him at all? Had their time together meant nothing at all?

He was about to explode with the need for answers. A million questions were in his mind demanding to burst free. But his primary desire was simply to touch her. Hold her. Confirm to himself that he wasn't dreaming. That this wasn't some morbid fantasy, a manifestation of years of wishful thinking taunting him so soon after his vow to put it all behind him.

Wade gently picked her up but then forcefully put her behind him. He wrapped his arm behind him to secure her solidly to his back, a barrier between her and everyone else in the room and especially Zack, whom he had pinned with a murderous glare that promised violence and retribution.

"Get the hell away from her," Zack barked. "*Now*."

He didn't want this man so much as touching her. Thinking

to protect her from Zack? This guy had shady written all over him. What the ever-loving hell was Gracie's association with Sterling and why was there possessiveness written all over the other man's face? As if Gracie belonged to him, was his to protect when she'd always been Zack's. But then maybe . . . God, he couldn't—wouldn't—go there. His sanity was already hanging by the barest thread and he was precariously close to losing all semblance of control, he who was always in control, his emotions always tightly in check.

Gracie let out an inarticulate sound of fear and even with her behind Wade it was apparent she was in full meltdown. Wade turned to his assistant, allowing Zack a brief glance at Gracie, whose face was red and swollen, tears streaking down her cheeks and so terrified that it broke Zack's fucking heart.

Beau intercepted Zack, putting his hand on Zack's shoulder.

"You need to back off, man," he said in a low voice. "Look at her. Is that what you want to do to a woman ever?"

Eliza was at his other side, her arm curled around his arm, obviously in support, but so too was her sympathy for Gracie evident in her eyes, her features as stricken as Gracie's own.

Gracie's fear and distress was palpable in the room. No one was unaffected, least of all Zack. But why was she afraid of *him*? It made no goddamn sense! The world had gone crazy around him and he needed answers. The longer he went without them, the more insane it was driving at him, eating at his very soul until he was about to go mad with it.

"Back the fuck off," Dane growled.

It pissed Zack off that members of his own team was putting themselves between him and Gracie, as if *they* feared him hurting her. *Him*. Jesus Christ. But then they'd never seen him so unhinged and out of control. They were likely having their own what-the-fuck moment and wondering just who the hell they'd hired when, until now, he'd always been cool and unflappable, even under the most extreme circumstances.

"She is—was—my goddamn *life*," Zack choked out in a gut-wrenching tone.

Gracie was struggling against Wade's hold on her, obviously in a bid to escape. To run. To get as far away from here—Zack—as possible. Wade's hold only tightened on her. And that only served to piss Zack off even more. This man had no right to touch her, to hold her against her will, even if he *thought* he was protecting her.

"Call the police," Sterling barked at his assistant.

Dane held his hands up. "Whoa. I think everyone needs to take a step back and calm the hell down. *You* called *us* here."

"And I've asked you to leave," Sterling said bitingly. "Which you've refused to do. So unless you get out in the next three seconds, the police *will* be called and you will be charged with harassment. One has only to *look* at her to believe that charge."

He nodded again at Cheryl, who seemed frozen in place, eyes wide, still clutching the painting that had started it all.

"We're leaving," Dane said calmly.

"No, the hell we're not!" Zack roared. "Not until someone gives me some goddamn answers!"

Eliza gently pulled him a short distance away from Beau and the others and said in a voice too low for the others to hear, "Hon, come on. You're doing more harm than good. Look at her. Really *look* at her. She's scared out of her mind. And this standoff isn't doing her any good. I understand that this is important to you. But you know where she is now. You know *who* she is. I'll help you. I swear I won't rest until I help you get the information you need. But right now, you have to leave or this is going to get even uglier than it already is. And if this woman is important to you, which she obviously is, then you aren't winning any points here. Don't do or say something you can never take back. Take the high road. Not out of respect for that egotistical asshole, Sterling. But for Gracie. Do it for *her*."

Dane and Beau both closed in on Zack, Dane gently nudging Eliza away with a soft directive to remove herself from the situation and then they both took Zack by the arms and hauled him toward the door.

It went against every fiber of Zack's being to simply walk away, as Gracie had apparently once done. To just give up, without a fight, for the single most important person in his life. The only person who'd ever meant the entire goddamn world to him. The woman he would have done everything for. Sacrificed anything for, no matter how important. Would have protected with his life. And would have spent the rest of his life loving and cherishing her to the exclusion of all else.

But his team wasn't giving him a choice. He struggled, but Isaac and Capshaw added their strength and they forced him past where Sterling stood, glaring them all down, his arm still tightly holding Gracie, who was firmly shielded behind his much larger body.

In the end, they simply subdued him, though it took them all, and with their combined strength they pushed him into the parking lot.

He wanted to hit someone. His fists were clenched and his body language was clearly defiant. The others knew it. Beau pushed him against his truck and got into his face.

"I don't claim to know what the fuck just happened back there, but you need to pull it together and fast. This isn't you, man. You don't treat a terrified woman like you just did. You don't push the issue when she's out of her mind with fear. I get this is important, but there has to be another way than you ending up in jail on assault and harassment charges."

Zack shoved him back and then closed in, going nose-to-nose with Beau.

"You tell me, if that was Ari. If someone got between you and Ari and then told you to back the fuck off. Would you just walk away? Take the fucking *high road*?" Zack roared, throwing the last two words out with the disdain they deserved.

Beau paused, his eyes flickering with instant understanding. Then he closed his eyes a moment and sighed. "Jesus. So it's like that."

Rage. Grief. Fury. Soul-deep sorrow. They engulfed Zack and despair slammed into him like a tidal wave. His shoulders sagged and he closed his eyes, leaning back against the vehicle and out of Beau's—his friend's—face.

Eliza's cool hand covered his arm, squeezing just enough to get his attention and wrest him from the fog surrounding him.

He glanced her way and saw bright emotion in her eyes as she inserted herself between him and Beau. Almost like she *knew* his story. As though his dark, stormy thoughts were displayed in real time and she could see right into his shattered mind.

"I'll help you, Zack," she said softly. "You just tell me what I need to know so I have a starting point. You don't have to tell me all of it. As little or as much as you're comfortable sharing. I swear to you on my life that I won't rest until this is resolved for you. I *won't* give up. You have my word." And left unspoken was the fact that Eliza's word was solid. She didn't offer her word lightly, and neither did she ever break it when given.

Before he could respond, Eliza pulled him into a hug, which was an impressive feat given her height and weight disadvantage. But her hug was fierce. Packed with emotion, solidarity. Loyalty. She was the sister he'd always wanted to have.

He'd grown up an only child, his mother ditching him and his father when Zack was still a baby. And Gracie had come from a broken home with an alcoholic mother who didn't even know Gracie existed most of the time. Her father? Some random hookup of her mother's. She didn't even know who the father of her child was, never mind Gracie ever knowing her father.

He and Gracie had both wanted children. As many as they were blessed with. They wanted to fill their home with absolute love and a strong sense of family. All the things he and Gracie had been denied.

"How soon?" he asked in a barely audible voice, one that was so strained it cracked with just the two words.

He didn't have to explain the two-word question. Eliza knew exactly what he meant.

"We can go into the office now," she returned. "Or if you prefer, I'll grab my laptop and meet you at your place. Or you can come to mine. It's up to you."

She was offering him a way out of further losing his shit in front of the others, something he was grateful for because he wasn't sure how much longer he could keep it together before he completely broke down.

It was like a ten-ton anvil had dropped from the sky and squashed him like a bug. He was still reeling from the shock of seeing Gracie in the flesh. No longer a ghost from his past, but a living, breathing woman—no longer a girl of sixteen—twelve years older but just as heart-achingly beautiful as ever.

"Your place," he managed to get out. "If that's okay."

It was the only place where he felt comfortable enough to spill his guts. He damn sure didn't want to have this conversation in front of all his coworkers at the office. He'd hidden his pain from the rest of the world for twelve years. Only since he'd gone to work for DSS had he formed any semblance of a friendship with others.

They'd just seen him at his lowest, but he knew it would only get worse, and he had no desire for the others to know the torment he'd lived with for so much of his life. He knew he was pathetic, but it didn't mean he wanted more witnesses to his weakness than necessary. Furthermore, now that finding Gracie was no longer an impossible dream but a stark reality, he didn't give two fucks how pathetic it made him that he refused to just let it go. As fucking if!

She gave his arm another reassuring squeeze. "Then run me back by the office so I can get my car. I'll just need to go in and get my laptop and then you can follow me over to my place."

"Thanks, Eliza," he said softly.

"No thanks necessary," she said just as softly.

SIX

GRACIE buried her face in Wade's back, her entire body trembling. She couldn't control the shaking. And the cold. God, she felt cold to her very bones. *Shock* wasn't even an adequate word for what she had felt looking up into the eyes of an older but still devastatingly handsome Zack Covington. If anything, he was more handsome. Gone was the boyish charm and easy smile and in its stead was a much harder looking man, one that appeared as damaged as she was herself.

She'd thought she'd felt pain over the years. Grief. Regret. She didn't think it could get any worse than what she'd already been dealt.

She was wrong.

Because never in that time had she faced Zack. Never since that night. No amount of imagining or mental preparation could have possibly prepared her for the reality of seeing him, when she'd made certain they would never again cross paths. Apparently fate wasn't on her side. Also apparent was that fate evidently didn't think she'd already suffered enough heartbreak for a lifetime.

Wade turned, sliding his arms around her in a comforting gesture. He gathered her to him tightly, hugging and soothing her with a low-pitched voice.

"He's gone now, Anna-Grace. He can't hurt you. I won't let him hurt you ever again."

His words seared through the chaotic tumble of her thoughts and through the numb that had settled over her body, paralyzing her. She shoved away from Wade sharply, catching her footing when she would have fallen again.

"I have to go," she babbled, searching desperately for an escape route.

She couldn't go out the front. What if he was out there waiting for her? What if he followed her? What if he found out where she lived? What if he already knew?

Oh God, he had to know where she was. How hard could it really be to find her despite the lengths she'd gone to over the years to ensure her privacy and make it so no one would ever discover her?

"I have to get out of here, Wade," she said, hysteria rising in her voice. "Please, you have to help me. I have to go *now*. But where? I have to think of someplace he can't find me. I can never come back here. I have to leave. I have to go. Tonight. Before he shows up at my apartment!"

She knew she was making no sense. She didn't care. She also knew that she was allowing irrational fear to override all else. But her sense of self-preservation had firmly taken over and she was content to let it do its thing. She hadn't survived this long by ignoring it.

Wade's hands slid up her arms and gently but firmly grasped her shoulders, holding her, forcing her to look at him. His expression was hard and anger glittered in his dark eyes. He wore that dangerous look that would scare the holy hell out of anyone else, but she'd learned that despite it, despite his appearance and the fact that there were things about him she didn't know—preferred not to know—that he was no threat to her.

"Anna-Grace, look at me," he said in a tone that brooked no argument.

Her eyelids fluttered and she lifted her gaze to meet his, desperately trying to keep the mind-numbing terror at bay.

He framed her face in his hands and gently stroked his thumb over her bottom lip.

"You will *not* allow him to control your life any longer," he said, soft reprimand in his voice. "You've allowed him too much control for too long. That's over with. He can't hurt you now. I swear to you, I'll never let him hurt you. Do you trust me?"

She bit into her lip, because God, that wasn't an easy question for someone like her. Someone who trusted no one. Who had no reason to trust anyone. And yet she'd already admitted that she did trust Wade. They'd established that point. One he was calling her on again. But before they'd been just words. Now they meant something.

She reluctantly nodded and he relaxed the slightest bit, almost as if he were afraid she'd deny it and run from him just as she'd run from everything else in her life for the last twelve years.

"You are *not* that frightened young girl any longer," Wade said gently. "You're strong. You've built a life for yourself. A career. A very promising career. You're talented. Far more talented than many of the big names in art right now. You've created a place for yourself in the world. Are you going to let him destroy all that?"

Anna-Grace frowned, because when put that way, while she hadn't had a choice over what happened to her all those years ago, now? She *did* have a choice. She was a different person than she'd been then. Older. Wiser. Not as young and naïve. Not as gullible. And yes, as Wade said, she was stronger now.

It was nearly laughable to consider any part of herself strong when she'd hidden for so long, scared of her own shadow. But she *was* strong. Stronger than she gave herself credit for. And Wade was also right in that she'd built a life for herself. Right here. Her showing was in a week. It was what could launch her entire career.

Wade leaned in and pressed his lips to her forehead in a gesture that looked decidedly intimate. To someone peeking in on them, they would appear to be lovers, clear affection between them. Only Anna-Grace and Wade knew better.

"Take a stand, Anna-Grace," he whispered. "You aren't alone. You'll never be alone. Don't allow your past to rule your present a single day longer. This is your moment to shine. Your moment in the sun. Don't let anyone ruin it for you."

She squared her shoulders and then lifted a hand to cup over Wade's that still rested on her cheek. She leaned into his palm and briefly closed her eyes.

"I'm not that sixteen-year-old innocent, naïve girl any longer," she said falteringly. But her voice grew stronger as she continued. "I'll never be that girl again."

She looked up at Wade with fire in her eyes.

"He took my life from me once. I won't let him do it again.

I'll never allow him—anyone—to have that kind of power over me again."

Wade smiled. "Now that's the Anna-Grace *I* know."

Anna-Grace took a deep breath. "I'm scared, Wade. I won't lie about that. You heard him. He thought I was dead. What if they were supposed to kill me?"

Wade's expression became hard. So hard that she shivered at the danger reflected in his dark eyes. His thumb rubbed along the indention of her chin and then moved to the corner of her mouth.

"I will never allow any harm to come to you, Anna-Grace. I swear it on my life."

SEVEN

ZACK paced the interior of Eliza's living room like a caged, rest-less lion ready to attack and kill. He dragged a hand repeatedly through his short, spiked hair until it was in complete disarray, shooting in a dozen different directions.

Sweat. He was sweating. His shirt was damp. His brow glis-tened with moisture. And a bead slipped down his spine, making him itchier and more irritable by the minute.

"Zack, sit down."

Eliza's voice was soft, but it carried a hint of command.

She glanced over the top of her laptop and motioned for him to sit down on the other wing of the sectional sofa. Eliza's apartment was a study in comfort. Decorated in warm earth tones with a splash of femininity. Not overdone. Not too girly. It was a place a man would feel welcome. A place he could call home.

He'd dreamed of surprising Gracie with a huge home. A two-story mansion with at least seven bedrooms, and jack-

and-jill bathrooms connecting the children's bedrooms in twos. He'd wanted four boys and then two girls. Six of the bedrooms would be connected by a bathroom so that only two children would ever have to share one. And of course he'd want the little girls last so they'd have older brothers to look out for them and spoil them every bit as much as he would.

Gracie had loved the house that Zack had grown up in. It was the epitome of the American dream. Two-story white frame house with homey dormers, a sprawling front porch with a swing and a white picket fence surrounding the house. It was precisely the sort of home she'd daydreamed about, though he'd never brought her over after that first disaster when he'd taken her to meet his father. The memory still enraged him. His father had completely humiliated Gracie. Had made her feel like a piece of filth. Hell, he'd even called her white trash. Had said that even the trailer park was too good for the likes of her. Given that Gracie was homeless for the most part, it had been a low blow. A trailer would have been welcome to Gracie. Anything that put a roof over her head.

After Gracie's uncle had died, Zack had been relieved, until he realized that Gracie had no place to live. Still, he recognized she was much better off homeless than under the power of an abusive relative.

Zack had found her a tiny motel on the Dover side of the lake. She landed a position as a room cleaner, which didn't provide much of anything in the way of a paycheck. But what it did provide was a place for her to live—a tiny bedroom on the first floor next to the office—and it provided her one meal a day, her choice of breakfast or dinner from the homestyle cooking restaurant attached to the motel. Zack gave her money for the other two meals of the day, and he often ate breakfast and dinner with her so that he ensured she didn't go without.

Every morning she rose before dawn to begin her day. She left in time to get to school and then she resumed her job afterward.

Zack came home at every opportunity. His father was disgusted by the fact he was so hung up on a girl that he was blowing what should have been the best years of his life. There were no frat parties or endless girlfriends, no living large with his star quarterback fame. No, he attended his classes and made all his practices, but he always looked forward to the end of football season, when he could come home to Gracie.

He'd never stayed at school over the weekend once football season was over. As soon as his last class on Friday had ended, he'd immediately get into his truck, having already packed the night before, and head straight home.

Though he'd never offered her the disrespect of taking advantage of her sexually—he, like her, had wanted to wait—Zack had spent most nights with Gracie, him taking the floor while she slept in the bed, and they'd talk for hours.

He'd hated that she'd be so tired the next day, struggling to get up early and get her duties done by check-in time, and so he'd often help her. The two had become a formidable team, coming up with an efficient method of cleaning the rooms spotless in twenty minutes. That made Zack happy because it meant she was his for the rest of the day.

Most high school football players' favorite night of the week was Friday. Friday meant football and the rush of adrenaline after pulling off an impossible play. Friday was Zack's favorite day as well, but not because of football. To him, football was a means to an end. A way for him to provide for Gracie and the children they'd one day have.

It was his favorite day because he knew that at the end of it, Gracie would be in his arms, her head pillowed against his shoulder.

Until the time he returned home to find her gone. For good.

He didn't understand it. Maybe he'd never understand it. But he sure as hell wasn't going to walk away without some sort of an explanation. If she didn't need him—didn't want him—then by God she'd look him in the eye and tell him so.

"Zack?"

Eliza's concerned voice filtered through his thoughts and he glanced over to see that evidently she'd been talking—or rather trying to talk—to him for the past several seconds, and he was unresponsive.

"Sorry," he muttered. "Just thinking."

"That much is evident," she said softly. "Want to tell me about it?"

Zack closed his eyes and sighed. "You're going to think I'm a head case. I mean, when I stand back for a minute and truly look at the situation, if it were anyone else, I'd think they were a complete idiot. I mean who the hell stays hung up on a girl— woman—for *twelve years*? Jesus. It's pathetic."

He winced, realizing just how much he'd admitted. He blew out his breath in a long, frustrated stream. What the fuck did it matter? Eliza was going to find out anyway. He wasn't going to hold back any information that might enable Eliza to track Gracie down, no matter how pitiful it made him look.

"I'd say someone who stays hung up on a woman for that long must have truly loved her," Eliza said quietly.

There was no judgment in her eyes. No pity. Nothing but unwavering support and friendship.

"Yeah," Zack murmured. "I did—do. Or at least I did. Hard to say what the fuck I'm feeling right now."

"So tell me what happened and why you lost your shit when you saw her again in the gallery. I'm assuming that's the first you've seen her since . . ."

He nodded and then sighed.

"There's honestly not much to tell. Gracie and I were high school sweethearts. I say high school, but I was four years older than her so we only attended school together my senior year. She was a freshman when we met. I had a full ride to University of Tennessee playing football. Quarterback."

"You played for the pros, didn't you?"

"Until an injury took me out," Zack said.

"You could have played still."

Zack didn't even respond to the fact she obviously knew his story. Or at least part of it. DSS would have done a thorough background check before hiring him on.

He nodded. "Yeah. I could have rehabbed. Missed one season at the most. Trained hard in the off-season and come back in the fall. The doctors thought I'd make a full recovery with intensive rehab."

"But you chose not to."

Again he nodded. The team owner, the manager and the coaches had been pissed. The fans had been pissed. He'd been labeled a quitter. A loser when for so long he'd been a winner. But without Gracie he didn't feel like he'd won fucking anything. Football wasn't enough to sustain him when he'd lost everything that meant anything to him. Football was only a means to provide for Gracie, for him to give her the kind of life he'd dreamed of. Without her, football didn't mean shit.

"Because of Gracie?" she asked gently.

He hesitated a moment, then met her gaze again. "Yeah. Because of Gracie. She disappeared. One day she was there. And then I came home and she was gone. No note. No word. No message. Nothing. It was as if she'd never even existed. Only, to me she did. She was my entire fucking world. School. Football. None of it mattered if she wasn't there to share it with me. I almost didn't even go to the pros. My old man was apoplectic. And in the end, the only reason I did go to the pros is because I thought that if I had a high enough profile, Gracie would know where I was. That she would even contact me. Come to me if she was in trouble."

"So you have no idea what happened to her?"

"None," he said flatly.

"Did you report her missing? Get the police involved?"

He emitted a harsh laugh. "My father *was* the police. The chief of police. He didn't lift one goddamn finger to find her. He was too busy *celebrating*. He fucking smiled when I told him about her disappearance. Told me it was the best news he'd heard all year. When I asked him to issue a missing person's report and actually look into her disappearance he told me his department's resources were much better used when not wasted on people who didn't matter."

Eliza frowned. "Excuse the observation but your father sounds like a real gem."

"Don't sugarcoat it for me," he said, his jaw clenching. "He's a bastard. A selfish, misogynistic chauvinist."

"You'll forgive me if I never go out of my way to meet him," Eliza muttered.

Zack lifted one corner of his mouth in a half smile. "You'd kick his ass."

"At least you fell pretty far from that tree," she observed. "And damn right I'd kick his ass. If he pulled that bullshit with me I'd rearrange his balls for him. Now, let's get back to Gracie. From what you've told me I can pretty well piece everything together. Or at least it suddenly makes sense. You get hurt. Choose to bow out instead of rehab. You enter law enforcement and go on to be recruited by a government organization until Beau stole you to our side. I assume you chose the career you did because of Gracie."

Her eyes were far too discerning. It felt as though she had crawled underneath his skin and now had a prime view of everything he'd hidden from the world. And it wasn't a very pleasant feeling.

He nodded, his jaw tight to the point of discomfort. "I wanted to find her. I looked fucking everywhere—have looked for her for twelve years. And then today, that closemouthed fucker at the gallery. Swear to God, Lizzie. I wanted to take him apart on the spot."

"Yeah. I noticed."

"I knew he knew something even before Gracie showed up. It was too coincidental. The painting was of a place only Gracie and I had knowledge of. Not that other people hadn't ever seen it. But she and I never came across anyone in the years we met there. She loved to draw and paint. It was her dream. Now suddenly a painting of that same place shows up in a gallery and it's signed 'A.G.'? And the name of the painting is *Lost Dreams*? And then the bullshit about the artist not mattering security-wise, that the artist preferred anonymity. I guess the reason why is now apparent. She's hiding. From me. But who else? And what the fuck is her connection to Sterling? Because that was not the reaction of a gallery owner to just another artist he plans to make money off of."

"So Anna-Grace is her real name, but you call her Gracie."

Zack nodded. "Only I called her Gracie. It was my pet name for her."

Eliza typed as he spoke, presumably taking notes. When she finished pecking, she glanced back up, her gaze meeting Zack's.

"I need you to grab a notebook and pen off the coffee table and write down every single thing you can think of that might help me locate her. Full name. Any known relatives even if they're deceased. This could take a while, so how about you order takeout while I run some searches. It could be a long night."

Hope eased a little of the burning sensation in his chest. His pulse sped up and he swallowed several times to keep the knot from forming in his throat.

"Thanks, Lizzie," Zack said in a low, utterly sincere voice. "You have no idea what this means to me."

Eliza shrugged and for a moment Zack could swear he saw a flash of pain in her pretty eyes. "We all have shit we deal with. We all deal with it our own way. I don't want to build up false hope, Zack. I may not be able to turn up anything, but I'm going to try my damnedest."

"Sterling has all the information I need," Zack bit out. "He's going to talk. I don't give a fuck how he does it. But he will. I'll fucking destroy him otherwise."

"Be careful," she warned. "He's involved in a hell of a lot more than just art galleries. The galleries are mostly a front for his other 'activities.'"

Zack lifted an eyebrow. "What does that mean exactly?"

"The preliminary background check that Quinn performs on all prospective clients turned up a few discrepancies."

His gaze sharpened. "You think he's dirty?"

"Can't tell you that for a fact."

"What's your opinion then?"

"He's dirty."

"So why were we even meeting with him?" Zack asked. "Beau doesn't operate like that. He'd die before ever doing anything reminiscent of his father."

DSS didn't take on any client who could potentially drag the company through the mud. They didn't have to. They could pick and choose at their leisure. They certainly weren't hurting for clients.

"Maybe Caleb made the decision. Beau may not have even seen the report yet," Eliza said. "And as I said. I can't tell you that he's dirty for a fact. It's merely and only my opinion. One that Dane doesn't share—at least for the moment. I'm judgmental, what can I say? Dane is more tolerant." She said the last with a shrug.

"Your instincts are good, Lizzie. I've never known you to be wrong about someone. So if you think he's dirty, I'm certainly willing to believe the same. And if he is dirty then what the hell is his connection to Gracie? Because you didn't see his eyes when I said her name. She's not just a faceless artist he gives gallery space to in order to display her work. And he clammed up quick when I started asking questions about her."

Pink dusted her cheeks and warmth reflected in her gaze at his assessment—confidence—in her skills. Lizzie, like Beau and everyone at DSS, were just good people. They'd certainly come along at a critical point in his life.

Instead of plunging recklessly into a risky career in law enforcement, one that came with a high possibility of burnout, he'd joined an elite agency. His job challenged him, made him focus on something other than the last twelve fucking years of his life. Made him feel as though he had a purpose instead of just going through the motions.

How ironic that just a couple of days earlier he had thought to himself, after a particularly bad night of tossing and turning, that perhaps it was time to let go—truly let go—and move on. Live his life and do something with it.

He didn't have that luxury now. Because now he knew she was out there. Close. Close enough that he could have run into her at the grocery store, or gas station. God, how long had she been in such proximity to him?

"We'll find her, Zack," Eliza vowed. "But you need to prepare yourself for the possibility that she could run. The showing could and will likely be canceled. She obviously feels threatened by you. And, well, you need to prepare yourself for the fact that she . . . left you. Willingly. Because from my position, that's what it's starting to look like."

Her words slid insidiously beneath his skin, cutting sharply to the very heart of him. Where Gracie lived, always a part of him, never leaving even if that's exactly what she'd intended.

Grief, a very different kind of grief, welled up in his soul, suffocating, like a swollen storm cloud heralding the rain.

Never once had he even given thought to the possibility that she'd left him for the simple reason that she no longer loved him. He'd tortured himself endlessly with all the possible reasons she'd vanished, as though she'd never existed at all. Maybe he had been the only person who'd ever cared about her. So why would she reject him and everything he'd ever promised her?

What earth-shattering event had caused two lives to be permanently altered, damaged, never to truly heal?

But then she'd hardly painted a picture of someone who'd endured hell on earth as he had for the last decade. For the first time, anger, something alien to him until now welled in his chest, traced acid to his stomach.

No, she'd been pursuing her dream all the while he had been chasing his.

Gracie.

His dream.

His beautiful, sweet Anna-Grace.

The memories of her that he'd held so firmly in his heart, fearing that they'd dull with the passage of time, eluded him for the first time in twelve long years.

No, he'd never, ever felt anger toward Gracie.

Until now.

It was the bitterest taste in his mouth, one he knew he'd taste at the mere mention of her name from now on. Because now he saw the future—Gracie's future. And nowhere was Zack a part of it.

EIGHT

ZACK stood outside the Sunshine Art Studio just a few blocks from Joie de Vivre, his fists curled tightly at his sides. He couldn't seem to catch his breath. Each one seemed torturous through his constricted airway and chest. Had she been this close all this time?

The irony wasn't lost on him. After he had spent a decade searching for Gracie, had she been in the same city? And for how long? Had she already lived here when he moved to Houston to take the job with DSS? After years of chasing his tail, how funny that he'd come across her in the line of his work.

As good as Eliza was, even she couldn't make information materialize out of thin air. Information was scarce on the re-clusive artist. Quite by luck Eliza had come across an obscure article in an art publication that had mentioned classes being held at the Sunshine Art Studio several blocks down on West-heimer. Three artists rotated through, teaching art to children who showed promise at a young age. One of the artists was the mysterious A.G.

And so here he was, a knot in his throat, his palms sweaty as he stared at the door. Minutes before, the studio had emptied. Smiling, laughing children had spilled from the doorway, all rushing to meet their waiting parents in the parking lot.

Now all was quiet. There were no other vehicles in the lot, which meant if Gracie was here she'd either walked to the gallery, taken public transit, or ... someone had given her a ride. Boyfriend? Lover? Husband? Wade Sterling perhaps?

It set his teeth on edge to entertain the idea she belonged to another man and was forever out of his reach.

He huffed another breath and berated himself for being such a coward. All he had to do was walk through the goddamn door. Only a door separated him and ... Gracie.

So why was he paralyzed with fear? Shouldn't he be eager to confront her and find out what the hell had inspired her epic meltdown in the gallery when they'd come face-to-face for the first time since she'd disappeared from his life?

Or perhaps he was simply coming to terms with the possibility that if she was alive and doing well, working as an artist, it meant she'd *chosen* to leave him without a word. No breakup. No closure. While he'd been unable to move on, to get over it, she evidently hadn't suffered the same.

He ran an agitated hand through his hair and then swore under his breath.

Get it together, dumbass. You've waited twelve fucking years for this. Just open the goddamn door.

He forced his legs to move, ignoring the tremble in his

knees. The door loomed closer until finally his hand grasped the handle. All he had to do was . . . push.

He shoved instead, disgusted by his hesitancy.

Then he was inside. Instantly, he was assailed by . . . hominess. Everything he'd ever imagined of a home with Gracie in it. The colors were warm and soothing and yet light and airy. He sniffed the floral-scented air. Around him papers were strewn on tables or affixed to easels. Paint was splattered over the dropcloths and smudged on the small kid-sized desks.

Nostalgia floated through him as he remembered all the times he and Gracie had talked about children. Their children. Did she have children of her own now? He didn't think he could bear to see a miniature little Gracie knowing he wasn't the father. That Gracie had pursued their dream without him.

He nearly turned and walked right back out of the studio. He wasn't sure he could bear to face the truth. That she simply hadn't wanted a life with him. But he froze when a familiar voice sounded in the distance.

"Wade? Is that you? I'm washing up, but I'll be out in a minute." Zack went stock-still as laughter, beautiful feminine laughter, rose. It sent a chill, a shock, straight down his spine. And only further confirmed his suspicions about her association with Sterling. "The children were rather exuberant today so I'm afraid I'll get paint all over your seats!"

Gracie.

His Gracie.

He'd know the sound of her voice—her laughter—anywhere, such a welcome change from the tear-stained, barely choked out words of terror from their "reunion." He stood, frozen, waiting for her to come forward when what he wanted to do was tear down the door of whatever room she was in and demand answers to all the questions tumbling out of control in his mind.

He was tempted to just turn his back and walk away. Much like she'd done twelve years ago. But unlike her, he needed closure. He needed an end to the torture he'd put himself through over the last decade imagining her hurt, dead and a hundred other dismal possibilities. Ironically, none of his imaginings had been good. And yet it appeared she was doing just fine.

"Sorry I kept you waiting," she said breathlessly.

And then she appeared and he drank in her appearance like a man starving.

She wore a paint-splattered smock that she was in the process of untying when she lifted her gaze and saw him.

After their first confrontation, he should have been prepared for her reaction, but a small part of him had hoped that it had simply been the shock of seeing him so unexpectedly. But he *wasn't* prepared, and it hurt his heart to see how she looked at him even now.

She froze. Went so still he wasn't even sure she was breathing. And just as before, fear—honest-to-God terror—entered her wide, shocked eyes.

She backpedaled hastily, throwing her hand out behind her to find the door she'd just appeared from. She stumbled, righting herself by planting her hand against the now-closed door, leaning heavily on it while scrambling for the handle as if desperate to put that door between them again. To lock herself away from him.

She was terrified of him.

What the ever-loving fuck was going on?

"Gracie," he said hoarsely. "It's me, Zack. For God's sake, I'm not going to hurt you. Do you have any idea what it's like for me to see you? Alive? Well?"

His initial shock was quickly replaced by anger as everything welled up. All the fear and grief he'd lived with for so long. And to be greeted like *this*? As if she hadn't been a major part of his life. Like he hadn't loved her for most of his life, and she wasn't the only woman he'd *ever* loved.

"My God, I thought you were *dead,* or hurt or somewhere out there suffering, that you needed *me*," he ground out. Jesus, he felt like a complete fool for thinking she'd ever needed him. What had changed? She'd been his world and he thought he'd been hers as well. He needed to know why. Didn't he deserve that much, at least?

"You disappeared off the face of the earth. What was I supposed to think? Didn't I at least deserve a goodbye, have a nice life?" He nearly choked on the last part. "Not even a 'fuck off,' or 'see you later'? No, you just disappeared, leaving me to think the worst. For twelve fucking years I've thought the worst. For twelve fucking years I've gone to bed every goddamn night sick at heart because I thought I had failed you in some way. That I hadn't been there when you needed me and that some sick fuck had hurt you, kidnapped you or murdered you. And all this time you've been happy as a lark, painting and moving on with your life while I've spent the last twelve years turning the earth over looking for you?"

She was pale as death and looked as though she was going to be sick. She was actively seeking escape routes, her gaze darting quickly but never meeting his, and God, he didn't think he could bear to see the fear in those eyes again.

Why the fuck was she afraid of *him*?

"Get out," she rasped, tears choking her voice. "God, just *get out*!"

Tears welled in her eyes and silently slid down her cheeks, and despite his rage and sense of helplessness, his insides twisted, because no matter that she obviously had dumped him and moved on, his first instinct was to comfort her because damn it, he couldn't bear to see her cry. Couldn't bear to see her hurting.

And the fact that he was evidently the cause of her distress?

"What the *fuck* is going on here?"

Zack whirled around in response to the male roar to see Wade Sterling standing just inside the studio, a murderous expression on his face. But as his gaze drifted to Gracie, his expression immediately became one of concern.

And what really pissed Zack off was that Wade immediately crossed the room positioning himself solidly between Gracie and Zack, and then, keeping his eyes on Zack the entire time, he firmly pushed her behind him. Just as he'd done at the gallery. A clear protective measure, as if Gracie needed protection from Zack. Of all people, Zack.

Sterling's stance was aggressive as he stared Zack down, clearly poised for a fight. And Zack was spoiling for one. There was nothing more he'd love than to knock the bastard on his ass so he'd take his hands off Gracie. But he couldn't afford to lose his shit a second time because God help him, he might not get a third. She might do just what Eliza had predicted and run. He couldn't lose her again. Not after finding her after so very long. Once had been devastating. Twice? He wouldn't survive. Not this time, under these circumstances.

"Why the fuck are you so afraid of me, Gracie?" Zack asked quietly. "You at least owe me that much."

Gracie emitted a strangled sound and it only served to further piss Sterling off. She wouldn't even get out from behind her "protector" long enough to look at Zack, much less offer any sort of explanation.

"I *owe* you?" she said with a sob. "God, just leave me alone. Haven't you done enough? You think I owe you *anything* after what you did? You ruined my life! You betrayed me. God, I can't even wrap my head around why you'd even bother to look for me unless that once wasn't enough. Or maybe you just wanted to finish the job."

She completely broke down, her composure melting. Sterling half-turned to put his arm around her in a gesture of comfort and when he looked back at Zack, there was absolute fury in his eyes.

"Look, I get it," Zack bit out. "You've moved on. You have a boyfriend, lover or whatever. But I have to say you have a shitty way of breaking things off with someone you supposedly cared about."

Sterling cut off any response Gracie might have made, though Zack doubted she would have responded because she was openly crying. It was a knife to Zack's heart. In all the ways he imagined seeing her again, this was never the way he imagined it going down.

"Gracie and I aren't romantically involved, not that it's any of your goddamn business," Sterling bit out. "I'm her *friend*. And as her friend, I look out and protect what is mine. You've got two seconds to get the fuck out of here and so help me God, if you come within a hundred yards of her ever again I'll slap a restraining order on you so fast your head will spin. If you violate that restraining order, I'll spend every dollar I own to ensure you never see the light of day again."

"You and what fucking army?" Zack said in a deadly quiet voice. "If you're her *friend,* then this has nothing to do with you. This is between me and Gracie and you need to butt the hell out. I'm not going to hurt her. Jesus Christ, I'd never hurt her. I loved her. I've loved her forever." His voice cracked as he said the last, and he broke off to save himself the humiliation of breaking down in front of them both.

"You disgust me," Sterling sneered. "It's obvious she wants nothing to do with you, so take the hint and get the hell away from her and stay away."

"I'd rather hear what Gracie wants from *Gracie,*" Zack said pointedly. "She owes me that much."

For the first time, Gracie stepped to the side of Sterling, her face red and tear-stained. Zack's heart clenched and his fingers curled into tight balls at his sides. He stared at her, really stared, absorbing every detail about her.

She'd always been beautiful but now she was even more so. Hauntingly so. She was thinner. She'd lost the glimmer of youth in her face and her eyes looked so much older than he remembered. As if she'd endured hell and back and had aged far beyond her years.

Her hair, which had always been shoulder length, with layers and bangs, was much longer now, the bangs gone, and as he studied her further, he realized she was really thin. There was a fragile, delicate air to her that had never been present even when she'd lived and endured terrible conditions.

His gaze narrowed, because where before she'd always had

a glow about her, despite the abovementioned living conditions, and she'd always been quick to laugh and had always been happy, she looked *nothing* like that now. What the hell had happened to her? What was all that bullshit about him ruining her life? His mind was ablaze with questions as all she'd said finally sank in.

She was quiet and subdued, as if the light inside her had been extinguished. She looked . . . sad. Not at all like his Gracie.

What the hell had gone wrong? What was she *thinking*, remembering? And why did his heart feel like it was shattering into a million pieces? Where was the self-righteous anger he'd felt just seconds ago? Why had it suddenly fled and left him with the feeling that the truth—whatever that was—would likely kill him? That he might never recover from the ugly revelation?

She lifted her gaze, almost as if she were having to force herself to look at him, to keep her gaze connected to his. There was so much sorrow in the depths of those sweet brown eyes that it took his breath away. And hurt. So many negative emotions that Zack felt them like hurled daggers.

"Please leave," she begged softly. "I never *ever* want to see you again. That's me speaking, Zack. Not Wade. Not anyone else. It's me. Think whatever you like, but don't you ever touch me."

Touch her? He hadn't been close enough to touch her. He could understand the never seeing or talking to her again, but why would she tell him never to touch her?

Something was terribly wrong and it frustrated the hell out of him because it was obvious that nothing was going to be accomplished today. For one, there was this fiercely protective guard dog looking for the world like he'd love nothing more than to beat Zack to a bloody pulp. As if this smooth-talking rich asshole had a chance in hell of taking Zack down in a fight.

Then there was the fact that Gracie couldn't even look at him. She was white as a ghost, shaken and obviously terrified. Of *him*, goddamn it.

All she'd said slammed into him like a bullet. He'd ruined her life. He'd done this awful thing and then the part about finishing the job?

The accusations she'd hurled at him swarmed in his mind like angry bees. He forced himself to look her calmly in the eyes and he took a step forward, which immediately made Sterling bristle.

"Read my mind, Gracie," he said softly. "All you have to do is read my mind. Whatever it is you think I've done, just look inside my mind. You'll get your answers, though it's evident you don't think I deserve them."

She closed her eyes, tears streaking down her cheeks in never-ending rivulets.

When she reopened them, there was raw, naked emotion.

"Even if I *could,* I wouldn't," she said, her voice cracking under the strain. "God, I never want to see into *anyone's* mind again. That's the only thing I can ever thank you for, because you took that from me too."

Her response took him aback. What the fucking hell was that? What did she mean he took her ability? There were so many questions tumbling through his mind that he had to make a concerted effort not to go off on a tangent, demanding answers right now.

But the last thing he wanted was a goddamn audience for what was certain to be a highly volatile conversation. Patience was not a virtue he possessed and this was frustrating him to the point of madness. So instead of bombarding her with the questions that were nearly tearing his lips off, he made his next statement with firmness just to make damn sure that the pussy Sterling didn't miss the message that Zack in no way would be deterred in his pursuit of the past and what went so horribly wrong.

"We need to talk, Gracie," he said grimly. "Without your little watchdog standing guard. You name the time and place. I don't care how public it is, if that's what will make you feel safe with me." He damn near choked on those words. Hurt her? Wanting her to feel safe from *him*?

"I'll even have the goddamn police present if that makes you feel better. But whatever the hell it is you *think* I did to you, I can tell you that you are dead wrong. And if it takes the rest of my goddamn life, we *will* have this conversation, Gracie. I won't give up. I won't go away. I won't forget. I've waited twelve years for this moment, and I'll be damned if I walk away from you like you walked away from me."

NINE

ZACK turned the corner of the street a few blocks down from his apartment, sweat sliding down his spine. He'd pushed himself harder than normal, and his usual two-mile run had turned into three. It wasn't until he'd seen the sign for his bank that he realized he'd far surpassed his routine run.

Not even taking a moment to rest or cool down, he propelled himself onward, blanking his mind to his inner turmoil as he made the jog back to his apartment.

The entire night before he and Eliza had searched exhaustively for leads on Gracie, and she'd been right here under his nose all along. Then for a second time, his quest for the truth had been stymied when he'd confronted her earlier today in the studio. He'd been put off, thanks to Sterling's interference, *twice*. He'd been forced to retreat and wait for a better opportunity, though now that Gracie was tipped off to his presence and very unwelcoming of it, he wondered if she'd tuck tail and run. As she'd apparently done before.

Which meant waiting. More waiting.

Goddamn it, but he was tired of waiting. He'd waited twelve fucking years for this moment. He was further frustrated because it wasn't as though he no longer knew where Gracie was. She was here. In this city. So close and yet so far away.

Never had he imagined their reunion would go as it had. She'd been afraid of him. Hell, not afraid, she'd been absolutely terrified.

His mind kept yanking him back to the look on her face. No shock. No pleasant surprise. No greeting for the man who'd loved—and searched for—her for more than a decade.

Why?

He knew he was missing one giant piece of the puzzle here. But hell if he knew what it was. If only she would talk to him. Give him *something*. Jesus, didn't he deserve more than what he'd gotten? She acted as though she were the wronged party here. But he sure as hell hadn't run out on her and left her to wonder if he was even alive for twelve goddamn years.

He'd given her everything. His heart, soul. He'd promised her forever. And he'd goddamn meant it. Not many college kids knew exactly what they wanted from the future. But he had. From the moment Gracie had entered his life, he'd had absolute focus. He'd known that his life would forever revolve around her.

Well, he'd certainly been right on that count. Because even when she'd disappeared, *everything* had revolved around finding her again.

He'd planned their lives together to the nth degree. He wanted her to have everything she could ever dream of. Though he planned to always take care of and provide for her, he knew an education was important to her. Her circumstances embarrassed and shamed her. He hated that, hated that he couldn't take that away for her. He didn't care if she had a degree or not. He knew he'd make good money playing pro ball and that she and their children would never want for anything he could give them.

But at the same time, he wanted her happy. And so they'd talked about her going to college after she graduated from high school. They were young. Had all the time in the world—or so he'd thought. No need to rush anything. He wanted her to have security. So she'd attend college, earn her degree, and only after would they think about having children.

Honestly, waiting to have children wasn't an issue for Zack. Yes, he had it all planned. But he wanted those years with Gracie—just the two of them—before they added children to their family.

Maybe he'd been so wrapped up in the future that he hadn't been paying enough attention to the *present*. Obviously something had gone extremely wrong. Something he'd been oblivious to, because he'd never seen this coming. He'd never forget the shock of finding her gone. Vanished. And the incessant question, one he'd hammered on repeatedly for the next twelve years. *Why*?

By the time he jogged through his complex toward the east wing, which was made up of three-level town houses, dusk had faded to night. His breath blew in a cloud and the evening air brushing his sweat-glistening skin caused a cascade of goose bumps over his arms.

He slowed to a walk when he neared the gate leading to his unit. Though the town homes were connected, the front and back yards were separated by privacy fences. And the gate at the end of the paved walkway to his front porch was opened via a security code.

He frowned when he saw the display was completely dead. Just what he needed. To be locked out of his own goddamn apartment. Frustration coiled through his blood like a venomous snake. He slammed his fist against the gate with an emphatic curse.

To his surprise, the gate wobbled and opened a few inches. Zack frowned, wondering just how good the supposedly high-tech security features actually were in this joint. Well, he wouldn't bitch too much. Having the gate open saved him the hassle of contacting the manager and being able to get into his own goddamn house.

His motion-activated lights were obviously a victim of whatever was wrong with the gate. A prickle of unease raced up his spine. His head came up, his nostrils flaring as he scanned the dark exterior of the house. The light was on in the midlevel TV room. But the outside light that illuminated the steps to the porch, and which he always left on, was off.

Cursing the fact that he didn't have his pistol, he paused at the bottom step. From his periphery, a shadowy form came into focus. His head yanked in that direction and he tensed, prepared to defend himself.

He blinked to narrow his focus and realized that he was looking at a *person*, obviously unconscious—or dead? Sprawled a few feet from the bottom step, hidden from the street by shrubbery, was a human body. It had to be a woman or a very small man. The only thing readily visible was two bare feet.

His pulse accelerated and he rushed to the body, his chest hammering in fear as he reached to turn the person over. The head lolled as he rolled her to her back and then all his breath left him when he saw who the person was. Oh God. Oh God. No. Please no.

"Gracie!"

Her name escaped him in an agonized cry.

His heart nearly exploded in his chest. He let out his breath in a long, visible cloud. His vision swam with moisture and he blinked, needing to see how badly she was hurt.

Oh dear Lord. She was beaten. Badly. Bruises marked and colored her swollen features. Dried blood was smeared down her chin and neck. Worse, her hands were tied behind her back. She'd had no way to defend herself. No way to ward off the blows she'd received.

Bile rose in his throat and it took every ounce of strength not to throw up. Tears burned his eyelids. His hand shook violently as he fumbled at her neck for a pulse. Let her be alive. Don't let him have found her after twelve long years only to lose her again.

With his other hand, he gently smoothed her hair from her face, wincing when he saw the extent of the bruising. God, where could he even touch her? What if she'd sustained internal injuries? She could be bleeding. He could still lose her!

He nearly wilted with relief when he felt the faint, erratic patter of her pulse. And then he shook the shock and utter confusion away and bolted into action. He yanked his cell phone up and quickly dialed 911.

As he spoke with the dispatcher, providing his location and Gracie's condition, he tried to make Gracie as comfortable as possible without moving her too much. The last thing he wanted was to cause her further harm by doing something careless.

His call ended, and he tossed the phone down so he could focus more carefully on Gracie. He bent down and gathered her gently against his chest, hoping his body heat would offer her some respite from the damp chill. He tugged at the ropes that had cut into her wrists. Then he frowned when he felt the rough abrasions on her skin.

She was so still. One could easily believe she was dead. Her breaths were so light that her chest barely made any movement at all. They were also shallow. He knew she needed oxygen and silently urged the ambulance to get there as fast as possible.

When he'd arranged her head so that it wasn't at such an awkward angle, he quickly assessed the rest of her body, his heart in his throat. Nothing looked broken, but how was he to know?

And then something else caught his eyes. Something familiar. He went utterly still, his gaze fastening on the tag affixed to her toe. No. Oh hell no. There was no fucking way.

An inarticulate sound of rage erupted from his throat as he ran his hand down her leg, checking for further injury before he carefully detached the tag from her toe. He was careful to only touch what was necessary and then he read the scrawled words, the now-familiar handwriting like salt poured on an already festering wound.

This is what happens to people who get in our way.

Son of a bitch! Gracie had been targeted because of him. He'd led the enemy straight to her! How could he have known?

His entire body was flushed with heat—rage. His skin and heart burned with it.

Months ago, they'd found another body with the same tag attached to the toe. Ari's biological father. He hadn't survived his beating. Would Gracie live?

He closed his eyes, unable to even consider the possibility. Were his worst fears of what had happened to her twelve years ago being realized *now*?

They had underestimated the enemy. Mistaken their silence and patience as them having given up. Now Zack realized that they'd simply been watching—and waiting—for the right moment to strike. To find a vulnerable target, since getting to Ramie and Ari, the two women married to brothers Caleb and Beau, would prove pretty damn difficult, given the fact that their husbands kept very close guard over the women they loved.

Zack was assailed by the knowledge that, just as he'd failed Gracie twelve years ago, so too had he failed her now. He hadn't even considered the risk of him seeking her out, doing nothing to cover his tracks. Never had he imagined the lengths this fanatical group would go to in their effort to strike back at DSS.

This would kill Ari. She was so tenderhearted, and the idea that someone had been so grievously hurt because of her . . . Of course it wasn't her fault. But she wouldn't see it that way. All she would point out is that until she came into the picture there was no way for her past to touch DSS and those associated with it.

With a curse he reached for his phone again. Where was the goddamn ambulance?

He punched in Beau's number, willing the other man to answer. He needed Beau to get the word out to the others. They weren't safe. None of them were. Beau and Caleb would be pissed and they'd lock down their women so neither would be touched by violence ever again. They'd suffered far too much in their young lives. They'd seen more damage and hurt than any ten people would in their lifetimes.

"Beau, we've got a problem," Zack said grimly when the other man answered.

"Talk," Beau said, his tone immediately matching Zack's.

"They got to Gracie," he said, nearly choking on the words. "The goddamn sons of bitches beat her."

"Whoa, back up. What the fuck?"

Zack closed his eyes in relief when he heard the distant wail of a siren.

"I've got to make this quick. The ambulance is almost here. The same people who beat Ari's biological father to death, the ones who also tortured and killed her biological mother, got to Gracie. Same MO. I found her body outside my apartment. Tag attached to the toe with the same message."

There was a horrified silence and then Beau's explosion of curses.

"Is she alive?" Beau asked.

"For now," Zack choked out, nearly beside himself with worry and grief. "It's bad, Beau. I don't know how bad. But she's breathing. For now. Look, I have to go, but you need to let the others know. And Lizzie. God. Make sure she watches her back. I was with her all night last night. They're obviously keeping close watch or else how the hell would they tag Gracie so soon after I saw her? Call Dane. Make sure Lizzie is safe. And make damn sure Caleb knows so he can protect Ramie."

Zack hung up before Beau could respond. The ambulance was right outside his gate and he took his hand away from Gracie with a whispered plea. "Don't give up, Gracie. Fight. You have to be all right. I can't lose you again."

He brushed his lips across her forehead and then surged to his feet so he could direct the medics to where Gracie lay.

TEN

ZACK paced the floor just outside the exam room they'd taken Gracie to. He'd firmly dug his heels in, refusing to leave her side until one of the nurses gently pointed out that they could do their job much quicker and more efficiently if he wasn't in the way.

Then she'd guided him to the door and told him he could return the minute the doctor finished his assessment and read the results of her lab tests and X-rays.

He couldn't even see inside, had no clue what was going on, and that sucked. What if she stopped breathing? What if she died, alone, with no one by her side to tell her she was loved?

He leaned against the wall, rocking his head back to rest, and scrubbed his hands over his face for the third time. His eyes felt like sandpaper. There was a knot in his throat that refused to go away. He couldn't speak more than a few words before his voice would break and then fall to an emotional, unintelligible tone.

"Zack."

Zack looked up to see Beau and Caleb a few feet away in the hallway.

"How is she?" Beau asked grimly as he and his brother approached.

Zack threw up his hands in frustration. "I don't know, damn it! They shoved me out of the room and told me to wait. That was fifteen fucking minutes ago."

Beau muttered under his breath and Caleb's face was strained, his expression intense.

Then realizing that the two men were here in front of him, alone, Zack yanked his head up. "Where are Ramie and Ari?" he demanded.

"Safe," Caleb bit out.

"Ari wanted to come. She was horrified," Beau said, anger etched on his face and in the twist of his lips. "She was crying when I left her. Jesus. I can't believe those motherfuckers would beat an innocent woman to prove some goddamn point. And *what* point?"

Caleb shook his head in disgust.

"It's not her fault," Zack said fiercely. "It's mine and mine alone."

"Bullshit," Beau said. "It's not her fault and it's certainly not yours."

"It doesn't matter anyway," Caleb said. "We have to move forward and we're going to have to take a more aggressive stance with these fuckers. I—we—all thought they were no longer an issue. They haven't reared their heads since everything that went down with Ari. I shouldn't have let it go but I just wanted us all to be able to put it behind us. Especially Ari. But now we're going to have to switch tactics and go on the aggressive."

"Fuck yeah," Beau said. "We need to hunt these assholes down and let them see what it feels like to be used as a punching bag. Jesus. It turns my stomach to think of at least two women they've beaten. One of them was killed!"

Zack shuddered, his hands shaking. He curled his fingers into tight balls to alleviate the twitch but he couldn't prevent the image of Gracie's bruised, battered body from hurling through his mind.

"I've already put Dane on it," Caleb continued. "Every single man employed by DSS is being put on this job. This agency's soul focus will be on locating and taking down every single person who had a hand in this. It is our *only* priority."

"Thank you," Zack said.

Beau hesitated, searching Zack's expression for . . . ? Zack wasn't sure, but uncertainty shone in Beau's solemn gaze.

"What?" Zack asked.

"Were you able to work things out. Before . . ." Beau broke off and lifted his hand toward the door to indicate Gracie.

"No," Zack whispered. "I went out for a run. I don't normally run as far. God, I wish I hadn't. If I'd gotten home sooner maybe I would have caught the fuckers. And she wouldn't have lain out there in the cold for God knows how long."

"She was just lying there when you got back?" Caleb asked.

Zack nodded. "My gate's security pad wasn't working. But the gate was open. The outside motion-activated lights didn't work either. When I got to the steps, I saw her on the ground out of the corner of my eye. They just left her there to die!"

"Does your apartment complex have security cameras?" Beau asked.

Zack nodded.

"I'll get Dane over there to pull what he can. Maybe one of the cameras caught the assholes and we can get an image," Caleb said.

"I bagged the tag," Zack said. "I tried to touch it as little as possible. Maybe we can get a print."

Beau nodded. "We're reporting this, right?"

"Absolutely," Zack said firmly. "I'll take all the help we can get. I want these fuckers, Beau. I don't care what we have to do in order to nail their asses to the wall, but I want their goddamn blood."

"Don't blame you," Caleb said softly. "If it were Ramie . . ." He shook his head.

Beau's expression tightened and rage glowed in his eyes. "It was Ari not too long ago and now it's Gracie. Fuck this. I'm with you, Zack. I want their asses and I'll do whatever the fuck it takes to take them out. But I think we go with Briggs and Ramirez. This may very well be out of their jurisdiction, but they're the only two I trust on this and they know the history."

Zack nodded his agreement. The two detectives had worked with them before and were familiar with the oddities that accompanied DSS's many jobs. They wouldn't be met with skepticism over some freakish story about a group of fanatics who targeted anyone they deemed as a threat to their "cause." Some fucking cause.

The door to Gracie's room opened and Zack surged forward, every muscle in his body coiled tight. He held his breath, barely able to speak through numb lips.

"How is she?" he demanded.

The nurse smiled at him. "The doctor will be out shortly to discuss her condition, but she's going to be okay. Nothing life threatening."

Zack closed his eyes. He staggered with relief and for a moment he weaved, unsteady on his feet. "Thank God," he whispered.

"Easy there, man," Beau murmured, grabbing Zack's arm to steady him.

"Can I be with her now? I don't want her to be alone when she wakes.

The nurse's eyes softened. "Of course. After the doctor comes out and discusses her condition, you can go in. She's woozy and confused though."

"Why?" Zack instantly demanded.

The nurse held up a hand. "It's to be expected. She awoke in awful pain so we administered IV medication to make her more comfortable."

"So she doesn't have a head injury?" Zack asked hesitantly.

"I'll let the doctor bring you up to speed on that," she said. "Oh look, here he is now."

She stepped away from the door so the doctor had room to get through. Then she hurried away, saying she'd return shortly to check on Gracie.

All three men focused intently on the doctor and some of what they were feeling must have shown on their faces because the doctor hesitated and took a step back, his expression wary.

"How is she?" Zack asked anxiously.

"She's undergone extensive trauma over ninety percent of her body."

"Jesus," Caleb muttered.

Beau swore and Zack clenched his fingers into fists at his sides.

"How bad is it?" Zack asked in a low voice.

The doctor grimaced. "She has a few broken ribs but fortunately she didn't puncture a lung or another vital organ. As odd as this may sound, the beating appeared to be calculated. As though her attacker intended to do as much damage as possible without her sustaining any mortal injuries. Because as I said she sustained bruising to ninety percent of her body and yet apart from the cracked ribs she has no other broken bones. But some of the bruises are deep and will require careful attention while she's recovering. She needs to be on strict bed rest for a few days and I can't stress this enough. She needs to limit her movement to only what is necessary. Someone needs to be with her when she showers or bathes. And she has to take her recovery slowly. There's no rushing this and no shortcuts. Her body needs time to heal. Period."

"She won't lift a finger," Zack vowed.

The doctor cleared his throat. "I assume the authorities have been contacted? By law we have to report any crime, suspected or real."

"They're on their way," Zack said. "My first priority was getting her to the hospital."

The doctor nodded. "You did the right thing."

"Can I see her now?" Zack asked anxiously.

The doctor nodded again. But as Zack started to pass him he stopped him momentarily.

"She must take her recuperation seriously. This isn't something that will go away overnight. She's going to hurt very badly for the first several days. It's imperative that she not suffer any emotional or physical upset during this time. And if I were you, I'd seek out professional counseling for her. After an attack, a common reaction is denial or the victim just wanting to forget about it and make it go away. That's not healthy and it won't work. You may have to push her and she likely won't thank you for it at first, but she needs to accept and work her way through what happened to her."

"I understand," Zack said quietly. "I appreciate your efforts, Doctor. And rest assured, she will not have to do anything other than rest and get to feeling better."

"I'm glad to hear that. And I dearly hope whoever did this to her is arrested immediately."

The doctor's expression grew fierce as he said the last and anger blazed in his eyes.

"I've been a doctor for twenty years and no matter how many times you think you've seen it all and can't possibly be shocked by what comes through the ER, there's always another case that leaves me shaking my head and wondering what kind of scum gets his rocks off by beating an innocent woman. Especially in the manner that Miss Hill was. I have no doubt this was a well-measured attack meant to do as much harm as possible without killing her."

"We know," Beau said in a savage tone. "And the bastards who did this to her *will* pay. You can take that to the bank."

"Good," the doctor said emphatically. "Now I'll let you see Miss Hill. I'd like to admit her for observation and keep her at least forty-eight hours before I release her. She'll be moved up to the floor when her room is ready and she's admitted. Do you happen to have her insurance information? The admitting nurse will need that and her other personal information as well."

Zack hesitated because he didn't know anything about Gracie. He knew everything and nothing, or at least what used to be. Who was Gracie *now*? The last forty-eight hours had shattered any illusions he'd had.

"It will be taken care of," Beau interjected.

The doctor nodded and then stepped away from the door to let Zack pass.

Zack sucked in a deep breath, squared his shoulders and braced himself before walking into the room.

He let out a strangled cry when he saw Gracie lying on the bed, eyes closed but her forehead marred with pain, her features tight and her lips firm in a thin white line. Even at rest, she looked as though she were in horrible pain.

How scared she must have been. If the doctor was right—and Zack had no doubt that he was—she had endured a cold, methodical beating. It hadn't been done in a rage. No, it had been administered impersonally. She'd been a job to someone. Nothing more.

But she hadn't known that. How long had she endured the pain? Had she been scared to death they'd eventually get bored and then kill her? Had she prayed for death? God, he hoped not.

He approached the bed hesitantly, his gaze anxiously searching the monitors and instruments. She was being given oxygen but there was no heart monitor. That had to be a positive sign that they weren't concerned she'd die. But then the doctor had said she'd be fine. Just in pain. That she needed to take it very easy. That was one vow he'd absolutely meant.

When she was discharged, she was going home with him. But not back to his current place. Not with those bastards still out there, circling like vultures. Her beating had been a message. To him. To DSS. His mind was already going full gear. He would have Beau find a secure location for him to move Gracie to. And security would be top-notch.

He eased his way to the head of the bed, careful not to wake her. For a long moment he stood, drinking in her fragile appearance. His heart ached. His chest was tight with discomfort.

He leaned down, cupping his hand over her brow, one of the few places left untouched by her attackers. Gently he rubbed his thumb over the bridge of her nose, wincing as he took in the extent of her facial bruising.

God, he wanted to kill those bastards for touching her. For laying their hands on what was his. Gracie had always belonged to him. The last twelve years no longer mattered. She was here now. And if he had his way, she'd never go anywhere else.

He lowered his head to press his lips against her brow. He closed his eyes as his breath blew warm against her skin.

"I'm so sorry, Gracie," he said bleakly. "God, I'm so sorry."

She stirred slightly and he quickly lifted his head, his gaze anxious. He held his breath when her eyelids flickered and then opened.

She blinked a few times, her face crinkling in confusion. And then she let out a low moan and tried to lift her head from the pillow. Her arms flailed out in a defensive gesture and more sounds of fear and desperation spilled from swollen lips.

"Gracie. Gracie, honey, you're all right. It's me, Zack."

She went utterly still and if possible she grew even whiter beneath the purple of bruises. Her head swiveled so that her gaze locked with his.

Terror swept through her eyes and her lips parted and then shut repeatedly as though fear had robbed her of speech.

Zack ran his hand lightly down her arm to where the IV attached at her wrist. He flinched when she withdrew so quickly it pained her. She emitted a soundless cry, hurt flashing in her eyes.

What the fuck?

He managed to keep the frown from his face. Barely. It took everything he had to stand there and take her response. If it had only been now he could understand. It was understandable for a woman who'd been attacked to have an instinctual defensive response. To be afraid.

But it wasn't just now. It wasn't because she'd been attacked. She'd reacted the same way on the two other occasions they'd come into contact. Like he was some kind of monster. She hadn't merely been surprised or afraid. She'd been fucking terrified. Of *him*!

"Do you remember what happened?" he asked softly, ignoring, for now, her fear of him.

She let out a small, defeated whimper. The sound nearly slayed him. He reached behind him to snag the lone chair, pulling it toward the bed so he could sit. So he didn't loom over her and frighten her more.

She visibly swallowed and then licked her lips.

"Would you like some water?"

For a moment she just stared at him with wide, frightened eyes. Then, slowly, she nodded. She kept her frozen gaze on him the entire time as he stood, went to the sink and ran water in one of the small cups.

He walked back to the bed, and holding the cup with one hand, he carefully slid his free arm behind her neck and lifted just enough that she could sip without spilling it on herself.

She took several long swallows and then broke away, coughing. Her face spasmed with agony and her arm went instinctively to her stomach, to her injured ribs, holding it while she tried to suppress the cough.

"Easy," he murmured, easing her head back down.

As he turned away, he saw that both hands were curled into tight fists, the backs of her knuckles completely white with strain.

When he was settled back in the chair, he reached for the fist on his side and carefully unrolled her fingers and then curled his around hers.

"Why are you so afraid of me, Gracie? I don't understand. God, there's so much I don't understand. But we'll start with this, the most important. Don't you know I'd never hurt you? That I'd kill—will kill—anyone who does?"

Tears welled in her eyes and silently leaked down her temple to disappear into her hairline. She fixed her gaze on the ceiling as those shiny rivulets continued to run.

"Please talk to me, Gracie. Tell me what's wrong. Why are you so goddamn scared of me?"

"I don't want you here," she choked out.

Her free hand went to her throat, rubbing as though it hurt her to speak. Fury raged inside him. Of course her throat hurt. There were visible hand and finger marks surrounding her slender throat. As if those bastards had choked her repeatedly.

Those words, those simple five words, gutted him to the core.

"Why?" he asked bluntly. "Why do you hate me so much, Gracie? I loved you. I always loved you. And you left. God, do you have any idea the hell it's been wondering what happened to you twelve years ago? Not knowing if you were dead or alive. Somewhere hurting. In need of help. Didn't I deserve more than what you gave me? Not even a goodbye. Or 'fuck off.' You didn't even do me the service of breaking up with me. You just . . . disappeared."

"How dare you," she spit out. "How dare you act the victim after what you *did*."

Alarm splintered up his spine. Finally they were getting somewhere.

"What did I do?" he demanded. "Tell me, Gracie, because I sure as hell don't know. If I were someone you loved then you would have at least given me a chance to explain. You would have told me what was wrong and given me a chance, at least, to make things right. I *loved* you. I would have moved heaven and earth to make you happy."

She looked utterly horrified. Tears swamped her eyes, making them bright and shiny.

"You didn't love me! Your idea of love is sick! It's twisted. I don't owe you anything. But you owe me more than you can ever repay. Listen to me carefully, Zack. There is nothing—*nothing*—you could ever do or say for me to forgive you. For you to even think it, for you to come in here and act as though I owe you something, is horrifying and so screwed up I can't even fathom your gall."

"What. Did. I. Do?" he bit out emphatically, emphasizing each and every word.

He was fast losing patience. He wanted to put his goddamn fist through the wall. He wanted to vent all the rage and grief festering inside him.

Gracie's hand flew to her mouth and she gagged, choking and then coughing.

"Oh God, I'm going to be sick!" she cried.

Zack flew to his feet and then reached over, lifting her head again while yanking the emesis basin from the stand beside the bed. He turned her as she dry-heaved, her entire body convulsing.

Her sound of agony cut through him like a serrated blade. He hastily punched the call button for a nurse and then shouted loud enough that hopefully Beau or Caleb heard him.

The door immediately opened and Beau filled the frame.

"What is it?" Beau demanded.

"Get me a nurse. Now!"

Beau disappeared and was back just seconds later with a nurse in tow.

The nurse frowned and rushed toward the bed.

"What on earth happened?" she demanded.

"She got sick," Zack said, stating the obvious. He hated when people asked the obvious. "And she's in pain from the dry heaving. Can you give her something more? I don't think her last dose of pain medicine is working worth a damn."

"I'll be right back," the nurse said, hurrying toward the door.

Beau stood to the side, a worried expression on his face as they waited for the nurse's return. Caleb entered quietly behind his brother and stood behind and just beside Beau, who'd taken position at the footboard.

Gracie stopped heaving long enough to cast a fearful look in Beau's direction, and then her attention settled on Caleb, her features freezing as if she had only noticed there were three of them, thus three possible threats to her standing right here in her hospital room. Her gaze darted between the two brothers as if she feared one or both would hurt her. Zack was going to explode if he didn't get some goddamn answers soon.

Finally the nurse returned, carrying two syringes. With crisp efficiency she stepped to the bed and lifted the arm that had the IV inserted. She rubbed and patted Gracie's arm in a comforting gesture.

"It'll be all right, hon," the nurse said in a sweet voice. "I'm giving you something for pain and also for nausea. It should fix you right up. But I'll check on you again in fifteen minutes. If you're still hurting, I'll call the doctor to see if we can up the order for pain meds."

Gracie laid her head back on the pillow, tears running endlessly from the corners of her eyes. Her silent sobs were taking a piece of Zack's soul, one by one. He'd never felt so helpless. How could he fix what he didn't know? Whatever the hell it was he supposedly did was apparently catastrophic in nature. What on earth could put such fear and revulsion in her eyes and such hatred in her voice?

This wasn't the sweet, loving Gracie he knew and had loved for most of his life.

"Try to get some rest now," the nurse said quietly. "We'll be taking you up to the room in an hour or so."

Gracie let out a sound of protest when the nurse started to leave. The nurse frowned and gave Zack a quick, inquiring glance.

"She's scared," Zack said truthfully. "Wouldn't you be?"

The nurse grimaced. "Don't worry, Miss Hill. You're safe here. No one can hurt you now."

Gracie's eyes only widened more and she cast a panicked look in Zack's direction. But the nurse missed it, having turned toward the door once more.

"Uh . . . Caleb and I will just wait outside," Beau said.

The entire room was weighed down by edginess, fear, even full scale panic. It was thick, it was nearly a tangible taste in Zack's mouth. He should know, because he'd tasted fear more times than he could count since losing Gracie so long ago.

"Who are you?" Gracie asked hoarsely.

It seemed she'd been having an argument with herself as to which of the Devereaux brothers to speak to. And since it was obvious she had no intention of addressing Zack, she was likely deciding which Devereaux posed the least threat to her. Not that either brother ever looked remotely harmless. But since she was looking directly at Beau and hadn't even acknowledged Caleb, it was obvious it was Beau she was asking the question of and Beau she'd decided posed the least threat of the remaining two men.

Zack couldn't blame her for choosing Beau over Caleb. Beau could be intimidating but he did have a sense of humor and he was always cognizant of how his actions, words and demeanor often made the difference in gaining a client's trust. Caleb, on the other hand, even on his best day, was intense and brooding-looking. He rarely smiled except when he was with Ramie or Tori Devereaux, the youngest of all the Devereaux siblings and the only sister to boot.

But then everyone was careful to shield the still very fragile and vulnerable Tori so she never feared the very people who loved her the most and protected her with their lives. At present, she lived with Caleb and Ramie, and from what little exposure he'd had with Tori, he doubted her living arrangements would change in the short term. According to Beau, Tori had made progress and was valiantly trying to do it on her own without her older brothers'—and now her two sisters-in-law's—help. Unfortunately for Tori, she possessed three of the most over protective older brothers a girl ever had. Some brothers threaten someone—usually a guy—when it comes to their baby sister. But Tori's older brothers wouldn't make threats. Threats are a waste of time and only useful to cowards who have no intention of ever trying to back up their threats.

Beau looked startled by Gracie's question, and for a moment, so too had Zack not registered it because his thoughts and focus weren't where they should have been. Here. With Gracie.

Despite his initial reaction to Gracie directly addressing him, his expression eased into a reassuring smile and he stepped to the foot of the bed so Gracie could better see him. When he spoke, it was with gentle, soothing tones.

"I'm Beau Devereaux, ma'am. I work with Zack. I run a security company with my brother, Caleb. I don't want you to worry any longer. We're going to put one hundred percent of our time and effort into ensuring your safety and into finding the bastards who did this to you. I swear it on my life."

She looked confused by Beau's passionate statement. Her eyes flickered and then she turned them toward Zack. She seemed puzzled, as if she were trying to make sense of it all.

"But who's going to keep me safe from *him*?" she whispered, staring directly at Zack.

ELEVEN

"WHAT are you going to do, man?" Beau asked in a hushed voice.

Zack ran his hand through his hair in a ragged, agitated motion.

The two men stood just outside the open door of the room Gracie had been moved to. Zack was leaning against the wall, exhaustion from two sleepless nights catching up quickly.

After Gracie had dropped her bomb of a question, one that Beau had been speechless to respond to, she'd drifted off under the influence of the meds and an hour later she'd been moved to a private room on the sixth floor.

"I don't fucking know," Zack said. "What the hell am I *supposed* to do? She hates my guts. She's terrified of me. And I don't know why. She keeps mentioning this 'horrible' thing I did. Said it was *unforgivable*."

"Ouch."

"Yeah, ouch. This runs deep, Beau. She had the same reaction at the gallery and the art studio. No way of faking that much fear. But Jesus, *why*? I don't get it. I *loved* her, man. She was *it* for me. You know, the trite cliché that so many men, especially men like us, cringe over and roll their eyes? Not me. She was The One for me. And God help me but there will be no other woman for me."

"I had our entire future planned. House, wife, kids. The American dream. I'd play pro ball for ten years if I were lucky. Bank the money and then retire and spend my time spoiling my wife and children rotten. Have a mini football team of our own if we were so blessed. She was on board. She said she loved me, and she *did*. No one is that good an actress. And she sure as hell wasn't using me. If that were the case she would have stayed and milked me for every dime. No, she cut out before I even *made* the pros. I came home one day and she had vanished, leaving me to think the absolute worst."

He blew out his breath and wearily closed his eyes.

"This is killing me, man. Think how you'd feel if you went home and Ari was just . . . gone. And you never heard from her again. And then twelve years later you find her, only she's terrified of you, accuses you of some horrible betrayal and she hates you."

"No thanks," Beau muttered. "That's some heavy shit you're toting around, dude."

"Tell me about it."

Zack looked back in to the room to check on Gracie, but she appeared to be resting comfortably, devoid of the nightmares he was sure were haunting her.

Also encouraging was that the strain around her eyes and on her forehead had eased after the last injection of pain medication had been administered.

But as much as he knew she needed as much rest as possible, he was also impatient for her to awaken so that maybe, when she wasn't in so much pain, and perhaps the horror of what she'd endured wasn't burning as brightly in her consciousness, then maybe, finally, she'd talk. To him. And only him. No one to interrupt them. No one to come to Gracie's rescue when she was already in the safest place she could be. And once she was discharged, he was taking her to an even safer place so she'd have time to heal. He only prayed that in that time, he and Gracie could talk about the past, something he knew caused her as much pain as he'd endured.

Please God show me the way to help her past this. Grant us both the courage to face our pasts. And for the both of us to heal. Together. So that we can finally live the dream we wanted so much instead of a twelve-year-long nightmare.

If only the beating of a few hours ago was the only thing currently causing her terror. Even if she did awaken better able to comprehend and put enough distance between the attack and where she was now, there was still the issue of her fearing Zack more than she had the assholes who had beaten her so brutally. And if that wasn't enough to make him vomit in the nearest trash can, he didn't know what was.

"I know it's risky but . . ."

Beau's unfinished statement was enough to break the stranglehold of panic and the litany of what-ifs and he glanced up to see what his partner was going to say.

Beau broke off, uncertainty flickering in his eyes. Beau was in no way indecisive. It wasn't like him to hesitate. Zack cocked an eyebrow and mentally braced himself as he waited for his partner to continue.

"What's risky?" he prompted when Beau wasn't forthcoming.

"I just wondered if having Ramie and Ari here *would* help. I mean make her feel more at ease," Beau added. "I'm sure it *was* startling to wake up in the hospital and have a bunch of surly-ass, pissed-off men in her room."

"No way," Zack said emphatically. "No fucking way. No way I'd risk them like that. I can't believe you'd even suggest something like that. Caleb would lose his damn mind."

"Just hear me out," Beau said, holding his hands up. "Of course we'd have heavy guard, and those fucking bastards are cowards anyway. They won't show their heads in public or broad daylight. They do their shit off the grid and in the shadows. And if it helped ease Gracie's fears and convinced her you weren't going to murder her in her sleep, then it would be worth it, don't you think?"

"I think it's a bad idea," Zack said stubbornly. "And even if we wanted to do it, Caleb would never agree. Hell, can you imagine if Ramie accidentally touched Gracie? Or if Gracie touched her, not knowing what it would do? Then not only will Gracie have gone through hell, but then Ramie will experience that same hell."

"True," Beau grudgingly admitted. "I hadn't thought of that. Still, there has to be something we can do. When Gracie is released from this place, she isn't going to want your help and she's an absolute target. Short of kidnapping her, I don't see what you can do."

"I *will* kidnap her," Zack said fiercely. "She already hates me. If making sure she stays alive until we bring down these assholes means she hates me more, then I can live with that. As long as she's *alive* to hate me."

Beau rubbed the back of his neck and sighed. "Okay, so we won't bring the girls here. But I still think it's a good idea to get them together with Gracie as soon as possible. This has cluster-fuck written all over it."

Zack mused a moment, glancing back through the doorway at Gracie a second time to make sure she was still resting quietly.

"There's also the issue of Sterling," Zack said, a foul taste in his mouth at the mere mention of the other man's name. "I doubt the bastard will just stay away. They're involved even though he says not romantically. But it would appear he keeps close tabs on her or at least has more than a passing acquaintance, so I'd expect him to roll in before she's discharged."

"I'll get a man on him to monitor his comings and goings. At least you'll get somewhat of a heads-up if he heads this way."

"Lizzie is working on getting me another place to stay. I'm not going back to my apartment. The security there sucks. Ramie and Ari could come then as long as we have all safety measures in place."

Beau nodded. "That's a good idea. Let me know when Eliza finds you something. I'll make sure it's furnished and stocked with groceries and I'll damn sure tighten security so you'll know when an ant farts on the property."

A light sound came from Gracie's bed. Zack jerked around to see her stirring. The frown and strain were back on her face and she turned restlessly, a small sigh escaping her swollen lips.

Answering pain registered in Zack's chest. He should be there at her bedside comforting her. Touching and holding her. Not be on the opposite end of the room because he couldn't bear to see so much fear in her eyes when she looked at him. When she would look at him, that is. So far she'd avoided his gaze except for a very few times. As if she couldn't bear to look at *him*.

"I'm going to run," Beau said in a low voice. "But I'll check back periodically. Text or call me if anything goes down or you need anything. And I'll send Eliza over with dinner for you and Gracie, provided she feels up to eating. Maybe having Eliza here will ease some of Gracie's fears."

"Good idea," Zack said. "I should have thought about her when you suggested bringing Ramie and Ari. But make damn sure Eliza doesn't come alone. I'm not disrespecting her or her skills in the least, but I don't want her going solo while these nut jobs are gunning for us."

"No, I agree absolutely. I'd rather none of us fly solo anytime soon. They obviously have a hard-on for anyone remotely involved with DSS so all bets are off and I wouldn't assume anyone is safe."

"I want these guys, Beau," Zack said in a low, fierce tone. "I want their blood."

"You'll get it if I have anything to do with it," Beau vowed. "I have a few shots of my own to get in for what they did and tried to do to Ari."

"Make damn sure she isn't blaming herself," Zack said.

Beau nodded and then clapped a hand over Zack's shoulder.

"Okay, then I'm out of here right now. Seeing Gracie makes me want to get back to Ari and reassure myself she's okay. This scares me, Zack," Beau admitted. "If anything happened to Ari . . ."

"I get it," Zack said in turn. "Believe me, I get it. Hey, do me a favor. When you call Eliza about dinner, ask her to buzz me on her way up so I can step outside to talk to her."

"Will do," Beau said. He blew out a long breath. "I'm sorry about this, man. Everything. I know it has to suck. I wish to hell there was something I could do—some way to help."

"You can. By helping bring down the people who did this to her. I won't rest until every last one of them is six feet under. Preferably in pieces."

Beau nodded and then quietly walked away. Zack turned back to go inside the room and return to Gracie's side, eager but at the same time reluctant for her to wake up again. Maybe this time he'd get some answers. There was only so much he could take, and this was eating him alive.

TWELVE

ZACK stood in Gracie's cracked doorway as he waited for Eliza to make her appearance. After checking with the nurse to see if Gracie was under any dietary restrictions, he'd asked Eliza to bring soup. The nurse had told him that while there was nothing to prevent her from eating, it could very well be painful for her to chew and she might just not feel well enough to keep anything down.

He was going to sit by her bed and feed her himself if she needed it. He hated to think of her in any discomfort at all. He couldn't take away the pain brought on by her injuries but he could at least ease any hunger she might have.

And hopefully Beau's idea that another woman might make her feel more at ease was spot-on and Eliza would deliver in spades. No one could resist Eliza's warm, earthy charm. She was as genuine as they came and could make anyone feel comfortable.

He just prayed today wasn't her first failure.

A moment later his gaze caught Eliza turning the corner of the hallway and striding toward him at a brisk pace. When she approached, bags in hand, she automatically enfolded him in a fierce hug.

"How you holding up?" she asked gently as she pulled away.

"Not well," he said.

There was little point in lying to her. Any idiot could see he was not okay.

She grimaced in sympathy and then handed a plastic takeout bag to him.

"I got the soup you asked for and I got you a sub, fully loaded, and there's a bottle of my home-brewed tea for you in the bag as well."

He smiled at her. "Thanks, Lizzie. You're the best."

"Beau brought me up to speed, so you don't have to. I hope I can be of help to you, Zack. I know this has to be horrific for you, to not know what's upset her so badly and for her to hate you. Man. I can't even imagine what you're thinking right now, what you're going through. But listen. You know I'm only a phone call away and if you need anything, I mean anything at all, you call me. Got it? Day or night. I don't give a crap what time it is."

He reached for her and pulled her into another bone-crushing hug. As pathetic as it might have sounded, he just needed another of her hugs. She gave the best.

She kissed him on the cheek and followed up with a gentle hand to his face, patting lightly before withdrawing.

"Come on then. Let's go see about Gracie."

"She's mostly slept since Beau left. She came around briefly but was in so much pain I had to call the nurse to get her more medicine. I probably shouldn't wake her up. She needs the rest, I'm sure. But I'd feel better if she could keep some food down and also, you're here, and I'll be honest: I'm desperate. I'm willing to try anything to get through to her."

"I'll do my best."

"I know, Lizzie. I know. I love you dearly. You and Beau. The others . . . You're the only friends I have. I mean I stay in touch with a few buddies from high school but we see each other maybe once a year, although I haven't seen them in the last two."

"Can't get rid of me," she said lightly as she put the bag she was carrying down on the table by the bed. "Once you're my friend, my friend you stay."

Eliza turned to the bed and studied it for a moment.

"I assume this an adjustable bed and you could raise the back up a bit. Would make it far easier for her to eat."

"Yeah. It does. I just have to be careful that movement doesn't cause her even more pain. The doctor said she had a few cracked lower ribs. I don't imagine that feels good with any sort of pressure on her abdomen."

Eliza looked contemplative for a moment. "Actually, lying flat like she is, only elevated a bit is probably less comfortable than sitting up more. I had abdominal surgery several years ago and for a week after, the only way I could sleep was in a recliner. Lying flat on a bed? Agonizing."

Zack frowned. "Damn. I didn't think of that. I hope to hell she hasn't been uncomfortable all this time."

"Do you want to wake her or do you want me to?" Eliza asked quietly.

He hesitated, staring at Gracie's closed eyes for a long moment. Then slowly he nodded. "Yeah, let's give it a try. Maybe if you're the first person she sees when she wakes up, instead of me, she won't freak as badly."

"I'm so sorry, Zack. I know that has to hurt you."

He didn't deny it but neither did he respond.

"Okay, well, you step back and get the soup ready to go. I'll see if I can get Gracie to come around for me."

Zack took a position by the sink, where he wasn't directly in Gracie's sight path but he could see her and Eliza both from where he stood. He found himself holding his breath when Eliza bent over Gracie and curled her own hand around Gracie's.

"Gracie. Gracie, honey, can you wake up?"

Eliza was infinitely patient and she kept her tone low and soothing the entire time.

"Gracie. I have soup for you. You're probably starving and could likely eat a horse by now, but I bet that jaw hurts like hell. Not to mention your poor mouth."

Zack's pulse accelerated when Gracie blinked and slowly turned her head in the direction of Eliza's voice. Eliza smiled down at her and reached up with her free hand to push back the hair that fell over Gracie's brow and partially obscured her sight.

"Hey, there you are," Eliza said affectionately.

To a stranger, it would appear that Eliza and Gracie knew one another. That they had a close relationship. But that was the magic of Eliza.

Gracie's face crinkled in confusion. She blinked again and moved her head slightly to the side as though she were trying to place Eliza.

"Do I know you?" Gracie asked, her voice hoarse and strained.

Her throat was probably swollen from the trauma and it

likely hurt like hell to swallow. He was doubly glad he'd gotten Eliza to get soup. Chewing and swallowing would both be a bitch.

Eliza's smile widened. "No, or at least you didn't until now. My name is Eliza Cummings. How are you feeling? Okay, don't answer that. Bad question, I know. Of course you feel like shit. And hon, not to offend you, but you look like someone ran over you, reversed and backed over you again."

Gracie looked startled for the space of a moment before she visibly relaxed and let out a short laugh that ended with a cough and a groan.

"Do you think you could get down some soup? It's nice and hot but not so hot it'll burn your mouth. I'm sure your lips are pretty tender. It had time to cool off a bit on the drive over."

Gracie nodded. "That sounds nice. Thank you."

"Zack," Eliza called softly. "Can you bring the soup over?"

Gracie's gaze immediately tracked the room and she froze when it settled on Zack. A hurt, confused look simmered in her eyes and she glanced at Eliza as though she'd been betrayed by the other woman.

"Hon, don't look like that," Eliza said. "Zack is a great guy. He asked me to come. He thought you might feel better with another woman here. And hey, we need to even the odds at every opportunity, don't you think?"

"Are you his wife?" Gracie asked, her stare returning to Zack.

It was the longest she'd ever looked at him at one time. She seemed to study him dispassionately. Almost as if she were analyzing him. What astonished him, though, was the look of pity she gave Eliza when she asked if Eliza was his wife. God, just what sort of sick fuck did she think he was?

Eliza let out a laugh. "Wife? Oh Lord no. I love him to pieces but we'd kill one another in the first twenty-four hours. We work together. Have been for a while now."

Her expression grew confused again. He could see questions in her eyes but she closed her lips in a firm line and turned her face away from them both.

With a sigh, he held out the soup bowl to Eliza, and when she took it, he walked around to the opposite side of the bed so that Gracie was between them. Gracie averted her gaze to the ceiling as if shutting them both out.

One eyebrow cocked, Eliza shot him a quick look that clearly said, *What now?*

Zack pulled up the only other chair in the room and sat so close to the bed that he could prop his arm on the rail.

"Eat, Gracie. Eliza won't bite. She's the very best kind of person. If you won't believe it of me, at least give *her* the benefit of the doubt."

But first he needed to elevate her bed so she wouldn't be wearing her meal.

He fiddled with the buttons on the side of the bed until he found the one that raised the head.

"I'm going to lift you up a bit so you can eat," he said. "Let me know when to stop and tell me if it causes you more pain."

Not waiting for a response, he pressed the button and a whirring sound started as the head half of the bed slowly elevated. At the first movement, Gracie's hand flew to the railing as if to steady herself. Then she relaxed more, waited a moment and said, "That's good."

She sagged against the pillow and took several shallow breaths.

"Hurt?" he asked.

She shook her head. "No. It's ... better, actually."

What a concession it must have been for her to speak directly to him. It beat screaming at him, or accusing him of doing whatever the hell it was he'd done, but then again, her yelling at him would be better than this icy silence between them.

He was silently begging her to talk to him. To tell him what had gone so horribly wrong in their relationship.

"Think you can handle it or do you want me to spoon it to you?" Eliza asked gently.

A rose color bloomed in Gracie's cheeks, or at least the few places she wasn't colored purple. She lowered her gaze as if shamed. Then she looked back up and slowly reached for the bowl.

"I can do it," she said quietly.

She wiggled just a bit, repositioning herself before taking the bowl from Eliza's grasp. Then she sank back down against the bed, seemingly exhausted from such a small task.

He was absolutely going to heed the doctor's instructions to a T. And he'd use her period of recovery to wrestle whatever demons she had. Not to mention his own, since it was obvious that *he* was her demon.

Each spoonful was painstakingly and slowly rendered. The hand holding the spoon shook, splashing some of the soup onto the sheet covering her lap.

Eliza immediately rose and ducked into the bathroom to get a towel. Then she placed it over Gracie's lap so any further spillage wouldn't get the sheets wet.

"Do you want to talk about what happened?" Eliza asked after a long period of silence.

Gracie was so shaken from her question that she dropped the spoon. Thankfully she'd already sipped the contents and had been on her way for another spoonful.

"The police have come by already," Zack interjected. "They asked me to call them as soon as she woke up so she can give them a statement."

Gracie closed her eyes and a thin stream of tears leaked down her bruised cheeks.

Eliza immediately took the hand that had been holding the spoon and she squeezed it but didn't let it go. Instead she rested their linked hands on the mattress at Gracie's side.

"Would you prefer then to wait until they arrive so you don't have to repeat it?" Eliza asked.

"I don't know anything," Gracie said in a bleak voice. "One minute I was there. Alone. The next minute they were there. I don't even remember most of what happened afterward. Just the horrific fear that it could happen again."

Zack immediately stiffened. "That *what* could happen again?"

Gracie closed her eyes and the hand Eliza held went white as she squeezed Eliza's. Hard. But Eliza didn't even flinch or act like she noticed.

All the color had leached from her face and she looked very much like she was going to be sick again. Eliza must have picked up on that fact as well because she immediately made a grab for the basin by the bed.

She merely slid it onto Gracie's lap, taking the bowl that was still half full and putting it away.

"Gracie?" Zack prompted. "What could happen again?"

"In my worst imaginations did I ever think you capable of

the things you've done, but to sit there and act like you don't know, that you're innocent ..."

She turned her warm chocolate eyes on him, emotion simmering, shiny with unshed tears.

"Why, Zack? Did you hate me *that* much? Could you not just have broken up with me? Were you afraid I'd turn into some psycho stalker? Or were you worried I would make you look bad when you entered the pros? God, what you must have thought of me."

She turned away again, tears running in endless streams. Zack was so dumbfounded by her barrage of heated questions that he couldn't even form a coherent sentence. Eliza immediately found his gaze, her question evident but not vocalized. Did he want her to leave?

As much as he'd like her to do just that so he and Gracie would be alone to hash everything out, he knew that if he rushed this, he was going to lose big. He had to gain her trust in some way. No matter what it took.

He gave a quick shake of his head but kept his gaze fastened on Gracie and her tear-stained and bruised face.

"Gracie, look at me please," Eliza said in a firm but gentle tone.

With seeming reluctance, Gracie complied.

Eliza gave her hand another squeeze. "Listen to me, hon. I don't know what happened in your past. Only you know that. But what I do know is that Zack has looked for you—thought about you—every day for the last twelve years. He's a good man. The very best. And he's worried about you for so very long. Will you at least talk to him?"

"I just want to forget. *Everything*," Gracie whispered brokenly.

His heart was in his throat. No matter that he knew he hadn't done anything wrong. *Gracie* thought so. She was convinced. Heartbreakingly so. How awful must it have been that she hadn't even confronted him about it twelve years ago? And she couldn't bring herself to even talk about it. She hated him. She wanted *nothing* to do with him.

He surged upward from his chair and stalked to the foot of the bed, his hand gripping the back of his neck. He closed his eyes in utter frustration and despair. He was getting nowhere fast. He'd never wanted anything as badly as he wanted her trust. Her love. How the hell was he supposed to get both back when it was clear she neither trusted nor loved him?

"I'm tired," Gracie whispered. "And I hurt. Can you push the call button?"

The question was obviously directed at Eliza. She never even looked his way while she made her request. Even so, he pushed forward and pressed the button himself.

For the briefest of moments their gazes locked as he once again stood to his full height. Her lips trembled and her eyes were still glossy with tears. The look of defeat in her features nearly unhinged him and broke his heart at the same time.

"Listen to me, Gracie," he said in a quiet, firm voice.

He waited until she finally lifted her gaze to his, and he winced at the stark emotion in her eyes. The bareness. Like a desert.

"I need you to talk to me, but I understand that right now you're upset and you're hurting. But I'm not going away. Not until we have this—whatever this is—worked out between us.

I won't allow you to walk away from me again. Not when I've looked for you for so damn long. So here's the way it's going to be. While you are here, in this hospital, I or someone I work with will be with you 24/7. And when you're discharged, you are going home. With me."

She let out a strangled protest and he gently touched the tip of his finger to her swollen lips.

"Shhh, and hear me out."

She went silent and he let his finger fall away instead of tracing the outline of her lips and imagine what she tasted like, if she still tasted as sweet as she had the last time he'd kissed her. Only, he hadn't known it would be the last time. If he could only have that moment back.

"The men who attacked you went after you because of me—because of the people I work with. And you aren't safe as long as they're out there. Targeting their next victim. And I will not allow you to be at risk. Someone will have to go through me to get to you. Now, we can do it the easy way, which is you agreeing to come with me. Or we can do it the hard way and I carry you out of here."

"What kind of people do you work for?" she asked, fear sparking in her eyes.

"The best, Gracie. The absolute best. Eliza works with me." He nodded in Eliza's direction. "I work for Devereaux Security Services. We protect people. Provide security. Any job that requires muscle and high technology."

"Ironic," she bit out, her eyes flashing with fire for the first time.

Well, he'd take anything over the fear and utter desolation that had seemed a permanent fixture in her soulful brown eyes.

She lifted her chin a notch higher, and she stared directly at him.

"Is this your penance?" she asked softly.

He swore violently, barely able to keep the blistering epitaphs from erupting off his tongue. He breathed in through his nostrils for a few moments as he sought to keep his temper in check.

He'd never been angry with Gracie. Never had a reason to. He wasn't sure he had a reason *now* but the anger was there all the same.

"Tell me what the hell it is I supposedly did," he demanded. "It's kind of hard to defend an action when you have no clue what it is!"

"Are you for real?" she asked incredulously.

Eliza leaned forward, interrupting the tense exchange. She squeezed Gracie's hand in a gesture of reassurance but Gracie appeared to be as angry as he was. Again, he'd take that over defeat and sorrow any damn day of the week.

"Gracie, in order to atone for one's sins, one has to know what sin has been committed," Eliza said quietly. "You and Zack obviously have very differing accounts of what happened twelve years ago. Talk to him. Tell him why you're angry. If nothing else, tell him to go to hell, but at least give him the opportunity to defend himself. Surely he deserves that much."

"Deserves?"

Gracie's voice cracked under the weight of emotion and tears rapidly filled her eyes once more.

"He deserves. God, that is so . . . I don't even have words!" Gracie said tearfully. "I sure as hell didn't deserve what he did to *me*—what he had *done*. I can't even think about that night or I get sick to my stomach."

As if to drive home her point, she gestured wildly for the basin, which Eliza promptly shoved onto her tray, just as Gracie heaved the contents of her stomach inside it.

THIRTEEN

ONCE again, Zack had been forced from Gracie's room while the nurse did an assessment and made her more comfortable. Eliza stood next to him, watching the goings-on through the narrow glass panel above the knob.

She shook her head, her eyes awash with sympathy. "I don't know what to say right now," she murmured. "I can't even imagine. I'm so sorry, Zack. This has to be hell for you."

"Evidently it's hell for her too," Zack said bleakly.

He rubbed his face tiredly, lack of sleep fast catching up to him. Maybe he'd never sleep again. How could he when whenever he closed his eyes, all he could see was terror blazing in hers. The shadows under her eyes. How utterly fragile and breakable she appeared.

Breakable.

No, that wasn't accurate. She was already broken. Anyone with eyes could see that.

God, it scared him to death to see her in such a state. What the hell had happened twelve years ago? He was getting damn tired of the issue being dodged and Gracie's refusal to let him in on the big goddamn secret. Especially when he seemed to be the only person who didn't know what the fuck was going on.

"I wonder if you shouldn't have a psychologist brought in," she said in a low voice, ensuring it didn't carry through the door. "She looks so . . . fragile."

"I've used the exact same word to describe her more than once since seeing her in the art studio."

"It's evident she truly is frightened. Whatever it is she thinks you did is very real to her."

"Tell me about it," he muttered. Then he cupped the back of his neck and dug his fingers into the aching muscle. "Can you do some looking? You know where I'm from. Where we're from. Can you go back twelve years or around that time, before and after the last time I saw her, and see if anything pops up? Something major? If it happened in our pissant little town then you can be sure it was all over the bloody place."

"I can try, though I did a fair bit more poking around after you left my apartment this morning. And so far, I'm hitting a brick wall."

Which is exactly how he felt, only in his case, it felt as though he were *beating* his head repeatedly against that wall. And he was starting to feel the ache all the way to his soul.

"Oh, here she comes now," Eliza said, hastily moving back from the doorway.

Zack surged to attention, scraping at the bristle of his unshaven face. He needed to get cleaned up. He looked—and smelled—like a goat. He was surprised the nursing staff hadn't thrown him out or at least into a nearby shower.

The nurse quietly closed the door behind her as she stepped into the hall to join Eliza and Zack.

"How is she?" Zack asked urgently.

The nurse's pretty face twisted into a grimace. "Exhausted. Hurting. Scared. At the end of her rope. Pretty much all apply here."

Zack bit back a sharp curse.

"I gave her a sedative to help her relax. She should sleep soundly for the next several hours. You should go home. Get freshened up. There's nothing more you can do here today."

"I'm not leaving her," Zack said emphatically.

The nurse hesitated and then blew out her breath in a long sigh. "She doesn't want visitors. At least not today. So you should go. Let her rest. Get some rest yourself."

Eliza nudged him in the ribs and stared pointedly at his unshaven jaw and his unkempt clothing.

"Let me make myself clear, ma'am," Zack said, forcing calm he didn't feel into his words. "Gracie has no one. And I mean no one. She is completely alone in the world apart from me. Now, do you really think it's a good idea to leave a woman who just endured a horrific traumatic event completely alone? What if she wakes while I'm gone? Who the hell is going to be here to reassure her that those sons of bitches can't hurt her anymore?"

The nurse's entire face went soft and she reached out to squeeze his arm.

"She's very lucky to have you then, if she has no one else. And she won't be alone. I promise. We are monitoring her very closely and will continue to do so overnight. But you staying here at her bedside while she sleeps does neither of you any good. Go home. Grab a shower and something to eat. Try to sleep if you can, even if it's only for a few hours. Then, when you come back tomorrow, everyone will be in a better frame of mind."

Zack shook his head. "You aren't getting this. Gracie was attacked and brutally beaten in a methodical, planned way. And you want me to leave her alone. Unguarded. Where anyone at all could walk into her room and kill her. Hell, they could kidnap her. Who on this floor would be able to stop them? And I can guaran-damn-tee you that they'll be armed. They have absolutely no compunction about using violence to achieve their means. You see what they do to defenseless women. They tortured and killed another young woman who'd just given birth. So while I appreciate your concern for Gracie and her mental well-being, right now I am most concerned with her physical safety."

The nurse went pale and she swallowed nervously. "Why weren't we told this? No one told us!"

Her voice was rising, on the verge of hysteria. Zack put a hand out to ease her panic.

"I'm not going to allow them to hurt anyone here. The police are coming when Gracie wakes up next. In the meantime, someone from my security company will be here round the clock, and no one who isn't medical staff or employed by DSS will be allowed access to her room. Someone will be stationed here at all times."

"I understand your priorities, sir," the nurse said, sincerity ringing in her voice. "But just as you have to take into consideration what is best for her in order for you to do your job effectively, so too must I prioritize her well-being, both emotional and physical, as long as she is a patient on my floor. And she was quite adamant that she wanted no further visitors today. So if someone is posted here—and they are more than welcome as the staff here would feel much better if there was tight security—then they must take position outside her room."

"Ouch," Eliza said, her lips twitching with humor. "I guess you've been schooled now."

Zack shot her a glare. He was in no mood for her sharp wit. He needed about twenty-four hours of sleep, a hot shower, a pot of coffee and to get his hands on the bastards who'd hurt Gracie before he would be remotely mollified.

"It wasn't my intention to be rude," the nurse began.

"Oh no, you weren't rude," Eliza said, her eyes sparkling with laughter. "Not at all. It's nice to see the men of DSS taken down a notch or two. It keeps their egos in check."

The nurse smiled. "That bad, huh. Let me guess. And you're the only female in the ranks."

"Got it in one," Eliza said with a grin.

"I'm Jacquie," the nurse offered, extending her hand to Eliza.

"Hi, Jacquie," Eliza returned. "I'm Eliza and this surly guy is Zack. We both work for Devereaux Security."

Zack's head was about to explode. He started to ask Eliza if she was high on something. How could she be out here, ribbing, teasing, *joking* when Gracie lay on the other side of the door, curled into a ball, having cried those silent silver streaks until the nurse had administered the medication, at which point her eyelids had fluttered slowly until her lashes finally came to rest against her cheeks.

Jacquie gave him a thorough assessment, staring intently enough to cause heat to flood his cheeks. He *hated* being the object of scrutiny.

"I tell you what, Zack," she said, using the name Eliza had provided. "I just came on an hour ago, so I'll be here for the next eleven hours. You and Eliza run home, change, grab something to eat. I'll call down to security and have them post a guard outside her door and I'll also stay on this end of the floor so I can eyeball her door until y'all get back."

Okay, so Eliza was a bloody genius who now had the nursing staff eating out of her hand. He silently groaned when Eliza turned her smug smile in his direction. He flipped her the bird when Jacquie's attention was drawn to Eliza—and her cheeky victory smile. He shook his head. Sassy little heifer.

"Well, you heard the lady. And we *are* intruding on her turf," Eliza said pointedly. "But we don't get all riled up like you men do and start pissing on everything to mark your territory."

Jacquie laughed. Zack just rolled his eyes. God save him from incorrigible females.

Zack wasted no time when he arrived at his apartment. Eliza had insisted on coming with him, so he'd have backup, since his security had been breached. But he still hurried, not wanting to expose Eliza—or himself—to further risk. If Gracie weren't in the picture, then hell yeah. He'd bait a trap and he and Beau would run round-the-clock surveillance until the fuckers bit. But she *was* in the picture. And she needed him, not that she'd admit or accept that, no matter what denials burst off her tongue.

His only thought was to get back to Gracie. He could be relentless. He *was* relentless. He hadn't gotten this far by wimping out. One had to be ruthless in order for the cards to fall one's way. If anyone had ever thought him savage and single-minded, focusing on one goal and one goal only, then they'd know he'd locked on to his target and nothing would deter him from crossing the goal line this time.

Third and long. There's the snap. Fake to the wide end. Looking . . . looking. He's tucked the ball! Cut to the inside. Another fake! Oh wait! He just hurdled the defensive end! Folks, does this young man have moves or what? He breaks the tackle! Running . . . running. . . . Ladies and gentlemen! He could go. All. The. Way! Touchdown! With twenty-eight seconds remaining in the fourth quarter, Zack Covington has just scored what is potentially the game-winning touchdown!

Remnants of that night. First-round playoffs. They'd been a Cinderella story from the onset of the season. No one ever expected them to make the playoffs. They were rebuilding. Replacing key positions vacated by trades, retirement and injuries.

Even the coach had admitted that they'd surpassed his wildest imaginings. With a majority rookie team plus a few irreplaceable seasoned veterans, they'd stormed onto the football field in week one of the regular season and they hadn't looked back once. Sixteen and O. The start of the perfect season. Bye in the first round. The W in the second playoff. One more week until the big game.

It had been a huge night. Maybe the biggest night of his life. His *old* life. He wasn't that starry-eyed, optimistic kid he'd once been. And the brief respite from so much ice and cold surrounding his heart had been glorious. It had lasted for maybe two minutes. Two wonderful minutes where the numbness couldn't find him.

And then he'd seen a few of his teammates looking toward the boxes in the stands. One of them balled his fingers into a fist, pounded it against his chest before kissing it and flinging it skyward, straight in the direction of where the player's wife and baby son sat somewhere in the sea of fans.

It had taken a space of a moment for Zack's feet to touch back down on earth. There was no one for him to share this with. Gracie was gone.

This time his dream wouldn't elude him. This time, for once, he wanted something for himself.

He wanted her not to look at him as though he were some monster. He wanted the fear in her eyes to be replaced with laughter and happiness. He wanted to love her.

And he wanted her to love him.

He finished shoving the clothing he needed into an overnight bag and then collected the few toiletries he required from the bathroom. He'd need to go shopping for Gracie after her release from the hospital. Or perhaps Eliza would be willing to pick up a few things for her.

He hurried back to the kitchen area, where Eliza had posted herself so she had a clear view of the front door.

"You ready?" he asked.

Eliza nodded. "But Zack, Jacquie is right. You need to eat. You look terrible."

He grunted. "Gee, thanks."

She shrugged. "Just keeping it real."

"I'll grab something at the hospital when the cafeteria opens. Gracie will probably want something then too, provided she can eat."

"Her throat looked pretty bruised. I'd stick with soup or broth for now. That's likely what they'll send up on her meal trays anyway."

"On your toes, Lizzie," he murmured as they exited his apartment.

"Always," she said lightly.

Their feet made the lightest of sounds on the concrete sidewalk. At the gate, Zack gave a gentle push, irritated that it squeaked loudly. Fuckers had obviously broken it when they'd broke in to dump Gracie.

They were nearly to Zack's SUV when a dark, shadowy form appeared just a few feet in front of them.

"Down!" Eliza barked, shoving at Zack.

He dropped and rolled. Before he could get back to his feet, he was hit by what felt like a truck full of concrete. He let out a guttural sound and immediately went limp.

Surprised by the move, his attacker stumbled, unable to bear Zack's weight. Zack took full advantage, ramming his shoulder into the guy's midriff and taking him down hard on the asphalt surface.

Zack was just pissed-off enough, and he'd had to keep his fury leashed the entire goddamn day, that he let the lion out of his cage with a roar.

His sound of rage echoed across the parking lot. His attacker hit the ground, Zack down on top of him. He felt the harsh exhalation of the other man's breath against his neck. Zack swung, punching viciously.

He reeled back when one of his attacker's fists connected with his jaw. Goddamn it.

Zack rolled, remaining in motion, not wanting to present too easy a target.

He was tackled, his motion abruptly ceasing. And then, before any more blows could be landed from either side, Eliza's command cracked the night.

"Hands up where I can see them, asshole! Give me a reason to shoot. Go ahead. You'll make my entire week," she snarled.

Zack was freed and the man slowly stepped away. Zack shoved to his feet and was on the guy in a split second. He grabbed one arm and twisted it hard behind his back, whirling the guy into motion. His forward momentum made the rotation easier and Zack pinned the guy's arm high behind his back to render him immobile.

"Get me a goddamn light, Lizzie."

A second later, a flashlight turned on and the beam tracked up the attacker's body and then to his face.

"What the fuck?" Zack demanded. "*Sterling?* What the hell do you think you're doing?"

FOURTEEN

BLOOD trickled down Sterling's nose and his eyes blazed with fury, reflecting eerily by the flashlight Eliza was currently blinding him with.

"What the fuck is your problem?" Zack roared. "How about you take a trip downtown on assault charges. *After* I beat the shit out of you."

Sterling's lips curled with contempt. "You fucking pussy. You couldn't take me in a fight. You're too much of a goddamn pansy to ever get your hands dirty. No, you have others beat up on women *for* you."

Zack punched him squarely in the jaw, sending the other man reeling backward. Sterling regained his balance and lunged for Zack, propelling both men to the asphalt parking lot.

A shot sounded, jerking Zack up. Sterling reacted no differently, hitting the ground with speed that told Zack the man was trained. His instincts were too good. Too practiced. The suave, wealthy and polished exterior he crafted covered up the raw, street-smart man underneath.

"What the fuck, Lizzie?" Zack roared. "Are you trying to kill me?"

Eliza huffed out in exasperation. "Look, we don't have time for this shit. We're out in the open. Not good. You're calling attention to us. Not good. Need I go on?"

"And you didn't just shoot a giant fucking firework into the sky?" Zack asked incredulously.

"Someone had to do something," she pointed out. "Now, what do you say we have this conversation somewhere other than the middle of a public parking lot."

"We're done here," Zack said flatly.

He didn't know what Sterling's issue was, but his insinuation that Zack had been purposely responsible for Gracie's beating? What the fuck? Zack couldn't even see straight, his vision was so clouded with red rage.

"No, the *hell* we're done," Sterling said. "Where is Anna-Grace? What did you do to her?"

Zack looked at Sterling like he'd grown a second head. "What the fuck are you talking about?"

"She's disappeared, but that shouldn't be news to you. Coincidentally, she disappears the day after you show up in my studio, harass her and scare the living hell out of her. It doesn't take much effort to connect the dots here. But you fucked up this time, Covington. Maybe she had no one who cared about her then. But she does now. She's important to me. And I *will* protect her even if it means taking you down for good."

The roar in Zack's ears was nearly deafening. He was tired of

Gracie's—and now Sterling's—hints of some past horrific event. He was tired of being found guilty for something he knew goddamn well he hadn't *done*.

He'd *harassed* Gracie? Since when did wanting to know if the woman you loved more than anything in the world was okay constitute harassment?

And now this polished, prissy motherfucker was going to threaten him? Take him down? What the *hell*?

"I've about had enough of this dancing around the issue shit," Zack growled. "Someone is going to tell me what the *fuck* it is I supposedly did to Gracie twelve years ago. Because looking at things from my side? I got dumped. Not only did I get dumped but I didn't even get the courtesy of a 'have a nice life' or 'goodbye.' Not even a 'fuck off, I never want to see you again.' I got nothing. So for twelve years—*twelve fucking years*—I've thought the worst. And believe me when I say I have a rather vivid imagination. Then I finally locate her, only she's not hurt. She doesn't need anything. She's happy. Started a new life. But the icing on the cake? She acts like I'm some kind of goddamn monster. Like I'm going to hurt her when she knows it's the last fucking thing I'd ever do. I would have given her the entire world, but she pissed that into the wind when she disappeared, leaving me to think the absolute worst."

Sterling stirred and looked very much like he wanted to start round three. Zack bristled, every muscle in his body tensing in readiness. Sterling wanted a fight, and Zack was spoiling to give him one.

"Damn it, you two!" Eliza exclaimed. "Swear to God, the next one to throw a punch is going to get shot. I wouldn't even be prosecuted. They'd consider me to have saved the world from Dumb and Dumber here."

"You are *not* helping, Eliza," Zack said through his clenched jaw.

"Listen up, because we don't have a lot of time," she said in a brisk voice. She pointed her finger—the one not curled around the trigger of her pistol—at Sterling, irritation evident in her eyes and words. "You're coming with us."

"No—!"

The automatic denial was said simultaneously by both men. Zack shot the other man a glare and then turned his glare on his current pain in his ass.

"You're right. We don't have a lot of time, which is why I'm not wasting it on his sorry ass," Zack said, gesturing toward Sterling.

"The only place I'll follow you to is hell," Sterling bit out. "Just to make sure you stay there."

"Shut up! Jesus. And they say women never shut up," Eliza grumbled. "Now get in. *Both of you!*"

She gestured with the gun, indicating that Zack and Sterling should both get into Zack's SUV.

"You drive, Zack. Don't give a fuck where. But long enough that I can have a little chat with our friend here and so I can keep a gun on him in case he decides to do something really stupid like pissing me off even more."

"You're serious?" Zack asked in clear astonishment.

"Do I *look* like I'm joking?"

Sterling didn't look any more pleased than Zack but it was clear he had a healthy respect for the gun Eliza held.

Eliza yanked open the door to the backseat and pointed her gun at Sterling, then whipped it sideways, motioning for him to get in.

Sterling emitted a string of curses and Zack could swear he heard the other man mumble something about crazy-ass women with guns. If this weren't such a what-the-fuck moment, Zack would laugh at the other man's bemusement. It was always fun to watch people's realization that Eliza wasn't a harmless ball of fluff. She was always underestimated, a fact she'd told Zack had benefited her on more than one occasion.

Shaking his head and having his own sour thoughts about women—a particular woman—with guns, Zack climbed into the driver's seat and cranked the engine.

"Where we going, Lizzie?" Zack asked in resignation.

He absolutely believed she'd shoot one or both of them. She wouldn't kill them, but she'd certainly do some minor damage. She was a crack shot and could hit a target the size of a dime smack in the middle. So if she decided to permanently rearrange a guy's balls, he knew she was absolutely capable.

"Don't care," she muttered, obviously still aggravated. "I need a few minutes and then you can drop him back off a block from here and let him walk back to his vehicle. By then the cops will likely be here."

"And I'm supposed to explain how I arrived on foot at an apartment complex I don't live in, to my vehicle that is parked there?" Sterling snapped.

"That's your problem, not mine," she said sweetly. "I'm sure you'll have no interest in talking to the cops, seeing as you assaulted one of the tenants. A night in lockup might do you good, although you'd be sprung in under an hour, I'm sure."

"Thirty minutes," he snarled. "And so help me, you little wench. This isn't finished, nor will I forget it."

"Yawn," she said, dragging out the word as if she had indeed yawned.

"So speak, Lizzie," Zack said impatiently. "We don't have all night."

There was a pause. Silence filled the interior of the SUV and then Eliza finally spoke.

"Zack is getting pretty damn tired of the jabs about some mysterious event that transpired twelve years ago. Hell, *I'm* tired of it and I'm sure he's hit his head against the brick wall more often than I have."

That was the fucking truth. And then he realized what Eliza was doing. He'd been so focused on getting into and out of his complex that Sterling's reference to what had happened twelve years ago had bounced off him and hadn't been followed up on. Damn it.

His fingers curled around the steering wheel, the skin over his knuckles stretching thin. He was careful to make no sound. His respirations even shallowed as he strained to hear whatever it was Sterling had to say.

"You're kidding, right?" Sterling asked in disbelief.

"Does it look like I'm joking?" Eliza ground out. "Start talking, Sterling. Either that or I'm going to start shooting, and in these close quarters, I can't guarantee I won't hit anything vital, although I'd really prefer not to have to clean up your blood from all over the inside of the vehicle. Blood makes me sick."

"Unbelievable," Sterling murmured. "I wonder, has he got all of you believing this innocent-victim act? Are you supposed to feel sorry for the asshole? Has he been telling you that Anna-

Grace walked out on him without explanation, without a word, and he never saw her again?"

"I want to hear *your* story," Eliza persisted. "We know Zack's story. Now we want yours. Or what you *say* really happened. Cough it up."

Zack went completely silent. Hopefully Sterling would get over his issues with Zack long enough to give them the information he so badly wanted—needed. But at the same time, he braced himself, holding his breath, because it had to be bad.

Instinctively, he knew it wasn't something minor. It had to have been huge to send Gracie running. Away from him. And twelve years of silence? Of thinking he had betrayed her? Zack had always made it clear that Gracie could come to him for anything. He'd thought she always did. But it seemed when she needed him the absolutely most, she'd turned away from him and left without a word.

"Christ," Sterling muttered.

"Just say it, for fuck's sake," Eliza pressed.

Zack knew that tone. Knew she was fast running out of patience, and if Sterling didn't start talking soon, she would likely lose her temper and start doing bodily injury to the man.

"He had her *raped*," Sterling said in disgust.

Zack slammed on the brakes so hard the SUV fishtailed, swerved left and right before he wrestled the steering wheel enough to screech to a halt on the shoulder of the highway. He whirled around in his seat, the seat belt flying as he disengaged it.

Rage smoldered through his veins and he fixed Sterling with the full force of his wrath.

"What the *fuck* are you talking about? You better not leave a goddamn word out and you better have a solid goddamn reason for even suggesting such a thing. I *loved* her. I fucking *adored* her. She was my entire *life!* I worshipped the ground she walked on. I would have killed the bastard who laid hands on her. Tell me it isn't true. *Tell me she wasn't raped."*

Sterling's brows drew together and he looked at Zack in confusion. His gaze flickered as he continued to study the seething man. The air in the SUV crackled with electric tension. Zack had never wanted to take someone apart with his hands more than right now.

Was Sterling telling the truth? Had Gracie been raped? And what the fuck was he saying *he'd* had her raped? He was near to exploding and Eliza must have sensed it because she hurriedly intervened, putting her hand up to squeeze Zack's hand that gripped the back of his seat.

"Don't you leave a fucking word out," Zack said around his clenched jaw. "So help me God, if you fuck me around on this I will make your life a living hell."

Sterling continued to stare at him and Zack could see the wheels turning in the other man's head. And Zack was beginning to grow antsy under the other man's scrutiny. Almost as if Sterling was passing judgment over Zack. Fuck that. He didn't need this goddamn pansy-ass bastard's approval or his belief. He didn't give a fuck what Sterling thought. The only person Zack needed to get through to was Gracie.

"Jesus Christ," Sterling breathed, finally responding after his intense analyzation. "You didn't do it, did you?"

"Didn't do *what?"* Zack yelled. "No one will *tell* me what the fuck happened! I'm tired of everyone speaking in riddles. Just tell me what supposedly happened twelve years ago."

Sterling rubbed a hand over his face, sagging back against the seat.

"Jesus," Sterling muttered. "Anna-Grace is convinced you betrayed her. It's not something she merely suspects. She knows without doubt that you orchestrated the entire sordid mess."

"So why do you not think Zack did it now?" Eliza asked curiously.

"No one can fake that kind of reaction," Sterling said in a low voice. "That kind of shock and surprise. Fuck. He didn't even know about it. Am I right, Covington?"

Zack gave a clipped nod.

"But *you* know what happened," Eliza pressed. "She confided in you."

"Finally," Sterling admitted. "It took a long time. I mean I knew something bad had happened to her. She was so fragile. And sad. There was so much sorrow in her eyes that it hurt to look at her at times."

"Christ," Zack said, nearly choking on the knot forming in his throat. "She thinks I did that to her? That I set it up?"

He couldn't wrap his mind around it. What the hell could he have done to ever make Gracie think he would do such a thing?

"Did she say why she thinks Zack was behind it?" Eliza asked curiously.

Sterling shook his head. "I asked. I mean from the way she described your relationship I found it hard to believe myself. But she was so adamant. Said she knew without a doubt that you'd horribly betrayed her. And after that one time, she never spoke of it again. She refused. I could tell it still hurt her even after twelve years."

"Duh," Eliza muttered. "Women don't get over shit like that overnight."

"But I didn't do anything!" Zack said, his voice rising. "You can't think I'd do something like that, Lizzie."

She squeezed his hand again. "No, I don't think so at all, Zack. But she does. And she's the most important person in this equation. It doesn't matter what I think. She's the one who is convinced you fucked her over. Until you can convince her otherwise, nothing changes."

"I have to get back to her," Zack said resolutely.

His gaze flickered over Sterling.

"We'll dump him back at his car and then we have to go."

"Whoa, wait a minute. So you *do* have her," Sterling said with a frown.

Zack sighed and quickly brought Sterling up to speed on the events of the last twenty-four hours. He wasn't sure when he'd stopped viewing Sterling as the enemy—a competitor—but it was clear the man cared about Gracie. Gracie had confided in him something she likely had never confided in anyone else. So whether Zack liked it or not, it would appear that Sterling was an important figure in Gracie's life. Perhaps her only friend and ally.

"Son of a bitch!" Sterling spat out. "Who the fuck beats up an innocent *woman* just to send a message?"

"Cowards. That's who," Eliza said, her features wrinkling in distaste.

"How is she?" Sterling demanded. "I'd like to see her."

Zack hesitated. The very last thing he wanted was for Sterling to have access to Gracie. But then again, perhaps allowing it would go a long way in rebuilding her trust in him.

"Just what is between you and Gracie?" Zack asked carefully.

He wasn't agreeing to anything until he had a clearer picture of Sterling's relationship with her.

Sterling studied him for a long moment. "It's not like that," Sterling began. "I'm her friend. Her only friend. I care a lot about her. She's like a little sister to me."

Zack's eyes narrowed in disbelief. Gracie was hardly the kind of woman most men would view as their sister. She was beautiful. So beautiful it hurt to look at her.

Sterling let out a sound of exasperation. "Okay, sure, in the beginning I was interested. But after getting to know her, I realized that the last thing she needed was a relationship. But what she *did* need was a friend. Someone she could trust. And it took a long time for her to trust me."

Zack felt grudging respect for the other man. It certainly appeared as though he'd been good to Gracie. Had been there when she needed someone. But it burned like acid in his mind and heart that *he* hadn't been the one she leaned on. He hadn't been her rock, her friend, her lover. He'd been . . . nothing. When she'd been everything in the world to him, she'd thought he'd betrayed her in the worst way.

He wanted to throw up.

"I need to know everything," Zack said quietly. "We'll drop you back by your truck so you can follow us back to the hospital. You can see Gracie. Maybe it will appease her fears if she sees a familiar face and understands that I'm not going to . . . hurt . . . her."

He nearly strangled saying the last. As if he'd ever hurt her. But she didn't believe the same. She believed he'd *already* hurt her.

"Okay, but I really don't know that much. Sorry. She wasn't very forthcoming on the details. All she said was the man she loved had set her up and wanted to get rid of her. She then told me that you arranged for her to be raped by . . ."

He broke off and glanced warily at Zack as if afraid of the impending outburst.

"Just say it," Zack said through his teeth.

What could be worse than what Sterling had already related?

He should have known it could get worse. It could *always* get worse.

"She was raped by three of your friends," Sterling said softly.

Zack's mouth flapped open and shut. He was utterly robbed of speech. His mind was such a red cloud of fury he couldn't breathe. He didn't think it could get any worse than Gracie being raped and believing it was at his instigation. But she hadn't simply been raped. She'd been gang-raped. By people he trusted! People he called *friends*? He was a hair's breath from completely and utterly losing all control and turning over the entire goddamn world to find the sons of bitches who'd violated Gracie in the most demeaning, dehumanizing manner possible.

"*What friends?*" he demanded hoarsely.

"I don't know. I swear," Sterling said. "She didn't get into much detail. All she said was that three of your friends raped her at your request. That you wanted to get rid of her for good. It happened while you were at school. The day before you were due to come home again. She said you wanted the job done and for her to be gone by the time you got home from school."

Tears of rage and anguish swirled chaotically in his eyes. This was insane. It was something straight out of fiction or some bizarre movie. This shit didn't happen in real life, did it?

His *friends* had raped the woman he loved? Supposedly at his behest? And she *believed* that?

How could she have had so little faith in him? She should have come to him. Immediately. God, he would have killed every last one of them. He would have done anything in the world to protect her, to make it better. He would have gladly spent the rest of his life in jail if it meant seeking justice for the horrific crime committed against her. He would have spared no regret and he would have made damn sure that Gracie was taken care of for the rest of her life. Had whatever she needed. And she damn well would have known that he loved her with every piece of his soul.

What friends?

Someone he'd trusted had violated the woman he loved? It was no secret that Zack was solidly in love with Gracie. That he'd planned his entire life around her. Everyone knew it. Even his asshole of a father. Even his father had resigned himself to the fact that Gracie was going nowhere. That she'd forever be a part of his son's life. That for Zack everything, *everything* revolved around her and her happiness. There was nothing he wouldn't do, wouldn't sacrifice for her love and happiness.

"So you know nothing at all other than she was raped. By my friends. Because I asked them to."

He could barely even get the words out. They choked him. The taste was so bitter in his mouth that he gagged.

This wasn't happening. After twelve years without her, he'd dreamed of this moment. The moment when they were reunited. Perhaps he'd imagined it a bit too optimistically. Maybe he'd truly thought that whatever misunderstanding had driven them apart could be overcome with a few words and that everything would be okay. That they'd resume their life together and live happily ever after.

How the hell were they *ever* going to be able to overcome this? He didn't even know where to start.

Why would his friends rape her? Why would they try to tear them apart? Well, they certainly hadn't tried. They'd succeeded beyond his wildest imagination. But it still kept coming back to . . . *why*? Had they hated her so much? Had they hated him so much? Was it jealousy? Resentment for what they deemed his perfect life? How could anyone do something so utterly despicable?

He searched his memory, trying to remember how they'd acted around her. Granted, she hadn't been exposed to them often. Zack hadn't wanted to share her with his friends or anyone else for that matter. He was extremely possessive of Gracie and his time with her. Had they resented being second best to a mere girl? Had they set out to ruin not only her life but his as well? He couldn't wrap his head around any of it.

But he didn't remember any animosity. His group of friends had been polite and respectful. They'd even teased and played around with her in an effort to make her feel comfortable. Gracie had been terribly shy. Her self-esteem and self-confidence hadn't been strong. He'd used every opportunity to build her up. To make her secure in the knowledge that she was perfect to him. That he loved her, would *always* love her.

The only person who'd been overtly hostile toward her and had never made the effort to disguise his dislike of her had been his father. But after that first time he'd brought her home to meet his father, he made sure the two were never exposed to one another again.

He couldn't put his finger on a single guy from his large group of friends who he truly believed would do something so despicable. And yet Sterling had said she'd been raped by *three* of them.

Oh God.

Bile rose in his throat, threatening to erupt from his churning stomach. She'd been raped by three men. One was bad enough for any woman. But three? It didn't bear thinking about. He was devastated. So heartbroken that he didn't even know what to do, to say. How could he possibly make something like this go away? She'd live the rest of her life reliving the trauma of that event and there wasn't a goddamn thing he could do to make it better.

Had she cried while they were holding her down? Had she called for him? Had she begged him to save her? What had she felt when she had been convinced that he had been the one to orchestrate the entire thing? And what the hell would *ever* give her that idea in the first place?

He was going to lose it. His hands shook around the steering wheel as he pulled back onto the road. His pulse was thumping wildly in his heart, at his neck, at his temples. The road stretched and blurred in his vision. Tears burned his eyelids and he rubbed them away with the back of one arm.

He had to keep it together. He couldn't confront Gracie this way. Not when he wanted to rage at the world. He wanted to destroy something. He wanted the names of the men who'd done this because he would not rest until they had all paid for hurting Gracie. He would destroy every last one of them. He would not rest until justice was served.

Sweet, beautiful, good-to-her-toes Gracie. What kind of

monsters would do that to her? And to somehow convince her that Zack had been behind it all? That he wanted to wash his hands of her in the worst possible fashion?

It was so sick and twisted that Zack couldn't even comprehend such evil. From his friends. Guys he'd called friends. That they would gang up on a defenseless girl and ruthlessly torment her, degrade her and destroy her, driving her away from Zack forever.

How the hell had she made it alone? No degree. No training. No skills. On her own without anyone in the world to lean on at such a young age. God, he wanted to cry like a damn baby.

How many nights had she cried herself to sleep? How hard had it been for her to heal from such devastation without anyone to help her, to love and support her? He had been Gracie's only source of support. No one else had given a damn about her, and in his youthful exuberance and optimism, he'd been convinced that he was all she needed. That he could provide everything for her. That she didn't need anyone else and neither did he.

God, how wrong he'd been.

Because Gracie had no one.

Gracie thought the man who'd professed to love her had set her up for a horror no woman should ever endure.

She thought the man she'd loved had lied to her. Had played her, manipulated her, and ultimately betrayed her and thrown her away like she was nothing more than a piece of trash. Not important. Like she was no one. Like she was a nuisance and a hindrance to Zack's life.

"Zack," Eliza said softly, shaking him from his torturous thoughts. "You okay?"

"No," he said, his voice cracking with emotion. "No, the hell

I'm not okay. I'll *never* be okay. How could I be after hearing that? She thinks I had her *gang-raped* by three of my *friends,* Lizzie. She thinks I discarded her like yesterday's garbage. How am I supposed to ever get over that? How am I supposed to ever get her to trust me, much less love me again?"

Eliza sighed. "I'm sorry, Zack. I don't even know what to say. This is one fucked-up situation. Any idea which 'friends' it could have been?"

"No. But I *will* find out," he said in an icy, frigid tone that promised retribution like never before dished out. "So help me God, when I found out who touched her, who hurt her, who put their filthy goddamn hands on her, I'll rip their fucking nuts off and shove them down their throats."

"I'd be glad to help you," Sterling said mildly. "I'm not without resources myself, and perhaps, as I'm not you, and the three in question would understandably be more wary around you, then I would have better luck finding out what we need to know."

"I may take you up on that," Zack said.

"Call me anytime. Gracie is my friend. Yes, at one time I entertained the idea that I'd like her to be more. But it was obvious she most needed a friend and so I filled that requirement. And now? I honestly do view her as a little sister, so you needn't be worried about me influencing her one way or another."

How ironic that a day before Zack would have gladly laid Sterling out for even breathing Gracie's name and now the two were actually joining forces. But if everything Sterling had said was true, then Zack could only be grateful that Sterling had been there for Gracie when she needed someone so desperately. When she'd had no one else in the world.

That was over now.

Gracie might not want him but she had him. He was hers.

And by God, before it was over, regardless of whether Gracie was ever able to forgive him for what she thought he'd done, the bastards who'd hurt her would pay.

He wouldn't rest until he'd brought his own brand of justice to his "friends."

"JESUS," Sterling said, his expression one of horror as he stared down at Gracie's sleeping figure.

He lifted his gaze to Zack, who stood on the other side of the bed, shock and disbelief mirrored in his eyes.

"What kind of animal does this to a defenseless woman?"

The incredulity in his voice was echoed by Zack's own. He didn't get it. Maybe he never would. He saw violence and ridiculous shit every day in his line of work. But this? A cold, methodical beating meted out for the simple purpose of a message? Whatever happened to writing a letter? Or a threatening phone call, for God's sake. Or better yet, not being a goddamn coward and bringing the fight to someone who could damn well defend themselves against such an attack.

Just come straight to the source. Bring the fight to *him*. He was positively itching to administer a dose of payback.

"They're fucking cowards," Zack said, the words rumbling through his chest.

Sterling leaned over, concern etched on his face, and he gently trailed his finger over her forehead to her cheek and then to her jaw. Zack might resent the other man's relationship with Gracie, but he at least seemed to genuinely care about her, so Zack couldn't very well find fault with Sterling for being a source of support to Gracie when she needed it the most. Even as he burned with jealousy that Sterling had what he didn't. A connection to Gracie, romantic or not.

Gracie obviously trusted Sterling, whereas Zack might never have or earn her trust again. It was a thought that formed a lead ball in his gut. His love for Gracie hadn't diminished in twelve years, as would be the case for most people. He hadn't been able to let go even when faced with the unlikelihood that he'd ever see her again. Never touch, kiss or simply hold her.

His biggest regret was never having made love to her. She would have given herself—her virginity—to him, but he'd wanted to wait for the sanctity of marriage. A marriage that had never happened.

He would never have disrespected Gracie by taking advantage of her. He was four years older than her, twenty to her sweet sixteen. He'd thought they had all the time in the world and that when they did make love, it would be as man and wife. Her virginity would be the most cherished of gifts. And now, to know that it had been ripped from her, with no care, no regard, none of the tenderness he'd planned? It made him so sick to his soul that it was a wound that would never heal. For her or for him.

"Zack."

Eliza called softly from the door and he lifted his head, turning his attention away from Gracie and Sterling.

"The police are here," she said in a low voice. "It's the second time they've been here and they aren't going to be put off this time. They want to question Gracie."

Zack sighed. He didn't want to upset Gracie, but the police did need to question her if anything was going to be done. Though he seriously doubted the cops would find one damn thing on the men who'd done this. It really didn't matter, and in fact, Zack almost hoped the police *wouldn't* find the bastards. He'd much rather exact his own brand of justice and personally take down every single person involved with Ari's and Gracie's abuse. It would sure as hell save taxpayers time and money.

"Show them in," Zack said quietly. "Sterling is here so maybe that will put Gracie more at ease. It would appear she trusts him, if no one else."

Eliza winced in sympathy. "This is six ways of fucked-up."

"Tell me about it."

Eliza ducked out and a moment later returned with detectives Briggs and Ramirez. They quietly greeted Zack and introduced themselves to Sterling when he stepped away from Gracie's bed to meet them.

"It would be better if you woke her up," Zack said, nearly choking on the words. "And stay with her while they question her. I'll be here, but she'll likely be more comfortable with you in her direct line of sight."

Sterling nodded and then led the detectives to the bed. He glanced up at Zack in question and Zack nodded to indicate Sterling should wake her now.

Eliza moved closer to where Zack stood just inside the doorway. He was leaning against the wall where he had a clear sight path to Gracie. Eliza put her arm around his waist and gave him a fierce hug.

"I know this has to be so hard for you, Zack," she murmured.

He hugged her to him and dropped a kiss on the top of her head. For a moment he simply held her. He needed this personal contact. The fact that he wasn't alone was the only reason he hadn't already lost his shit completely. As it was, he was hanging on to his sanity by the thinnest of threads.

He had to be strong for Gracie. He did her no good if he were an irrational, pissed-off ball of fury. Not to mention he'd scare the shit out of her when she was already frightened out of her mind by him.

His chest ached. His heart *hurt*. He wanted to be alone so he could grieve over all he'd discovered—and lost—in the last twenty-four hours. But he could do none of those things because time was of the essence and he didn't dare give Gracie the chance to slip away or else he may *never* see her again. It was obvious enough that she'd planned to never cross paths with him. He would have spent the rest of his life never knowing her fate, if not for the happenstance of him recognizing the scenery in her painting.

"What if she hates me forever?" Zack whispered, confiding his deepest, most devastating fear.

Eliza squeezed him in a comforting hug. "Shhh, don't do that to yourself. There's no sense torturing yourself with the worst-case scenario. You're going to have to be patient and take it one minute, one hour, one day at a time. She's fragile. Not only are the events of the past alive and well in her mind, but now she has to contend with what happened to her now. Once is enough to break a woman. But two instances of her being attacked, being completely helpless?" She broke off, shaking her head.

"Yeah, I know," he said in a low voice. "Damn it, Lizzie. I

don't know what to do! How am I going to convince her that I had nothing to do with her being raped?" He dragged a hand through his hair in agitation. "I don't even know which so called friends did this to her and why. *Why*, for God's sake? She never did anything to anyone. She was nothing but sweet and caring and gentle. God, it makes me sick to think of what happened to her. And I wasn't *there*," he said brokenly. "I wasn't there to protect her. I swore I'd never let anything hurt her. And I *failed* her, goddamn it!"

"You couldn't have known, Zack. Especially if they were your friends. How *could* you have known? You don't think people, much less people who were your friends, have the capacity for such evil. You can't blame yourself for what happened."

Zack went still and straightened, homing in on Gracie's bed as Sterling leaned over and gently began shaking her awake. The two policemen stood on Gracie's other side, their expressions grim as they surveyed her bruised and battered face.

Gracie's world was a haze of confusion and unease. She'd retreated into a drug-induced fog where pain and fear faded away, replaced by a false sense of security. Here she was able to block out her reality and avoid it. Things she'd sworn she'd put behind her had come storming to life the moment she'd seen *him* again.

She hadn't thought she could feel such pain ever again. That she'd become immune to anything regarding Zack Covington. She'd thought she'd put his betrayal behind her, that he couldn't possibly hurt her anymore. But some wounds simply didn't heal. Some wounds continued to bleed, no matter how much time had passed. Worst of all, she now realized she'd merely been in denial all these years. Now it was as if the bandage had been ripped from a wound, causing it to bleed fresh all over again.

She'd been wrong. She hadn't been remotely prepared for the wave of anguish that had consumed her when coming face-to-face with the man she'd loved with every part of her heart and soul. The man who'd betrayed her so horribly that she still couldn't fathom it.

It had been crippling, robbing her of breath. It had shamed her, that she was so weak. That the day he'd shown up in her studio she had been completely helpless, unable to say or do anything in her fear-induced paralysis. If Wade hadn't appeared when he had she didn't know what she would have done. What *Zack* would have done. A man she would have never dreamed she needed to fear. A man she'd never imagined being capable of such . . . evil.

And now? The past had repeated itself. What did the two events have in common?

Zack.

Why did he hate her so much? What had she done to make him despise her? What kind of person went to the lengths he did just to get his message across? And what message? If he hadn't wanted her any longer, if he hadn't loved her anymore, then why not just break things off with her? Why punish her for sins she knew nothing about? That she hadn't committed!

Please, please God, let him be gone when she awakened again. She couldn't do this again. She couldn't face him, not after twelve years. She'd worked so hard to put the past behind her, to recover from something she hadn't been sure she would survive. But she *had* survived. It had taken her *years*, but she'd put the pieces back together. She had a life now. And the moment her past caught up to her, she was thrown into a world of pain and violence and . . . heartbreak. Again.

"Anna-Grace. Come on, honey. I need you to wake up for me. There are people who need to talk to you."

Her brow furrowed in confusion. She didn't want to leave the warm cocoon formed by the pain medication. It was safe here. She felt nothing here. Just a blank, empty void filled with warmth and soothing light.

She drifted away once more, shutting out the voice that had infiltrated the fog surrounding her.

But it was persistent. Someone called her name again. Louder this time. She frowned and shook her head, wincing when the motion sent shards of pain through her skull. Why wouldn't they just leave her alone? That's all she wanted. Just to be left alone. She'd been alone for so very long. It was the only way she knew. The only life she knew. She didn't dare trust anyone. Not after Zack's betrayal.

Zack had been her entire world. Her love, hope and trust had been solidly wrapped up in him. If she couldn't trust him, then whom else could she trust? No one. And that's a policy she'd adhered strictly to for the last decade. Except . . .

Wade had befriended her despite her best attempts at holding him at arm's length. He'd been persistent, not allowing her to remain indifferent to him. But the sad part was she was just waiting for *him* to betray her as well. Even in their easy friendship, she was wary, convinced—having been taught the hard way—that betrayal was inevitable.

"Anna-Grace, you have to wake up. You've been sleeping long enough."

Wade?

A surge of relief overwhelmed her. Oh thank God. Wade was here. He wouldn't hurt her, would he? Was she a fool for putting her trust in any man?

It had taken a long time for Anna-Grace to relax around him. She'd been understandably wary of him. But he'd patiently outwaited her, slowly and carefully wearing down her defenses until she'd finally let him in.

But even so, she hadn't confided her past until recently. Some hurts were too private. Too painful. Telling him hadn't been a relief, like ripping a bandage away quickly. It had been the most difficult, most heartrending thing she'd ever done. And afterward, she hadn't been able to face him for days. She'd hidden, embarrassed and mortified at what she'd confided in him.

Only when he'd forced a confrontation and been firm with her that nothing had changed between them, that he was still her friend, had she finally acted rationally and accepted his offer of . . . friendship.

She wasn't a fool. She knew Wade's interest had been more personal when they'd first met. But after she'd finally confided in him her terrifying past, he'd never again suggested there be anything more between them than close friendship.

Going forward he'd been her rock. Her best friend. Even as she chided herself for allowing anyone close to her, for trusting someone again, she'd been unable to help herself. She needed human contact. Twelve years of isolation had worn on her, beating her down and dragging her further and further away from humanity. Wade refused to let her continue to hide. He'd pushed her, encouraged her and refused to let her shut him out.

He called her name again.

Her eyelids flickered open and she frowned at the effort it took. The entire room was fuzzy and for a moment she forgot where she was. She turned her head to the side, seeking out Wade, and the pain that splintered through her head reminded her of just where she was. And why.

Tears welled, stinging her eyes. Weakly she lifted her hand, flailing outward in an attempt to grab Wade's arm. Then his warm hand curled around hers and she was imbued with his strength and support.

"Thank God," she whispered hoarsely.

She frowned harder when she heard her raspy voice. Her free hand flew to her throat to massage absently at the sore muscles. It felt as though her throat was nearly swollen shut. Remembering the huge hands wrapped around it, squeezing, nearly choking her time and time again, she understood why it hurt so badly now.

Her attacker had wanted her to believe she was dying. He'd closed off her airway until she nearly passed out, only to relax his grip so she could gulp in more air. Then he'd done it all over again until she'd lost count and had prayed to lose consciousness so she could escape her current hell.

"Wade?" she croaked.

He bent and pressed his lips to her forehead. "Yes, Anna-Grace, it's me. You're safe now. I swear it on my life."

Tears streaked hotly down her cheeks and she gulped back a betraying sob.

"The police are here, sweetheart. They need to talk to you. Ask you some questions. I know you hurt. I know you're tired. But it's important that we catch the bastards who did this to you.

If I help you sit up some, can you try to answer a few questions at least?"

Her heart pounded violently and her entire mouth went dry. Police? Questions?

She cast her fearful gaze to the side only to collide with two tall, somber looking men. Both wore short, clipped hair that made them look more military than plainclothes detectives.

"Miss Hill," one of the detectives said politely. "My name is Detective Briggs and this is my partner, Detective Ramirez. We'd like to talk to you about the attack on you. Are you up to answering a few questions for us?"

She almost said no and took the coward's way out. But determination gleamed in the policemen's eyes and she got the impression that even had she said no they wouldn't have simply given up and walked away.

So she nodded hesitantly.

"I'm not certain I'll be of any help," she said in a low voice. "It all happened so fast. I mean on one hand it seemed to last forever. I thought they were going to kill me. I thought I was going to *die*. I wanted to die," she said painfully, closing her eyes in shame.

Beside her Wade cursed, and she could swear she heard it echoed from across the room.

"When I try to remember, it's all one big blur. I don't know who they are or what they wanted."

It was on the tip of her tongue to accuse Zack. To tell them they should be questioning *him*. But she was too afraid of retaliation. She had to leave this city. She wasn't safe here. He knew where she was. God, he'd said he'd looked for her. Why? Hadn't he been determined to get rid of her? Or maybe the men who'd raped her were supposed to have killed her. Silence her for good. And for what? For loving him? What had she done so wrong that he would have such a terrible thing done to her?

She closed her eyes and more tears spilled over the swollen, scratchy rims of her eyes. Wade curled his hand around hers and squeezed reassuringly. Then he slid his arm behind her and eased her upward while telling one of the detectives to elevate the back of her bed.

A low whirring noise sounded and soon the bed was elevated enough that she could sit up without too much pain or discomfort.

But then she got a good look at her hospital room. Her gaze homed in on the two people who stood in the background, beyond the foot of the bed close to the door, and she froze, fear paralyzing every muscle in her body.

Completely stricken, she stared helplessly at the monster who'd haunted so many of her dreams. Standing beside a woman who was vaguely familiar to Anna-Grace. She let out a low whimper of terror and desperately clung to Wade's hand, her only anchor in a sea of madness.

Her nightmare come to life was standing at the foot of her bed staring intently at her.

The man she'd loved with every fiber of her being. The man she'd given her heart and soul to. The man she'd saved herself for, vowing she'd never be with any other man, only to have that precious gift ripped from her in a violent, horrific, soul-shattering act.

Zack.

SIXTEEN

ZACK felt as though he'd been punched right in the gut. All his breath left him and pain rolled over and through his chest—his heart—and tightened every one of his nerve endings. As soon as Gracie's gaze found him, her expression turned to one of stark fear . . . and then utter revulsion.

God, he couldn't bear the fact that she thought . . . He couldn't even repeat it to himself. The very idea of orchestrating her rape—the rape of *any* woman—was so repulsive that nausea rose from the depths of his stomach and swelled in his throat. What kind of sick bastard would do such a thing?

And then it hit him even harder that people he knew, people he'd trusted, people he'd called friends had horrifically assaulted her. In a way he *was* responsible because he'd introduced these "friends" to Gracie. He'd exposed her to them. What possible threat to them could she have been that they'd taken such extreme measures? Were they just sick, twisted fucks whom he'd sorely misjudged?

He couldn't bear the way she looked at him. The horror on her face and then how she gripped Sterling's hand even harder and looked to him as if for ... protection?

"Get him out!" Gracie said in a near shriek, her voice breaking under the strain.

She choked on the words and ended in a coughing fit that obviously pained her.

The detectives whirled around as if expecting to find someone new in the room. Their looks grew puzzled when they saw that only Zack and Eliza stood there. Detective Brigg's gaze sharpened and then he glanced back at Gracie's sheet-white face and back at Zack, a frown twisting his lips.

"What's going on here?" Ramirez demanded.

Gracie was shaking like a leaf now, her panic escalating into a full-blown anxiety attack. The hand that wasn't holding Sterling's flew to her mouth but jittered so much her fingers were tapping her lips in a nervous staccato.

"Make him leave!" she said, her hysteria rising.

"Shhh, Anna-Grace," Sterling said soothingly. Or rather he tried to calm her. But Gracie was a mess. A terrified mass of anguish that ripped Zack's heart right in two.

She shook her head, her teeth chattering so violently that when she tried to speak, her words died in a garbled mess.

Sterling turned to Zack, regret lining his forehead. "Maybe you should go," he said in a low voice. "For now. Until Anna-Grace answers the detectives' questions."

"Why are you so afraid of him, Miss Hill?" Detective Briggs asked, still staring holes through Zack.

Any other time Zack would appreciate—and commend—

the detective's solicitousness and his attention to detail. But right now he really just wanted the two men to ask their questions and get the hell out. They had assholes to catch that didn't include Zack.

To Zack's surprise, Sterling looked up at the detective while soothing Gracie with one hand and said, "She's understandably afraid of a lot of men right now. Can you blame her? She's been brutalized and I'm sure she'd like to get this over with as soon as possible. So, please, ask your questions and leave her to rest."

Ramirez frowned but didn't pursue the matter further. But Zack still held his breath as the detectives refocused their attention on Gracie. Sterling leveled a stare at Zack and lifted his chin to indicate Zack should leave.

Damn it. As much as he hated the idea of not remaining to hear Gracie's account of what happened, he couldn't afford to upset her further.

Eliza nudged him toward the open door and he reluctantly stepped into the hallway. When he was well enough away from the room, he slammed his fist into the wall, emitting a sound of rage that had been bottled up far too long.

Tears coursed down his cheeks, carving harsh grooves in his skin. Then after three successive punches, the last forming a crack in the paint, he leaned forward, pressing his forehead against the wall.

Eliza put her hand on his back and simply held it there in a gesture of silent support. Finally, when he felt capable of words, he swallowed back the throbbing knot in his throat and turned to face Eliza.

"What am I going to do, Lizzie?" he asked brokenly. "Jesus, I don't even know what the statute of limitations is for aggravated rape in Tennessee. What if she decides to prosecute, for God's sake? I mean I *want* her to. I'd like to see those bastards rot in prison for what they did, but to think I engineered it? I could well go to jail along with those assholes."

"It could never be proved," Eliza said grimly.

"And that's supposed to make me feel better? I *want* justice for her. But I'm not going to take the fall for something I could never—would never do. But how can I ever convince her of my innocence? For twelve years she's thought I've set her up. That's just under half her lifetime! She's believed in her heart and soul for over a *decade* that I betrayed her in the worst possible way. And why would she ever get such an absurd idea if they hadn't planted it? So in essence I was betrayed by guys I considered friends. I can't fathom any of my college friends doing such a sick, twisted thing. And to set me up? This is all insanity. It's like something out of a goddamn soap opera. Shit like this doesn't happen in real life. Only it *is* happening. To me. To Gracie."

Eliza blew out her breath. "I don't know what to tell you, Zack. I wish I did. I wish I could make this all better for you."

"I just want to talk to her, to explain. To have an opportunity to make her trust me again." He broke off and hesitated before saying the last. "To make her love me again," he whispered. He lifted his gaze to Eliza's once more. "I'm an idiot. Go ahead and say it. What kind of moron remains in love with his high school and college sweetheart for twelve years?"

"There aren't any rules when it comes to love," Eliza said softly. "Unfortunately we don't always get to pick who we love or how long we love. Love is . . . inexplicable. It can fuck you up and tie you in knots, or so people say. Can't say I've ever had the pleasure, nor can I say I'm very sorry about that. Seems like loving someone is opening oneself to all kind of pain. No thanks."

Eliza's nose wrinkled in distaste and in that moment Zack wholeheartedly agreed with her. Love sucked. Love made you entirely too vulnerable and it gave far too much power over yourself to someone else.

Zack's cell rang and he glanced down, pulling it from his pocket to see Beau's name and number flash on the LCD screen.

"Hey, man," Zack greeted lamely, knowing he sounded like a man for whom talking on the phone was the very last thing he wanted right now.

"Got everything worked out for you and Gracie. Untraceable residence. Fully stocked and completely secured. Once you and Gracie get settled, at least two of our guys will be stationed at watch on the premises with a third making periodic drive-bys. I also called in a favor with HPD and they're going to add you to their routine patrols around the clock."

"They may not want to do me a favor for long," Zack muttered.

If Gracie launched her accusations against Zack to the two detectives, he might well find himself behind bars and then extradited back to Tennessee, where this entire sordid mess began.

"What was that?" Beau asked.

"Nothing. Continue on. I need to get back to Gracie," he lied.

"Any idea when they're discharging her?"

A jolt of panic blew through Zack. He wasn't ready for her to be discharged. She'd freak over going home with him. But at the same time maybe that's precisely what he needed. Time alone with her to convince her of his innocence. Provided she didn't scream the walls down around him and get him arrested for kidnapping.

Maybe he should rethink having Eliza stay with him and Gracie or even bring Gracie to Eliza's place.

He sighed, closing his eyes.

"No. I wouldn't think they'd discharge her any sooner than tomorrow afternoon. She's pretty banged up and she looks like hell."

"We're working on this around the clock, Zack," Beau said, his voice serious. "No stone is being left unturned. We *will* nail these bastards. No matter what it takes."

"Thanks, man. I appreciate it."

He hesitated before bringing up what was weighing most heavily on his mind. He almost didn't confide in Beau, but Beau was solid. The closest thing Zack had to a best friend after most of his life had been in solitude and self-exile. He'd grieved for Gracie for years and he'd purposely closed himself off from other people. He hadn't allowed anyone close. Not until he came to work for the Devereauxs. And, well, Eliza knew, so it followed that the others would know soon enough as well, though he doubted Eliza would break his confidence.

"I need your help with something else too."

"Anything, man. You know that. Name it."

Zack put a hand to the back of his neck and glanced at Eliza, who sent him a look of support, as if she knew exactly what it was he was going to talk to Beau about.

"I need some discreet digging done on some people back home in Tennessee. Old . . . friends of mine."

He nearly choked on the words. Hatred consumed him.

He'd never before knew what it was like to hate as much as he hated the people who'd done this to Gracie. He shook with rage, could barely see through the haze of fury clouding his vision.

"Okay. What am I looking for here, Zack?"

Beau's voice had gone somber, as though he sensed the importance of Zack's request.

Praying he didn't break down over the phone with his partner, he quietly recounted everything that Sterling had told him earlier.

At the end there was a shocked, prolonged silence. Zack could well picture Beau's open mouth as he put together all the information Zack had just given him.

After a long pause, Beau, in a raised voice, said, "What the fuck?"

Zack could hear him seething through the phone and could easily imagine Beau's big body bristling with anger.

"That's insane!" Beau sputtered out, before Zack could offer anything further. "Jesus, that's just . . . crazy! She believes that? She honestly *believes* that horse shit?"

Again, Zack closed his eyes as weariness—and relief—blew over him. It was nice to have unconditional trust from the people he worked with. Not only worked with but considered close friends. His only friends, ironically, since parting ways with the group of "friends" back home. The same group of guys he still kept up with. The same fucking assholes who'd destroyed his and Gracie's lives. The same men who had horribly abused the woman he loved.

"She believes it," Zack said quietly. "She gets hysterical every time she sees me."

"Shit. I'm sorry, man. That has to suck. What are you going to do?"

"Somehow convince her that I had nothing to do with her rape," Zack said quietly. "It's all I can do. And in the meantime, I need to do whatever I can to dig up the truth so I can get justice for Gracie. For me. For . . . *us*. And for all the time we lost."

SEVENTEEN

ZACK fidgeted and impatiently paced the hallway in front of Gracie's door. He checked his watch for the sixth time and blew out his breath. It had been an hour since the police had arrived to question Gracie. What the fuck was taking so long? He hated being out here, out of the loop, like he didn't figure prominently in Gracie's life or well-being.

She might not want him in any loop, but Zack wasn't backing down and he damn sure wasn't walking away from Gracie, even if that was what she repeatedly demanded. Maybe it made him a complete bastard. Maybe he should comply with her wishes and disappear. It was obvious his presence was causing her extreme emotional distress.

But damn it, he just couldn't do that. He couldn't let her go without a fight. He had to find a way to make her believe that he hadn't done this terrible thing. If only she could read his mind.

He stopped his pacing and froze.

Eliza immediately picked up on the change in mood because she approached him, concern mirroring in her eyes.

"What is it, Zack?"

He huffed out his breath, remembering Gracie's emotional tirade. That she couldn't read minds anymore, that she *wouldn't* even if she *could*. She'd said he'd taken that from her too. What the hell had she meant by that? It was the simplest solution. If only she would reach into his mind, then she'd *know* the hell he'd been through the last twelve years. She'd know that he'd spent more than a decade searching for answers—for *her*. And she'd damn sure know that he had nothing to do with her rape, that he would *die* before ever hurting her.

"Do you remember, when all that shit was going down with Ari, when I said that I used to know someone who read minds?" he asked quietly.

Her brow furrowed in thought, and she was silent for a moment, as if trying to recall the incident. Then her eyes flashed in recognition as she evidently remembered his long-ago statement.

"Yeah, I remember. But you never expounded. I'd forgotten all about it, to be honest."

"I was talking about Gracie. She could read minds. I know it sounds crazy, but you of all people shouldn't have a problem believing it. I mean after Ramie and Ari and all the crazy assignments we've had."

Eliza's features bunched into confusion. "But Zack, if she can read minds, then surely ..."

"Yeah, I know," Zack said, cutting her off in midsentence. "The second time I saw her, in the art studio when she lost her shit and freaked out. When she was so terrified of me and hinted about this horrible thing I did. I told her to read my mind. It would be so simple, right? I told her to read my mind if she had any doubt, that she'd quickly know the truth and that whatever the hell she *thought* I'd done, she'd know I didn't!"

Eliza continued to look puzzled. "So did she? You're right in that if she truly has that ability it would be a simple solution. Then she wouldn't be on the other side of this door scared out of her mind and upset over the idea of being in the same room with you. Obviously she didn't—or couldn't—otherwise she'd know, right? Why didn't she, Zack? Wouldn't she *want* to know the truth?"

Zack dragged a hand through his hair. "She told me she couldn't. She said even if she could she wouldn't. Then she said that I took that from her as well, and that it was the only thing she could ever thank me for. What the hell did she mean by she 'can't'? She made mention of never wanting to read anyone's mind again. Said something about people being evil."

Eliza's eyes and expression were troubled. "Whatever it is, it doesn't sound good. I think you should start there. Find out how or *why* she lost this ability. And you're sure she was the real deal? I mean, was it something she claimed to be able to do or do you know for a fact she could?"

"Oh she was the real deal," Zack said softly. "She hid it from everyone but me. She was terrified of what would happen if people knew. That she'd be treated like a freak and that she'd be a social pariah. You have to understand. Gracie lacked self-confidence. She was intensely shy and her self-esteem wasn't the greatest. Her ability to read minds is what made her believe in my feelings."

He broke off with a harsh laugh.

"Amazing, huh? She was able to read me like a book. She knew, and was confident in the fact, that I loved her. That what I felt for her was genuine. Her ability to read minds is what convinced her that I wasn't fucking around with her or just trying to get into her pants. God, we waited. I never made love to her. She was too young and I thought we had all the time in the world. She would have given herself to me. She trusted me and believed absolutely that I loved her. But I wanted to wait. I didn't want it to ever be in question that I, at twenty years old, took advantage of a sixteen-year-old girl. So it was my decision to wait. I wanted our wedding night to be special. It was a big deal to me that I would be her first—and only. That I would be the only man who ever made love to her."

He broke off and covered his face with his hands.

"God," he said, his words muffled by his hands. "Her first time was horrific, violent, painful. Nothing like what I had planned. I wanted it to be tender, exquisite, loving. To be the ultimate expression of my love for her. Instead her virginity was brutally torn from her by fucking animals."

Eliza's arms went around him, circling his waist as she leaned in and pressed her cheek to his chest. She simply held him as his body heaved with emotion. He wanted to cry like a damn baby. He wanted to weep for all that he'd lost, all that *Gracie* had endured—and lost. And for what they could never get back.

"So she was able to read minds—your mind—and now she can't?"

Eliza's tone was skeptical. Zack found it hard to believe, himself. Or was she simply refusing to open herself up to more potential hurt? Maybe she was *afraid* to confirm her accusations.

Maybe she couldn't handle having her worst suspicions proved true.

No, that couldn't be. Gracie had always been able to read every part of him. His deepest, dearest feelings. She knew the heart of him—had always known it. And she'd known he was utterly sincere in his love for her. She'd laughingly told him that being able to see his love for her was the best possible gift. That she never had to doubt because all she had to do was open her mind to his and his love for her flooded her heart, mind and soul.

And yet, despite being witness to his innermost thoughts, seeing the depth—and sincerity—of his feelings, knowing he loved her with all his heart, she honestly believed that he had taken part in something so horrific? That he was capable of doing such a thing to *any* woman, much less a girl he adored ... How could she think such a thing for even a moment?

He was growing angrier by the minute. He'd been shocked. Devastated. Completely unhinged. Destroyed when he'd discovered the shocking truth. But now, after fully digesting it all, after the initial numbness had worn off, he was angry. No, not angry. *Pissed*.

He'd given her *everything*. His heart, his soul. She *knew* how much he loved her. So how the fuck could she, even for a goddamn minute, believe, honestly *believe* that he would have three of his *friends* horrifically violate her?

What kind of sick fuck did she think he was? And how ... how could she possibly claim to have loved *him* if she was so willing to believe—to accept—that he had done this terrible thing?

He felt as betrayed as she believed herself to be. It didn't make any goddamn sense.

"I'm pissed, Lizzie. God help me. I know it's probably all kinds of fucked-up, but I am so goddamn pissed that I want to put my fist through a wall. How could she believe it? How could she have so little faith in me that she believes I did this to her?"

"I understand," Eliza murmured. "I wish to hell there was something, anything I could do to help. This is so twisted and fucked-up. I mean I've never come across something like this, and believe me when I say, I thought I'd pretty much seen it all."

Zack squeezed her tighter in his embrace. "Thanks for that. I feel so guilty for being angry, but goddamn it! It all goes back to how she could possibly think that I would do this. She knew me better than anyone!"

Eliza pulled, lifting serious, somber eyes to his. "There's something missing here, Zack. Something we aren't aware of yet. Something huge. Until you know what that missing piece of the puzzle is, nothing is going to make sense. Hopefully she'll open up to you. So the two of you can talk and make peace with the past. Neither of you will ever be able to put this behind you until everything is revealed."

"I just wish I knew what that was," Zack muttered. "She's not exactly giving me much. I only found out about what happened because of Sterling. I don't think Gracie would have *ever* told me. And now I don't know what to do. Do I pretend I don't know what happened? Do I play dumb and wait for when or *if* Gracie opts to confide in me? Or do I confront her with what I know and demand to know why she's so convinced that I had a part in it?"

"That's a hard one," Eliza admitted. "I don't know what to tell you. Maybe you should play it cool, for a little while at least. Get her to trust—and confide—in you. Then go from there. But if she continues to shut you out and won't acknowledge or talk to you then I think you have to address the situation with the information you got from Sterling. Because the problem is, even though she eventually confided in him, she didn't say a whole lot. He didn't have much to offer other than she was raped by your friends at your instigation. She didn't tell him how or why she 'knows' you were involved. It sounds to me like she told him very little about the whole thing."

Zack grimaced. "If I push her, that makes me a huge dick. If I lay off, I'll never find out the truth. So either way I lose."

"Maybe not," Eliza murmured. "It's not going to be easy, hon. But if you prove to her that you can be trusted, if you're there for her every single day, then eventually she'll relax and let down some of her guard. If she isn't willing to confide in you relatively quickly then I do think you have to come clean with her and tell her what you know. Maybe that will be the impetus for her to tell the entire story. Not the abbreviated version she gave Wade. At some point she has to let it all out. It's been festering inside her for twelve years. And in that time, if she hasn't ever confided in anyone or dealt with her demons on her own, then sooner or later she's going to break. It won't be pretty. And she's going to need you more than ever."

"If I have my way, she won't ever be alone again," Zack said quietly.

The door opened, and the two detectives stepped into the hallway, glancing down as if looking for Zack. Zack hurried toward them, his expression seeking.

"Did you get any leads whatsoever?" Zack asked.

Detective Briggs scowled. "No. Unfortunately we don't have much at all. I think you'll be of much more help than Miss Hill.

It sounds like she was just an innocent woman who was in the wrong place at the wrong time. It was a crime of opportunity."

Zack tried to keep the murderous rage from his features. But it was hard.

"It's an opportunity that they won't ever have again," he said tightly.

"Can we walk down to the cafeteria and get a cup of coffee?" Ramirez asked. "My partner and I have a lot of questions for you and Ms. Cummings." He nodded his acknowledgment of Eliza and the fact he remembered her name.

"Yeah, we fucked up, guys," Eliza huffed out as though it pained her to admit DSS's shortcomings. "After last time, these assholes just fell off the radar and Beau and Ari were only too glad to put it all behind them. With the complete annihilation of their compound and Ari taking out most of their men, we wrongfully assumed they were no longer an issue. They're obviously out there waiting and watching, wanting payback."

Briggs nodded. "Let's find a more comfortable place to talk. I'll need about an hour of your time."

Zack hesitated. He glanced back toward the room, but Sterling hadn't come out yet.

"How was Gracie when you finished?" he asked the two detectives in a quiet voice.

"Upset," Ramirez said truthfully. "Scared. Confused. She summoned the nurse when we were finished. She was in quite a lot of pain."

"Give me just a minute," Zack murmured. "I just want to check in on her before we go down to the cafeteria. I have to make sure Sterling can stay with her so she isn't alone until Eliza and I return."

The detectives nodded and Zack stepped away. He eased the door open, peering in at the bed where Gracie lay, Sterling still standing at her bedside.

Sterling's gaze lifted and turned toward the door when he heard it open. Zack sent him an inquiring look, asking without words how Gracie was. Sterling grimaced and shook his head at Zack, clearly indicating he shouldn't come in.

I'll stay.

Sterling mouthed the words to Zack. Zack stood there a long moment, warring with himself over what he should do. Finally he nodded and retreated from the room, closing the door behind him.

Tomorrow Gracie would be going home. They would be in forced proximity soon enough. Until the time he could bring her to his home, where for all practical purposes she would be a captive audience, he would force himself to be patient. This was the most important thing he'd ever do in his life and he couldn't afford to fuck it up and lose her forever.

EIGHTEEN

ANNA-GRACE emitted a soft groan as she tried to sit up in the bed. It took forever to move her legs to the edge so she could slide off and plant her feet on the floor.

Once she managed that feat, she stood for several long seconds, grasping the bed rail tightly as she swayed. When the spinning around her abated somewhat, she carefully let go of the rail and tested her balance.

Other than the protests from her bruised, stiff muscles and the fractured ribs, she was fairly steady on her feet.

She took a step, wincing at the effort it took. Then another. God, at this pace it would take her forever to walk out of here. How on earth would she get past people charged with ensuring she stayed? But they couldn't force her compliance, could they? Surely it wasn't legal.

All she knew was that if she stayed, Zack would kidnap her from the hospital and bring her home with him. He'd *told* her that's what was going to happen. And why? So he could protect her from the animals who'd attacked her? Who the hell was going to protect her from *him*?

The idea of being alone with him scared her. It *should* scare her. And yet, there was something about him. Something she couldn't quite put her finger on. Maybe it was the genuine confusion on his face when she spoke of the past.

She shook her head, refusing to even go there, and promptly regretted the action. The room swayed and the floor seemed to reach up and swallow her. She promptly closed her eyes and sucked in deep breaths through her nose.

"Damn it, Gracie. What the hell do you think you're doing?"

Her eyelids fluttered open, and she saw Zack standing right in front of her, concern burning brightly in his eyes. She stiffened when he reached out to steady her, but his grasp was infinitely gentle.

With complete tenderness, he started to guide her back to the bed, but she dug in her heels and put a hand up to stop him.

He frowned, but it was more in worry than displeasure. His gaze swept over her, taking in every detail, every bruise and hurt.

"I need to go to the bathroom," she said in a low, embarrassed voice.

It was true. Yes, she had planned to leave, but not before making a much-needed trip to the bathroom. And in hindsight, she'd been stupid to think she could manage the task of escaping on her own. Better to wait and ask Wade to help. God, where was he? Why wasn't he here?

Zack's features softened and then he slid his arm around her waist and anchored her to his body.

"Here, hold on to me," he said. "I'll help you. Why didn't you call the nurse?"

She flushed as a surge of guilt swept over her. Then she was disgusted with herself. Why should she feel guilt? So what if she'd planned to leave without him ever knowing? Yes, she'd planned to disappear, and if possible *never* see Zack again. It hurt too much to look at him and think of all that could never be. Of what used to be and what she lost.

A different kind of hurt assaulted her. More aching and piercing than the worst bruises she suffered. For so long she'd shut herself off from pain, betrayal, of feeling anything at all. Her life had been hollow. Devoid of any emotion. Because allowing herself to feel was opening herself up to a lifetime of pain and regret.

A sob welled in her chest, in the deepest part of her soul, and she quickly stuffed it down, forcing the cold nothingness that she kept herself permanently enveloped in to come back. She couldn't allow a single crack. No opportunity for past hurts and betrayals to haunt her.

It was far better to feel nothing at all.

"Gracie? Are you all right?"

Zack's worried, anxious voice jerked her from her self-battle. She blinked to see that they were standing just inside the bathroom.

"Do you need help?" Zack asked gently.

Heat stained her cheeks. She was mortified. She shook her head even as she pushed him away.

"I'll be fine," she said firmly.

He cast her a doubtful look but didn't argue, thank God. Nor did he insist on leaving the door open.

"I'll be right outside. Holler if you need me," he said softly.

She'd die before ever asking him for anything.

As she slowly and painfully completed her business, her mind raced with how to get rid of Zack. She would ask Wade for help. He was her friend—her only friend. But maybe she'd been a fool to trust him. The first person she'd trusted or remotely allowed close to her since . . . Zack.

If only she'd been awake when Wade left. She could have immediately left and been gone before Zack returned. She should have known better. Not only Zack, but people from his security company, not to mention hospital guards and the police were a constant presence.

She was being released in the morning and then Zack would take her to God knows where and she had no idea what her chances of escape would be. Just how long did he intend to keep her barricaded—prisoner—in whatever place he was taking her to?

Being forced to be in his presence—alone—for an undetermined length of time was the cruelest of punishments. And what had she done?

Tears burned her eyelids like acid. She rubbed furiously at them, trying to alleviate any sign that she'd been crying. Zack's discerning eye didn't miss much, and he'd pick up on it right away.

She wouldn't cry. She refused to let him make her cry again. She'd spent weeks and months doing nothing but crying, mourning the loss of something truly magical. But she had been just a girl. Sixteen. She hadn't known better. Now, at twenty-eight, she was beyond girlish infatuation. No longer did she dream of happily ever after. She'd learned the hard way that there was no such thing.

She closed the toilet seat cover and then sank down onto it, burying her face in her hands. Maybe if she stayed in here long enough Wade would return and she wouldn't be alone with Zack.

If that made her a coward, she could certainly live with that. She couldn't even look at him without it nearly destroying her. She'd truly thought she'd put her past behind her. Until Zack had appeared very unexpectedly in the gallery and again in the studio. In just a few seconds, everything she'd done to survive the last twelve years had unraveled.

Twelve years of numbing herself to heartbreaking pain and sorrow. And grief.

Because even though she hated Zack for what he did, she still grieved for that sixteen-year-old girl dreaming of forever. She'd mourned the loss of innocence and of believing there was good in the world.

Ironically her horrible childhood hadn't defeated her, having no father, having an alcoholic mother who hadn't even remembered Anna-Grace's existence for the most part, much less that she was her daughter.

Anna-Grace should have been accustomed to people leaving her. Of being betrayed. But not even her mother running out on her and then Anna-Grace being shuttled to her mother's brother, also an alcoholic, and who was verbally and physically abusive, had been able to knock her down.

And when her uncle had died, leaving her homeless, Zack had come and taken Anna-Grace away.

Zack had very much wanted to move Anna-Grace in with him, but he'd known and had lamented the fact that his father despised her. It seemed no one in the world had cared if Anna-Grace lived or died. Except . . . Zack.

He'd even wanted to move in to the tiny motel room he'd found for Anna-Grace so she wouldn't be alone, but his father had hit the roof. Zack himself hadn't cared, but his father had threatened to withhold his financial support, which would interfere with him going to the University of Tennessee.

Again, Zack hadn't cared. He threatened not to go to college at all, which only served to infuriate his father even more. It was only when Anna-Grace had pleaded with him to stay at home, make peace with his father and go to school that Zack had reluctantly capitulated.

He'd hated that Anna-Grace had been alone, had lived alone and had no one to look out for her. He'd tried to find a way to move her to Knoxville with him so she'd be close to him at school. So he'd never even have to come home on weekends or breaks.

But finding a place they could afford had been impossible, and there was no way for her to get to school unless Zack drove her to and from it, and with football practice that was impossible.

Anna-Grace hadn't minded the solitude of living at the motel with only the elderly caretakers for periodic company. For the most part, she'd done her job quietly and efficiently. The kindly couple who managed the motel and restaurant had even offered to drive Anna-Grace to school every day.

But the best times had been when Zack came home from school. They didn't get out much. He helped her with cleaning the rooms so she'd finish early in the day and then they'd spend the afternoon and evening in her little room watching the tiny television, snuggled up together on the twin bed. Dreaming of the future. Making plans for when Anna-Grace completed high school and Zack was drafted to the pros.

He'd promised her the world, but she had only wanted one thing. Him. His love.

And in the end, none of it had been real.

Despite her best efforts, a tear slid hotly down her cheek. Instead of wiping it away, she drew up her knees, wrapped her arms around her legs and buried her face against her thighs as more tears fell.

She should hate him. But despite saying so, despite the fact that she should utterly despise him, she was still in love with the boy she once knew. She grieved the loss of a dream as if he had truly died. And in essence he *had*. Because the young man she'd loved as she would never love another would never have done something so horrific.

What had caused him to turn on her? Had he met someone at college?

What he'd done was insane! Most people simply broke up with their girlfriend and moved on without thought or remorse. His actions implied a deep and abiding . . . hatred. As if he'd wanted her to pay for and suffer for some unforgivable sin.

What could she possibly have done to make him despise her so much that he would go to such great lengths to retaliate?

And why did he now so violently deny having done anything wrong and pretend his innocence? Did he fear reprisal? Or did he merely seek to undermine her and make it appear that she was crazy and delusional?

How could he seem so . . . *sincere* . . . in his claim of having searched for her the entire twelve years that had passed? Dear God, could he possibly want . . . forgiveness? Did he seek atonement for his sins? Did he feel guilty for what he'd done?

The thought that he would think for a minute that she could possibly forgive such a betrayal made bile rise in her throat, burning as she swallowed it back down.

And yet, he seemed so . . . haunted. No one could fake the pain she'd seen in his eyes nor the shadows present in them. He acted as though *she* had hurt *him*. And he seemed so sincere.

She shook her head. He was a consummate actor. Hadn't he already proved that? She couldn't allow herself to be sucked into his twisted world. If she ever doubted what he truly was, all she had to do was go back to that terrifying day when she'd been attacked, violated and discarded like trash.

More tears fell as she squeezed her eyes shut against the painful memories. They'd laughed at her. Told her how pathetic she was. That someone like her would never be good enough for Zack.

And God help her, when she'd been blasted by their thoughts, when they'd consumed her as if playing out in real time, she'd learned the horrifying and devastating truth.

Zack had instigated it all.

A forceful knock on the door startled her so much she nearly fell off the toilet.

"Gracie? Gracie, are you all right? What's going on in there? Do you need my help?"

She hastily scrubbed at her face, but before she could respond, the door burst open and Zack filled the doorway, his expression grim and worried. Then he evidently saw what she'd tried hard to conceal and his entire face softened.

He knelt on the floor of the small, enclosed space and took her hands.

"Hey, are you all right?" he asked gently. "Are you hurting? Do you need help getting back to bed?"

She closed her eyes again, shutting out his image. He'd aged well, although his eyes had changed. They looked older, haunted, as though he'd endured hell. As though he had grieved—was still grieving. But why?

Her head pounded, and she ached, but it had nothing to do with her injuries and bruises. Some hurts went beyond the physical. Some ran soul-deep and did far more damage than those inflicted by her attackers.

Those injuries and hurts would heal, would go away and be gone as if they'd never occurred. But the hurt Zack had inflicted would never go away, would never cease to hurt, and she'd never recover from them.

"Gracie, talk to me."

She opened her eyes to see his narrowed eyes blazing with concern. God, there was nothing she could do. No way for her to avoid him.

"I-I'm okay," she stammered out.

"You don't look okay," he muttered.

"Look, Zack, this is hard for me. Can you blame me? After what you did? How can you sit there and look at me and expect me to act as though nothing ever happened? God, are you some kind of sociopath?"

She choked the last of her statement out and then angrily brushed at new tears that slipped down her cheeks. Damn it. She hated being so vulnerable in front of him, of him seeing her so weak. Hated that old wounds were once again raw and bleeding, as though they'd never truly healed. And she supposed they hadn't. They never would. She could lie to herself, be firmly in denial just so she could endure each day, but in the end, nothing had changed. She could never get back all that she had lost.

His lips thinned and his jaw ticked. Anger blazed in his eyes and it looked very much like he wanted to say something but he remained silent. Then he rose to his feet and simply reached over and carefully picked her up.

Ignoring her surprised protests, he carried her back into the hospital room and laid her on the bed. Then he arranged and plumped her pillow, briskly fixing her bedding as if the incident in the bathroom hadn't occurred.

When he was done, he pushed her hair from her face and forehead, his fingers lingering against her skin. His expression grew sad and distant. It looked very much like tears welled but she had to be imagining that.

He trailed a fingertip down her cheekbone as though he couldn't resist touching her in some way. She should shrink away. She should be repulsed. And yet she closed her eyes, trying to keep her own tears at bay. Hadn't she cried enough? At what point would the past cease to make her cry?

His touch took her to another time, a sweeter, happier time when they were together and she was convinced they'd be together forever. Before she lost everything that mattered to her. Before her life was destroyed and she'd been left to pick up the pieces alone and shattered.

But when he leaned down and pressed his lips to her forehead, it was simply too much. She turned away from him, the tears coming faster.

He let out a sound of pain, as though *he* were the one

wounded. She wanted to laugh—or cry more—over the irony. He hadn't suffered as she had.

"We'll work this out, Gracie," he said in a low, anguished voice. "Now that I've finally found you I'm not letting you go. If it takes the rest of my life I'm going to make you understand."

Understand what? The question tugged relentlessly at her lips but she pressed them together to prevent the words from spilling out.

She didn't want to understand why he'd done the unthinkable. She just wanted him to leave and never see him again.

Was that too much to ask?

NINETEEN

ANNA-GRACE had dozed off after a sleepless night when she was awakened by noise in her room. It had been impossible for her to sleep with Zack propped in a chair in the corner. She could feel his gaze on her even when she wasn't looking at him.

Conversing with Wade had been impossible, and so the room had remained awkwardly silent until the two men had finally drifted off to sleep. She had spent the entire night agonizing over her situation and wondering if there was a way out.

From beneath slitted eyelids she watched as Zack tiredly rubbed his face and walked out of the room. Her heartbeat accelerated and she hurriedly glanced around to find Wade, who was awake and using his laptop by her bed.

"Wade," she called softly.

His head yanked up, and his eyes narrowed in concern. "You okay, Anna-Grace? Do you need anything?"

"I need your help," she whispered.

His brow furrowed and he got up and walked to her bedside,

sitting on the edge so that he faced her. He picked up one of her hands and held it in a comforting manner.

"You know I'll do anything I can," he replied.

She licked her lips, nervously glancing at the door to make sure Zack hadn't returned and would overhear her conversation.

"I need to get out of here. I mean now, before I'm discharged. He is insisting I leave with him, that I *stay* with him."

She couldn't even say Zack's name and choked when she referenced him.

Consternation wrinkled Wade's features and he sighed as he gripped Anna-Grace's hand tighter.

"You *should* go with him, Anna-Grace," he said in a low voice, shocking her with his response. Her mouth fell open but before she could respond—how did she respond to *that*?—he continued. "You're in danger. Until the animals who attacked you are caught, you shouldn't be alone. Zack can protect you. It's what he and his associates do. He has the resources necessary to ensure your safety."

She had to force herself to suck in a breath. She'd been unconsciously holding it and had begun to get light-headed and dizzy. Wade's features swam before her, blurring, his face stretching and yawning ghoulishly.

"Do you forget what he *did*?" she said in an incredulous voice. "Do you honestly think I could stand to be in the same room with him? And certainly not *alone* with him, staying God knows where for an indefinite period of time. Who's to say I don't have more to fear from him than I do the men who did this to me?"

She gestured at the bruises on her face in agitation.

"He could do anything at all to me and who would know?

You're the only person I know, the only friend I have. I could disappear forever and no one would even bother looking for me."

Her chest was heaving with agitation and her voice had risen to the point of shrillness.

"Calm down, sweetheart," Wade said, his tone soothing.

He gripped her hand and rubbed his thumb over her knuckles in an attempt to dispel her rising hysteria. Like that was going to happen.

She could admit that she didn't *feel* threatened by Zack right *now*. Or at least she didn't sense any danger from him. He'd been nothing but . . . gentle. Like the man he'd been when they were together, and that was the worst because it was like teasing her with what could never be again. But his current demeanor didn't matter. She couldn't afford to trust her instincts because she had never dreamed twelve years ago that he was capable of orchestrating such a horrifying crime. And yet, after what he'd done, he'd chosen a career in security? Protecting others from the very sort of people he'd coerced into doing his dirty work for him?

It was a joke. The irony was laughable. Maybe he regretted his choices. Maybe this was his way of atonement. But for Anna-Grace it was just too late. He could seek restitution and assuage his guilt by his own means. She'd be damned if she were the instrument by which he made peace with himself. Some sins were forgivable. This one was not.

"I want you to listen to me," Wade said in a firm voice. "You know I care about you. You *know* I'd never do anything to hurt you, don't you?"

She inhaled sharply, her lips quivering, dreading what he was about to say. But she nodded, agreeing that he wouldn't hurt her, even if it was hard for her to trust anyone. It was obvious she couldn't trust her instincts. And in no way would she ever allow herself to be that naïve sixteen-year-old girl who looked at Zack with adoration. A girl who thought he looked at her the same way. How his friends must have laughed as she cried. The truly humiliating part of it all wasn't the fact that she'd been violated repeatedly. No, what mortified her the most was that she'd been more devastated by Zack's betrayal and the knowledge that he didn't return her love.

"I think you should go with Zack."

When she would have launched an immediate protest and denial, he put his fingers to her lips to hush her.

"Let me finish," he admonished. "I also think you should listen to him, Anna-Grace. You might be surprised to hear what he has to say. You should confront him, talk to him, tell him *everything*. And then listen—really listen—to all he has to say."

Her mouth fell open as she stared at Wade in stupefaction. What on earth was going on? He had been *furious* when she'd confided what had happened. Wade had very nearly taken Zack apart when he'd walked in on Zack and Anna-Grace in the studio. And suddenly Wade was taking up Zack's cause? Had the world gone crazy? Or was it some male code of honor? Men sticking up for the brotherhood?

"Wade, you *know* what happened," she said. "How can you even suggest that I listen to anything he has to say? There is no excuse, no apology, no *forgiveness* for what he did. Do you have any idea how terrified I am to be trapped somewhere—*anywhere*—with him?"

She was shaking violently. Her skin felt damp and clammy and she recognized the signs of an impending anxiety attack.

She could feel her heart beating frantically in her chest, could feel her chest constricting, her throat closing off her airway.

She tried to suck in a steadying breath, tried to make the horrible panic go away. She hadn't suffered extreme panic attacks for eight years now. It had taken four years after the traumatic event to manage the attacks and learn to stave them off.

Wade cursed and then leaned forward, framing her face in his hands.

"Look at me, Anna-Grace," he commanded harshly.

Responding to the authority in his tone, she focused her stare on him, locking on to his features.

"You have to calm down. You're breathing far too fast. Look at me and breathe with me."

He went silent and in an exaggerated manner he noisily breathed in through his nose, held it a moment and then breathed out through his mouth. His thumb caressed her cheekbone and then he slipped one arm behind her, leaving one hand cupped to her cheek. He rubbed up and down her spine, spreading warmth and comfort with his hand.

"Try to relax," he murmured in a gentler tone. "You're way too tense. It's only going to make the pain from your bruises worse."

Her eyes filled with tears and she closed them, hating her weakness, hating that she couldn't control her wayward emotions. After so long living in a vacuum, after so many years of refusing to feel anything at all and living each day robotically, on autopilot and refusing to get close to *anyone* until Wade, it was as if the ice had cracked and was rapidly falling away, allowing pain and grief to consume her all over again.

And now, once again, she felt the sting of betrayal. Once more, someone she trusted was abandoning her. What was wrong with her that this kept happening?

"Honey, don't look at me like that," Wade said, his eyes sorrowful.

"Why are you doing this?" she whispered. "Why would you refuse to help me? Why would you encourage me to listen to *anything* he has to say?"

She could feel the reins of control slipping away. Grief consumed her at the loss of someone she trusted. Again. She closed her eyes as tears continued to trickle down her cheeks.

"You're breaking my heart, Anna-Grace. I'm not abandoning you. I swear. I want you safe, and Zack can keep you safe. If I thought for one minute that he would hurt you in any way, I'd never allow him anywhere near you. Do you understand that?"

He tipped her chin upward, forcing her gaze to meet his.

"Look at me, Anna-Grace. Do you really understand that? Are you really hearing what I'm saying to you?"

The gravity of his tone gave her pause and her eyes narrowed with confusion.

"There are things you must discuss with Zack, Anna-Grace. Things that are eating you alive. You've pushed them away, refusing to deal with them for too long. You can't continue like this. It's not healthy. I want more than anything for you to be happy. And you *aren't* happy. You haven't been happy the entire time I've known you and it hurts me to see you so sad. You're still a young woman with her entire life ahead of her. Why deny yourself the basic right to peace? I will *always* be your friend and I am never more than a phone call away. I don't want you to be angry with me because I'm encouraging you to talk to Zack. Because I'm encouraging you to do what is best for *you*."

She stared at him in abject shock. His intuitiveness made her feel horribly exposed, as though he could see every single thought—memory—in her mind. Her chin wobbled in his grasp, and his gaze grew tender with understanding. Why couldn't she have returned Wade's attraction? He was a good man. She couldn't be wrong. Not like she'd been about Zack. But in a lot of ways, she was still that young girl, hopelessly in love, and she'd never felt the stirrings of attraction. Maybe she was ruined for anyone but Zack, which meant she was destined to a life alone, devoid of love, companionship. A family. Children.

"Talk to him, Anna-Grace," Wade said firmly. "Promise me you will. Don't do it for me. Do it for you. If you ever hope to have peace, to come to terms with your past and be able to move forward, then the past has to be put to rest."

He thumbed a tear from her cheek and she curled her hand around his wrist, holding on and absorbing his comfort and strength.

A noise alerted her to Zack's presence and she turned her fearful gaze to him, worried about how long he'd been there and all he'd heard.

His expression was bleak and her heart sank. He must have heard most—if not all—of her conversation with Wade.

If she hoped that he would at least *pretend* he hadn't heard, she was sorely disappointed.

"He gave you very solid advice, Gracie," Zack said, his jaw tight. "Hopefully you'll heed it."

Gracie swallowed and Wade dropped his hand from her

chin. She turned her pleading stare on him. "Don't leave me," she whispered brokenly. "*Please.*"

Zack ran his hand through his hair and sighed. He looked hopeless, like he'd lost . . . what? What could he possibly have lost? She was the one who'd lost everything. How dare he act the victim here?

"If Wade stays with us, will you agree to go home with me?" Zack said wearily.

Wade gave Zack a startled glance as if that was the last thing he'd expected.

"That is, if he's agreeable," Zack added. "But if it makes you feel better, Gracie, then I don't have a problem with it. But it means you go home with me and you stay there. No running. No exposing yourself to potential danger. They may well kill you the next time just to send another 'message.'"

Gracie's heart was pounding. He was making it harder and harder for her to extricate herself from an impossible situation. Wade had already sided with Zack for some unknown reason. She could feel her options dwindling away faster and faster and it made her feel helpless. She *hated* a sense of helplessness.

"I'll stay if that's what Gracie wants," Wade said to Zack, though he looked at Anna-Grace the entire time. And then he spoke to her as though Zack weren't even in the room. "I'll stay under one condition."

She lifted her eyebrow in question even though she knew she wouldn't like his condition. But then again, how could she refuse and end up alone with Zack for an indefinite amount of time?

"You have to promise me to talk to Zack and tell him *everything.* Leave nothing out, Anna-Grace. You have to make peace with what happened to you. And you just may be surprised by the results. After you've been completely honest with him, and him with you, if you want out, then I'll take steps to take you away and provide protection for you myself."

"But if you are able to provide protection, then why do I even need to go with Zack?" she demanded, her panic rising once again as she realized she was trapped with no way out of the situation. "Why are you forcing me to go with him?"

She sounded like she was begging, like someone at the end of her rope, and God, maybe she was. Maybe he was right, and in suppressing it for so long and not really dealing with it she'd created an inevitable firestorm when things finally boiled over.

"Because you—and he—need this," Wade said gently. "You may not think so now. And I know you're afraid. But I'll be with you and I promise nothing will hurt you."

"That's what he always promised too," she said painfully.

She saw Zack flinch and go pale as if she'd landed a blow.

"I'm your friend," Wade reminded her again. "I'll always be your friend. And I promise you on my soul that no one will hurt you this time."

"I guess I don't have a choice," she said in a dull monotone.

He leaned over and kissed her forehead. "This is for the best, Anna-Grace. You may not think so now, but you'll realize it soon enough. I promise. Now, if I'm going to an undisclosed location with you and Zack then I need to run home and stop by my office to make arrangements to be away for a period of time."

"How soon will you be back?" she asked fearfully.

"An hour. Maybe an hour and a half."

"We'll wait," Zack interjected. "We won't leave the hospital until you return. My partner is arranging for transportation and a disguised escort so we can be on our toes and be watching for a tail."

"Anna-Grace needs clothing and personal items, I'm sure."

Anna-Grace flushed as they blithely discussed her as though she weren't present.

"Eliza is taking care of that. She has a good eye for sizing people and she's shopping for clothes, shoes and all the feminine accessories Gracie will need. She should be here within the hour," Zack said. "Gracie's exposure has to be limited and there's no way in hell I'll let her go back to her home. I'm sure the bastards have it staked out."

"They know where I live," Gracie whispered. "It's where they attacked me. I can't ever go back there again."

She closed her eyes as painful memories assailed her. Things she'd tried very hard to put out of her mind, much as she'd attempted to block out her attack twelve years ago. And yet now, she was assaulted by memories of both incidents together as though they had merged and had become one. Flashbacks of her rape were as clear as if it had happened yesterday. The clarity of each of those memories tore another piece of her soul.

Zack's curse made her flinch and when her eyelids fluttered open, cold fury blazed in his eyes. She stared at him, truly dumbfounded by his reaction. Nothing made sense and her head ached from trying to sort through it all.

"I'll have someone pack up your apartment, Anna-Grace," Wade assured. "When this is all over with, I'll help you find another place." He glanced up at Zack and then added, "That is, if you still need it."

TWENTY

ANNA-GRACE breathed a huge sigh of relief when Zack finally pulled into the long, winding driveway of a large house that sat atop a hill. The ride had been interminable and she'd been rigid and tense the entire way, which wasn't helping her sore, bruised muscles.

When she'd insisted on riding with Wade to wherever it was they were going, both men had acted as though they hadn't heard her. Or perhaps they simply ignored her. Wade had walked briskly away to collect his vehicle while Zack helped her into the SUV that he'd pulled to the entrance of the hospital so she wouldn't have to walk a long distance.

It was thoughtful of him. She begrudgingly gave him that much. But then he'd been nothing but solicitous of her since reappearing in her life. It was a mystery to her, and trying to ponder the whys and wherefores just mentally exhausted her.

To prevent awkwardness—though she failed miserably on that count—she'd rested her head on the rest behind her and closed her eyes, pretending sleep. At least Zack hadn't called her on the pretense though she highly doubted he bought that she was asleep. Perhaps he was content in getting his way after successfully strong-arming her into acquiescing to his demands. It was wise to pick one's battles, and it certainly appeared as though Zack adhered to the same motto.

She'd watched him through a barely discernible slit in her eyelids, and he seemed grim and utterly focused the entire trip. His gaze darted like clockwork between all the mirrors as if he was truly expecting someone to be following or an attempt to run them off the road.

Admittedly, Zack appeared to be good at his job, but then again, if he and the company he worked with were such hot-shot security experts, why the hell were the "enemies" he spoke of able to get to her as soon as Zack made contact with her? So far she hadn't been very impressed with their "skills."

She didn't understand the extreme paranoia or Zack and his partners being so worried that she would be targeted again or killed. It didn't make any sense to her. If they'd intended to kill her, why not have done just that? They'd certainly had ample opportunity when they'd beaten the crap out of her. It seemed far more risky to beat her, then let her go, only to return to kill her another time, when the others would be on their guard. What purpose would that serve anyway? It was risky, not to mention inefficient. But perhaps protecting her was an ulterior motive and was Zack's way of forcing a confrontation with her.

Zack had said she'd been used to send a message. To the people Zack worked with. So in essence it had been a crime of opportunity since everyone associated with the security company evidently had security up the ass. It hadn't even been personal to her—thank God. All the same, she had Zack to thank since he'd made their association known by visiting her at the gallery *and* the studio. If he'd stayed away, she likely wouldn't have spent the last two days in the hospital.

She barely stifled the urge to wrinkle her nose as Zack rolled to a stop. God, she hated how bitter and cynical she sounded. Life hadn't taught her to be anything but that, though. She'd never known hatred before she'd been raped. She hadn't hated her father for deserting her and her mother. She hadn't hated her alcoholic, negligent mother. Nor had she hated her abusive uncle.

It had taken the ultimate betrayal by someone she *loved*—the only person she'd ever loved—to make her truly hate for the first time in her life.

Had it taken over all else? Was this who she was now? Wary. Withdrawn. Miserable. Afraid . . . She was so tired of living with hatred *and* fear. Maybe forgiveness wasn't for the person who'd committed a sin against her. Perhaps forgiveness was really for *her*, enabling her to move on, free of the weight and oppression so many years of anger had caused.

It was an epiphany far too long in the making, in her view, but a much-needed one nonetheless. After living so long chained by her past, and in order to achieve peace, she had to provide it for herself. No one could do it for her.

"Gracie, we're here," Zack said, touching her lightly on the arm.

She'd been so lost in thought that it had been as if she had dozed off and was miles away. Her eyelids fluttered open and she blinked several times to gain her bearings. Wade pulled up beside where they were parked and got out, removing his expensive designer sunglasses.

She stared at him a long moment before sighing with unhappiness. It hit her then and there that she knew why she'd allowed Wade to become so close. She hadn't been attracted to him whatsoever and so she'd deemed him safe, unable to possibly hurt her as she'd been hurt before.

Even after all Zack had done, it was becoming more obvious that there would never be another for her. It didn't only boil down to trust issues. She was simply incapable of looking at a man and feeling desire. Happiness. Seeing her future in another man's eyes. Only Zack had ever elicited that kind of response from her. Damn him for ruining her life—her dreams. And her only chance at happiness.

"Gracie? Are you all right?"

Zack's softly spoken question shook her from her dour thoughts and she reached clumsily for the door handle, unlocking her door when she realized that Wade had tried to open it for her from the outside but had been unable to do so. She'd drifted off and hadn't even noticed.

"I'm fine," she mumbled.

Her lie was obvious. Zack knew it, but he let it go.

She shoved harder at the reluctant door and it opened. Wade extended his hand to gently help her from the vehicle. She took it nice and slow, having already discovered at the hospital, when she was on her feet just those few seconds of getting from the wheelchair into the SUV, that she was anything but steady.

Every bruise made itself known in a hurry and a low groan, part pain, part frustration at her inability to move well, blew past her lips before she could call it back. Zack appeared just behind Wade, his face a mask of concern.

Her brow furrowed as she truly looked at him. His concern

was real, not faked. He was utterly genuine in his worry and it puzzled her to no end. He kept vowing that he . . . cared . . . and yet she'd never bought that "lie" until . . . *now*.

It was as though her eyes had only just been truly opened and she could see the truth. Or perhaps she'd been unwilling to see the truth before. And she had no idea what she was supposed to do with this particular revelation.

Unwilling to ponder the perplexities of that, she eased another step forward, directing her focus to Wade instead of analyzing Zack's sincerity. No amount of genuineness *now* made up for past betrayals.

With Wade by her side, one arm curled firmly around her waist, she shuffled through the open garage door and into the door leading into the house. It took seemingly forever to make the short journey into the warmer interior and she sighed with pleasure when a heated draft of air blew over her face, dispelling the chill that had scuttled up her spine after she had gotten out of the vehicle.

"Do you feel well enough to eat, Gracie?" Zack asked. He was still wearing that worried frown. "You need to eat. You barely had anything the last two days."

She wanted to separate herself from the discomfort of his company and the tug-of-war with her emotions that was becoming increasingly more prevalent when it came to him. How easy it would be to fall back into their old routine. Zack taking care of her. Zack looking out for her. Zack loving her. Her loving him.

Pain that had nothing to do with her injuries assaulted her. She hadn't imagined he could affect her so strongly. Not after so long. But on the heels of pain came grief. Over what could have been.

"Anna-Grace?" Wade said sharply. "What's wrong?"

She shook her head, briefly closing her eyes. "Nothing. I'm okay. Really."

Wade's lips thinned with disapproval but at least he didn't call her on her blatant lie. Then, to her dismay, he excused himself to go shower and put his things away after asking Zack which room he should take.

She stood, frozen, unsure of what she should do now. They were standing in the kitchen and silence descended into awkwardness. Much like the ride from the hospital had been.

Then Zack tucked his hand underneath her elbow and as Wade had done he wrapped his other arm around her waist and began guiding her to the small table in the breakfast nook, where a bay window overlooked the meticulously landscaped backyard.

"Just sit here and take it easy. I'll take a look at what was stocked and whip something up right quick."

He cupped his hand over the crown of her hair and for a moment she could swear he was going to try to *kiss* her. But then he dropped his hand away after running his fingers down her long tresses to the ends and letting them fall away from his grasp. He curled his fingers inward and then flexed them outward as though warding off the urge to continue running his hands through her hair. Then he turned and walked back into the kitchen, leaving her sitting there, her lips tingling as if he *had* kissed her.

She hastily lifted her hand to her mouth, rubbing to rid herself of the sensation. God, she was losing her mind. How could she have even thought it for a minute? Worse, if he had tried to kiss her, she wouldn't have done anything to stop him. It made her the worst sort of person and guilt and self-loathing nagged relentlessly at her. But so too did the longing for his kiss, which she put down as remembering the sweetness of their kisses before everything went to hell.

Zack was the only man to ever kiss her. He was the only man she'd ever loved. Would ever love, for that matter, even if that emotion was dead to her now. But she could still remember how glorious it felt to be young and in love, to have the entire world at her feet and to dream of beautiful things together.

He'd been her dream. And then he'd become her nightmare.

Several long minutes later, in which she'd spent staring down at the table in front of her as though she were in a daze, Zack returned bearing two plates. She hadn't even registered him cooking, had no idea what he'd concocted.

It smelled divine, though, and her stomach immediately rumbled a sharp protest after being neglected for so long.

He put the plate in front of her and put his hand on her shoulder, squeezing gently before taking his own place across from her at the table. Her foolish body still reacted as though it had no knowledge of his betrayal. It acted as though it were starved for his touch having been bereft of it for so long. Goose bumps cascaded down her arm and a heated flush rushed through her chest and down into her belly. She was so disgusted that she wasn't sure she'd be able to eat.

Tears burned like acid, welling up from nowhere. She was an emotional wreck, so conflicted and torn that she felt positively unhinged. Was she going crazy? Had she held on to her sanity for this long only to let it go now, when she needed it the most?

"Gracie."

She refused to lift her head, embarrassed beyond words for him to see her tears. She should have known he could see them anyway.

"Look at me, damn it," he said fiercely.

Closing her eyes, she slowly raised her chin and after drawing several steadying breaths, she opened them again only to see him through a cloudy sheen of moisture.

He looked furious . . . But he also looked as sick at heart as she felt. Something had to give. She wouldn't survive such proximity without completely breaking down. If she thought for a minute that she wouldn't face-plant by getting up on her own and fleeing, she'd be up and running in a heartbeat.

"We've got to talk." He was positively seething. How could there be so much fury and sorrow both vying for control in his eyes? "This has gone on too goddamn long. Enough. I've tried to wait. I've tried to be patient. I'd hoped like hell that you'd talk to me but that's obviously not going to happen. You look like you're going to break apart and shatter into a million pieces any second and *I'm already there*. Torturing yourself—me—hell, *us* does no one any damn good, so I'm done with this. After you eat, you and I are going to have a long, honest conversation and I will *not* let it go until that happens."

She stared at him in abject shock, absorbing his impassioned, angry outburst. He was furious, yes, but oddly, *not at her*. His words and tone said one thing, but his eyes said something entirely different. There was pain—anguish—glimmering in the depths. And . . . regret? Worry for her? Maybe she was imagining it all, but she'd always been especially intuitive with him. She'd assumed it was because she could read his mind, but she didn't have that ability now, and yet she could easily pick up his emotions.

She knew what was going on in his head—not because she could read his thoughts, but because his eyes and expression broadcast them in startling clarity. She was numb with confusion because he seemed utterly sincere. If she shrugged off her anger and bitterness for just a brief moment, she was able to see that he genuinely cared for her. Maybe even loved?

A gasp nearly escaped her lips, but she snapped them shut to prevent her audible reaction. Her mind was buzzing with so many differing emotions, she was dizzy.

Confused didn't begin to describe her state. She dropped her gaze because it was uncomfortable to see the naked emotion written starkly on his features and mirrored in his eyes. Eyes are a mirror to the soul, or so the saying went. The eyes didn't lie. And if all of that was true, then she had one giant contradiction on her hands.

Because if everything she was registering was true, then he *did* care about her. Deeply.

Her mind was in chaos. Complete turmoil as she quickly replayed every sequence of events since he'd barged back into her life. Every single word he'd spoken. Each expression. The look in his eyes. They all said the same thing, but could they be believed? Or was it all one very elaborate charade?

Her lips pursed in consternation. Zack would have to be one damn good actor to pull that off as consistently as it had played out, and Zack was no actor. He had always been refreshingly blunt, unable to hide his true thoughts or feelings. You never had to wonder where you stood with him. If ever in doubt, all you had to do was simply ask him. He certainly never shied away from giving his honest assessment of anything, even at the risk of hurting someone's feelings.

Her head ached vilely, her pulse pounding at her temples. It was all too much to take in. She was clinging to the edge by her fingertips, having already gone all the way over the cliff and dangling haphazardly. One little slip and she'd be gone. She wasn't sure how much more she could take.

She risked another look up at Zack and saw real concern and agitation in his eyes but at the same time his features were unyielding. He wasn't budging and she knew him well enough to be certain that he wouldn't be swayed once his mind was set on something.

Which meant they were about to have a serious come-to-Jesus moment and for only the second time since the horrible nightmare twelve years ago she was going to tell someone what had happened in exacting detail.

God help her but she wasn't sure she would survive facing the man responsible for destroying her and recounting in detail the pain, sorrow and humiliation she had suffered at *his* instigation.

TWENTY-ONE

ZACK'S heart pounded viciously against the wall of his chest. After his forceful declaration, he and Gracie had eaten the rest of the meal in silence. He could sense her fear. Hell, it was tangible, completely enveloping her. And it broke his heart.

Never, *never* would he have imagined that Gracie would be afraid of him. He was the very last person she needed to fear. He'd always been her protector, had always handled her with the utmost care and respect.

He had put her on a pedestal and had worshipped the ground she walked on. There was nothing in the world he wouldn't do for her, and he'd made sure he told her that every single day. He never let a moment pass when she wasn't completely confident in his absolute love and devotion. She'd been the most precious thing in the world to him.

She still was.

But Gracie wasn't the only one who was afraid. He was fucking terrified. This was the single most important moment of his life. Everything was riding on this. Right here, right now. If Gracie refused to believe him . . . and, God, how could she have ever believed it in the first place? It was so baffling that he couldn't wrap his head around it.

Had these so-called friends who'd raped her told her that he had *asked* them to? Who the hell asked someone to rape someone as a favor, for God's sake? It sickened him. It was so abhorrent to him that nausea curled in his stomach at the very thought. And what sort of sick fuck did she think he was to have believed that shit?

He swiped his hand down over his face and stared down at the dishes he'd placed in the sink. Once they'd finished eating, Zack had broken the stony silence by telling Gracie that it was time for them to talk—really talk. And then he'd received a punch in the gut when panic had buzzed across her features.

After helping her into the living room, he'd returned to clear the table. Not that it was important at all, but Zack needed time to compose himself and bolster himself for the revelation of the demons that haunted Gracie's past—her present. And to prepare himself for her assertion that he was the biggest demon of them all.

He'd racked his brain trying to figure out which of his hometown friends would have done something so despicable. And he kept drawing a blank. Gracie was such a sweetheart and people couldn't help but love her on sight. He knew he certainly hadn't escaped her infectious smile and laughter. He'd fallen and fallen hard the first time he laid eyes on her. He'd known without a doubt that she was it for him. And then he'd taken the necessary steps to ensure that she was his.

But again, who—and why, for God's sake—would hurt

Gracie? And blame him? It made no sense! Nothing made sense anymore. Not one thing in this entire fucked-up situation made a bit of goddamn sense.

He closed his eyes, braced his hands against the edge of the sink and breathed deeply for a few seconds in order to gather strength for the ordeal ahead. Sterling was staying put in his bedroom making business calls, at Zack's behest. He'd absolutely planned that the moment he got Gracie established in a safe place, where they could have privacy, they would finally air out the past. He hadn't been pleased that Sterling would be occupying the same quarters as him and Gracie, but if it gained Gracie's cooperation, he'd get over it. But he'd made sure that Sterling was for the most part going to stay the hell out of the way.

Zack glanced over his shoulder into the living room, where Gracie sat like an ice sculpture on the couch and he knew he was merely delaying the inevitable when before he'd been frustrated as hell with the lack of information.

He slid his hand over his stomach and grimaced. The food he'd consumed was swirling in his gut like a goddamn Tilt-A-Whirl and his nerves were completely fried. So much rode on this conversation and whether or not she'd believe in his innocence. If she'd been convinced of his guilt for twelve years, what were the odds of her changing that belief anytime soon?

Man up and stop being a fucking pussy.

He sighed at the admonishment but paid heed nonetheless. Turning from the sink, he walked back to the living room where Gracie sat at the end of the couch leaned against the side, pillows surrounding her. Likely an intentional barrier or a protective wall.

He gave her the space she was demanding and he eased down on the same couch, but on the other end so they faced each other with an entire vacant spot between them. It went against every natural instinct for him not to be close enough to touch her. Hold her. Offer her comfort, something she would undoubtedly need when recounting such a traumatic event.

She wasn't the only one who would need comfort, and he sincerely doubted he'd find any himself.

He locked gazes with her, observing the way she twisted her fingers in obvious agitation. His chest physically hurt for all she would soon reveal. He was still reeling from the bombshell Sterling had dropped on him. Grief had hovered incessantly over him, and he'd tortured himself endlessly, imagining her at the hands of three men who mercilessly violated her. Men that apparently he *knew*.

"Tell me what happened, Gracie," he said quietly.

Even knowing the story already, he wanted—needed—to hear it directly from her. He wasn't going to throw Sterling under the bus and hurt Gracie by revealing that someone she trusted had broken her confidence. She needed people she could trust. But goddamn it, he wanted to be one of them.

She was pale and strain was evident on her face. Her eyes were weary and pain filled, as though she were reliving hell. Guilt plagued him. He didn't want her to have to recount the horror of what she'd endured, but it was the most important thing in the world for her to know he had nothing to do with it.

It was his only chance of ever making her love him again. And God help him, he wanted—needed—her love. If there had been any question of his feelings for her diminishing with time and distance, with him being older and very different from the idealistic college kid who thought he had it all, there wasn't now. The moment he saw her again, even with her unexpected fear of him, he'd been overcome with the knowledge that there would never be another woman for him. He couldn't lose her now. Not when he'd looked for her for so very long. He nearly hadn't survived the first time he lost her. This time? It would destroy him.

He watched helplessly as she struggled to find the words. She looked utterly lost and so forlorn, and though he simmered with impatience, he didn't rush her. But he could no longer tolerate the distance that separated them. He slid forward on the couch, steeling himself for her rejection but determined to show her he wasn't a monster.

He reached for her hand and she visibly flinched and tried to pull free of his grasp. He didn't let her tug it away, and gently, so as not to hurt her, he tightened his hold.

She shuddered, shame clouding her delicate features. "Don't touch me," she begged softly, her eyes awash with tears. "Please don't touch me."

Her aching plea tore at his heart. "Why, Gracie?"

She closed her eyes and then reopened them, her eyelashes sparkling with tears.

"Just . . . don't."

She rubbed her free hand up and down her arm as if trying to scrub away some invisible taint. As if being so close to him made her feel *unclean*.

"I make you feel dirty?" he asked hoarsely.

Even knowing the answer, he had to hear it from her. Somehow they had to navigate through a myriad of pain and betrayal and he *had* to convince her of his innocence. His entire life hinged on her somehow regaining her faith in him. He could wait for her to love him again. He'd wait forever if that was what it took. But he knew he didn't have a chance in hell of getting her back if he couldn't unravel this fucked-up mystery and convince her that he'd had no part in it.

"Not you . . . I mean not right now. *Them*. Oh God . . ."

She choked on the last part and looked very much like she'd be sick on the spot. She was shaking violently from head to toe as though she were freezing, and her lips were stiff and clumsy. Each word seemed agonizing for her; she was clearly exhausted even though they'd only just begun. And they still had a long way to go.

"Them who? Tell me what happened, Gracie. Did someone hurt you?"

He couldn't control the fierceness of his question even though he already knew. He couldn't even think about what had been done to her, without rage consuming him. Even now he had to flex his fingers to prevent curling them into tight fists, but he didn't want to display any outward sign of his fury. He had no desire to make her more afraid of him than she already was. She expected pain and violence from him when in fact he'd die before ever doing or allowing harm to her.

Her face crumbled in her distress. She made no effort to hide her tears and a sob welled from her throat, a sound that sent despair quaking through his heart.

She turned toward him then, her eyes wild and flashing, anger and distress rolling off her in waves.

"How can you sit there and *ask* that? *You* hurt me," she raged. "*You!* How dare you sit there and pretend you don't know what happened? Does it satisfy you to see the results of your handiwork? Or was that not enough and you want to push the knife a little deeper?"

He captured her other hand as it flew to her face in an effort to wipe away the signs of grief—and rage. Gathering them, his hands shaking violently as she had been shaking, he looked her in the eye, but God, it was hard. It was devastating to see the raw agony reflected in her gaze. He'd give anything in the world to go back. He would have never left her alone. If only he could have the last time he saw her back again. *If only.* There were so many regrets. So many mistakes. His greatest one had been not bringing her to college with him or him simply remaining at home with her until she finished school.

"I would never hurt you, Gracie. *Never.* I loved you. I've loved you *forever.* Tell me what happened. We have to get this out in the open or things will never be resolved between us. And we will resolve them. I won't accept any other alternative," he said fiercely.

She stared at him with obvious disbelief, her eyes flashing wildly. "Do you honestly think I could ever just get over you having me *raped*? That it's something that can be resolved between us?"

Her voice rose to a shrill almost-shriek. Color rose in her cheeks and her chest heaved with exertion.

The words cut him like a knife. It brought to mind horrific images of Gracie. Helpless. Being savaged. And her thinking the *entire time* that *he* was responsible. His eyes burned as though he'd poured acid in them but he was determined not to lose it. She needed him to be strong right now. He had to be strong for *both* of them.

Even having heard parts of the story already, hearing her say it, seeing the accusation and pain in her eyes, nearly brought him to his knees. Every drop of blood fled his face.

He was still trembling, his hands clumsy and inept as he

lifted her hands so they were solidly between him and her. Then once more he stared her directly in the eyes, praying she'd see sincerity—and *truth*—in his.

"I don't know what the hell you're talking about, Gracie. But you listen to me and listen very close. You were my entire *world*. The very *best* part of it. I would never, *ever* do anything to hurt you. I'd lay waste to anyone who ever did. I have no goddamn idea where you got such a fucked-up idea like that. Jesus. Did you have so little faith in me then?" he asked, unable to keep the thread of hurt from his own voice.

He tried. God, he tried so hard to keep the hurt and betrayal out of his voice. But he just couldn't fathom why she'd ever believe for a minute that he was even capable of such an atrocity. She wasn't the only one with a deep sense of betrayal in this whole fucked-up mess.

"I believed in you more than anyone I've *ever* believed in," she said, her voice trembling and raspy after her impassioned outburst. "If I hadn't had irrefutable proof I would have never even *considered* that you were involved."

"Irrefutable proof?" he asked, incredulity evident in the echoed words. "What the hell kind of proof?"

He was so goddamn tired of dancing around the issue. His frustration, which had simmered for days, was near its boiling point and he felt ready to explode.

"Just tell me what happened. Who did this to you? And what kind of *proof* makes you believe that I would ever be a party to *any* woman being horribly violated? Much less a girl I loved. A girl I planned to marry. A girl who I planned to be the mother of my children. The girl I wanted forever with. I get that you hate me, Gracie. But for fuck's sake, the least you can do is tell me what the hell happened. Who put their goddamn hands on you? Who hurt you? *Who raped you?*"

His teeth were firmly clenched and his pulse was racing a mile a minute. Despite his best efforts to remain calm and keep his emotions in check, he was a ticking time bomb ready to explode.

He hadn't imagined anything could hurt more than when he'd come home to find Gracie gone. Disappeared as though she'd never been the most important part of his life. He hadn't thought anything could feel worse than the desolation that had become rooted in his soul for the last twelve years when, despite his best attempts, he continued to come up empty-handed in his search for her.

But this . . . This had the power to destroy him all over again. That she thought so little of him. That she had believed all this time that he'd turned on her. Hell, now the cryptic statement she'd made in the hospital about him finishing the job made sense. She thought he'd had her beaten in addition to having her raped twelve years ago. What kind of sick, twisted bastard did she think he was?

"Don't you act like the injured party!" she yelled, tears running fast and unimpeded down her cheeks. "*You* aren't the victim here. Do you think I just came to the conclusion you orchestrated the rape? Your *friends* raped me, Zack. *Your* friends. And no, they didn't tell me you had them do it. They didn't say anything at all. They were too busy laughing while I *cried*. But their thoughts were broadcast like a neon light. It was like reading a transcript to some horror movie. All three had the exact same memory of you asking them to do you a small *favor*. Like I was some pesky little nuisance you wanted to be rid of. Couldn't you have just broken up with me like normal people do? Couldn't you just *tell* me you didn't want me anymore?"

Zack bolted to his feet, his hands dropping hers as he stared at her in shocked disbelief. The room was spinning around him in dizzying circles. Blood rushed to his ears and the roar nearly deafened him. He searched her features for some sign that he'd heard wrong. But no, every single word was branded into his mind with painful clarity. This was a nightmare. One he had no hope of waking up from. In that moment, he wanted to die.

"*What friends?*" he asked in a horrified voice.

He was barely able to choke out the words as his chest constricted to the point he couldn't even squeeze air into his lungs. He was paralyzed, unable to move, to think, to process the terrible truth.

She sagged back against the couch, and it was as if the life had seeped right out of her, leaving her drained and listless. There was such a look of despair and hopelessness that it gutted him to look at her.

"Kevin, Stuart and Bryan," she said dully.

Zack went rigid with shock. No. *Hell no.* This had to be some sick joke. He couldn't even coherently formulate his thoughts enough to question her further. Kevin, Stuart and Bryan? They weren't just friends. They were his best friends. He'd known them since kindergarten. Hell, he still saw them once a year or so. He'd been to their houses. Met their wives and kids.

And they not only terrorized and raped a girl they damn well knew he adored, but their *thoughts* implicated him? God, he was going to be sick. He'd cried on their fucking shoulders when Gracie had disappeared. They'd even helped him look for her. No one else gave a damn, and for that matter most of the people in his town didn't even know who she was. His father had laughed when Zack had gone to him in panic and despair. He'd told Zack that she very likely ran off just like her mother had and that he was better off without her.

Jesus Christ, no wonder they kept up with whether Zack had ever managed to find her. No wonder they so easily accepted that she was alive when most people would have gently suggested to their friend that Gracie was likely dead and that he'd never know what happened to her. Every time he got together with them in the ensuing years, they always asked if he'd ever found Gracie. They'd probably inwardly rejoiced in the fact he hadn't, because then, surely the truth would have come out. Just as it was coming to light now. And then he'd know every detail of their foul deed. Especially that they'd implicated him in the crime.

A terrible sound of anguish made him wince and then he realized that it had come from him.

"No," he whispered. "Oh God no. No. No. *No!*"

He shut his eyes and curled his hands into tight balls at his sides. He was falling apart piece by piece and was on the verge of coming completely undone.

He staggered, his legs no longer able to hold up. He fell to his knees, his hands covering his face as raw sounds of despair welled in his chest and boiled out his throat. Tears blurred his vision and he scrubbed angrily at them, determined that he would keep it together. For Gracie. For them both. If they ever had a chance. If he ever had a chance to gain her trust again. He had to *hold it together*.

Knowing he had zero chance of standing, he crawled the short distance to the couch where Gracie sat, eyes drenched with despair, her anguish mirroring his own.

His chest was so tight he felt like he was about to explode. A knot formed in his throat, making breathing next to impossible. And yet this was important. The most important moment he'd ever face. This was his life. His love. His happiness. And the woman who held all three in her small, delicate hands thought he had done the unspeakable.

TWENTY-TWO

ANNA-GRACE was rigid with shock as she took in Zack's grief-ravaged face. Her mind was a mass of seething confusion and she felt much as she had at the hospital just after being injected with pain medication. Was she having some drug-induced psychosis? Was this all some bizarre dream and she was really *still* in the hospital? Had she imagined the entire chain of events up to now?

But no, this was real. His touch was real and he curled his hands so tightly around hers that it made her wince. She stifled her reaction, though, because she didn't want him to know he'd hurt her. How messed up was that? Shouldn't she *want* him to hurt? Bleed just as her heart had bled every time she thought back to happier times? When she was in love and thought *she* was loved in return?

Numbly she stared as he shakily drew her hands up to his lips, and closing his eyes, he bowed his head slightly so that his mouth rested atop her knuckles. The gesture was so tender, so filled with aching emotion that her breath caught in her throat and just remained until she was forced to exhale because her chest protested the lack of oxygen.

None of this made sense. She hadn't made a mistake. Her attackers' thoughts—memories—had all been *identical*. Zack telling them to fuck the bitch up and get rid of her. She was dead weight he no longer wanted to carry. Every single word, every single image had hurt her far worse than the physical pain and humiliation they'd meted out. She'd cried, not because of the pain. No, she'd been numb with shock and completely grief stricken, shutting out the horror of their violation. Her tears had been for Zack. And for what she knew then she'd lost. What she'd never *had*, because it had all been a *lie*.

He'd never loved her. He didn't know what love was. And maybe at sixteen she hadn't known either, but she knew what it wasn't. Love wasn't shameful and degrading. Love wasn't callously discarding her like trash after reducing her to that level.

She could still feel how dirty she'd felt lying there on the ground, weeping brokenly and praying to die. How later, when she'd dragged herself into her tiny room at the motel, she'd scrubbed herself for hours in a shower that had long gone cold. But the chill of the water on her skin was nothing compared to the bone-deep cold that had settled to the depths of her soul.

Never would she forget sitting on her bed, naked, trembling, skin red and raw from the endless scrubbing and considering—wanting—what only someone with no hope ever contemplated. And worse, in those darkest hours, very nearly *giving in* to the overwhelming temptation that whispered so insidiously through her shattered mind.

And he was asking, not for her forgiveness—some things

weren't forgivable—but for her to believe something that contradicted what her gift had enabled her to see, to *know*.

Zack's reaction wasn't one of shame, remorse or guilt or even distress over being found out. She saw someone who was completely . . . *wrecked*. Despair and utter heartbreak were evident in every line of his face. There was such overwhelming devastation in his eyes that it *hurt* to look at him.

She began to tremble and it quickly progressed to shaking that spread through her body like wildfire. Her throat seemed to close in, until each breath was torturous to squeeze in and out. An odd wheezing noise echoed in her ears and it took her a moment to realize that it was the sound of her *breathing*—or rather her attempt at breathing.

Zack opened his eyes and her wheeze became more pronounced. For a moment she simply stopped trying to get more air into her starved lungs as she tried to make sense of his reaction.

His tears were readily visible and he made no effort to disguise his grief. Such terrible grief. Never had she seen such naked emotion reflected in another person's eyes. It was gut-wrenching for her. It mirrored her own sorrow, was like a window into her soul and her own suffering. Suffering he was responsible for.

"Gracie," he said, his voice thick with all the emotion so visible in his features. "You have to believe me, baby. *Please*."

He eased her hands down to her lap and then leaned forward, his fingers shaking as badly as she was. He lifted his hands to her face, hesitating as if he feared she would recoil, and then carefully cupped her cheeks.

"I don't care what you read or *think* you read from those bastards' sick, twisted minds. It doesn't matter. I had *nothing* to do with them hurting you. I swear it on my life! I would *never* do anything to hurt you. I could kill them for what they did. So help me I *will* kill them if it's the last thing I do."

His voice had gone hoarse, each word vehement and impassioned. Her eyes were wide with shock because he was begging. He'd never begged anyone for anything. He was too proud and too determined to go his own way. And she couldn't even comprehend what he was begging for! He was denying it? Everything? Was he crazy? Or was he saying *she* was crazy?

"I loved you. I have never and *will* never love anyone like I loved you. Do you know what it *did* to me to come home and find you gone?" he asked, his eyes blazing. "You simply vanished. No trace. No hint of where you'd gone. And I looked. God help me but I looked everywhere for you. I never *stopped* looking."

His expression grew fierce, more earnest. His gaze was piercing, as though he was willing her to understand—to *believe* him.

"I don't know what happened that day or why. But I will find out, Gracie. Because not only did those sons of bitches put their hands on you"—he broke off and shuddered visibly and then took several steadying breaths as if to compose himself again—"they violated you; they drove you away from me. They knew I loved you. They knew I planned to spend the rest of my life with you."

He stopped his impassioned plea and went silent, studying her face. She was sure what he saw wasn't good. All the blood had long since fled her face. Her eyes were wide with shock. And she was still shaking like a leaf and struggling for every single breath.

"Gracie?" he whispered tentatively.

His gaze was imploring, silently begging with her to accept

his emotional plea. His hands stroked lightly over her cheekbones, mindful of the bruises. Then his thumbs gently wiped away tears she hadn't realized had fallen.

"Please say you believe me."

She closed her eyes, and she felt herself slowly give way, her tenuous grip on her composure snapping. She tried to respond but couldn't breathe, much less manage to articulate her shattered thoughts.

Her eyes flew open in panic when her chest constricted to the point that she could no longer squeeze in the slight breaths she had before. Her arms flailed wildly, shoving at Zack's hands, which still framed her face.

She heard a distant, muffled curse but couldn't make out anything else as the roaring in her ears escalated to the point that it sounded like a freight train bearing down on her.

And then she did something she'd sworn she'd *never* do again.

She looked frantically at Zack for help and she managed to gasp his name before the room faded to black around her.

The last thing she registered was Zack's grim, worried expression, and him enfolding her in his arms.

His familiar scent, unchanged in twelve years, enveloped her. Being in his arms gave her a deep sense of . . . homecoming.

And nothing had ever felt so sweet.

TWENTY-THREE

ZACK held Gracie in his arms, savoring the moments of quiet in the dimly lit bedroom. He'd made sure to leave the bathroom light on and the door open enough so that if she woke up, hopefully she wouldn't panic to find herself nestled firmly against him. Something he'd dreamed about on more nights than he could count. And finally his prayers had been answered, even if the two of them had a very long way to go in their journey back to one another.

He clung to hope, though. He had to or else the very thin strings holding him together would snap, leaving him clinging desperately to his last vestiges of sanity and plunging him into a dark world of despair.

He buried his nose in her hair and inhaled her scent, then ran his fingers through the strands. Memories of so many nights spent just like this were bright in his mind. Gracie in his arms, her small frame curled into his. Him looking forward to many more nights spent in the same manner once they were married and he'd made love to her for the first time.

A fresh wave of grief rolled through him all over again at all she'd lost. What *he* had lost. Just a sixteen-year-old girl, brutally violated by men Zack had trusted. Had called friends. No, he didn't have anything to do with their sick crime, but in a way he was guilty all the same because Gracie would have never been exposed to them if not for him.

Her head was pillowed on his shoulder and she slept deeply, and he hoped dreamlessly, devoid of the memories of her past. In forcing her to relate all that she'd endured, she'd been taken back to that awful day all over again, thrust right back into the horror of her worst nightmare. And he'd lived it—envisioned it—right alongside her. It had taken a piece of his soul that he would never get back again. He'd live the rest of his life knowing she'd suffered the unimaginable, all the while believing that he had done this to her. He couldn't even think about it without becoming completely undone.

He wasn't sure if having to relive her ordeal had instigated the panic attack that had left her unable to breathe to the point of passing out, or . . . if him protesting his innocence had finally sent her over the edge.

He'd never felt such a lack of hope in his life. Except when he'd had to face the fact that Gracie was gone and wasn't ever coming back. He couldn't survive losing her a second time. If she refused to believe him, if she ran as far and as fast as she could, he would never be whole. He'd forever be a hollow shell of himself, wandering aimlessly through life with no purpose, no hope. None of the joy that only Gracie could bring him.

But before he could even think about regaining the precious gift of her trust and acceptance, her belief in his fervent denial, there were other important matters to tend to.

His jaw locked and his hand went still against her slim back. Hatred consumed him, clouded his mind and formed a red haze in his eyes. While his bastard friends enjoyed their lives, their wives, children, Gracie had been out there alone, damaged, carrying invisible scars—*permanent* scars. Zack had been denied the very things his friends took for granted. Because they had made certain that he and Gracie had nothing of the future Zack had planned.

Why? Goddamn it, *why?* It was so bizarre and fucked-up that he couldn't even wrap his mind around it. What purpose could they possibly have had in doing something so vile? Jealousy? Had they resented that his time was split between Gracie and school, with no time for anything else in between? And if that was the case, who the hell went to such extreme, criminal measures because they were fucking jealous? It was *insane.*

No, he didn't have the answers. Not yet.

But he would.

He hated to leave her. It was the very last thing he wanted. But until he confronted the men who'd destroyed an innocent girl, he and Gracie didn't have a chance. Because she wouldn't believe him by his word alone. He'd find out the truth, no matter what he had to do. He was going to make them bleed, just as they'd made Gracie bleed, make them hurt just like Gracie had hurt. They'd find out real damn quick how well they fared when up against a man their size instead of abusing a much smaller, delicate girl.

It made him want to vomit. The men who raped Gracie had been twenty years old, four years older than her. They'd raped a *minor*, for God's sake.

His breath stuttered from his lips and caught, making a sound almost like a sob.

He was supposed to be her first.

They weren't going to make love until their wedding night.

Because more than anything he'd wanted to give Gracie the respect she was due and not precipitate his vows. He intended to make their first time together special. A night she'd remember the rest of her life. One he would as well.

He'd wanted to give her time to grow and mature more, to fully bloom into the woman she was about to become. And as she was coming to their marriage never touched by another man, so too had he wanted to honor her by giving himself *only* to her.

She was adorably shy when they spoke of making love, and they spoke of it often, sharing their hopes and dreams. He would whisper to her how glad he was that he would be the only man to ever make love to her and that he would honor her gift by giving her the same assurance. She would be the only woman *he* ever made love to.

The night he'd lost his virginity, his first year in the pros, he'd lain there beside a woman whose name he didn't even remember and he'd never felt so sick in his life. He'd stared up at the ceiling, his eyes burning like he'd wiped them with sandpaper, and grieved the loss of Gracie all over again. He'd rolled out of bed and barely made it to the bathroom before throwing up into the toilet.

He hadn't had sex again until after he'd quit football and was working as a cop. In time it got a little easier. He even managed to enjoy it eventually. In a physical sense. But never once had he been emotionally engaged. Never had he experienced the euphoria and mental satisfaction of making love with someone he cared about. Someone he *loved*.

Had Gracie ever managed to have a healthy relationship with another man after such a traumatic experience? The idea of another man holding her, touching her, kissing her, loving her . . . sliding into her soft, sweet body. It made his chest tighten to the point of discomfort and filled him with envy for this hypothetical lover.

He recognized the hypocrisy of his reaction and in truth, despite wishing with all his heart that *he* had been the one to comfort, love and pleasure her, and show her the beauty of making love to wipe away the ugly memories of pain, degradation and rape, he truly hoped she *had* found someone who cared enough about her to make the experience beautiful and pleasurable for her.

The idea of her shutting herself off from any sort of intimacy, and living alone—afraid—unwilling to trust anyone because of *his* perceived betrayal, broke his heart.

Despite his hope that she'd been able to overcome such a horrible life-altering incident at *sixteen*, such a fragile and impressionable time for any girl, he had the sinking feeling that she'd never allowed anyone close enough to establish the kind of trust necessary to allow such intimacy.

Though he'd certainly not had a very favorable impression of Sterling from their first meeting, he'd been wrong. It appeared that Sterling was a good man and that he'd been good to Gracie. But Sterling had made it clear that he and Gracie were just friends. Nothing more. Not that Sterling hadn't been interested. He'd admitted as much. But Gracie had shut him down, and yet they had become friends.

She seemed to trust him, yet she hadn't allowed more than friendship, which told Zack that she likely hadn't ever gotten that far with anyone else.

That knowledge should have given him satisfaction, but all he felt was hollow regret that she'd never had anyone to show her tenderness and . . . love.

He wanted to be that man. He wanted it more than he wanted to breathe. But unless he could somehow offer Gracie tangible proof of his innocence and not just his word, he knew in his heart that he'd lose her all over again.

At that thought he went rigid, his jaw clenching to the point of nearly breaking his teeth. He couldn't—wouldn't—allow that to happen again. Murderous rage swelled within him and his mind was consumed with revenge. Justice. For Gracie. Truth for himself. Freedom. For them both. So that maybe—*maybe*—they could move past this. Together.

The soft strands of her hair that were wrapped around his fingers slipped from his grasp as he formed a rigid fist. He knew what had to be done. He wanted to seek vengeance. For Gracie. For them both. His thoughts were consumed with violence and making the pieces of shit who'd hurt his Gracie *pray* for death.

He'd *make* them confess every sordid detail of their sickening attack on a girl who legally was still a child. And then their wives could decide whether they wanted to remain married to a rapist or ever trust them with their own daughters.

His pulse thudded at his temples and he forced himself to

calm his raging thoughts of retribution. Just for now. He lay his cheek atop Gracie's head and pulled her a little closer to him.

"I love you, Gracie," he whispered. "And if I ever hope to make you love me again, there's something I must do. I have to leave you for a while, but I'll be back. I swear."

He turned his cheek, sliding it against her hair just enough so he could press his lips to her forehead. Closing his eyes, he inhaled deeply, capturing the feel of her, soft and warm and so very precious.

He would carry this memory of her in his arms, when, for just one exquisite moment in time, everything was good and perfect. It would be all that sustained him until justice was served and he came back to her with the answers they both desperately needed—and deserved. Because while Gracie was the biggest victim in this tragedy, they were both victim to something all encompassing and completely life changing. And it would take time—and understanding from them both—to possibly right past wrongs and to move forward from a past that would haunt them both for the rest of their lives.

TWENTY-FOUR

GRACIE awoke with a heavy sense of lethargy. Her limbs felt heavy and slack and it took much effort to even turn over in bed. She felt exhausted, like she had lead in her veins, and her reflexes were dull and sluggish. It was as if she'd been drugged or heavily sedated.

She wrinkled her nose trying to remember if she'd taken any of the medication the doctor had prescribed when she'd been discharged, but no, she hadn't had a chance. As soon as she and Zack had arrived at this place, things had been thrown into turmoil.

She went still as memories began sliding back into place, like pieces to a puzzle. Snapping together at a speed that momentarily disoriented her. Then some of the fuzziness dissipated and the fog lifted, revealing with painful clarity all that had transpired the night before.

Her hand tentatively reached out and she turned, wondering if Zack was still beside her in the bed. She didn't remember him taking her to bed after her debilitating panic attack, but at some point in the night she'd briefly roused only to find herself firmly nestled against his body, his arms surrounding her like a protective wall. It had felt . . . nice. For the first time in years, she'd felt *safe*. And how screwed up was that? Nothing had been resolved. Nothing had changed. Or had it?

All her hand encountered was a bare space. Not even an indention or warmth to indicate that he'd recently vacated the bed. She frowned and was puzzled at the instant surge of disappointment upon finding him gone. All she wanted was to be next to him again, his arms around her, to experience just for a moment the reassurance that nothing could ever hurt her again.

But he had been the one who hurt her the *most*.

She couldn't be swayed by words, no matter how persuasively they'd been rendered. But . . . what if . . . No, she wouldn't go there. Her gift was infallible—when she still possessed the ability to read minds. But that was gone along with her innocence and belief in good.

She *hadn't* been mistaken. There was no way all three rapists would have identical recollections of the same event.

And yet Zack had been utterly devastated by the revelation. No one could possibly feign that kind of reaction. He'd looked sick at heart and there was no faking the tears and anguish. Never had she seen such raw agony in another person.

She could make herself crazy trying to make sense of the insensible. There was no point in even attempting it. But she *could* make sure she was never again in a position of being betrayed by someone she trusted when the solution was so simple.

She wouldn't give him—or anyone—the opportunity. And that was no way to live. Never allowing herself to get close to

someone. Never having friendships, close relationships. Or sharing her life with someone she cared about. Hadn't she already
wasted too much of her life as it was? Living in a self-imposed
void, carrying out the motions of each day, never dreaming of the
future. Not having dreams at all?

The idea filled her with sadness, and, disgusted with herself
for already weakening under his influence after only forty-eight
hours, she shoved the covers back and gingerly sat up, sliding her
legs around and over the edge of the bed.

Taking it slow, she eased up, holding on to the headboard so
she didn't end up in a heap on the floor. Her body groaned its
protest. A hot flush washed through her body, and the stiffness
and pain had her panting lightly as she weaved around like some
drunk sorority girl. She paused a moment to gain her bearings,
and after she steadied herself enough that she felt confident that
she wouldn't take a header, she took a purposeful step, pleased
when she didn't so much as wobble.

She was still dressed in the clothes she'd worn the day before.
Wrinkling her nose in distaste, she made her way to the closet.
Zack had said Eliza had shopped for her and she was curious to
see what the other woman had chosen.

If she had been worried, she needn't have been. The clothing
was a study in comfort. Soft—not stiff—denim jeans were folded
neatly and arranged on the shelves. There was an array of tops to
choose from as well as shoes, socks and, to her embarrassment,
an assortment of panties and bras. It appeared as though Eliza
had covered all the bases.

Bypassing the jeans, because she didn't feel up to wrestling
with the formfitting denim, she instead chose a pair of athletic
pants and then selected one of the comfortable-looking shirts.

She'd kill for a hot bath and to soak for a couple of hours, but she knew she didn't have a prayer of being able to get out of the tub once in, and she wasn't about to ask Zack for help. Later she would attempt a shower and hope that she was steady enough not to slip and fall.

After brushing her teeth and taming her tangled hair into a much more manageable ponytail, she braved leaving the bedroom and carefully walked toward the living room. To her surprise, she saw Wade and Eliza—not Zack. Where was he? In the last few days, she hadn't been able to move without him being no more than a foot away at most.

Eliza was cheerfully making a cup of coffee, and Wade . . . well, he didn't look pleased by Eliza's company. Anna-Grace wondered what that was all about. Wade certainly wasn't immune to a pretty woman and Eliza was very attractive. Not to mention capable and self-sufficient. All the things Anna-Grace wished she was.

Wade turned down the coffee Eliza offered, and with a shrug, Eliza sank down onto the couch with her mug cupped in her palms as though she had a cup of ambrosia. The look of bliss on her face was comical.

Then Eliza glanced up and saw Anna-Grace in the doorway. Immediately she shot to her feet and set her coffee on the table in front of the couch and hurried over to where Anna-Grace stood.

"How are you feeling?" Eliza asked.

She put her hand under Anna-Grace's elbow to lead her farther into the living room and then firmly deposited her in one of the armchairs.

"Would you like some coffee? I just brewed it so it's nice

and hot, and I do make a pretty mean cup of coffee if I do say so myself."

Wade also walked over to Anna-Grace, concern darkening his face.

"Are you all right, Anna-Grace?" he asked quietly. "Are you hungry? Is there anything I can get you?"

To her surprise, Anna-Grace *was* hungry. After a few days of sipping, at best, a few spoonfuls of soup, her stomach was protesting loudly.

"Coffee and breakfast sound heavenly," she breathed.

Eliza beamed. "I'd say that's a good sign that you're starting to get better."

Wade turned to Eliza and grudgingly asked, "Would you like something to eat as well?"

Eliza's eyes twinkled mischievously, almost as if she knew she annoyed Wade—and didn't care one bit, and she smiled sweetly with exaggerated innocence. "Why thank you, Wade. I'd love something to eat. Gracie and I can eat together."

"Her *name* is Anna-Grace," Wade growled.

Eliza's gaze shot to Anna-Graze, apology evident in her eyes. "I'm sorry. It's just that Zack has always called you Gracie and that's what I know you by. Would you prefer that I call you Anna-Grace?"

Anna-Grace gave her a reassuring smile. The other woman was so nice and the last thing Anna-Grace wanted to do was make her feel as though she'd done something wrong.

"You can call me either. Truly. I don't mind. Zack is the only one who ever called me Gracie. It was his pet name for me."

She couldn't control the spasm of pain that wrinkled her features when she spoke of Zack, and recalled the giddy pleasure she'd always experienced when Zack had used the affectionate endearment.

Eliza gave her a look of sympathy and impulsively reached out to squeeze her hand.

"Where . . . where is Zack?" Anna-Grace asked hesitantly.

She didn't want to appear eager, but after spending every single minute with her since her attack, it seemed odd that he was nowhere to be found. Had the revelation from the night before unnerved him? Was he through keeping up his pretense of innocence and had left as a result?

But he'd been so . . . adamant that he'd done nothing. And Zack had always been stubborn. She couldn't imagine him simply giving up and walking away.

Eliza and Wade glanced uneasily at one another and tried to cover that they had, but Anna-Grace didn't miss the quick exchange. She frowned and pinned Wade with her stare since Eliza was likely more loyal to Zack and may or may not tell her what was going on.

Wade sighed and ran a hand through his immaculate hair, and astonishingly didn't mess up a single strand. But that was Wade. Always impeccably dressed and perfectly put together. Anna-Grace had no idea how he managed it. But his appearance—like everything else in his life—was well ordered, without a single thing out of place.

"He left," Wade said hesitantly.

Anna-Grace was stunned, but more unsettling was the fact that she was . . . upset? Disappointed? After the events of last night, she couldn't imagine him simply leaving, but perhaps she shouldn't at all be surprised.

"Oh for God's sake," Eliza said in exasperation. "Leave it to a man to completely fuck up an explanation."

Wade shot Eliza a glare and she glared right back at him. The animosity between the two was tangible, and it puzzled Anna-Grace. They'd disliked one another on sight, but then they'd had contact before Anna-Grace had been pulled into the picture, so perhaps something had occurred between the two that she had no knowledge of. Whatever it was must have been serious to have sparked such an intense reaction.

"Come on, Gracie," Eliza said, taking her hand and gently pulling her toward the breakfast table.

She pinned Wade with an imperious stare. "Make yourself useful and get Gracie something to eat while I pour her a cup of coffee, and *I'll* explain everything to her."

Wade didn't look at all pleased to be ordered about by Eliza, but then he was a man used to doing the ordering. But he didn't argue and began taking out items from the refrigerator and banging pots and pans about as he pulled out two skillets.

Eliza set a steaming cup of coffee down in front of Anna-Grace and then sat down catty-corner to her with her own cup.

"First, and most important, you will *not* be left without protection," Eliza said emphatically. "Wade and I are staying with you here, and members of my team will rotate through so that there is always a third present here as well. And well, also because Wade is a civilian, so he doesn't really count."

Wade slammed down one of the skillets and turned, a fierce scowl on his face.

"I'd pit my skills against one of your pansy-ass operatives any day of the week," he said in an icy tone. "And I can damn sure protect Anna-Grace better than *you* can. You aren't much bigger than she is, for God's sake. What exactly are you going to be able to do if faced by two or three much larger and stronger men who aren't exactly deterred by the fact that you're a woman? Are you just *trying* to get yourself killed?"

Anna-Grace's eyebrows rose because she could swear mixed in with the obvious irritation was actual *concern* for Eliza.

"I wasn't dick-sizing you, Wade," Eliza said dryly. "Nor was I implying that you were some ball-less pussy."

Anna-Grace coughed trying to stifle her laughter and ended up wheezing when her mouthful of coffee went down the wrong way.

"I was merely suggesting that as refined and as highbrow as you are, you likely aren't used to what I—and my coworkers— deal with every day."

Wade's eyes glittered, and his expression grew deadly, suddenly giving Anna-Grace the impression that despite his outward appearance, he was something quite different underneath. And his next words confirmed that fleeting thought.

"Don't let the outward trappings fool you even for a moment, Eliza," Wade said, his tone sounding . . . *lethal*. And dangerous.

Anna-Grace shivered, because he suddenly sounded like someone you did *not* want to cross. Ever.

"You may very well be surprised by what I'm capable of. I didn't get to where I am with good looks and charm."

Eliza didn't seem ruffled at all by Wade's declaration.

"And you may be surprised by all I know about you and your various business practices," she said airily. "So, in that regard, no, I doubt I'd be surprised by anything when it comes to you. And that's quite an ego you have there. Who said you were good-looking and charming? Personally I find you to be a royal pain in the ass."

Wade's eyes narrowed at the insult. "What the hell does that mean? What exactly do you know about me? And there are plenty of women who disagree with you," he added in a silky, mocking voice.

Eliza laughed, ignoring his comeback about other women, who were countless, Anna-Grace was sure. It was a mystery to her why Wade had ever been interested in her on a more personal level than casual friendship.

"I'm a wiz at uncovering information on people that they don't necessarily want the rest of the world to know. It's useful in my line of work. It frustrates my computer geek boss—one of them—that I'm better with technology than he is and he knows it even if he won't admit it."

Wade's scowl deepened. "I don't even want to know," he grumbled and then turned back to the stove, muttering about all-knowing, interfering women.

Eliza's eyes were sparkling with laughter when she turned her attention back on Anna-Grace. "Now that we've got certain egos in check, I'll continue telling you about Zack."

Anna-Grace got the impression that Eliza quite enjoyed yanking Wade's chain, and even more interesting was the fact that she clearly got under Wade's skin when not much ever seemed to bother him. He was the epitome of cool and calm, and Anna-Grace had never seen him remotely ruffled.

Eliza's expression sobered as she reached over to place her hand on Anna-Grace's. She squeezed lightly in a gesture of comfort.

"Zack specifically asked me—hell, he demanded—that you

be protected around the clock and that you not go anywhere if possible, and if you absolutely must, then you were to have a full security detail. And he asked me to tell you that there were things he had to do, things that had to be taken care of and that he would be back as soon as possible. But, and he was very adamant about this, he said to tell you he *was* coming back—to you—no matter what."

Eliza hesitated, clear concern marring her pretty features. A sense of dread overtook Anna-Grace as she took in Eliza's words. And their meaning. Surely . . . *surely* he wouldn't. But he'd been so angry—*furious*.

"Gracie, do you have any idea where he would have gone?" Eliza asked. "I'm really worried about him. I can't imagine what could be *so* important that he'd take off—on his own—when his primary focus is—has *always* been—you. He said nothing, other than he had something he had to do. He didn't ask for help or backup. And we do nothing without backup. It's the only way we do things at DSS, which tells me this is very personal and that he didn't want to confide whatever it is he's doing in anyone."

Anna-Grace closed her eyes, shame and embarrassment overwhelming her. How could she tell Eliza—someone who obviously cared a lot about and respected Zack—what she suspected was the thing Zack had to do?

"Gracie?"

Anna-Grace opened her eyes to see Eliza's imploring gaze locked on her, a silent plea in her eyes.

"You can talk to me," Eliza said softly. "I know you don't know me, and I know it's hard for you to trust anyone. But you can tell me anything. I won't judge. Nor will I betray your confidence. But Zack is very important to me—to everyone at

DSS. And if he's in trouble, we want to help him. Just as we'll do everything we can to help *you*. You're important to Zack, which makes you important to us as well."

Tears simmered in Anna-Grace's eyes and she looked down for a moment, indecision weighing heavily on her mind. Then she took a deep breath and glanced Wade's way.

"If you want to speak privately, I can ask him to leave," Eliza said in a voice too low for Wade to hear.

"No," Anna-Grace said just as softly. "He knows part of it. And he needs to know the rest, or at least what I've told Zack. Because he hates Zack because of what I told him sometime ago, and now..."

"Now what?" Eliza prompted.

Anna-Grace lifted her head and stared directly into Eliza's eyes and admitted what had been nagging at her ever since witnessing Zack's reaction the night before.

"Now I'm not so sure that I was right. Maybe...maybe I was wrong." Tears flooded her eyes and sloshed over the rims, streaking down her cheeks in wet trails. "And if I was wrong... Oh God, Eliza. If I was wrong, then I've made a terrible, unforgivable mistake. If I was wrong, then I punished Zack for *years* for a sin he didn't commit. I don't know *what* to believe anymore."

"Oh, hon," Eliza said, her voice filled with sympathy.

"He'll hate me," Anna-Grace whispered. "Just like I've hated *him* for the last twelve years."

TWENTY-FIVE

ZACK jammed the rental car into park, got out and strode up the walkway to Stuart's house. Stuart was the weak link in the chain. The one who never had an original thought in his head and went along with whatever the group was doing. And yet Zack wondered just how much persuading and nagging Kevin and Bryan had really had to do in order to get him to participate in their gang rape of Gracie.

Nausea boiled in his stomach all over again and he had to shove back his visceral reaction to what three men he'd called friends had done to an innocent sixteen-year-old girl or he'd lose his tenuous grasp on what was left of his sanity.

If Zack had any hope of getting a confession out of all three—and he'd beat it out of them if he had to—he needed to start here. And in truth he relished the thought of exacting punishment and cold-blooded revenge. Justice for Gracie. And for himself. But most of all Gracie, who'd suffered the most. Lost everything. As had he.

His hands itched, curling into fists as he knocked forcefully on the door. Never in his life had he experienced such an intense need for blood. And more than anything he wanted to know *why*. What could have inspired men he would have never suspected of such depravity to attack a defenseless young woman in such a horrific, degrading manner?

The door opened and Zack's vision clouded with rage as Stuart stood staring back at him, blinking in confusion. And then to Zack's complete surprise, Stuart's eyes went dull and he sagged like a deflated balloon. Guilt and resignation were stark, and he simply stood there, unmoving, unspeaking. Almost as if he knew exactly what was coming.

Zack's fury reached its boiling point and he rammed his fist into Stuart's jaw, smashing his nose with his knuckles. Stuart flew back and landed on the floor, his hand covering his now-bleeding nose. And he simply stayed down, looking at Zack with so much guilt and regret that it made Zack physically ill.

"Get up, you son of a bitch," Zack snarled.

With a defeated sigh, Stuart slowly crawled to his feet and staggered when he stood upright. Blood smeared his nose and mouth and he made no further effort to stanch it. He merely looked at Zack like a condemned man awaiting his execution.

Then he closed his eyes and when he reopened them, a sheen of moisture glistened.

"I knew this day would come," Stuart said in a weary voice.

Shame was evident in every feature. He looked like he very much wanted to throw up. Well, that made two of them. Zack's rage was so great that he couldn't even form the words he wanted to hurl at his former friend.

"Why," he finally managed to grind out between tightly clenched teeth. "For God's sake, *why*?"

"You have no idea how sorry I am," Stuart whispered. "It's eaten me alive for years. Still eats at me. At times I can't eat. I can't sleep. All I can see are her tears. All I can hear are her sobs. And her asking why over and over. Jesus, I'm going to be sick."

Zack hit him again and stood over Stuart's fallen body, fists clenched as each and every one of Stuart's words flayed him open inch by excruciating inch.

"You sick son of a bitch," Zack hissed. "Did you enjoy brutalizing a sixteen-year-old girl? Did you get off on seeing—and hearing her cry? How many times did she beg you to stop and where was your fucking conscience *then*?"

"Kill me. I deserve it," Stuart said dully. "I don't have anything to live for anyway. My wife left me. She took the kids. I told her what I did. God, I had to. It was eating me alive. I couldn't continue living a lie. She'll never forgive me. And I don't expect you to either."

"And it never occurred to you to tell *me* what you'd done?" Zack roared. "You knew she was my life. My goddamn world! And you damn well know the hell I went through when she disappeared. That I looked for her for years. Never stopped looking for her! And you're fucking worried about your wife and me forgiving you when the person you should be begging forgiveness from is the woman whose life you completely ruined!"

Stuart dragged himself up and sagged onto the couch, burying his bloody face in his hands. His shoulders shook with sobs and Zack hadn't thought his disgust could have gotten any worse. Was he supposed to pity this pathetic piece of scum because he'd lost his wife and kids? What about the family he and

Gracie had lost? The children Gracie had never held in her arms. The wife and children Zack would have even now if not for this sick fuck's interference.

"You make me sick," Zack said in a barely controlled voice.

He was perilously close to losing his shit and completely coming unglued. So many lives ruined. And why?

He got into Stuart's face and grabbed his shirt, fisting the material and hauling him up until they were nose-to-nose.

"You're going to tell me every goddamn detail. You're going to tell me why the fuck the three of you thought the entire time you were raping Gracie that I had put you up to it and how the hell you knew Gracie could read minds. Because this was a complete setup. It's too pat. Too coincidental. You set it up so Gracie would *think* I set you loose on her to get rid of her and make her think I was done with her. Why would you do something like that? Did you hate me that much? Did you resent that I had a great girl and a future in the pros? What the hell is *wrong* with you?"

Stuart's face was haggard, and already swollen, bruises rapidly forming from the punches Zack had landed.

"It's fucked-up, man. You have *no* idea how fucked-up."

Zack shoved him back, releasing his hold on Stuart's shirt. Stuart landed with a thud against the back of the couch, his head snapping back and then forward.

"Then how about you clue me in," Zack growled.

"It was your old man," Stuart muttered. "Jesus Christ. He was fucking obsessed with getting rid of Gracie."

Zack went stock-still, his knees locking painfully as shock splintered up his spine. He shook his head, certain he hadn't heard correctly. Then he advanced on Stuart, ready to beat the ever loving fuck out of him for coming up with such a lame-ass, trumped-up excuse to divert responsibility from himself.

Stuart put up his hands to ward Zack off and began talking fast.

"Listen, Zack. Just give me a minute to explain, okay? I have no reason to lie to you, for fuck's sake. I'm guilty. Guilty as hell. But I'm not lying to you about your old man. If you'd just give me a chance to explain, I'll tell you the whole twisted story."

"So help me God, if you're fucking with me, I'll twist your balls off and shove them down your throat," Zack said in a dangerous low tone.

Stuart was visibly agitated. Pale, jittering like a junky in withdrawal and sweating profusely. He nervously licked his lips and his eyes were wild and unfocused.

"He was pissed that you were so obsessed with trailer park trash—his words not mine. He saw you as his ticket to easy street. He had it all planned out. He was going to convince you to let him act as your agent and manager and when you went to the pros he was going to retire as chief of police and live it up. Off your money and fame. When Gracie came along, your focus shifted entirely, and you were only concerned with her, your future with her, and suddenly your father found himself on the outside looking in."

So far Zack could see exactly what Stuart was saying. It certainly matched up with his father's actions and words. But to suggest he had something to do with Gracie's rape? No matter his faults, he was still an officer of the law. Being an asshole wasn't against the law, and his father was a straight arrow when it came to the law.

"He became increasingly agitated and honest to God he

went off the rails. He started asking me, Bryan and Kevin all kinds of questions. Wanted to know if you and Gracie ever fought. If Gracie was manipulating you. If you ever talked about breaking up with her. And when we told him you were absolutely serious about her, he lost it.

"And then, Jesus, he told us some crazy shit. About how Gracie could read minds but it was some big fucking secret and that you and she didn't know he knew. He overheard you talking to Gracie on the phone or some shit like that. And he came up with this insane plan."

The blood leached from Zack's face and a knot formed in his stomach that felt like a giant bolder. No way. It was too . . . crazy. So far-fetched no one would ever believe this crap.

"He told us that she'd cut off your balls and was leading you around by the dick. That you hadn't even made it with her because she was holding out for marriage. Said she was manipulating you and trapping you into marriage. Hell, he was so convincing with examples—examples that we had all witnessed—and we began to wonder if he was right. And then . . ."

Stuart closed his eyes and covered his face with his hands.

"Then *what*?" Zack said harshly, though he knew, goddamn it. He knew and he was sick to his soul. But he had to hear it. Had to hear it said aloud. Had to *hear* what a complete twisted bastard his father was.

"Then he set us up and he blackmailed us," Stuart said bleakly.

"How?" Zack snapped.

He was reeling, his mind spinning out of control. His life had been a farce. The only real thing in his life had been Gracie.

And he'd lost her. He'd lost her in the most horrifying, repulsive and heartbreaking manner possible. He was utterly gutted and his grief was overwhelming. He would never recover from this. How could he?

"He pulled us over for a bullshit traffic stop and planted enough drugs to charge us with possession with intent to distribute, a felony. Locked us up and told us he'd throw the book at us. Unless we did him a 'favor.' He then explained exactly what he wanted us to do, and Zack, he was off his rocker. He was unhinged and incoherent. Kept mumbling about how that bitch was going to ruin things for *him*. He snapped, I mean *completely* lost his shit and all sense of reality. Told us he would ruin our lives like she ruined his.

"God, the stuff he told us. At first we thought he was having paranoid delusions. But he was absolutely serious when he said that Gracie could read people's minds. Well, imagine how nervous that made us. I mean what the fuck? Then he said he had a plan to make it look as though you were behind the whole thing and that it was up to us to be convincing enough that she believed it."

"And you just went along with it," Zack said bitterly. "You just violently raped a young girl and why? Did it never occur to you to come to me and tell me what the hell my father was planning? You didn't think I'd put a stop to it?"

"We were facing felony charges and serious jail time," Stuart said wearily. "We were young and scared. Had our whole lives ahead of us."

"And it didn't scare you that if Gracie had pressed charges you would have gone to jail for aggravated rape of a minor?" Zack asked incredulously.

Stuart sent him an uneasy glance. "Your father told us not to worry about that. He said he'd provide us all an alibi. He'd say we were all out at his place the night in question and that no one would believe some girl from the trailer park over the chief of police. He was smug about it. Patted himself on the back for having such a foolproof plan."

"And so you just did it," Zack said, his rage mounting with every breath. "The three of you raped her. And obviously you staged your fucking thoughts so that when she saw into your twisted, fucked-up minds, she saw *me*. You made her think that I put you up to a completely reprehensible and unforgivable act of violence."

"I couldn't do it," Stuart said painfully. "I mean I tried. But I couldn't . . . Jesus, it disgusted me. I couldn't finish."

Zack's stomach lurched and he closed his eyes, taking deep breaths in an attempt to steady his raw, exposed nerves.

"You think that makes it better?" Zack asked hoarsely. "Am I supposed to feel better that you couldn't keep it up long enough to get off raping the girl I loved? I hope you rot in hell, Stuart. That's where you belong."

Stuart's expression was bleak. "I'm already there."

Zack couldn't form a coherent thought. His hands shook, his knees kept buckling and it took all his concentration and focus to remain upright. He was floored by the revelation that his father had orchestrated the entire thing. God, the thought and planning that had gone into it was mind-boggling. And how the fuck had he known about Gracie's ability to read minds?

He had to have overheard Zack on the phone with her at one point, but Zack had always been so careful to guard Gracie's secret and it made him sick that he'd evidently failed. He'd given his father the means to strike out at her in a believable way that would have destroyed her. *Had* destroyed her. No wonder she believed the worst. No wonder she was so convinced of Zack's guilt. The evidence was overwhelmingly not in his favor.

He couldn't even stand to look at the pathetic excuse of a man he used to call his friend any longer. It was repulsive. The entire sordid mess was repugnant.

"I hope you go to sleep at night with the sound of Gracie's tears in your head," Zack rasped. "I hope you go to bed seeing the disgust on your wife's face and know that you'll never get her or your children back. And I hope when you die that hell will be waiting for you with open arms."

TWENTY-SIX

ZACK stared out over the sprawling expanse of Kentucky Lake, hands shoved into his pockets, his thoughts in utter turmoil. The landscape had changed dramatically since he and Gracie used to come here so many years ago. And their tree had been cut down, only a rotting stump remaining. A place they'd spent many a night gazing at the stars and dreaming of their future. A future that had never happened.

In many ways the irrevocably ravaged landscape was symbolic of his broken dreams.

He pulled the small recording device from his pocket that had every damning piece of evidence Stuart had spilled. And it was a good damn thing he'd had the foresight to record the conversation, because who the hell would ever believe the outlandish, unthinkable events Stuart had confessed to? Hell, he wouldn't believe someone with that kind of story. It was inconceivable that someone could be that diabolical. And that his own father, despite their many differences, had gone to such lengths to ruin his son's future? For his own perceived selfish gain?

It defied all reason. His father was a psychopath in every clinical sense of the word.

In the distance, headlights shone and the faint sound of an engine registered, then shut off, followed by the headlights. Zack tensed, anger throbbing through his veins as he braced for the impending confrontation with his father.

He refused to go back to the house he was raised in. He'd give no physical evidence that he'd ever been there. Instead he'd called his father and told him to meet him here. He hadn't responded to the questions, his father asking when he'd come back into town or why. He'd simply said he had something important to talk to him about and hung up, leaving him to make what he wanted of Zack's cryptic statement. He hadn't even known if his father *would* come.

Curiosity must have gotten the better of him. And as the old saying went, curiosity killed the cat.

A few moments later, his father shuffled up, a shadow in the darkness that blanketed the area above the lake.

"Zack?" he called.

"Here," Zack said grimly.

The beam of a flashlight bounced erratically over the ground and then his father came into view. His appearance was shocking. He looked every bit his age, if not older. He had a beer belly that protruded well over his cinched belt, and he had the look of a longtime alcoholic. His hair had thinned considerably, a bald spot on top, and what was left was completely white.

The years hadn't been good to him, a fact Zack took savage satisfaction in.

Harsh lines cut grooves in his father's face and he had the haggard appearance of someone who didn't sleep at night. Maybe his demons—and guilt—tormented his dreams. Zack could only hope that he endured half the hell that Gracie had suffered, though he doubted his father was capable of guilt or remorse.

"What the hell is going on, son? Why did you ask to meet here, for God's sake? You should have come to the house. We could have had a beer and caught up. It's been three years since I saw you. Not even a telephone call in that time. Christmas. Birthdays. Is that any way to treat your old man?"

Zack was seething. It took every ounce of effort he possessed not to lay his father out right then and there.

"I know what you did, you son of a bitch," Zack bit out. "And don't you dare fucking stand there, look me in the eye and deny it. Because swear to God, I'll *beat* the truth out of you, you bastard. I'll pull out every lie you ever told. Every law you broke and every sin you committed. And when I'm done, you'll have nothing and you'll *be* nothing."

His father's face flushed with anger. His cheeks mottled with rage, and his eyes bulged outward in clear agitation.

"Goddamn weak-ass pussies," his father bellowed, spittle forming on his lips. "Which one was it? I bet it was Stuart. I should have known the spineless idiot didn't have the stomach for it. It's probably the reason his wife left him a while back. The dumb fuck probably couldn't live with his conscience and told her everything. What a pathetic excuse for a man."

Zack stared back at his father in shocked horror and complete incredulity. God, he wasn't even going to deny it. There was no remorse whatsoever. No guilt. Just anger that he'd been ratted out. And he called Stuart a pathetic excuse for a man? What kind of man engineered the rape of a teenage girl? A girl young enough to be his daughter. The girl his own son was in love with and planned to marry.

Zack felt like he was stuck in some bizarre nightmare he couldn't rouse from.

"You don't even *deny* it?" he asked hoarsely. "What kind of a sick, twisted bastard are you? How could you *do* that to just a girl? She was a virgin, for God's sake, and her initiation was a brutal gang rape that *you* instigated? A grown-ass adult man. A man sworn to uphold the law and protect the people of his town as their chief of police. Or did that protection only extend to those you deemed worthy?"

His father snorted in disbelief, ignoring Zack's outrage and the issue at hand.

"You expect me to believe you hadn't gotten in her pants already or that she wasn't spreading her legs for anyone who looked twice her way? You're a naïve fool if you believe that bullshit."

Zack lost it. He laid his father out with one hard punch to his jaw. His father went down with a thump and just lay there rubbing his jaw with an expression of disbelief. As if he couldn't believe that Zack would be furious or why. Was Zack supposed to thank him for single-handedly ruining the lives of an innocent girl and a boy, his son, whom he was supposed to love?

"You'd honestly *defend* the little slut? What is *wrong* with you? Isn't it enough that she ruined your career? That even now you could still be playing ball? You could have won a Super Bowl, for God's sake. You led a shitty-ass team to the playoffs the first *two* years you quarterbacked for them, and then you just walked away. And if you hadn't been so fucked-up over her and had your head in the game you would have never gotten hurt to begin with."

Zack's fury exploded and he hauled his father up and rammed his fist into his gut and then sent him reeling with another blow, this time to his nose. The sickening crunch and the gush of blood indicated it was likely broken but at the moment Zack could kill him and suffer no remorse whatsoever.

He was out of his mind with rage. It boiled and erupted like a volcano and twelve years of worry, grief and anger were suddenly unleashed in a violent tornado of pure hatred for the man who'd fathered him. God, he'd do anything in the world to cleanse himself of his father's blood and he wished with all his heart that they weren't biologically related. Never would he be the kind of man his father was. He'd die first.

"I'll have your ass for this," his father wheezed as he took a wary, unsteady step away from Zack. "I'll nail you for assault on a police officer. I don't give a damn if you're my son or not."

"You do that," Zack spit out. "Just realize that you stand to lose far more than I. I have nothing more to lose because I already lost everything that ever meant anything to me thanks to you. *You* took everything from me. But if I go down, so be it, because I'll take you down with me and never suffer a single regret. I'll make damn sure you spend the rest of your life behind bars. Not to mention the entire town will know what a complete sick fuck you are and you can kiss your reputation, your career and your pension goodbye."

"You can't prove a goddamn thing," his father said in a smug tone that only infuriated Zack all the more.

"Can't I?" Zack asked softly.

The two words and ensuing silence visibly unsettled his father. Worry entered his eyes and he jittered nervously, his earlier bravado fading under the confidence in which Zack spoke.

"The statute of limitations for aggravated rape hasn't elapsed," Zack continued. He pulled out the small recording device from his pocket and hit play, Stuart's confession filling the stillness of the night. "If you don't think the others will turn on you on a dime, then think again. You blackmailed them into a despicable crime and the DA will be far more interested in taking down a dirty cop than they will three losers who've gone nowhere in life. Think what it'll do for his career. Expose a crooked lawman, the chief of police in a small town. It will be a sensationalistic story and will hit the AP like wildfire. In a matter of days, you won't be able to show your face anywhere because everyone will know what you did. I'll make sure of it. If it takes the rest of my life, I'll make you suffer the way Gracie and I have suffered for the last twelve years. And as God as my witness, you'll pay, old man," Zack seethed. "You'll pay."

"You're bluffing," his father hedged. But it was obvious Zack's vow was convincing because now his father had lost all his previous bluster and looked scared shitless.

"Oh? You should know me well enough to know that I don't bluff. But if you don't think I'm serious, *try* me."

The challenge in his voice was unmistakable and there was tangible anticipation for his father to disregard the threat he'd issued. And his father quickly recognized it.

"What can I do?" his father asked, panic rising in his voice. "I'll do whatever you want, but you *can't* go public with this. It will *ruin* me and I don't have much left as it is. Just my pension, and if this is exposed, I'll lose that too and be left with nothing. You can't do that to me, son."

Zack's temper flared. "Don't you ever call me son. I'm not your son. And I sure as hell don't claim you as any blood of mine." And then he laughed, the sound brittle, cracking like ice. "Do you think I give one fuck about you? You've certainly never given a shit about me. All I was to you was a ticket to the good life. You were counting on being the father of a pro football player and riding my star, milking me for every dime you could. How it must have pissed you off when I walked away from a multimillion-dollar career, because you saw the life you envisioned for yourself disappear in a flash. But you never gave a damn about the life *I* wanted. What made *me* happy. You destroyed the best thing in my life, and I'll *never* forgive you for that. Better hope you live a long time, because when you die, I'm going to dance on your grave, and Satan will be there to greet you and usher you personally into the bowels of hell."

His father blanched and then began pleading. He lost all semblance of control and started blubbering like a baby, begging Zack to have mercy. And all Zack could think about was Gracie begging for the same. For them not to hurt her. And they hurt her anyway. His heart screamed with the need for vengeance, to make every single person involved in her violation hurt as much as she'd hurt, suffer as much as she'd suffered. And for them to never have another day's peace in their lives.

"You're going to confess everything while I record it," Zack said coldly. "Every single sordid detail and why you did it. If you leave so much as one detail out, I'll nail you to the wall and ruin you. You'll admit that you knew of Gracie's ability to read minds and how you manipulated the situation to make it appear that I was behind her rape. And then, I never want to see you, hear your name. Nothing. You are nothing to me. You aren't my father."

"W-h-what are y-you going t-to do with the confession," his father stammered, his eyes frantic and bulging with fear.

"I'm going to give it to Gracie so she knows what a complete, ruthless bastard you are."

"What if she decides to press charges?"

His father was sweating now, the stench of his fear palpable in the air. And he was whining, which just sickened Zack and made him all the more ashamed that he shared DNA with the worthless piece of shit standing in front of him about to piss his pants.

"That'll be her decision," Zack said. "I hope to hell she *does*, but I won't ever force her to do anything that will cause her further pain, just as I'll support her one hundred percent if she chooses to seek justice for the crimes you and others committed against her. Because let there be no doubt. You are every bit as guilty and reprehensible—if not more so—as the men who actually raped her. Your fate is now entirely in the hands of a woman you irrevocably damaged and inflicted your sick abuse on and whose only crime was loving me."

His father's cheeks puffed outward and he exploded in anger. "I only wanted what was best for you! The same as any father wants for his only son."

"Bullshit! No father has his son's girlfriend raped and abused and made to think her boyfriend set it all up, you sick bastard! What was best for me was *her*!" Zack shouted. "And what's best for me *now* is to forget you were ever a part of my life and that in all ways you're nothing more than a sperm donor. I used to resent my mother for leaving us, but I can't blame her now that I know what an asshole you really are."

"So this is it. You're just going to leave things like this and write me out of your life," his father said bitterly.

Zack advanced, his finger up in his father's face. "*You* did that. You did that twelve years ago when you initiated a brutal assault on an innocent young girl for your own selfish gain. I wish to hell you had *never* been part of my life and that it had been *you* who left and not my mother or that she would have taken me with her. Because you were probably the worst thing to ever happen to her life and I *know* you're the single worst thing that's ever happened to mine."

"What the fuck took you so long to check in?" Beau demanded when he answered Zack's call. "Do you have any idea how worried we've been? This shit doesn't fly, man. You don't go off half-cocked solo on some vigilante mission."

Zack sighed. "I know. I get it, okay? But this was something I had to do. And I didn't want any of y'all involved in my fucked-up situation."

"That's bullshit," Beau said rudely. "I'm your friend, not just your partner. You have to know I would have had your back no matter what."

"I do know that," Zack said quietly. "But some things are private, man. And like I said, this was something I had to do. That had to be done."

There was a long pause.

"And did you get it taken care of?"

Zack sighed wearily. "Yeah. No. Fuck it all. It will never be okay, but I got the answers I wanted. But if Gracie doesn't accept that or forgive me then it doesn't mean a goddamn thing."

"Is there anything I—we—can do?" Beau asked quietly.

"Just keep Gracie safe until I come back home to her," Zack said in a soft voice. "I can't lose her, Beau. And I know it looked like a dick move to cut out on her when she was just beaten nearly to death, but this . . . this had to be done or I will never have a chance to get her back."

"You don't have to worry about Gracie," Beau said adamantly. "She has to go back to the doctor so he can check on her recovery and she needs to refill her prescription for her pain medicine. She's stubborn and has been refusing to take it but Lizzie and Sterling have been leaning on her, making sure she takes what she needs. She's been in a lot of pain, and hell, who wouldn't be after the beating she took? So they're going to make sure she not only gets the medicine but takes it as well."

Fear squeezed Zack's insides at the thought of Gracie leaving the confines of the safe house they'd installed her in, even if it was a necessary evil.

"Make damn sure she's protected. Those bastards are out there, waiting and watching for another opportunity to strike. Hell, they waited months after the shit that went down with Ari. They aren't going to give up. They've proven that much."

"She'll have a full security detail," Beau reassured. "Private clinic. She needs follow-up X-rays and blood work or we would have had the physician come to her."

Zack swore. "When is her appointment?"

"Tomorrow morning. Before the clinic opens."

Damn it. There was no way for him to get back in time to go with her. And, well, he didn't want their first face-to-face meeting after he'd ducked out to be in public or with others present. Nor would he subject her to the devastation of having to listen as the people who'd abused her so callously admitted to such an atrocity.

"I'll be home tomorrow afternoon. Take care of her for me, man. She's my entire life."

"You know I will. You went to the wall for Ari, and I'll never forget that. I know how you feel. Ari is my life too, and I wouldn't survive something ever happening to her."

Zack reluctantly rang off, frustrated by the time it would take to get back to Gracie. He was tempted to just rent a fucking car and drive through the night to get back to her, but he'd still miss her appointment, and he'd be in no mental or physical condition to take her back to hell. Not that he was prepared to brave the bowels of hell either, but one of them had to be strong, and he certainly didn't expect Gracie to be when she was the one most affected by the events of the past.

He needed to get some sleep so he could catch his early morning flight back to Houston, but he already knew sleep would be a long time coming. He'd never sleep another night until Gracie was back in his arms for good.

TWENTY-SEVEN

ANNA-GRACE sat in the nearly empty waiting room of the doctor whom she'd been referred to for her follow-up appointment. She'd been assured that this doctor was someone DSS used because he was utterly discreet and often made house calls, or, as was the case currently, if he needed access to medical equipment he arranged for times when the clinic was either closed or before it opened to the public. And, well, from what Beau Devereaux had told her, most of his patients were those who had need of complete anonymity, so he didn't take on "normal" patients. And judging by the posh, expensively decorated waiting area, it didn't appear that he was hurting for money.

As empty as it was of actual patients, the room was crowded with Eliza, Wade, Dane, Isaac and Coop. There were two others she'd been introduced to but she couldn't recall their names.

And then there was one other man in the waiting room, who at first she'd assumed was just another person in her ridiculously large security escort. Well, and as silly as it sounded to be surrounded by mountains of testosterone—excluding Eliza, of course, though she was more of a badass than most men!—it *did* make her feel safer. Especially with Zack gone.

But the man had garnered suspicious glances from the others and raised eyebrows among her security detail as though they had no liking for his presence.

But he was inconspicuous and didn't pay any heed to the rather large contingent of fierce-looking men surrounding him.

Arrogant bitch. The whole lot of them think they're invincible.

Anna-Grace's head snapped up, her mouth dropping in surprise at the sound that had popped out of nowhere, but not a single person in the room reacted in any way to the terse, angry statement. In fact, they acted as if they hadn't heard it.

So smug. They think they can get the best of us. They have no idea of our resources or what we're capable of. And the ballsy bitch who works for them needs to be taken down a notch or two.

There was a sound of triumphant glee that accompanied the next statement.

She'll soon find out that she's not as invincible as she thinks she is. It's a lesson I'm very much looking forward to.

Gracie's graze swept over the occupants of the waiting room, convinced that someone was having a cell phone conversation and not being in the least concerned with being overheard. But again, she saw nothing to indicate anyone *using* a phone. Not even the hands-free kind.

And then her gaze settled on the other side of the waiting room, where the man she'd been observing hadn't changed position. He stared intently at Eliza, his jaw ticking with agitation, while the others all were expressionless and seemed bored.

Was she going crazy? Was she ultra-paranoid after her attack and the traumatic sequence of events of the last few days? Had she reached her emotional limit?

It was almost as if . . . She shook her head. No, that was even crazier. She had lost her ability to read minds twelve years ago and hadn't missed that gift in the least. Clearly she was imagining it all.

All went quiet in her mind and she was convinced that she'd imagined the entire thing but then she was instantly flooded with images—horrifying images of Eliza lying on her back with some sort of cloth over her face and someone pouring water over it.

She couldn't keep the revulsion from her face, and Dane immediately picked up on the change in her demeanor. He was sitting closest to her and leaned over, concern flaring in his eyes.

"What's wrong, Gracie? Are you in pain?"

She shook her head, unable to formulate the words to explain her reaction. How could she? Instead she put up her hand to wave him off and carefully schooled her expression so that he'd know she was okay.

To her profound relief, the door opened and a cheerful-looking young nurse motioned for Anna-Grace to come back. She stood so quickly that she nearly fell over, and would have if Dane hadn't lunged for her, wrapping one strong arm around her to steady her.

"Careful now," he murmured. "Take it nice and slow."

Eliza stepped to Anna-Grace's other side. "Do you want me to go back with you?"

Unspoken was the question of whether she'd feel more comfortable with another female in the exam room with her instead of a man or men she didn't even know.

She nodded because she was suddenly besieged by the desire to have Eliza close, not because she herself was scared, but because the terrifying images she'd had involving Eliza made her fear for Eliza.

Dane frowned. "Of course, we won't go into the exam room with you, Gracie, and yes, I do think it's a good idea for you to have Lizzie there with you, but someone will be posted outside the door as well as at any exit and entry points."

"That's fine," Anna-Grace said faintly. "You can let go now, Dane. I'm all right. Truly. I just stood too quickly. I can make it on my own."

Dane looked doubtful but he relinquished his hold on her and shot a look at Eliza that clearly said, "Help her."

Eliza kindly curled her arm around Gracie's waist and eased her to where the nurse stood in the open door. As soon as they were through, the nurse started to close the door but not before Dane and Wade pushed through the door too, startling the nurse.

Then Dane turned and secured the lock so no one could gain access.

The nurse started to open her mouth to protest but was silenced under Dane's chilly stare. "She goes nowhere without us. We will take position outside the exam room. I trust there are no windows or alternative entries or exits from the room she'll be in?"

The nurse vigorously shook her head and stammered out a no.

Dane nodded. "Good then. Show Gracie to her room so we can get this over with and get her back home so she can rest and recover."

The doctor briskly and efficiently checked her over and proclaimed that she was fast on the mend with only bruises to show for her ordeal. He said it in a tone that suggested she was lucky. Forgive her, but she didn't exactly feel lucky to have been beaten senseless by a bunch of thugs, regardless of whether they'd *intended* to kill her or not.

Fifteen minutes later, they were on their way and Gracie anxiously looked for the man who'd been in the waiting room with them. But he was nowhere to be seen. Had the nurse called him back to a room after she'd called Gracie?

She couldn't shake her sense of unease, nor did the imprint of those voices—thoughts—leave. They were still strong in the waiting area, and she shivered involuntarily, which only made Dane frown harder.

"Did they even check her for a fever?" Dane demanded, though he directed his question to Eliza, not Gracie herself.

"They gave her the full physical," Eliza responded, a hint of amusement in her voice.

She looked at Gracie with a sympathetic look only females shared when encountering a forceful, dominant man. Then she rolled her eyes, and Gracie had to choke back her laughter.

Dane scowled. "Then why the hell is she shivering? She looks like she's freezing to death."

"Well," Eliza drawled out. "It could be the weather. It's a might chilly today. Or it could be the fact that she was only recently brutally attacked, is not only still hurting from that attack but is scared shitless that she isn't in a more secure place and not out in the open."

She shrugged her shoulders. "Or maybe she's just afraid of you and your broody-ass expressions. Take your pick."

Gracie bit into her bottom lip, wondering how she could possibly find humor in something as macabre as her situation. And leaning on the very last people she would have ever accepted help from. Zack's friends. Acquaintances. Coworkers or whatever he considered them. That he had a connection at all with them should have sent her on the run after that very first encounter with Zack.

But Wade had talked her down, ever the reasonable, unflappable one. And coldly dangerous. However, she'd known that had she not seen the light and realized that Wade was right about her needing to stop running and to embrace the life she'd made for herself, he would have helped her if she'd truly wanted to relocate somewhere else. All she would have had to do was ask.

Perhaps it was the stubborn streak in her. And . . . well . . . recent events had her questioning every single thing she'd been made to believe for the last twelve years. Zack had been utterly devastated and so enraged that in that moment she truly did fear him. Not that he'd hurt her. And that was insane enough after what he purportedly did. No, she feared he would kill every last man who had a part in her rape. And that gave her no joy. No sense of justice. Because it meant that Zack would have to pay the price, just as she'd had to pay the price for more than a decade, and she wouldn't wish that on her worst enemy. Whether he'd betrayed her or not.

She opened her mouth to ask a question and froze because she sounded too . . . eager. And she wanted to remain indifferent. As if none of this mattered. Particularly Zack. She knew enough about herself to know she'd never love another man as she'd loved Zack. Sixteen or not, she'd know—known—that he was it for her. Every time she looked at him, she saw forever in his eyes and when she read his thoughts. God, they were bursting with love. So much love and pride. And possession.

She had belonged to him. The only person she'd every truly belonged to. And he'd belonged to her.

So what had happened?

None of this was adding up!

There was no faking the gut-wrenching grief and regret in Zack's face when she'd told him what happened. He hadn't been able to speak and when he had, tears had rolled down his cheeks and he'd crawled to her, unable to stand. A proud, arrogant, dominant male, crawling to her just so he could gently touch her face. So he could apologize and beg forgiveness for something he'd sworn to her he hadn't done.

None of this made any sense in her already senseless world. The only question that stood out to her during this whole thing was . . .

What if he hadn't done it? And what if because she ran from him twelve years ago without hearing his side of the story, he now hated her every bit as much as she'd hated him?

She closed her eyes and warm tears slid soundlessly down her cheeks. That one word held a wealth of meaning. Capitulation. Surrender. Admittance of wrongdoing. God. Was she crazy?

She had said she'd hated him. Past tense. As if that were no longer the case and she loved him still. Did she? Had she ever truly stopped loving him even in the darkest moments of her grief and despair? It was a question that disturbed her on many levels.

But the one thing that kept creeping into her consciousness, despite her best effort to keep it at bay, was the fact that he'd been so vehement in his denial that he'd had any part in her rape. And God, he'd seemed so sincere. What if she'd been wrong? All these years?

Nausea and unease churned in her stomach.

"Gracie?"

Eliza's soft voice interrupted the volatile mix of Gracie's thoughts. "I know you're upset, but please just give Zack a chance. He'll be home in a few hours. His flight was delayed and he was furious because he wanted to be here for your doctor's appointment. But he's coming."

Gracie's thoughts immediately shifted to Eliza as overwhelming fear and anxiety swept over Gracie. Should she tell Eliza what she'd "heard"? And had she heard anything at all except her own scrambled imagination?

She bit into her lip, not knowing what she should do. Wondering if she was losing her mind after so long trying to keep it together and survive.

"Gracie?"

This time it was Wade who softly spoke her name. There was concern and a slight edge to the softness. She glanced up to see his eyes sharp, taking in every aspect of her appearance, almost as if he were reading *her* thoughts.

But he didn't need her gift to read people. He was very discerning and had an uncanny knack for reading people. Their intent. Whether they posed a threat or not. And given that she was the only person he'd allowed close, to her knowledge, she must have some way passed his scrutiny.

Several things came to her at once. Voices. Random echoes.

It overwhelmed her and she clamped her hands over her ears as if to somehow shut out the barrage of thoughts around her. Oh God. She wasn't crazy. It was coming back.

She closed her eyes tightly, because given a choice between the two, she would have preferred to be crazy.

TWENTY-EIGHT

GRACIE paced the interior of the safe house, tension growing increasingly more difficult to bear. Her palms were sweaty, her pulse raced and her respirations were rapid and light, making her dizzy.

Where was Eliza?

They'd split off several hours ago as they'd left the clinic. Eliza had stated she needed to retrieve her laptop from her home, run by the office to do some digging and then she would be back at guard duty at the safe house. She anticipated an hour and a half, two at the most. That had been four hours ago.

Gracie had a very sick feeling that she wasn't crazy. That she had recovered some of her powers and that everything she'd "heard" in the doctor's office was indeed directed at Eliza.

She glanced Isaac's way. He'd been given guard duty in Eliza's absence. He didn't seem unruffled or worried in the least. Wade, however, wore a grim expression and seemed deep in thought. Was he worried like Gracie was? Or was he contemplating something altogether different?

There was at least one other DSS agent outside the house. Where, she wasn't sure. But she knew he was carefully watching the house. It should make her feel safe, but she couldn't rid herself of the horrible feeling that she was no longer even a target and that the focus had now been shifted to Eliza.

What if she was already in the hands of the people who'd abducted and beaten Gracie, and by account, had also taken and done grievous harm to Ari, Beau Devereaux's wife?

Her pacing sped up and she turned quick turns, walking back and forth in a short line, her mind trying to come up with a possible solution. If she just blurted out to Isaac that she used to be able to read minds, but then couldn't—but oh wait, now all of a sudden she seemed to be regaining her power, and oh, by the way, I think Eliza is in great danger—he'd think she was a raving lunatic.

Not to mention if she got them all hot and bothered and focused on Eliza and something did happen, Gracie would be responsible.

And yet the growing dread wouldn't leave her. It only swelled until her chest was constricted and she could barely draw breath. The images of Eliza had horrified her. Was that what she was enduring even now?

She shook her head. She couldn't—wouldn't—simply shake this off. Eliza had been kind to her, had put her life on the line to protect someone she didn't even know. She was loyal to Gracie because, in her words, Gracie was important to Zack, thus it made Gracie important to the rest of DSS. Gracie wouldn't reward such selflessness by remaining silent out of fear of being wrong or thought a lunatic.

An idea popped into her head, so crazy and ridiculous that it was absolutely . . . brilliant. Her breath hitched in excitement. Of course! She knew exactly how it could be determined if Eliza had been kidnapped, if she was suffering. And they certainly had the tools to mount a full-scale assault and take out every single person responsible for the harm that had come to DSS, as well as take out anyone associated with them.

And it had nothing to do with a single DSS agent. No, the real power and skill for this operation was in the women who'd married DSS agents: Ramie, who could discern Eliza's location by simply touching an object belonging to Eliza; and Ari, whose powers were enormous and not even fully tapped yet. There was no telling just what she was capable of, but she'd already taken on these men once, and annihilated an entire compound in the process. And Gracie . . . Her powers weren't as awe-inspiring or as helpful as Ramie's and Ari's, but she could read minds, and if there was pertinent information to be had, a way to bring about the complete end to this madness, then she could be of some small help.

Her gaze leapt to Isaac. From all Eliza had imparted, getting to Ramie was as hopeless as getting into Fort Knox undetected. She bit her teeth into her lip and then glanced Wade's way. Wade's allegiance wasn't with DSS. It was with her. It was why he was here. And . . . Gracie knew in her heart, though she chose to deny it, Wade was not always a good man. He was steeped in shadows and had connections no ordinary man should ever have.

But she'd never questioned him. In truth, she didn't want the answers. She preferred to live in ignorant bliss and consider him the friend he'd indeed become.

Wade turned as if sensing her gaze and his eyes sharpened as he stared at her. Then he glanced Isaac's way, as if knowing Gracie had something on her mind she wouldn't want the DSS agent to hear.

He headed toward Gracie and tucked his hand underneath her elbow and gently guided her into the bedroom he occupied, leaving Isaac alone in the living room. He didn't shut the door. It would likely arouse suspicion, but he took Gracie into the bathroom, to the farthest point away from others.

"What's wrong?" he asked bluntly.

Gracie swallowed. "Wade, if I asked you . . ." She sucked in a deep breath. "If I asked you to do something no questions asked, would you do it?"

His gaze narrowed even further as he studied her. Then, as if reaching a decision, he simply said, "Yes, of course. Name it."

Her shoulders sagged in relief. "I need to get in touch with Ramie and Ari Devereaux. Eliza is in great danger, Wade. I shouldn't have waited this long. God, if she's been hurt or killed, it's my fault. But I didn't believe that my power had come back. I questioned it. But I can't wait another minute and the only two people who can help are Ramie and Ari. And their husbands can't know about it, because they would never allow them to be involved in what I plan to do."

Wade frowned. "I'd very much like to know exactly what it is you plan to do."

She placed her hand on his arm and squeezed gently, a gesture of friendship and gratitude for all he'd done for her.

"I need you to trust me," she said in a low voice. "I don't have time to explain it a dozen times. I'd rather do it once so we can act as quickly as possible. I know I'm asking a lot, but Wade, I know Eliza is in trouble and that she's hurting. And I can't— won't—just sit here and do nothing because it might put me in harm's way," she said fiercely.

Wade cupped her jaw and tenderly caressed her cheek. "Yes, all right. As long as you fill me in before you act on whatever this plan of yours is, then I'll get you what you need."

"I swear it," she said. "But hurry, please. I'm so worried about her, Wade. You know how dependable she is. She said she'd be gone two hours at the most and that was now over four hours ago. She wouldn't just flake like that."

Wade's expression grew grim. "I know. I've been worried as well."

Relief made her sag a little more. Okay, so she wasn't the only one that suspected Eliza was in very real danger. Even though she knew, it was nice to have validation.

"I'll need you to tell them how to get here," Anna-Grace said in a low voice.

Wade nodded. "Not a problem. I can send transportation to get them since the chances of them getting out on their own past their husbands is zero."

She squeezed him again. "Thank you for believing me, Wade. For not thinking I'm crazy."

His entire expression softened. "I'll never not believe in you, Anna-Grace. Now, let me go and make some calls so that we can go find our Eliza."

TWENTY-NINE

RAMIE and Ari Devereaux stared curiously at Gracie as they took a seat in the living room of the safe house. Isaac had been apoplectic when the two women had shown up, escorted by three burly bodyguards who were *not* employed by DSS. Wade had taken proper precautions, but then, Gracie would have expected no less.

And Isaac was most assuredly on the phone with either Caleb or Beau or both this very minute, so Anna-Grace figured she had fifteen minutes tops to convince these women she wasn't crazy and to help her—help Eliza—before their husbands burst in losing their minds that the women had escaped their temporary safety restrictions.

Though there was a hint of impatience that Anna-Grace picked up from both women, neither had malevolent thoughts about her cryptic call to them. There was only concern for Eliza and puzzlement over why they were called and not their husbands.

Anna-Grace nervously put her hands together, clenching

them until her knuckles were white. "We don't have much time, so I'll explain quickly. I'm not crazy. You two of all people should have the easiest time believing me. And you two are the only ones who can help Eliza now."

Concern darkened Ramie's eyes. "Are you sure she's in danger?"

Anna-Grace hesitated a brief second and then scolded herself. She was not crazy. She knew what she'd heard. What she'd seen in the other man's head. And then Eliza disappeared mere hours later? There was no such thing as coincidence. Eliza was being held prisoner and she was hurting.

Her stomach clenched, remembering her own pain and terror at their hands. Her beating had been a message. Not an intention to kill her. But could she say the same for Eliza? The hatred in the man's thoughts didn't give Anna-Grace any reassurance they wouldn't kill Eliza just to prove that DSS wasn't impervious to the threat they posed.

"I'm positive," Anna-Grace murmured.

In as few words as possible and as to the point as she could make it, she explained everything: her ability to read minds, the loss of that power when she'd been so brutally attacked and her belief that her mind had simply shut out the power as a protective measure. Why it was reasserting itself now she wasn't sure, but then she realized it was because she'd come to care about Eliza. She'd relaxed around the other woman. And her consciousness had picked up on the threat to her.

"She's been missing for three hours," Anna-Grace said grimly. "Does this sound like the Eliza you all know so well?"

She received worried answering frowns from both the other women.

"No," Ramie muttered. "Eliza is as solid as they come. She's gone to the wall for us all. What's your plan? I'm in."

Anna-Grace blinked. She hadn't even outlined her plan or explained that it could cause Ramie immeasurable pain. And yet Ramie had signed on with no reservations.

"I am too," Ari said with a growl. "I still owe those bastards some serious payback and I'm dying to reek some serious havoc."

Anna-Grace almost smiled.

Then she looked at Ramie. "I'm asking for a lot. I know. I know what using your powers does to you. The price you pay. But I also believe it's the only way we can locate Eliza in time to save her. I believe they mean to kill her to send a stronger message than the one they sent using me."

Ramie merely nodded. "I'll do it. Is there anything here belonging to Eliza?"

"There has to be something in her room," Wade said, speaking up for the first time. "I'll go find something."

Anna-Grace leveled a look at Ari. "You are powerful. Magnificently so. They don't stand a chance against you." Then she lifted her shoulders in a rueful shrug. "My gift isn't as intuitive or as powerful as yours. I'm not sure how much help I'll be. But I can read minds, and if there is information that helps us locate the other members of this . . . organization . . . then they can be taken out and will pose no further threat to any of us."

Ari stepped forward and slid her cool hand over Anna-Grace's arm. Then she squeezed it in silent solidarity. "Your gift is as powerful as mine and Ramie's. We just have different powers, and that's a good thing, because the three of us together? Those assholes don't stand a chance."

"No one is going anywhere, goddamn it!" Isaac roared.

He'd reappeared from the adjoining room, where he was no doubt calling in the troops. Fury was radiating from him in waves.

"Do you honest to God think that any of us would put the three of you in harm's way? Caleb's and Beau's heads just exploded when I told them they better get their asses over here pronto because their wives were *not* where they were supposed to be."

Anna-Grace looked helplessly at the two women whose husbands would likely burst through the door any moment now. Would they buckle under pressure from their husbands, who only wanted to keep them safe? Anna-Grace didn't fault them for that. But she refused to leave Eliza to her fate, and only Ramie could help locate her, because she could be anywhere.

The impressions that Anna-Grace had lifted from the man's mind hadn't given a location. Any recognizable place. All she'd seen was Eliza with that cloth over her face and the water being dumped over it repeatedly.

"We're not bailing on this," Ramie said softly. "We're going to find and rescue Eliza no matter what our well-meaning husbands think or say. Besides, if they give us too much grief, Ari can take care of that matter for us."

A slight mischievous gleam entered her eyes while Ari outright laughed. She turned a smug smile toward Anna-Grace.

"She's right, so stop fretting. As soon as we get a lock on her location, we're out of here. With or without the husbands."

Isaac let out an inarticulate string of what Anna-Grace assumed was a combination of curses and protests but none of the women paid him any heed.

Just as Wade strode from Eliza's room carrying the item of

clothing she'd worn last, before what she had on today, Caleb and Beau did indeed burst into the house, their expressions black, fear stark in their eyes.

"Don't you dare give that to her," Caleb barked, inserting himself between his wife and Wade.

Wade stared back at Caleb just as hard as Caleb was staring him down and neither man gave an inch.

Anna-Grace could admit being intimidated by Caleb Devereaux. Even Beau to an extent, although he'd been nothing but gentle and kind to her. But Wade was clearly unruffled by the dangerous glitter in Caleb's eyes. And, well, he did have three huge mountains for men, who were loyal to him and not DSS, so the odds were even. The victor would be decided by which side Ari aligned with since she could incapacitate them all if she wanted.

Anna-Grace shot a quick look Ari's way just to see if she'd faltered upon her husband's arrival. But what she saw was a good sign. Or at least she hoped.

Ari looked annoyed, though she tried to mask it. But Anna-Grace could pick up fleeting impressions from Ari's mind, including her repeated efforts to demonstrate that she was more than Beau's equal and she resented that he put her in a gilded cage where nothing could ever hurt her when in fact, it was she who could prevent anyone from ever hurting him. Or any other DSS agent, for that matter.

And part of her thought pattern was hurt, because a tiny part of her regarded his obstinance as lack of trust in her and her abilities, and she'd demonstrated on numerous occasions that she wasn't weak. She was capable of awe-inspiring things.

She could protect Eliza better than any man in this room. The women knew it, acknowledged it. But the men couldn't see past their fear to accept that.

Ramie shoved Caleb aside forcefully so she was once more standing in front of Wade. She didn't immediately take it from him but her lips were in a determined line even as Caleb pushed forward again.

She turned to her husband, her eyes hard.

"Do *not* interfere," she said in a voice that could possibly crack stone. "Eliza is in trouble. She could die. She could be dead already. And I'm the only one who can track her quickly enough to give us a chance of saving her. You do not make my decisions for me. Eliza helped me, no questions asked. She's never asked for a single thing in return. I will not abandon her because of your misguided notion that I'm too weak to suffer temporary agony in order to get back someone who is very dear to us all."

Caleb went stock-still. Anna-Grace wasn't even sure he was breathing. He seemed to be waging an internal war with himself because his thoughts were so chaotic and jumbled that Anna-Grace couldn't get a clear sense of what he was thinking. The only word that came from his subconscious was *no*! In a litany. Over and over. As if he couldn't bear the thought of her suffering even for a moment.

"That explains why Ramie is here," Beau said gruffly as he stared his wife down. "It does not explain why *you* are here."

She sent him a breezy smile as her words, though lightly said, still sent a chill down Anna-Grace's spine as they filled the room.

"Because I'm going to take these bastards out. They are no

match for me and my powers. They have one of our own. I would no sooner remain behind than I would allow harm to come to any person who is important to me."

Beau opened his mouth to argue, but Ari turned her back to him to look at Ramie.

At first, Ramie's movements were hesitant and then more forceful as she reached for the piece of clothing from Mathew's hand.

But Anna-Grace quickly caught the shared thought between Caleb and Beau, that once Ramie determined where Eliza was, they were in no way allowing any of the women to go anywhere and would have their men sit on them. Which was pretty stupid considering no one could keep Ari anywhere she didn't want to be. Anna-Grace rolled her eyes but she too sent the women a look and hoped they could sense what she was saying with her expression.

A small smile flirted at the corners of Ari's mouth. She was far enough away from Beau that she could whisper to Anna-Grace and not be heard.

"I may not be able to read minds, but I know my husband very well, and I knew from the beginning he was going to throw the mother of all hissy fits about me going anywhere. Even though I'm far more capable of death and destruction than any of his men are."

Her expression softened a brief moment as she looked over at her husband.

"It's just that . . ." Her expression became wry. "I can't fault him for his fear. I fear for him every time he goes out on a dangerous assignment. I almost didn't make it out alive when we last encountered these fanatics. So I understand his fear. But I've

grown stronger since then. I'm more self-aware. I know my limitations, or at least the ones I've discovered so far. But I also know
that there is more that I don't even know about, that I haven't
discovered yet. He's just going to have to deal because I'm not
staying home on this one."

Anna-Grace's admiration for Ari grew even greater. And she
only had to look at the resolve in Ramie's features to know that
she would present a united front with Anna-Grace and Ari.

If only Zack were back.

Anna-Grace went still. For a moment she didn't even
breathe as the shock of the unconscious thought floated through
her mind. When had she shifted from hatred and fear to a sense
of not feeling safe when he was gone?

She rubbed at her temple, but quickly lowered her hand
when she realized it was shaking. The thought had rattled her.
And right now she couldn't afford to be shaken. Not when
Eliza's life was at stake.

It seemed the entire room sucked in their breaths, the moment Ramie finally took the article of clothing from Wade's
hand. Caleb immediately stepped forward, inserting himself
between his wife and Wade. And becoming a barrier to the rest
of those assembled as well.

"Do not do anything to distract her," Caleb hissed out quietly. "Do not touch her or speak to her. It won't be easy, particularly if it's bad for Eliza, but everyone has to keep their cool or
Ramie suffers more."

A chill ran down Anna-Grace's spine. It was one thing to
imagine the horrors Eliza might be facing. Anna-Grace had
gotten a glimpse of something she didn't quite understand. All
she'd known was that Eliza was suffering. But it was a thought,

or rather a fantasy held by the man. One not yet performed, so there was no way of knowing if what she had glimpsed would even become reality.

It was another matter entirely to see in real time precisely what was happening to Eliza—and Ramie—and know that it was real. Not hypothetical.

Ramie let out a strangled gasp. Both hands went to her face and she struggled violently. She staggered and would have fallen had Caleb not caught her and eased her gently to the floor.

She lay on her back and it was evident she wasn't breathing. She struggled wildly, making choking, gurgling sounds. Anna-Grace froze in place as dread took over her entire body. It was eerily reminiscent of the image she'd picked up from the man's mind. Eliza had a cloth over her face. A wet cloth. What did it mean?

"Goddamn it," Caleb swore viciously. "Breath, goddamn it. Breathe Ramie!"

Just when it seemed Ramie would succumb and pass out, she suddenly sucked in a huge gasping breath. Her entire body heaved as if she were starved for oxygen.

"Go fuck yourself," Ramie said hoarsely, her voice odd sounding. She sounded almost like . . . Eliza. As though she were Eliza in this moment and transmitting to everyone present precisely what Eliza was experiencing, feeling, hearing and saying.

No sooner had the words escape her lips than she began struggling again and making those awful choking sounds, her hands raking at her face until Caleb defied his own order and held her hands back to prevent her from harming herself.

Her body writhed. Her chest arched upward and tears streaked from the sides of her eyes, disappearing into her hair.

"What the fuck is happening to Eliza?" Beau whispered, his rage terrible to look at.

"I can't tell you much," Anna-Grace said quietly. "But earlier today, when we were in the clinic, I picked up on the thoughts of the other man who was in the waiting room."

For a moment, everyone's attention focused solidly on her, their expressions intent. It made her uncomfortable, but she pushed past it because Eliza needed their help before it was too late.

"He hated Eliza. He was focused entirely on her. And his thoughts were not good ones. They were full of violence. And through his mind, I saw Eliza, lying on the floor as Ramie is now, but she had a cloth over her face. A wet cloth. And she struggled to breathe. I don't know what that means but it seems to match with what Ramie is currently experiencing."

"They're fucking waterboarding a woman?" Wade roared.

His reaction startled Anna-Grace and her gaze quickly swept to him. He was bristling with fury, his jaw set in a hard line, his eyes as cold as ice. His hands clenched and unclenched into fists at his sides. For a man who was always in control, he appeared to be on the very verge of losing it right now.

"Jesus," Isaac muttered. "Fuck!"

"Ramie. Ramie!" Caleb said more forcefully. "Come back to me, baby. I need you to come back and tell us where to find Eliza."

He gently stroked her hair, his expression worried and furious all at the same time.

From the moment Anna-Grace had explained what she'd seen, the entire room vibrated with terrible anger. And fear. For Eliza. There was a heightened sense of urgency. Everyone was tense and ready to explode into action.

It took several more long moments before Caleb was able to get through to Ramie and pull her from the grasp of Eliza's nightmare. Slowly her eyes focused on Caleb and then sorrow swamped her entire face, and the tears came faster than before.

"We have to go *now*," Ramie said hoarsely.

Even as she spoke, she shoved away from Caleb and scrambled to her feet.

Beau's face froze into an implacable expression even as he held his hands out.

"Tell us where, Ramie. We'll get her, but you, Ari and Gracie are staying here where it's safe."

The three women exchanged quick looks, once again confirming their solidarity. Then Ramie's chin came up.

"We aren't staying here or anywhere else," she said calmly. "We're going to get Eliza. She needs us, and we aren't going to let her down."

THIRTY

ONE could break a stone on the faces of all the men assembled, including Wade's, which surprised Anna-Grace because she'd thought he was accepting of the women's plan. But then maybe he, like Beau, had thought that the women would only provide pertinent information and then be left behind wrapped in cotton while the menfolk handled the dangerous stuff.

Annoyance gripped her but she shook it off. It didn't matter what the men wanted. Ramie would know where Eliza was and no one was going to keep Ari where she didn't want to be, so regardless of whether the men gave in gracefully or pitched a fit, the end result would be the same.

"I don't think you understand," Ramie said in a measured tone. "We aren't asking to go. We are going. Furthermore, I am the only person who has the knowledge of her location, so without me, you—and Eliza—are fucked."

"You're weak and hurting," Caleb said bluntly. "You need to

rest and recover from your ordeal. I can't—I won't—put you in harm's way, Ramie. I can't do it. It scares the hell out of me."

"My gift may not be as powerful as Ari's or as intuitive as Gracie's, but I can read things by touching items and you may need me to see, to discern information that we otherwise wouldn't have access to. And we need to pool all our resources so that we take out every last person in this organization so that no more people are hunted, tortured or murdered."

Ramie moved to stand beside Anna-Grace and Ari and they all stared resolutely at the men.

"They are no match for my powers," Ari said in a calm, confident tone. "They cannot hurt me."

"Bullshit!" Beau exploded. "They *did* hurt you! Or don't you remember the fact that you almost died! I was this close to losing you."

His eyes were so haunted that it hurt to look at him. It was then she grasped Ari's words about understanding Beau's concern for her. It was written all over his face. Fear. Abject terror.

"And I can read their thoughts," Anna-Grace said quietly, taking the focus from Beau's imminent meltdown. "Which means I can gather valuable information that we may otherwise not be able to get."

"And this is all why we're going," Ramie said firmly. "With or without you. It's your choice. But only I know where Eliza is and none of you are a match for Ari. Walking out of here will be a piece of cake with minimal effort on her part."

Caleb closed his eyes. "Fuck."

Wade shot him an incredulous look. "You aren't seriously considering this insanity, are you? Isn't one woman hurt enough? Hell, make that two since they already got to Gracie."

Beau's expression went utterly grim. "Oh, they got to Ari as well. They are due some serious payback."

"Then why the hell would you risk them again?" Wade roared.

"Okay, Superman," Isaac drawled sarcastically. "You lead the way. Tell us where Lizzie is. We're more than happy to take them out and keep our women out of harm's way."

Wade's eyes narrowed as he stared pointedly at Ramie. "Every minute you withhold the information you have is another minute Eliza undergoes indescribable pain. A minute that could mean the difference between her life and death. This is not the time to make a stand against the confines your husband places on you."

Ari bristled next to Anna-Grace, who flinched, wondering just how close Wade was skating the line. A pissed-off Ari certainly couldn't be good news. For Wade.

Ramie stared coldly back at Wade. "I don't give a damn what you think or think you know about my relationship, but get it through your head. We are not the ones wasting time. It's every one of you men. We're going. Right now. With or without you. So make your choice. And make it fast. Because Eliza is our friend, and we aren't leaving anything to chance when we get her back."

There was resignation in the eyes of every man present.

"Fuck," Beau muttered. "Goddamn it."

Anna-Grace shared a look of triumph with her new partners in crime. They all knew they'd won.

"Whoa, Superman," Isaac said, holding out a hand when Wade would have gathered with the others. "The women may have us by the balls but you don't and you aren't part of this mission. You aren't going."

"Fuck off," Wade said crudely. "Anna-Grace goes nowhere without me. Now stop wasting fucking time and let's go. I won't be a hindrance. I think you'll find me to be a valuable asset."

Wade's eyes grew cold. "I suffer no fits of conscience over killing a man who would waterboard a woman, who would beat a woman as they beat Gracie. In fact, I would relish it."

The other men exchanged raised eyebrows. Anna-Grace picked up on the current of surprise and unease as the men absorbed Wade's blunt statement.

"Okay, you're in," Beau said. Then he turned his stare to Ramie. "You win. It's a fucking rescue party. Everyone is going. So *now* can you tell us where we're going?"

As soon as the plane touched down in Houston, Zack turned on his cell phone and then frowned when he saw his screen light up with more than a dozen notifications. Unease gripped him as he saw they were all from Beau. Beau knew he was traveling, in the air, so if he'd been blowing up Zack's phone it wasn't good news.

He didn't bother reading texts or listening to voice mails. He went straight to the source and punched the call button.

"Come on, come on," Zack muttered when Beau didn't pick up on the first ring.

His gut was churning like hell and he had a tight grip on the handrest with his free hand. His knuckles were completely white and he wouldn't be surprised if he didn't end up breaking the damn piece of plastic.

"You on the ground?" Beau demanded after the third ring.

"Just landed."

"Fuck."

Zack didn't like this at all.

"What the hell is going on?" Zack demanded.

"It's Anna-Grace." Beau cursed again. "And Ari and Ramie. It's a fucking mutiny and there's not a damn thing any of us can do about it."

"You better start talking," Zack said in a deadly voice.

Beau sighed. "They got to Eliza. And there was this guy at the clinic when we took Gracie in for her checkup. Gracie said she was able to read his mind."

Zack frowned. Hadn't she said she'd lost that ability?

"What she saw, it wasn't good, and worse, it turned out to be true. The guy was imagining waterboarding Eliza. Ramie confirmed that when she touched an item of Eliza's. The women hatched this plan, you see. They pooled their resources and are hell-bent on getting Eliza back. Not that I'm not with them on that count, but goddamn it! I don't want them anywhere near these bastards."

"Back the fuck up," Zack said. "Tell me you aren't saying what I think you just said. You are *not* allowing any of the women and especially Anna-Grace to participate in a fucking takedown and hostage retrieval exercise! Are you out of your goddamn mind?"

"We didn't have a choice," Beau said harshly. "Ramie wasn't coughing up the info unless they came and Ari threatened to incapacitate us all and the three women would go on their own, so our only real choice was to let them come with us so that at least we could offer them protection."

Zack bit out a string of curses that had the neighboring passengers lifting eyebrows and staring agog at him.

"Tell me where, and then, Beau, swear to me you'll keep Gracie safe for me. Swear it on your life. You have to give me the chance to make things right with her and I can't do that if she gets herself killed."

"I know, man," Beau said quietly. "Believe me, I know. And we *will* protect her, all of us will—and Ari and Ramie—with our lives. Just get here as soon as you can. We could use all the backup we can get, because I have no idea how this is all going to go down once Ari unleashes her fury on them."

THIRTY-ONE

DARKNESS shrouded the empty-looking warehouse on the outskirts of the city. But Anna-Grace knew better. It wasn't empty. Somewhere in its bowels, Eliza suffered.

A knot formed in her stomach, dread gripped her in its menacing hold and squeezed until she could barely breathe. She clenched her fingers into a fist, anger rushing like fire through her veins. She was well acquainted with hate—or so she'd thought. But even when thinking she truly hated Zack, she knew there was still—would always be—a part of her that would never stop loving him. Or rather the young man she'd fallen in love with before he became another person entirely. Except . . . maybe he hadn't? But the hatred she'd used simply to survive, to keep it together the many times she nearly fell apart, because she knew if she ever did truly break down, she would never recover . . . that hatred didn't even come close to what she felt toward the people who'd beaten her, who'd nearly killed Ari and even now were putting Eliza through unspeakable torture.

Then she went utterly still as thoughts, a confusing mass of them, faintly brushed the edges of her mind. She closed her eyes while those around her stopped and she could sense their puzzlement—and impatience. They were in as much hurry to get to Eliza as Anna-Grace was.

Still, she focused on only those alien voices, narrowing her focus as well as she could since her gift was rusty from her not having been able to use it for so long.

Finally she managed to push everything else out and only listen to what was inside that building. Swearing vehemently, she suddenly strode forward because the sounds were just too faint. She needed to be closer to the source.

"Anna-Grace," Wade hissed, making a grab for her. "What the hell are you doing? You go *nowhere* without our say-so."

But Anna-Grace paid him no heed and picked up her pace, determined to get close enough to the warehouse, though she did keep to the shadows, avoiding the few places where light would expose her. The others had no choice but to follow or leave her without protection. Though she could feel their disgruntlement, even as they surrounded her protectively, leaving no part of her vulnerable, they didn't order her to keep back, unlike Wade. Perhaps they picked up on her urgency because every single DSS agent was staring sharply at her, waiting for her to tell them what she was picking up on.

And then, like before, she stopped. She halted so quickly, Capshaw ran into her back, and with a muttered curse he made a grab for her so she didn't topple forward. But she ignored him, her mouth widening in horror. She tried to speak, but nothing would come out. She slapped a hand over her mouth to stanch

the silent cry. She stared at the ominous-looking building—
hell—in horror.

"We've got to get in there. *Now*," she hissed, her entire body
shaking. Even her teeth chattered, sounding too loud. "They're
going to kill her. She's been of no use to them. They're even
angrier than before because a 'mere' woman wouldn't give in,
no matter what they did to her. They couldn't break her so now
they're going to kill her and send her body to DSS in pieces.
They feel they're wasting their time and should pursue an easier,
more vulnerable target."

Dane's expression became murderous, unbreakable and un-
forgiving. It was an expression that promised retribution. And it
was echoed by every one of Eliza's teammates.

"Of course she wouldn't break," Caleb said in a soft voice
that hinted of pain and guilt. "She's one of the toughest women I
know. And she's loyal to her bones. She would never sell out her
team, even if meant dying in the process."

Just hearing those words—a confirmation of what Anna-
Grace had already discerned on her own—sent panic shuddering
through her body. Her airway constricted to the point of pain
and light wheezing noises emanated from her flared nostrils.

It was Ari who jumped to the forefront, leaving Beau scrambling to catch up, swearing the entire way. Anna-Grace took off
just as quickly, close on their heels. Her heart was beating so fast
that she was light-headed and disoriented, but she couldn't afford to hold the others back. Not when Eliza had so little time
remaining.

Wade and Isaac both quickly caught up to Gracie, flanking
her, guns drawn, their eyes constantly darting back and forth,

looking for any movement, any possible way to pinpoint her location within the huge, sagging building.

It was startling to see Wade carrying a gun. How easily he fell in with the other operatives, though it shouldn't have surprised her. She already knew there was a lot more to him than his polished exterior.

Caleb pulled Ramie back with him, putting her behind him and Capshaw. But there was still a keen sense of unease between the men. It was killing them to put the women they loved at risk for even one moment.

It made her suddenly feel an outsider to something so very precious and all consuming. The memory of when she had that with Zack. And how she'd lost it all. Her dreams. Her passion for life.

But right now she'd give anything for him to be here, because with all of DSS's resources focused on bringing Eliza home—alive—she now knew in her heart that he simply wasn't capable of doing what was done twelve years ago. Was she crazy for even contemplating forgiveness so they could both move on, live their lives and try to find the kind of happiness they once shared?

She wanted Zack with her, because every time they were together she felt that nothing could ever touch her, or hurt her, or ever bring her down. Because he loved her. He could have had any girl he wanted with the snap of his fingers and yet he'd chosen a girl four years younger than him and it was like . . . magic. When you see that one special person who you know has just altered your entire destiny.

And then to find out she'd been completely wrong about the man she loved, the man she planned to marry and spend the rest of her life with, the man who'd discussed with her a desire for a large brood of children, at least six, and Anna-Grace couldn't have been happier on that day.

Because for the first time she'd truly seen a future with Zack. Not just one of dating, passing the time, doing menial and mundane things. No longer did she worry that when he was drafted into the pros she would be left behind. At that time, it had been understood—taken for *granted*—that their fates were intertwined. Unbreakable, endless, eternal. For all time.

Beau called a halt, close to one of the entryways to the warehouse. He turned to Anna-Grace, leveling a hard stare that held no malice. Just determination and not wanting to wait a second longer than necessary.

"What do you know, Gracie?" he asked in a low voice. "Did you see *where* in the building they are? Their position? How many?"

Regretfully she shook her head. "There were so many thoughts, some stronger than others, but they all have the same intent."

Ramie stepped forward, shrugging off Caleb's hand. "They are in the far left corner from our current position. But there is a lot of clutter and debris on the floor, and though it won't be difficult to get there, one sound and they'll know they have company."

"I need to be the first in," Ari said in a harsh tone.

Anna-Grace easily picked up on the other woman's thought patterns. They were loud, as though Ari were screaming into Anna-Grace's head. Sorrow, guilt, regret emanated from Ari in waves, but also rage, hatred, the desire to serve justice for the women these men had hurt.

Ari felt great responsibility for what had happened to both Anna-Grace and Eliza. The force of Ari's thoughts hurt Anna-Grace and made her ache to tell Ari she wasn't at fault. To somehow offer comfort and solace for what was not Ari's doing. But they didn't have time. Eliza didn't have time.

"Hell no, you aren't going in first!" Beau snapped, his eyes flashing as he stared his wife down.

His fear was overwhelming, filling Anna-Grace's mind until it shut out all else. Anna-Grace closed her eyes and narrowed her focus in an attempt to break free from the hold the people closest to her had on her mind and to extend outward and reconnect with the men preparing to murder Eliza.

When she reopened her eyes, she saw Ari turn her gaze, an aquamarine that held glints of gold, to her husband, those specks nearly glowing with ferocity.

"Yes, I do. Because once they know we're here, they'll kill Eliza. If I get close enough to her, I can erect a barrier around her so that she comes to no further harm while the rest of you take these assholes out."

The group went silent. Anna-Grace knew that Ari had scored a point. How could they hold her back at the cost of Eliza's life? But no one liked it. No one wanted any part of falling in behind the deceptively fragile-looking woman and allowing her to go directly into harm's way.

Clearly it went against their grain to, in essence, hide behind a woman. To take cover and allow her to risk so much. They were warriors. Protectors. They led, never followed.

A small smile curved the corner of Ari's mouth. "They can't hurt me. Remember? Or have you forgotten what happened the last time they tried to take me on?"

Beau flinched, his eyes raw with remembered pain. And for the briefest of moments before Anna-Grace once more shut out the thought patterns around her, she picked up on the memory of Ari lying limply in Beau's arms, soaked in blood and Beau begging her not to die.

A chill scuttled up Anna-Grace's spine and she shivered at the image so clear in Beau's mind. She didn't blame him for his reluctance. Not when he'd come so very close to losing the woman he loved.

"I think that what most of us remember is you very nearly dying," Beau said hoarsely.

"Just get on with it," Dane said sharply.

Anna-Grace jumped, startled by how shaken Dane sounded. He was always so . . . not human? He reminded her of a robot, programmed not to feel. Just to act. But right now he was extremely pissed. His nostrils flared and he was sucking in deep breaths through his nose.

And Wade as well. Anna-Grace couldn't ever remember Wade displaying any outward emotion and yet every cell in his body seemed to be rigid with impatience. He was clearly agitated and restless as though at any moment he'd barge through the doors, with or without the others.

Without waiting for Beau's okay, Ari walked to the door but stood back a short distance so that she wasn't touching anything. Even knowing of Ari's gift, it still made Anna-Grace's eyes widen when the locks and chains quietly lifted from their resting places and hovered in the air as though waiting for Ari's next command. Then they simply floated effortlessly away and settled quietly onto the ground several yards from where the group stood.

Ari closed her eyes and the doors slowly and soundlessly opened, just enough so they could each fit through. She disappeared within, Beau nearly glued to her backside. Dane was hot on Beau's heels and the others quickly followed. Anna-Grace was herded forward, she and Wade positioned between Isaac and Capshaw.

Sweat beaded and rolled down Anna-Grace's back as she concentrated on stepping around all the debris on the floor. The closer they got to where Eliza was being held, the more overpowering the thoughts broadcasting from her tormentors sounded in Anna-Grace's head.

Silently she urged Ari to hurry. Anna-Grace's pulse ratcheted up in response to the captors' own. They were preparing for the kill. Her stomach clenched and nausea welled, forcing her to swallow. They were *relishing* the idea of dismembering her while she was still *alive*.

She cupped a hand over her mouth and held it firmly there, afraid she was going to throw up at the horrific images that flashed through the men's minds. Each had his own idea or rather fantasy of how it should go down. No one wanted her end to be quick and merciful. She had embarrassed them by proving stronger than they could have possibly imagined and now they wanted revenge.

Ari turned her head, staring directly at Anna-Grace, obviously picking up on the sudden tension emanating from her. Her eyes glowed with an eerie light, growing brighter as she summoned her powers for the fight for Eliza's life. Then, as if understanding the depth of Anna-Grace's distress and knowing every second counted now, she turned and sprinted toward the back of the warehouse.

The DSS men took off after her, no longer caring whether they made a sound or not. Ari skidded to a halt and then gunfire erupted. Anna-Grace's heart nearly exploded. She could no longer make sense of the thought patterns because they were all panicked and none made sense. All she could translate was their fear. That had to be a good thing. They wouldn't be afraid if they thought they had the upper hand.

Anna-Grace ran toward Ari, determined that the other woman wouldn't be vulnerable while she wielded her powers like a warrior of old. Wade made a grab for Anna-Grace's arm, but she wrenched free, needing to see for herself that Eliza was alive.

And then suddenly she was flattened. Not by Wade but by Dane. His much bigger and heavier body covered her completely, pinning her to the floor.

"Do *not* distract her," Dane barked in her ear. "*She* is safe, but you are an open target. And she can't protect Eliza and herself if she has you to worry about too."

Anna-Grace tilted her gaze upward as much as was possible with a boulder on top of her. She sucked in her breath, staring in awe at the force of nature that was Ari.

It was as though a tornado had struck the warehouse, only there was no debris flying around. Only men.

Screaming, shrieking, terrified men. Men who'd terrorized an innocent woman.

Anna-Grace watched in awe as one by one, the men were thrown high up against the walls, seemingly glued to them. They struggled against invisible bonds but to no avail. Nothing else in the area was disturbed. No flying debris that could accidentally injure them. In fact, it looked as though no one had even been here.

Where was Eliza? Try as she might, Anna-Grace couldn't angle herself to see the entire area. What if they'd been too late? But no. Wait. There were no thoughts of satisfaction. No glee that the others were too late to save Eliza. There was only fear and rage . . .

Anna-Grace's pulse sped up. It was hard to breathe beneath Dane's weight but he hadn't moved. Fear was foremost in the minds of the men pinned against the walls. But a very close second was fury over being thwarted.

They hadn't killed Eliza yet!

"She's alive," Anna-Grace whispered up to Dane. "They're pissed because they didn't kill her in time."

It might have been her imagination, but it seemed as though Dane sagged in relief, weighting her down even more.

"Thank God," he said in a nearly inaudible voice.

Beau stood and immediately shouted orders. "As they drop one by one, make damn sure they're restrained and pose no threat. Ari can't withstand this for long."

Anna-Grace glanced anxiously up at Ari and caught her breath. Blood trickled from Ari's nose and ears and her brow was furrowed in obvious pain. Dane quickly rolled off Anna-Grace and bounded to his feet. Caleb issued a harsh command for Ramie to stay back and then he too rushed toward where the men were suspended in the air.

Now free, Anna-Grace scrambled up, her sole objective to get to Eliza. With the men incapacitated and the DSS agents ready to subdue them, *someone* had to see to Eliza.

Anna-Grace's heart thumped forcefully as she darted to the far corner where Eliza lay, still as death. Panic surged in her chest. What if they'd been too late? What if she'd died before her captors' macabre plans had even been carried out?

She stumbled and nearly fell and then let herself pitch forward so that she hovered over Eliza's body. Eliza was so very pale and for a moment it appeared as though she wasn't breathing.

Fear and grief formed a hard knot in her throat as she slipped her arm underneath Eliza's shoulders and lifted slightly, hugging the other woman to her chest.

"Don't die, Eliza," Anna-Grace choked out. "You're safe now. I swear it. Please don't die. You have to be okay. You're stronger than they are. You can't let them win. You *can't*."

There. There it was. The softest whisper of breath on Anna-Grace's neck. She sagged in relief and both women collapsed onto the floor. A low moan escaped Eliza's lips and then her eyelids fluttered weakly, but she clearly lacked the strength to open them fully and keep them that way.

"You're okay now," Anna-Grace whispered. "We're here to get you out. They'll pay for what they did to you. And me. And Ari. They won't hurt anyone ever again."

Anna-Grace knew she could very well not be stating truth. She didn't know what brand of justice DSS adhered to when it was *personal*. If simply turned over to the police and the justice system, they could end up going free.

The savage thought crossed her mind that she hoped they'd just kill them all. And then she was shocked to her bones that such a thought *had* crossed her mind. Yet she still didn't recant. They didn't deserve to live. Evil needed to die.

So absorbed in Eliza's well-being, Anna-Grace never saw it coming. But one moment Eliza was in her arms, cradled protectively, and the next Anna-Grace was painfully wrenched away, a strong arm wrapped around her neck. His strength was bruising and she struggled to breathe. He yanked her upward and backed toward the corner so there was no threat to him from behind.

Anna-Grace glanced frantically over the room, confused by how one of the men had gotten free of Ari's hold. But when her gaze settled on Ari, she understood. Ari had collapsed under the enormous strain of maintaining the barrier around Eliza and the captors pinned to the wall. All but the man with a choke hold on Anna-Grace were subdued.

Everyone froze and time stood still as the DSS agents stared warily at the man holding Anna-Grace. Beau hovered protectively over Ari even as his gaze was directed outward to detect any threat to his wife.

It didn't escape Anna-Grace that the man crushing her against him had her positioned so that no one could safely make a kill shot without risking shooting her in the process. He'd lifted her so that only the tips of her toes touched the floor and his head was behind hers.

"If anyone moves, she dies," the man growled.

It was then she registered the cool metal of a knife between his forearm and her chin. The edge was against her throat, so close that blood seeped from the shallow wound inflicted by the blade.

And his thoughts were broadcast in her mind as if he spoke them aloud. He *would* absolutely kill her. If he died, he was taking her with him. In fact, he considered his death inevitable. He didn't truly believe he'd escape unscathed. His resolve to exact a small measure of vengeance before he drew his last breath was as clear as a beacon.

Terror paralyzed her. She was so scared that she didn't even feel the nick of the blade. She was numb because she didn't see a way out of this. The others couldn't make a move or he'd slice through her neck. And Ari was out of commission, so she couldn't wield her deadly powers on this man.

"Give us the woman and you go free," Dane said, his features stony, eyes sparking with rage. "All we want are the two women. Let her go and you walk."

Her captor barked out a harsh laugh. "Do you think I'm stupid? She's my only insurance. If I let her go, I die. That's not going to happen. What *is* going to happen is that she and I are slowly going to leave. No one is to follow us. If even one of you takes so much as a step, she's dead. When I get to my vehicle, I'll let her go."

But Anna-Grace could clearly read his thoughts. He had no intention of letting her go. If he actually succeeded in getting to his vehicle—and doubt was still strong in him—he planned to slice her throat when they got to his car and then he would escape.

She sent panicked looks in the others' direction, silently pleading with them not to believe him. Not to let him take her. If they did, she was dead. God, she was dead no matter what because either way, whichever of the two possibilities prevailed, freedom or death, *she* wouldn't live. She closed her eyes in despair and suddenly wished with all her heart that she could have seen Zack one more time. That she'd given him more of a chance to explain—to defend—his part in her rape.

She opened her eyes again, but the room was blurred by the sheen of tears welling in her vision.

Wade gave a nearly imperceptible nod as if to say he understood. The others didn't look as though they believed the lie, even without her trying to convey his intentions.

Everyone was frozen in place. It was as if they were all holding their breaths. Anna-Grace didn't dare breathe too deeply. If she did, the blade would slide deeper into her flesh. And then she began to shake.

She squeezed her eyes shut and tried to rein in her utter terror. She couldn't lose it now. One wrong move and she'd end up killing herself with no help from the asshole holding the knife against her throat.

"Just take it easy and let up on the knife a bit there," Dane said in a controlled tone.

His words had the opposite effect because the man tightened his arm around her neck until she was wheezing for air.

And then the strangest thing happened. The man behind her jerked. His arm flew away from her throat and the knife fell off her skin but as he dragged his arm over her shoulder, the blade sliced just under her shoulder blade. Fire lanced through her veins and she let out a cry.

She registered the warmth of blood sliding down her back and her knees buckled. She went down, landing atop the man who'd been holding her at knifepoint.

The room burst into action and through her hazy consciousness she heard a single, explosive word.

"Gracie!"

THIRTY-TWO

ZACK watched in abject horror as the knife sliced down Gracie's back, blood immediately welling, bright red and rapidly staining her shirt. Dear God, what had he done? He was sure he could make the kill shot without endangering Gracie. He had the advantage of no one knowing he was there and so he'd set up the perfect angle. The only area he had a clear path to make a head shot was through the temple so there was no chance of a bullet penetrating Gracie from the front.

And he'd fucked it up. She'd been knifed anyway.

Around him the room erupted as his teammates scrambled to assess the injuries to Eliza and Ari. But Gracie was Zack's alone. No one else would touch her.

He ran full out toward where Gracie lay atop the man who'd hurt her. He had to force himself to calm his seething rage because Gracie needed tenderness. But he wanted to kill the motherfucker all over again. Wanted to rip him apart piece by piece for putting his hands on what was Zack's.

He fell to his knees beside Gracie and hovered anxiously over her, putting himself in her line of sight. Her eyes were open, but she looked fuzzy and unaware. In shock. Not to mention she was bleeding like a stuck pig.

He touched her cheek with a featherlight caress.

"Gracie?" he said, worry and fear making her name nearly inaudible.

But she must have heard because her gaze tracked to his until finally she found him.

He lifted her hand and pressed his mouth to her palm, so overcome he was momentarily at a loss for words.

"Hi," she whispered. "When did you get here?"

"Not soon enough," he said, unable to keep the bite from his voice.

He was still furious that Beau had allowed this. That he'd put Gracie in harm's way.

She gave a half smile, her expression woozy. "Oh, I don't know about that. I'd say you got here just in the nick of time."

She became completely solemn.

"He was going to kill me no matter what."

Zack closed his eyes. He didn't register that he was shaking until Gracie made a small sound of pain and he realized he was still holding tightly to her hand and he was jarring her entire body, causing aggravation to her wound.

Gently he lowered her hand to her abdomen and then simply rested his hand atop hers. He had no idea what was going on around him and he didn't care. He simply knelt there, drinking in the sight of Gracie. Alive. Hurt but alive.

"Eliza," Gracie said, her features contorted with worry.

Zack swung around to see Dane and Wade hovering over Eliza. Wade looked coldly furious and yet his movements were extremely careful as he touched Eliza's face, almost as though he was afraid of hurting her.

To his further surprise, it was Wade who gently picked Eliza up and cradled her in his arms. He barked an order to one of the others to get him a blanket to cover her. Zack lifted an eyebrow to see other DSS members paying heed to his order. But then, when it came to a fallen teammate, any pissing matches were permanently put on hold.

Beau had wrapped Ari in a blanket as well and held her there, in the middle of chaos, rocking her back and forth muttering, "Never again. Fuck this. You are never doing this again, Ari."

She issued a faint smile without opening her eyes and whispered back, "You know that's not true, but if it makes you feel better to say it, then by all means roar away."

Zack felt a clenching in the region of his heart. Then he turned back to Gracie and yelled for someone to bring a med kit. He needed to get her to a hospital fast. The others could do cleanup and get the information they needed from these assholes.

Already Isaac, Capshaw and Caleb were interrogating the men. They started with the first downed one. Dane strode over, evidently satisfied that Eliza was in good hands, and he was a scary sight. It wouldn't have surprised Zack if the guy pissed himself before it was over.

But when they questioned him about how many more there were, where they were based, where could they be found, all they received was a smug, triumphant smile.

Gracie stiffened beneath Zack and struggled upward, attempting to push herself into a sitting position although it obviously pained her.

"Whoa, baby, where do you think you're going?"

Gracie turned earnest eyes on him and uttered in a low voice.

"Tell them not to spend too much time on each man. Have them question them all. No matter what they say, I can pick up on what they think. And when they asked the first one where the others were and how many, he immediately thought of the place and numbers even though he refused to say anything. They all need to be questioned quickly so I can glean what information I can."

Zack stared at her in awe. Here she was, having already been beaten to hell and back by these bastards. Because of Zack and his history with this fanatical group. And yet she'd gone to the wall for Eliza at great risk to herself. Jesus, if Zack's aim had been the slightest bit off, and God knows he'd been shaking like a leaf, Gracie would be dead.

He touched her cheek again, the sting of tears burning his lids. Then he lifted his head and quietly called for Dane.

Dane looked annoyed at being pulled off interrogation duty but he came, his expression inquisitive.

"Gracie says to question them all and not spend too much time on each one. She said that when you questioned the first one, he immediately thought of where the others were and how many. If we can get that kind of information from all of them, we can take them out for good."

Dane's sharp gaze flew to Gracie. It seemed to soften and admiration was reflected in his eyes.

"Are you sure this isn't too much for you?" Dane asked quietly. "You should be getting to the hospital right now. You'll need stitches. A lot of them," he added wryly.

Gracie shook her head. "This is important. They'll never talk. But they don't know what I can do."

Dane merely gave a nod and then stalked back over, pulling Isaac, Capshaw and Caleb away. After only a few seconds of conversing, they left the first guy entirely and moved on to the second, asking him the same questions. Each time Dane would glance at Gracie and she'd give a nod to let him know she'd picked up information.

The longer it went on, the more worried Zack became. Gracie was growing visibly weaker and she was completely pale. She didn't even have the strength to hold herself up and so Zack slid his arms around her, anchoring her against his frame, careful not to cause her further injury by aggravating her wound.

His jaw was tight and pained from clenching his teeth so tightly. It was all he could do not to haul Gracie out of there that instant and get her to the hospital. But she soldiered on, focusing her efforts on each of the men being questioned.

As she'd said, no one talked. They sneered arrogantly at each question and told Dane to fuck off. Dane was barely keeping it together. The tension was explosive and it looked as though the team leader was precariously close to taking out each and every one of them.

When the last man was questioned, Dane strode back to Gracie and then hunkered down so he could look her in the eye. He took one of her hands and gently held it, his expression gentle.

"Tell me, Gracie. Can you identify these men? Are they the same men who took you and beat you?"

She swallowed hard but slowly nodded. "I remember them," she whispered.

Dane looked almost . . . disappointed. He sighed, resignation lining his face.

"I'd prefer to just kill them," he said bluntly. "God knows it's what they deserve. But if you and Lizzie can both identify them, then we have an airtight case against them. And we have the others to go after now. Were you able to get enough information? Can you tell us enough to find them?" he asked Gracie.

Again she nodded.

And then Dane was all business again. He stood and barked orders to call it in to Ramirez and Briggs. Two ambulances were called, though Gracie insisted that Eliza be the first to go.

Gracie kept gazing anxiously in Eliza's direction, worry etched in every facet of her face. In response to her silent question, Zack gathered her more closely in his arms and gently lifted her and carried her over to where Eliza was being tended to.

When Gracie saw that Eliza was conscious, she lost it. Tears streamed down her face and she struggled from Zack's hold and wrapped her arms around the other woman.

"Thank God," Gracie said brokenly. "Thank God. I was so afraid we were too late."

Eliza held on to Gracie for a long moment, tears glimmering in her own eyes. Then she carefully pulled away, also mindful of Gracie's injury, and she looked solemnly into Gracie's eyes.

"I understand I have you to thank."

Gracie shook her head vehemently. "No. It was Ramie who was able to find you. And Ari . . ." Gracie swiveled and waved her hand at the captive men in various places on the floor. "Ari did the rest."

Dane snorted. And then he sent pained looks in Caleb's, Beau's and Zack's directions.

"It would appear we have three Valkyries hell-bent on saving our asses at every turn."

Eliza grinned. "Is this where I say 'yay girl power'?"

Ramie pressed forward, though she was careful not to touch Eliza. Once had been enough for Ramie to endure Eliza's torture. She wasn't eager to repeat the experience.

"Are you truly all right, Eliza?" Ramie asked anxiously.

Eliza's entire face warmed as she glanced between Ramie and Gracie. "Thanks to very dear friends—*girlfriends*—yes, I'm fine. Can't say I won't have nightmares after this, but give me a few days and I'll be back on the job."

Then she glanced fiercely at Dane as if daring him to refuse.

"I want in on the takedown, Dane."

Dane's jaw clenched as though it were the very last thing he wanted to allow, but he nodded tightly. "Of course. But only after you've had a few days to heal. It will take that time to coordinate a takedown of this size. They have no reason to suspect we know where they're hiding. They believe they're invincible and impervious to any danger."

"That's where they're wrong," Zack said darkly.

"Are you all fucking crazy?" Wade roared.

Gracie jumped, startled by the outburst. Eliza turned warily to look at Wade, who up to a few moments ago had been cradling her in his arms against his chest. But of course as soon as Eliza had felt steady enough she'd put up one hell of a fight and demanded Wade put her down. Eliza wouldn't take kindly to appearing weak in front of her team. Even if that was the very last thing any of them would ever think about such a fierce woman.

Wade was seething in anger and he shook his head back and forth, harsh expletives muttered under his breath the entire time. But it was Eliza he directed his fury at.

"You were just goddamn tortured. They *waterboarded* you. You're in no condition to mount a full-scale assault on this organization. What the fuck are you thinking? You should be in the goddamn hospital, for Christ's sake!"

Eliza smiled. "That's the way I roll, I guess."

"You need a fucking keeper," Wade muttered. "Someone with more sense than you so he can keep you out of trouble."

Eliza snorted. "I'd like to see a man try it."

Wade's eyes glittered at the challenge in Eliza's voice and he stared her down but Eliza didn't budge one inch. Defiance was bright in her eyes but so was anger and rage. Zack could well understand Eliza's need for revenge. It was a bitter, all-consuming taste in his mouth as well. He wanted these assholes to pay for every single woman important to DSS who'd been hurt by complete cowardice.

Eliza glanced at the group around her as though searching for someone. Fear and concern furrowed her brow.

"Ari? Where is Ari? Is she all right?" Eliza asked in a panicked tone.

"She's fine, Lizzie," Dane soothed. "Beau is seeing to her now. It was hard on her. It always is. But she seems to be recovering more quickly this time."

Eliza sagged in relief. She hugged herself tightly as though she were cold. Wade slipped his arms around her from behind and pulled her against him so she'd absorb his body heat. She acted as though she didn't even notice.

She closed her eyes wearily. "I'd never want my freedom at the cost of one of your lives. I couldn't bear it."

"Too fucking bad," Dane said rudely. "You risk your life for us all the goddamn time. So suck it up and deal when we do the same for you."

Eliza smiled ruefully. "Okay, boss man."

Then she frowned as if only just realizing that Wade was surrounding her, his arms wrapped tightly, trapping her against his body. She immediately shoved away, putting distance between them, and she scowled her displeasure at Wade.

In the distance the wail of multiple sirens sounded. Dane tensed and glanced back at the contained prisoners.

"Fuck, this is going to be a long goddamn night," Dane grumbled. "I hate paperwork and dealing with cops, even if they're on our side. I just hope to hell no reporters show up."

THIRTY-THREE

ANNA-GRACE lay on her side on the stretcher in the emergency room, half dozing, fuzzy from the pain medication. She wasn't complaining, though, because her wound required a lot of stitches and she was glad for the most part she'd been completely oblivious to what was going on.

It wasn't hurting, a fact she was thankful for. Because when the adrenaline had worn off in the aftermath of Eliza's rescue, the pain had screamed through her back, catching her completely off guard. She'd nearly hyperventilated on the way to the hospital, until the paramedic administered oxygen and then very nicely injected morphine into her IV.

The rest of the ride was a warm, fuzzy haze, her only memory arriving at the hospital and Zack's head appearing above hers when they unloaded her stretcher from the ambulance. He'd been grim and worried and lines of strain were evident in his face.

She'd given him a goofy smile and said, "Don't be sad, Zack. I'm a Valkyrie."

She nearly groaned as that memory came back to her. God, could she have been any more ridiculous? And apparently she hadn't been particularly quiet with her declaration because she'd heard laughter from several different sources.

Despite not minding the state between awake and sleeping, she forced her eyelids open and saw Zack slumped in a chair right next to the head of her bed. Her arm was outstretched and his hand was curled around hers through the bars of the bed rail.

She studied their clasped hands a moment, pondering how right it felt. As though they hadn't spent the last twelve years apart.

As if sensing her silent perusal, his eyes opened and then he became more alert, leaning forward so his face was closer to hers. With his free hand he smoothed his palm over her cheek, so much love and concern in his eyes that for a moment she couldn't breathe.

This was not the look of a man who'd brutally betrayed her.

And so she had to ask. Because she had to know. It was suddenly the most important thing in the world to her.

"Zack?" she said softly.

"Yes, baby, I'm here. Are you all right? Are you hurting?"

She shook her head but stopped when that *did* hurt.

"Where did you go?" she asked in a quiet voice.

He didn't pretend to misunderstand, nor did he ask for clarification. For a moment his eyes went so hard that she shivered. His hand trembled around hers and he swallowed several times as if trying to compose himself.

"I intend to tell you all about it," he said in a controlled voice. "There's a lot we need to talk about, Gracie. A lot you have to know. But not here. Please give me that much. The doctor said you'll be discharged soon. They aren't keeping you overnight. Just sending you home with antibiotics and pain medicine and instructions to rest and not aggravate your wound, which I fully intend to ensure you do. I swear to you, I will tell you everything when we're alone."

There was a pleading look in his eyes and for a moment he looked so very vulnerable. Her heart clenched and she squeezed his hand just to have an anchor.

"Okay?" he whispered.

"Okay," she whispered back. "How is Eliza? And Ari?"

His lips quirked into a half smile. "Eliza is raising hell because they want to keep her overnight for observation and she's not having it. However, Wade has threatened to sit on her and they're currently in a standoff and neither is budging. The rest of us are just staying the hell out of the way. I think Wade is going to win this one."

Anna-Grace smiled, imagining well the clash of those two stubborn wills.

"And Ari?" she prompted.

"Beau took her home," Zack said. "She was okay. Just very weak."

Anna-Grace heaved a sigh of relief.

"You scared the hell out of me," he said starkly, abruptly switching the focus to her. "Don't ever do that again, Gracie. My heart can't take it. Do you have any idea how helpless I felt knowing I couldn't get to you in time? Why in the hell did you do it?"

She shrugged. "It was the right thing to do."

Zack closed his eyes. "Jesus."

"I couldn't not do anything," she said defensively. "Eliza helped me. She was there because of me. Being tortured because of me."

She couldn't control the pain in her voice and she broke off, averting her gaze from Zack.

"For whatever reasons, my powers reasserted themselves when Eliza needed us the most. Maybe it was God's way of saving her. I don't know. But I knew that between me, Ramie and Ari we could find and save Eliza, and I was not going to just sit there while they killed an innocent woman. Especially a woman who has given so much of herself for others."

Zack smiled ruefully. "I shouldn't have even asked. Of course you would. You're incapable of turning a blind eye to anyone in need."

He caught her gaze and again she was consumed in a wave of so much love that she trembled under its force.

"You're still my Gracie," he whispered. "You haven't changed a single bit from that beautiful girl I fell in love with so many years ago. That I still love. Will always love."

She stared at him in shock, incapable of responding. How could she respond? What was she supposed to say?

She opened her mouth, but nothing came out. It just remained open as she stared helplessly at him.

He pressed a gentle finger to her lips. "Shhh. Not now. You don't have to say anything right now. It will wait. Until we're home and I can explain everything."

The door to her room opened and a nurse came in smiling at Gracie. "Are you ready to go home? I have your discharge instructions and your prescriptions. As soon as I take out your IV, you'll be all set. Just make sure you go straight home and rest. No strenuous activity whatsoever. If you put any strain on those stitches, they'll come out, and we don't want that happening."

The rest was a blur because all Anna-Grace could focus on were Zack's words. The vow in his voice. The utter sincerity ringing in his words. And how very close she'd come to telling him she loved him too.

And if that wasn't messed up, she didn't know what was.

THIRTY-FOUR

THE drive home was silent and strained. Anna-Grace kept looking sideways at Zack but he stared straight ahead, his hands clenched tightly around the steering wheel. His anxiety was palpable and once again she was struck by the vulnerability he displayed.

The crazy thing was that she wanted to reach over, take his hand and tell him it would be all right. That everything would be all right. But she couldn't tell him what she didn't know to be absolute truth.

And so she sat, as silent as him, and willed the drive to go faster.

She recognized the safe house as they pulled in. The same place they'd taken her after she'd been abducted. No other cars were there, which meant they would be alone. She swallowed nervously as Zack firmly told her to stay put. Then he got out and walked around to her side and opened the door.

He helped her out, careful not to jar her shoulder, and then he wrapped his arm around her waist and they walked slowly to the front door. Once inside he led her into the living room and settled her at an angle on the couch so she wasn't leaning back against her stitches.

And then he began to pace. For a long while he was silent as though he were collecting his thoughts and deciding what to say. Sensing just how important this was, she waited quietly, watching for when he would begin.

He dragged a hand through his hair and finally turned to her, his eyes raw and ravaged with grief and sorrow.

"I shouldn't put you through this right now. God knows it's the worst possible time. You've been through hell and here I am about to put you back through hell all over again. But I can't wait, Gracie. Because every day that passes that you believe I did something so repulsive and ... evil ... a part of me dies. I'm a bastard for doing this and I hope you can forgive me when all is said and done, but I'm a bastard who loves you with every breath in my body. And I can't, I just can't let you believe the worst of me a minute longer."

She sucked in her breath because yes, now she could read his mind, when before she couldn't. And she could sense undying sincerity. And love. His thoughts were chaotic, a jumbled mass of pain, anger and regret. But at the forefront of everything was love. For her.

And he'd always loved her. He'd never stopped. Oh God. Had she been wrong? Had she done this to them by not having faith in him?

"Tell me," she managed to say. "I have to know. I *need* to know."

And so Zack related every single detail of his trip to Tennessee. His confrontation with Stuart and then with his father. And finally the other two men involved. She was already numb, completely frozen by all he said, but then he took his phone out of his pocket and placed it on the coffee table in front of her before sitting down beside her on the couch.

"If it's too much, just tell me to stop. If it upsets you or hurts you too much, it stops. But this is proof, Gracie. In their own words. Stuart's confession. My father's. I didn't bother with the others. I was too bent on killing them."

Anna-Grace swung her gaze to him in alarm. "You didn't."

There was a savage fire in Zack's eyes. "I wanted to. God, I wanted to. But no, I didn't. I wouldn't doubt they spent a few days in the hospital though."

She stared at the phone as though it were a snake prepared to strike. Could she do this? Could she listen to the details of her rape all over again?

And then sudden peace descended and settled over her. Yes. She was ready. Because if what Zack said was true, then that recording absolved him of any participation in the crime. And if that was also true, then she'd made a terrible, terrible mistake that they'd both paid for over a very long time.

"Play it," she said hoarsely.

Slowly Zack reached over and pressed a button on his phone. She flinched when Stuart's voice filled the room. She closed her eyes, trying to shut out the instant bombardment of images from that day.

When the recording got to Zack's conversation with his father, she knotted her fist and it flew to her mouth, pressing deeply as she tried to prevent her sounds of pain from escaping.

Somewhere in the midst of it all, Zack's arm slid gently

around her waist and he pulled her to his chest, gently rocking her back and forth as the vile words his father had spewed rang in her ears.

"Stop! It's enough!" she cried.

Zack immediately ended the recording and then turned to Anna-Grace with dread and so much pain in his eyes.

He slid to the floor in front of her, getting on his knees, taking both her hands in his.

"I am so sorry, Gracie," he said, tears glimmering in his eyes. "I left you unprotected. I allowed this to happen to you. I should have taken you with me or just stayed with you and not gone away to college. I don't know that you'll ever be able to forgive me. God, I can't forgive myself. But I've never stopped loving you. I've never stopped looking for you. I've never stopped hoping that one day we'd be together again."

Tears slipped hotly down Anna-Grace's cheeks. Oh God. So much time wasted. So many years. If only . . . There were so many if-onlys. And no way to take back the past. No way to undo it all and start all over again.

Or could they?

"How do you not hate *me*?" she said in a stricken voice. "I didn't trust in you. I've hated you for twelve years. I said horrible, horrible things to you. Oh God."

She yanked her hands from Zack's and covered her face as sobs welled from her throat.

Zack was there in an instant, enfolding her in his strong embrace. He simply held her, rocking her and brushing kisses over the top of her head.

Then he gently pried her hands away from her face and

slowly lowered his mouth until it hovered just over hers. And he pressed his lips so very gently to hers.

It was a sense of homecoming so powerful, so overwhelming that it very nearly shattered her composure. Nothing had ever been so sweet. Not before. His lips moved with exquisite tenderness until her lips parted and his tongue brushed against hers.

She inhaled deeply, taking in his scent, oh so familiar and haunting. And she kissed him back, allowing all her grief, sorrow, regret and . . . love . . . to bleed into that kiss.

"I could never hate you, Gracie," Zack said against her lips. "Never. I've always loved you. I always will. Can you forgive the past? Will you give me another chance to make things right between us? I swear to you I'll spend the rest of my life making you happy. Protecting you. Loving you. And our children."

She leaned forward, pressing her forehead to his as more tears slid down her cheeks. "I have nothing to give you, Zack. They took it. I had nothing. I was nothing. All I had that was precious to me was my virginity. That was all I could give you when you gave so much to me. And they took that. How could you want me after what they did?"

"Oh baby, no," Zack said in an aching voice.

He pulled her away so he could look her in the eye, but she couldn't meet his gaze. He tipped her chin upward with his finger until she was forced to look at him.

"Read my mind right now, Gracie. See inside the heart of me. And then you tell me that I don't love you. That I don't want you with every breath in my body."

She hesitated, a little afraid to hope. But his gaze was steady and sure and his eyes so very warm and loving.

She released the tight constraints she'd put in place and allowed herself into his mind and she was immediately flooded by a wave of love so strong that she swayed. There was so much he was thinking. About their future. Their wedding. The children they'd one day have. And how he looked forward to waking up every single day with her next to him.

It was simply too much.

She leaned into him again, grasping him tightly as though she feared he'd simply disappear. Her sobs were raw and horrible sounding. Guttural, coming from the very depths of her soul.

"I'm sorry," she said in a terrible voice. "I'm so sorry, Zack. Oh God, I'm sorry. You should hate me. I didn't trust you. I wasted so many years hating you for something you never did. And yet you ask *me* for forgiveness."

Zack stroked her hair and then buried his face in the strands and she felt the warmth of his own tears against her head.

"There is nothing to forgive, Gracie. We were set up. Of course you believed that I orchestrated it. That's what they wanted. They are to blame. Not you. Not me."

She lifted her head, her vision watery as she stared back at him.

"I love you," she whispered. "I never stopped loving you. Even when I hated you, a part of me knew I'd always love you and mourn the loss of what we had."

Zack seemed to crumble before her very eyes. Profound relief and for the first time . . . hope . . . shone in his eyes.

He cupped her face in his hands and his expression became very serious.

"You didn't give them your virginity, Gracie. They took it. They took something very precious, but you know what? Virginity is more than a thin barrier that proclaims a woman's innocence. And on our wedding night, when you give yourself to me, you will have given me a gift more precious than any other. Because it *will* be our first time. Together. And just as we were going to wait before, I want to wait now. Until you're my wife. I want our first time together to be as man and wife."

She stared at him in wonderment. "Are you asking me to marry you?"

He laughed, though it sounded more like choked emotion. "Apparently not very well."

He went back to one knee and gathered her hands in his, his expression somber and so very serious.

"Gracie, will you marry me? Will you live with me and love me until this life is over and the next begins? Will you have my children and fulfill all the dreams we ever dreamed?"

She pulled one hand free and cupped it against Zack's bristly, unshaven jaw. For the first time in so very long, she felt . . . free. Happy. Optimistic. As though a terrible wrong had been righted and the world was as it should be once more.

"Oh yes," she breathed. "Yes, I'll marry you, Zack. I love you. I'll always love you."

He pulled her into his arms, ever mindful of her shoulders, and he simply held her as his body heaved against her. "Thank God," he whispered. "Thank God."

She closed her eyes, absorbing the sense of rightness, feeling true peace for the first time in twelve long years.

"I don't want to wait," he said gruffly. "But I also want you to have the wedding we always planned. I won't have it any other way. We'll invite our friends here, but we're getting married in a church, by a preacher, and you are definitely wearing white."

"How about we wait just long enough that I get these stitches out," she said with a smile. "It would kind of suck not to have our wedding night because I'm still recuperating."

He smiled back at her and suddenly she saw the boy she'd fallen in love with when she was just a young girl. It was as if the years fell away and his eyes glowed with happiness and renewed hope.

"Deal," he said. "Besides, it'll take that long to plan a proper wedding, and I plan to pull out all the stops."

THIRTY-FIVE

"WHY am I so nervous?" Gracie asked breathlessly, as butterflies scuttled around her belly.

She stared into the full-length mirror and saw a woman she didn't recognize. And yet, she also saw a sixteen-year-old girl who was finally getting the day she'd dreamed of.

Eliza and Ari flanked Gracie, their smiles broad and their eyes sparkling with excitement and happiness. It was contagious. No one in the small bridal room of the church was immune to the electric current of joy.

"You look beautiful," Eliza said, a sheen of moisture reflecting wetly in her eyes.

"Don't you dare make me cry, Eliza!" Ari admonished, scrunching her face in various ways to prevent her own eyes from tearing. "Weddings always make me cry, and this one more than most."

Gracie did her own blinking and then held her eyes wide open to dry. Her hair and makeup was perfect, but then it had taken over an hour to get it that way. And she wanted to look her absolute best when she walked down the aisle to Zack. Finally to Zack.

At the mere thought of him, the butterflies swarmed again, giving her a slight queasiness that had her breathing in through her nose.

"You're not going to puke, are you?" Eliza asked anxiously. "Because that dress is just too gorgeous to be puked on. I'll wrap you in a garbage bag if I have to, but the dress must be saved!"

Ramie and Ari laughed and Ramie poked her head between the mirror and Gracie, giving Gracie a final once-over, her brow furrowed in concentration as she studied every detail of Gracie's appearance.

Then Ramie smiled. "You're all set."

She reached for Gracie's hand and gathered it tightly in hers. When Gracie put her other hand on top of Ramie's and squeezed back—a gesture of thanks and unity—Ari and Eliza put their hands over Gracie's and the four women stood there in solidarity.

The last few months hadn't been the easiest. DSS had made three hits on facilities utilized by the fanatical group that had caused Ari, Gracie and Eliza so much pain. And not only had Gracie, Ari and Ramie been left behind to worry for the men of DSS, but they'd had to worry about Eliza as well, because she'd refused to be left behind.

Only one man had been taken back, shoved before Gracie under the guise of her identifying him. She hadn't even had to have him questioned. His defeat and rage over their entire organization coming down at DSS's instigation was as clear as if he'd said his thoughts aloud.

Gracie had merely nodded at Zack, Dane and Beau and then closed her eyes, her hands trembling. It had been over then.

She opened her eyes and once more she was in the bridal room, her dearest and only friends all gathered around her, staring back at their reflection in the mirror.

"Surely this is the granddaddy of all selfie opportunities?" Eliza announced. "No one move!"

Eliza reached back and fumbled with her phone and then inserted it in front of them, angling it and lifting it so it captured as much of them in the photo as possible.

"Think I'll send this to Zack now," Eliza said with an impish grin. "It'll drive him crazy."

"The groom is not supposed to see the bride before the wedding," Ari reprimanded.

Ramie snorted. "He drove her to the church this morning. While Zack is refreshingly traditional in many ways I wouldn't have expected, not seeing his bride for any extended period of time is not one he's going to be down with."

The other women laughed and Eliza sobered, once more gripping Gracie's hand.

"He went far too long without seeing the woman he loved," Eliza whispered. "One can't blame him for not ever wanting to do it again."

"She's going to make me cry," Ramie muttered in disgust. "Who would have thought our Lizzie was such a romantic?"

A knock sounded on the door, causing the women to jump and then they dissolved into laughter. Eliza sent a sheepish look toward the door and hung back.

"I'll, uh, let one of you get that. It'll be Wade, come for Gracie no doubt. He still hasn't exactly forgiven me for the incident involving his arm, so, uh, I'll just stay out of his sight for now," Eliza hedged.

Ramie snorted and she and Ari both opened the door to reveal Wade, who was indeed standing there, an expectant look on his face. Gracie pressed her lips together as her gaze slid over the sling wrapped around his left arm. She glanced sideways to Ari and Ramie, hoping for help. The last thing she wanted to do was even send a half smile in Wade's direction.

But they were no help. The traitors. Ari actually turned her head and Ramie was making suspicious noises behind the hand covering her mouth.

Wade scowled at all of them, which only caused Ramie and Ari to lose what little control they had left and they burst out laughing.

Traitors.

"So much for their makeup," Gracie muttered.

"I have no idea what the hell's so funny anyway," Wade growled.

Gracie managed to keep a straight face. Barely.

Wade had been pissed when Eliza insisted on being part of the takedown. He'd dressed her and her DSS coworkers down and when that didn't work, he somehow managed to finagle his way onto the team since in his words none of them had "the goddamn sense God gave a mule."

Convinced that Eliza was going to get herself killed, Wade had shadowed her every movement, in the process driving Eliza absolutely insane. And in the end, Wade ended up taking a bullet meant for Eliza, hence the bandaged arm and sling. He wasn't pleased to say the least, nor had he let Eliza forget about it.

"Tell the little coward that she's going to miss the ceremony if she doesn't come out of hiding," Wade said loudly.

He also knew just how to push her buttons.

Gracie exchanged sighs and aggrieved looks with the other women, and Gracie pulled at Wade to get him out of the doorway before the explosion from Eliza that was sure to come.

Once in the vestibule, all ribbing was forgotten and even Eliza came out to hurriedly arrange Gracie's dress. When all was perfect, the three women lined up in front of Gracie and the doors were opened partway—enough for them to walk through without revealing Gracie behind them to the occupants of the church.

Wade squeezed Gracie's hand, her arm looped through his, her hand resting on his palm.

"You look beautiful, sweetheart," he murmured. "Zack is one lucky son of a gun."

She smiled radiantly up at him, her eyes going moist with a sheen of tears. "Thank you, Wade. For everything."

He leaned down and brushed his lips across her cheek and anchored her arm more firmly against his body.

"You ready?" he whispered. "That's our cue."

Gracie sucked in a deep breath, squared her shoulders and squeezed his hand.

"Ready," she said, lifting her head as the doors opened to her future and finally closed on her past.

Zack stood at the front of the church, fingers balled into tight fists as Ramie, Ari and Eliza slowly walked down the aisle and then took their places across from where he stood. Behind him, standing for him, were Beau, Caleb and Dane.

There weren't many guests in the small church, but all were family. A family that had banded together to ensure that the women they loved never suffered at the hands of such evil again.

As much as Zack had wanted to marry Gracie as soon as humanly possible and to never let her go again, she'd needed time to heal, but most important, Zack refused to have their marriage ceremony until they were certain that every last person responsible for so much pain and death were extinguished.

His and Gracie's wedding day would be perfect and there would be no worry of retaliation. Their thoughts would only be of each other and the future they'd once mapped every inch of, a future they'd both thought lost to them. But no, it had only been on hold as fate waited for them to find their way back to one another.

The doors opened again as music swelled and filled the sanctuary. Zack's breath caught when he saw Gracie for the first time in her wedding gown.

She stood beside Wade, her smile as big as the sun, her eyes sparkling with joy. And then Wade slowly began walking her down the aisle.

Zack hastily wiped at his burning eyes, determined to hold it together and not ruin Gracie's day. It had touched him and Wade both that Gracie had asked Wade to give her away. No longer did Zack harbor any animosity toward the other man. He'd been a source of support Gracie had desperately needed, and well, he'd also taken a bullet meant for Eliza, which meant that the entire DSS organization owed him their gratitude for saving someone so important and beloved by all.

He shouldn't have bothered trying to disguise his emotion. As Gracie drew closer to Zack, he saw the shimmer of tears in her eyes and then watched as they traced silently down her cheeks.

Her gaze was locked solely on him, as if they were the only two people in the room. She walked toward him with no hesitation, Wade at her side. But when she reached Zack, she slipped her arm from Wade's but then took his hand, holding on to it for a long moment as she looked away from Zack for the first time and met Wade's soft gaze.

"Thank you for being the friend I needed so very much," she whispered.

To Zack's shock, he saw a faint glimmer in Wade's eyes, but then it was gone, leaving Zack to wonder if he'd imagined it.

Wade lifted his hand from Gracie's grasp and gently cupped her cheek, wiping the thin line of moisture away with his thumb.

"Be happy, Anna-Grace," Wade said quietly. Then he leaned down and kissed her softly on the cheek.

Afterward, he let his hand fall and once more curled his fingers around Gracie's hand, but this time he lifted her hand toward Zack. As Zack slipped his fingers through hers, Wade pinned him with his gaze.

"You are getting a rare and precious gift, Covington. Take care of her."

"Always," Zack vowed in a somber voice.

Wade stepped back and then seated himself on the front pew where other members of DSS sat.

Zack knew he and Gracie should turn to the preacher, who was waiting to begin the ceremony. But he couldn't break the magic of this moment, one he'd dreamed of for so very long.

"I can't believe you're standing in front of me in your wedding dress," Zack whispered, nearly choking on the words. A knot of emotion swelled rapidly in his throat, threatening to render him incapable of any speech. "I love you, Gracie. And never, ever will I forget today."

Another tear rolled down her cheek, but her smile—God. It was like being enveloped by the sun after a long, harsh winter. And her eyes. Liquid brown. So warm that he'd never feel the cold wrought by complete emptiness.

Unable to help himself, he framed her face in his hands and leaned down to capture her lips in a long, sweet kiss.

Hoots and laughter rose from the others. And then the ribbing began.

"Do you need cue cards there, buddy?" Beau asked from behind him. "I'm pretty sure that part comes *after* 'you may kiss the bride'."

Zack broke away to glare at all of them. "I'll kiss my bride any damn time I want to."

"Amen to that," Caleb muttered and was greeted by another round of amused laughter.

Beau shrugged. "The man does have a point. I do kiss my bride any damn time I want to."

Ari blew her husband a kiss from across the aisle.

Zack smiled down at Gracie, whose tears were gone thanks to laughter. She was so radiant that she glowed like a beacon. A ray of sun. His sunshine.

"What do you say we get properly married?" he asked with a grin.

Then to his surprise, Gracie defied ceremony and circumstance as she leaned up on tiptoe and fused her lips to his. All else fled his mind under the sweetness of her kiss. And when she finally pulled away, he was hard-pressed to remember his own name, much less what he was supposed to do next.

Smiling, she tugged him toward the pastor. "This is the part where we both say 'I do'."

"I do," he whispered so only she could hear. "I do, I will, I always will. And *never* will we be parted again."

THIRTY-SIX

ZACK stood in the bay window overlooking the ocean and inhaled the salty air in an effort to settle his nerves. It felt as though someone had their fingers wrapped permanently around his neck in a choke hold. For God's sake, even his palms were sweaty, and his fingers shook when he unrolled them from the tight fists formed at his sides.

He closed his eyes, lifting one of his fists to rub his hand through his hair and then he gripped the back of his neck with his palm, absently massaging as he tried to get himself together.

Gracie had been nervous the moment they got inside their suite. The tension was palpable when she'd excused herself to go change for bed.

Not wanting to move too fast or shove himself in her face from the start, instead of stripping down—as one might have done when about to embark on his wedding night—he kept his boxers and socks on.

He glanced ruefully down at his sock-covered feet and

shook his head, a light chuckle escaping. Socks? Really? The boxers were understandable. The socks were just a result of his own nerves. He quickly toed out of them and kicked them underneath the chair by the window.

He had to get his shit straight before he completely lost it and ruined the night for him and Gracie before it even began. This would be more difficult for Gracie than it ever would be for him. But at the same time, what if he made the wrong move? What if he ended up traumatizing her? The last thing in the world he wanted was for their wedding night to be a disaster because he made some boneheaded move or by him simply not knowing the right thing to do at the right time.

The latter was the more distinct possibility. He felt clumsy and inept, just like the virgin he would have—and should have—been for Gracie. He broke his promise to her but she'd kept her promise to him.

Tonight Gracie would give herself to him and only him. The knowledge that he was the first and only man who would be given such a precious gift nearly brought him to his knees. He was humbled and . . . ashamed.

"Zack?"

Gracie's wavering voice reached him, and he turned swiftly around, cursing the fact that he'd been so caught up in his deep shame that he'd failed to hear Gracie come out of the bathroom. He should have been there waiting for her, to reassure her instead of her having to be so vulnerable by, in essence, making the first move.

All the breath left his body in a long exhale when his gaze fell over her. His mouth went dry and his heart sped up until he could feel the hard thud against his chest.

She was wearing a white silk, lacy gown that fell in waves down her body to swirl at her feet. Only the tips of her dainty toes peeked out from beneath the hem. Bright pink. He wanted to kiss each and every one of those sweet toes. Just as he wanted to kiss and touch every inch of her satiny skin.

But the bodice. Good Lord, but that was a gown destined to give a man heart failure. He was standing, speechless, staring at her like a prepubescent boy seeing naked pictures of a woman for the first time.

The neckline plunged in a deep V between her breasts, all the way to the indention of her belly button. The material clung strategically to her breasts so they weren't bared, but the lace was sheer and he could see the shadow of her nipples. He could see their shape puckering against the gown.

Her lips trembled as they formed a smile, and he finally kicked himself into gear so he didn't remain there gawking at her like a moron for the entire night.

He had to form the words twice, because his first effort to speak just didn't happen.

"You are the most beautiful thing I've ever seen in my life," he said in a hoarse voice roughened by emotion.

She blushed but her eyes lit up and sparkled, her smile widening at his reaction.

"I'm afraid to touch you," he admitted. "I'm so afraid that if I touch you, I'll wake up and this will all have been a dream. The most wonderful dream of my life, but just a dream nonetheless."

She moved forward when again it should have been him going to her. Giving her reassurance, love and comfort. Her fingers slid down his arms until they caught and tangled with his, and it was then he felt her trembling and his heart softened. His entire body caved in.

He gathered her hands in between his and gently squeezed as he absorbed the image, the angel, standing before him. Tears burned his eyelids and he tried to swallow them back.

Tonight was not a night for tears. Or sadness. Or regret. Or even shame. Tonight was the night of his dreams. Of all the dreams he'd ever dreamed all rolled together in one wonderful, living, breathing moment.

And yet, he couldn't quite keep one thing from creeping into his mind and casting shade on all his joy.

"I'm sorry, Gracie," he choked out.

She looked baffled. She cocked her head to the side and tightened her hold on his hands as if offering him reassurance.

"I didn't keep my promise to you."

He had to look away as a single tear burned its way down the cheek he now hid.

"I promised you that you would be my first. That I would come to you as untouched as you were. You are giving me the most precious gift a man can ever hope to receive. You're honoring me as the first man you're allowing to make love to you. And I can't even say you're the second or third woman I've been with."

He closed his eyes, causing more liquid to slide down his face.

"Zack," she whispered. She gripped his hands tighter. "Zack, look at me please."

He slowly turned his head to meet her gaze and saw mirroring tears and emotion in her eyes.

"Did you ever give any of those women your heart?" she asked softly.

"No," he said emphatically, his tone harsher than he intended. God, to even think for a moment that any other woman than Gracie had ever held a piece of his heart. "Never."

She smiled and then leaned up until she was straining to reach his height and gently wiped the wet trail from his cheek. He wrapped his arms around her, gathering her tightly against him, lifting so she wasn't at such a height disadvantage.

"Just like always," she said, wrapping her arms loosely around his neck. "You holding me up. Never letting me fall. Always protecting me from the world."

"Forever," he vowed, staring directly into her eyes, allowing her to see, to feel the sincerity of his promise.

She lovingly cupped his jaw and stared back at him, so much love shining in her warm brown eyes that it nearly undid him.

"You never gave your heart to another woman but me," she said, her eyes growing as serious as her tone. "You never gave them a part of your soul as you've done with me."

"Not just a *part*," he said adamantly. "All of it, Gracie. My heart, soul, body and mind. I never gave to anyone else what was yours to keep."

"Then I fail to see how you broke your promise to me."

For a moment he couldn't even breathe. His vision blurred and he pulled her even closer so his face was buried in her hair and her head lay against his cheek. He inhaled her sweet scent and held it for as long as he could before allowing it to escape his body.

"I love you," he said, his voice breaking up under the weight of so much emotion. "I'll never love anyone else. It's always been you. Thank God you found your way back to me. Don't ever leave me, Gracie. I can't live without you. I'm not whole without you. The last twelve years have been so empty. I don't ever want to have to live that way again."

She turned her face so that her lips met the corner of his mouth.

"I love you too, Zack. And I'll never leave you again."

Slowly, Zack walked toward the bed, carrying Gracie molded to his body. When he got to the edge, he very carefully lowered her to the mattress. He straightened, staring down transfixed by the sight of her.

Her hair was spread out and disheveled looking. Her cheeks were pink and flushed with the same nervousness that assailed him. Her nipples puckered and strained against the confining material of her gown.

Unable to resist such delicious temptation, he lowered his head to where the neckline plunged to her navel and he pressed his lips over the shallow indention, fully intending to kiss his way up her entire body. No way he was rushing this. It would take all night and he was going to enjoy every single minute.

"I'm scared," she said in a quivering voice.

He immediately raised his head to meet her eyes. And then he lowered his body so he lay against her side, his leg going over the tops of hers possessively. But at the same time, he made sure he wasn't making her uncomfortable.

"What are you scared of, baby?"

She swallowed hard and then she turned her head to the side so she met his gaze.

"I don't know what to do," she admitted. "I've never . . . I mean not willingly."

She promptly closed her eyes, but not before Zack saw the shame darken the brown depths. He had to work very hard to control the rage building inside him. This was too important for him to fuck up. He had to handle her very gently.

"Of course you haven't," he said. "But neither have I, Gracie. I've never made love to a woman in my life. How could I have when I'm only in love with you?"

She blinked and swallowed again and he touched his finger to her cheek, running it over her silky skin.

"I'm scared too," he admitted. "Nothing has ever been more important than this night, this moment. I don't want to hurt you or scare you or go to fast. In fact . . ."

He leaned down to kiss her lips before continuing his thought.

"No one says we have to make love tonight," he whispered. "We have all the time in the world. The rest of our lives. I would be the happiest man in the world just to get to hold you in my arms while you sleep and know that you're finally mine. That you wear my ring and bear my last name."

Gracie pushed herself up and over Zack, her eyes blazing in the low light cast by the bedside lamp. "No," she said fiercely. Her hand slid over his chest until it rested just above his heart. There was sorrow in her eyes, but also determination. "I won't let them take tonight from me. I won't!"

Tears welled in her eyes and she leaned down so her forehead rested against his. Their lips hovered so close that their breaths mingled.

"I'm not afraid of you," she said. "Never of you, Zack. I know you won't hurt me. I've waited for this moment for twelve years."

The last words were nearly cut off as she choked them out. He cupped the side of her face with his hand, drawing her down so their lips met. He stroked her jaw as they kissed lightly, the only sound coming from the soft smooching.

"I'm only afraid because I don't know what to do," she whispered against his lips. "I want to please you, but I don't know how. I want this night so much that I'm afraid of messing it all up and making us both miserable."

Zack wrapped his arms around her and rolled until he was atop her, though he made sure to prevent his full weight from crushing her. He stared at her with eyes that surely blazed as hers had just moments before.

"You will never disappoint me. You will never *not* please me. It's impossible, Gracie. You married me today. You're wearing my ring. You've taken my name. I couldn't be any happier than I am right now and I don't give a damn if we make love or not. Just having you here, with me, in my arms is enough. It will always be enough."

"And if I *want* you to make love to me?" she whispered.

Savage satisfaction such as he'd never known gripped him.

"Then I'll make love to you," he said in a low growl.

"Please," she said sweetly. "Make love to me, Zack. We've both waited so very long for this."

He fused his mouth to hers, cutting off anything further she might say. This time he allowed his restraint to slip and he put every ounce of feeling, of love, into his kiss.

Their tongues met and slid hotly over each other. He tasted her, devoured her, then went back for more.

He let one hand fall gently down the side of her neck and to her shoulder where his fingers caught on the thin string holding her gown up. With infinite care, he pulled it over her shoulder and down her bare arm.

Goose bumps danced beneath his touch. She shivered even as she deepened their kiss and let out a low moan of desire—of need. Need that matched his own desperate desire for her, for this. For him to finally, *finally* make her his.

"Don't let me hurt you," he ground out as he slid her gown further down her body.

"You won't," she denied.

God, she was so beautiful. So perfectly formed. He paused when the gown was at her waist to stare at the supple curves of her breasts. Then, unable to wait a second longer, he lowered his mouth to taste them.

She gasped and arched upward when he sucked one turgid peak between his teeth. He licked and sucked until she was writhing beneath him. Then he turned his attention to the other, coaxing it to rigidity like he had done to the first.

Her hands flew over his arms, his shoulders, his back, up and down. When he hit a particularly sensitive spot, her hands would still and her fingers would dig into his flesh as if the pleasure was nearly unbearable. It certainly was for him.

He ached to slide into her welcoming body. His dick had never ached so bad in his life. Never had he wanted someone with the desperation he wanted Gracie. His Gracie. But he forced himself to go slowly, not wanting the moment over too soon. Instead he stoked and built the fire burning between them until it was an inferno of desire and need consuming them both.

He let out a groan when her mouth slid hotly over his neck and then up to his ear where she nibbled and teased. He was panting, so desperate was he for breath. But she did that to him. All he had to do was look at her and he was breathless. And he knew that would never change.

His mouth covered every inch of her skin, from head to her pretty pink toes. And just as he'd fantasized, he kissed every single toe.

After the last toe, he nudged her legs farther apart and began kissing his way up the inside of her leg, pausing when he got to the sensitive skin around her knee. He smiled when she flinched. Her knees were definitely her weakness.

But he was determined to find new weaknesses. New places he could drive her mindless with pleasure. She tensed when his mouth traveled up the inside of her thigh. Her fingers slid through his hair and curled just as he placed a tender kiss on her soft mound.

With a gentle touch, he parted the ultra soft lips between her legs and exposed her satiny opening and the tiny, pulsing center of her pleasure.

He laved his tongue over her clit first, stroking, enjoying each and every sigh of pleasure wrung from her. Then he grew bolder, sucking ever so gently until her hips bucked upward to meet his demands.

He was shaking with so much pent up need as he eased one finger inside her opening. The velvet walls closed around the tip, sucking him further inside and his eyes nearly rolled to the back of his head as he imagined his aching erection bathed in such plushness.

Gracie's legs trembled and shook. Her entire body was shaking. Her eyes burned brightly when he lifted his head to meet her gaze. The question was unspoken and yet she responded by nodding. Then as if to further convince him she put both hands on his shoulders.

"Please, Zack," she begged softly. "Please, I need you."

The hell she'd ever beg for anything he could give her.

He rose up and settled himself between her splayed thighs and he stared down at the beautiful feast of naked woman spread out before him.

"I'll never ask for another thing as long as I live," he said in a hoarse voice. "All I ever wanted was you."

A tear slid from the corner of Gracie's eye and over her temple to disappear into her hair.

Using every ounce of restraint he owned, he positioned himself at the mouth of her sweet, silken dampness and nudged forward, just enough that the head of his dick was bathed in her heat.

He closed his eyes and let out an agonized cry, one that sounded like pain but was the most exquisite of pleasures he'd ever experienced in his life.

Gracie's hands curled around his shoulders, her fingernails digging into his skin, urging him forward. And he needed no further urging.

He pushed, inch by delicious inch, carefully studying her for any sign of pain or discomfort. Her eyes widened as he gained depth, but they were glazed with pleasure and so he pressed on.

His skin was on fire. The flames licked over him, threatening to utterly consume him and push him over the edge. He could feel the sweat on his forehead from the toll of restraining himself.

"Zack, I'm okay," she whispered close to his ear. "You aren't hurting me. Let go now. Love me."

Her sweetly worded plea snapped the last strings of control he had in place. With a harsh groan, he wrapped his arms around her and plunged the remaining distance, completely uniting them as one.

Her taste was on his tongue as her heat enveloped him and pulled him in, again and again. Her legs came up and wrapped around the backs of his thighs and she arched upward to meet every thrust.

Then her eyes popped open and her fingernails dug into his skin with enough force to break it. "Oh God, Zack. Don't stop. Please don't stop!"

It was the final push he needed. With a roar he began to drive into her, over and over, deeper, wetter, harder.

Their hips met, their bodies jostling with the force of each of his plunges.

Gracie's mouth opened in a soundless cry and her eyes went cloudy as if she lost all awareness of time and place. He felt her spasm and tighten around his erection and he felt the sudden explosion of wetness, signaling her orgasm.

It was the catalyst for his own.

Bathed in her silken depths, and with a sense of homecoming he'd never felt before, he let go. Her name on his lips, his whispered "I love you" over and over, he poured himself into her.

He buried his face against her neck, felt his hot tears against her skin. He shuddered one last time and then finally went limp against her. When he could see and think straight again, he was aware of being sprawled across her soft body and of her stroking his back with her hands, her cheek resting atop his head.

When he would have moved so his weight wasn't crushing her, she protested and held on.

"No, I like you there," she murmured. "Stay."

And so he stayed.

Long after the last sighs and sounds of pleasure, they lay entwined, two lovers who'd been separated far too long. Two lovers who'd finally found their way back to one another and experienced the sweetest homecoming one could ever ask for.

Perhaps she thought he was asleep or maybe she intended him to hear. Zack couldn't be certain. But as she stroked her fingers through his hair, her soft whisper fell on his ears.

"I'll never let you go again."

He smiled as her solemn vow found its way to his very soul.